WRITTEN IN LOVE LETTERS
A MOONSHINE SPRINGS NOVEL

ZOEY DRAKE

Written in Love Letters

Copyright © 2021 by Zoey Drake

Cover Artist: Talia - Book Cover Kingdom
Photographer: Lindee Robinson
Cover Models: Travis Bendall and Sabree Alexandra
Editing: Amy Briggs at Briggs Consulting

WRITTEN IN LOVE LETTERS PLAYLIST

Are You Gonna Kiss Me or Not by Thompson Square
F-150 by Robyn Ottolini
Pretty Heart by Parker McCollum
What Hurts The Most by Rascal Flatts
The Nights by Chase Rice
Memory I Don't Mess With by Lee Brice
You Broke Me First by Tate McRae
Out Of Love by Alessia Cara
Tomorrow by Chris Young
Crazy for You Tonight by Kip Moore
I Love You by Alex & Sierra
Fishing in the Dark by Nitty Gritty Dirt Band
Somethin' 'Bout A Truck by Kip Moore
Never Stop (Wedding Version) by SafetySuit

PROLOGUE - FAITH

The first time I ever laid eyes on six-foot Remington Cole, I knew I'd never love another boy the same way. There comes a time in everyone's life where a first crush changes everything you thought you knew about life and for me, it was him.

I was shy. The girl who sat in the back of the class, avoiding the glances and whispers of my classmates.

I couldn't even say hi to him without my knees shaking. I'd open my mouth to speak, but no words would form past the clog in my throat. Awkward was my middle name. I was short and lanky, and still hadn't grown into my chest or ass. Something I couldn't live down with the guys who bullied me at my high school.

I can't say the number of times I tripped over my tongue and he'd smile at me like he knew I could do it one day. He was simply waiting for me to find an ounce of courage.

He was the first and only boy who ever stood up to my bully. The day he shoved Jimmy Moon into a locker for calling me a nerd, I knew we were meant to be friends. I took note of the slim-line his lips formed as he glared down at Jimmy crumpled on the ground, cursing him up one side and down the other.

When I peered up from my huddle against the lockers, I could see the hint of danger as it crept into his eyes. What kind of danger I wasn't exactly sure, but I didn't care because in a split moment he was my savior, my knight in dark shining armor. Well, my knight in a nineties rock band T-shirt.

Remington was a year older than me. Tall with tanned skin and muscles, obviously hitting a growth spurt early—he had short dark brown hair, gray-blue eyes, and a Kid Rock T-shirt stretched across his broad chest. No one messed with him. He was more of a move when you moved, listened but remained silent type.

They called him a loner. A loser. I felt a certain kinship with him, even though no words were exchanged between us. It's like knowing someone has your back because they've been where you are right now sorta feeling.

"You okay?" he asked, leaning his hand down to help me up from the ground.

I cleared my throat. Words eluded me, no matter how many times I opened my mouth to tell him I was okay. Instead, I simply nodded, letting my hand slip into his larger one. Warmth spread in my heart at that exact moment. Something I couldn't explain. Maybe it was an enlightened sense of new friendship or love at first sight. Or possibly it was the hints of a crush on the first boy who glanced my way, but the moment his warm hand crossed mine I didn't care. Whatever it was, I soaked it in like a sponge. My first brush with something more, emotions, flirting, a whole new me.

Once we were eye to eye, I took him in fully.

Fingertips sent a spark of excitement through my veins as they brushed against my skin. My cheeks flushed a lovely shade of red, feeling awkward and nervous. I pulled my hand away from his when I realized my palm was sweating and the thought of him realizing I was sweating sent me mentally running for the hills. He was reluctant to pull away, but eventually relented, and the expression on his face gave me pause.

Did he feel the connection sever too, or was it only me feeling the loss?

When he raised a hand and stroked his rough finger along my cheek, I bowed my head away. I couldn't handle the intensity of the moment as his eyes scrutinized me. No one had ever truly seen me before, and it was terrifying. Or at least it's what I would have thought had a small smile not been creasing his lips. My eyes met the ground, taking in his dirty boots and the books scattered across the floor from my fall. I bent down quickly to pick them up at the same time he did, our heads bumping together awkwardly.

"Ouch," I mumbled, reaching up to rub the spot I was sure would form into a knot on my head where it'd connected with his.

A curse left his lips as I groaned hard - but more in sheer embarrassment than anything else. "I'm sorry," I whispered, avoiding eye contact. I'd been shy for years, but he brought it out in me more.

His fingers gripped my chin softly, lifting my jaw to gaze at his face as a smile graced the hard jawline he was sporting. "Hey, it's fine. You don't have to be sorry. These things happen."

He seemed so calm for a sixteen-year-old. What I'd heard of Remington's family life wasn't the best, so his calm and collected posture confused me. Not that I was expecting him to act crazy or anything over a tiny bump on the head, but still.

For a moment I stood in his gaze and let myself get lost in him. I wanted to be calm, that carefree. His don't give a shit attitude intrigued me. It must be easy, freeing. Somewhere behind me voices broke my mind from the moment and my eyes drifted slightly from those grey ones boring into me. My eyes fell to the floor, and I resumed the task at hand.

Quickly collecting my books, he leaned down to help me again, mumbling something so low I wouldn't hear. The bell rang for my next class and I hurried to get there without turning back. In hindsight, maybe I should've stuck to my guns. Who knew the wreckage Remington Cole would wreak in my life at that point? I sure didn't.

Throughout the rest of high school, we were together because it's how things went. You were either with someone or you weren't. There was no hooking up simply for fun. Over those four years, Remy became my everything. My first kiss. My first love. My first time. He held my deepest secrets. My hopes and dreams laid in the palm of his hands. He told me they were precious moments to him. He was my shelter, my home.

Being with Rem meant my bullies stayed away. It meant I wasn't alone anymore. The awkward girl who used to sit in the back of the classroom and hope to not be noticed, she'd since disappeared.

I wouldn't ever be popular, but it's not what I wanted at the time anyhow.

Maybe I should have known from the beginning that starting anything with Remington would be my end, but young love lies to you. Tells you the first boy you fall in love with may be the one who sticks with you for the rest of your life. The tale of high school sweethearts whispered throughout the town. Again, thinking back, I should have known better. It sure would've saved me from what I didn't know was coming.

Late nights by the lake, holding hands, sitting in the back of his beat-up truck staring at the stars, stealing kisses, riding horses, and canoodling in the springs took up most of our time.

It's where we planned out our dream life together and carved our initials into our favorite tree. It was a huge Sugar Maple at Willow Springs stables, situated in the middle of the woods by the springs. I remember it like it was yesterday instead of a memory I'd rather forget. The way the breeze flipped my hair across my shoulders right before the first smell of fresh rain tingled my senses. We stood under the sugar maple tree trying and failing to escape the rainstorm. The way Remington had pushed me against it to try and shield me, followed by distracting me with his lips while we waited it out, is one of my favorite memories.

Later on, when we'd grown up, we'd have a little farm of our own. I would train horses and give lessons; Remington would take care of the day-to-day running of the farm. Maybe he'd help break a client's horse or train them to barrel race. We'd have a couple of kids with our barn full of horses, a couple of dogs, and cats. We would own a goat named Elvis. Anything to leave the real world behind, but no one told us they would only ever be dreams- never flowering into anything more or expanding. Our dreams would wilt away without the sunlight and water to sustain them.

Instead of moving to the big college I wanted to, I'd stayed behind to be with Remington. He was my soul; my heart who lived outside my body. My parents hated him for the decision I made, but it was mine to make. His daddy wouldn't let him attend college, and since they weren't overflowing with cash, he knew it wouldn't happen. So, I guess you could say I gave up my big dreams of leaving this little town for him, instead going to community college. I thought it was love at the time. It's what I'd chosen to believe anyway.

———

I met Sofia my first year of college and we became friends quickly. She was the picture of a model next to my cute, short, blonde hair style. Everything about her made people awestruck with her long dark hair, copper-toned skin, curves for days, bright shiny smile, and perfectly manicured nails. She was the Sofia Vergara to my Julie Brown.

There wasn't a day or time where full-grown boys and men wouldn't fall over themselves to be in her presence. She chewed her bubble gum extra loud and twirled her hair so they were eating out of the palm of her hand. She was like a sea siren lulling them into a state of calm before feasting on them.

A little twisted, I can't deny this, but she was what we called a maneater. She'd been through so many boyfriends in the first couple of months of college it made my head spin trying to keep up.

We slowly became best friends. I'd let her do my makeup and hair as she'd drag me along to the parties she could find. There weren't many because, hello, community college, but if there was one in fifty-mile radius odds are we were there. It was almost as if she felt sorry for me. I had no social life, but I was fine with it. Sofia would hear no such thing.

We were those friends, her the wildly popular one, me the less popular and odd-looking one. I kept her away from Remington, not because I didn't trust him, but because I thought for sure he'd fall to the lust surrounding her when men came into contact with my best friend. And for the first time, I realized I didn't exactly trust Sofia, not around the most important person in my life.

He didn't seem to mind; my Rem stuck to himself. He wasn't the go-out-and-party type. He didn't care if he might be missing out on the next big thing. A night in with dinner and a movie on the small screen in my apartment was perfect. Remington told me those were his favorites. Hiding away from the world so he had me all to himself.

Remington had his eyes on the prize, making enough money to get out from under his father. The last thing he wanted to do for the rest of his life was work for Cole's Junk Yard. I didn't blame him.

Willow Springs Stables offered Rem some work halfway through high school, doing odds and ends here and there. When I started my first year of college, Beau's dad hired him on the farm full time. He could live on the property and still make money. It was a win-win and he leaped at the chance.

Leaving his father was probably the best thing he ever did for himself. So many times he'd sneak in at mid-night with cracked ribs and bruises littering his face and torso. He didn't have to tell me what happened. Every black eye and wince told me a story all their own. His particular story bled with pain and sadness over something that probably wouldn't change. He'd tell me at the beginning it was his clumsiness at fault, but I knew a lie when I heard one. One day he finally came clean with me. His father was an alcoholic who beat the shit out of him because he could.

My blood boiled time and time again as my eyes found new bruises. I was outraged, the familiar patterns of abuse flaring time and time again. The pit in my stomach grew with each new round, but there was nothing I could do to change it. His body was powerful and magnificent, and somehow the scars seemed to give him even more beauty. Each bump and stitch scar showed a life still in process. He'd come out swinging on the other side of every shitty situation thrown his way.

People called him a rebel, a scoundrel, the son of a drunk. They said he wouldn't amount to much, but I saw him. The man was a survivor, a hero for not falling to the secrets whispered surrounding his name. He was sewn together beautifully with all the disjointed pieces of his life. A maze of twists and turns with a father who beat him and a mother who left them when he was a little boy.

He was raised to be let down constantly, by his parents, by his life. I couldn't blame his mother for leaving. Being married to a monster would've caused anyone to run. I wondered if she'd received a similar type of abuse. If she'd dealt with the physical and mental anguish Rem had also endured. But one question remained. *How she could leave her little boy with such a monster?*

I guess it was selfish in my own right to be happy she hadn't taken him when she ran. If she had, I wouldn't have known him. Knowing our lives would be entwined for so many years.

And that's how we lived. He would get up early and head to

the ranch. Call me on his break. I'd attend my classes and then we'd meet up in the evenings, even if it was to simply sit under the stars and reminisce about our dreams. It was a simple life, but it was ours. At least while we could hold onto it.

FAITH

It was the last party before the start of summer. I'd started working part-time at Willow Springs Stables giving kids horseback riding lessons, but tonight I specifically asked to not be scheduled.

Everyone would be at this party and for once I wanted to bring Remington and show him off to my friends.

They'd teased me for the last couple of months because I talked about him often, but they'd yet to meet him. They started to think maybe he was a figment of my imagination and lord knows I couldn't let it fly.

I knew it wasn't his thing, but when I asked him, he'd agreed. No questions asked. He was the one constant in my life when everything else fell flat.

My phone buzzed across the counter like a mini hurricane while I was getting ready with Sofia. "Hey, babe," I answered, knowing it was Rem.

"Hey, I'm stuck at the farm. A colt came in late today and they need me to help before I can get away. I'll meet you at the party, text me the address."

My shoulders dropped even though he couldn't see it. The

silence hung between us for a couple of seconds before I respond. "Oh...okay. I guess I'll see you when you're done."

"Faith, don't be upset. I didn't know we were getting this colt today. I thought he was coming in tomorrow. I promise I'll be there; I'll just be a little later."

I sighed. "I know you will, Rem." I didn't know why I was upset other than for the purely selfish reason of showing up to the party without Remington on my arm. I knew he was hot; girls would fawn over him. The truth was I felt insecure with myself. I knew Remington loved me as he told me often, but the little voice inside my head still told me he wasn't mine.

Thirty minutes later, Sofia and I were on the road, excitement pumping through our veins. The drive was quick, and we didn't talk much. Maybe we were both psyching ourselves up for the night, I wasn't sure.

A slew of partiers littered the front lawn when we pulled up to the house. Getting out, we made our way through the crowd, music pumping through the loudspeakers as we slipped into the kitchen. The counters were lined with booze, every flavor and bottle imaginable.

"Shots first," Sofia said, laughing as we danced to the music.

We filled up two shot glasses, unaware of the crowd gathering in my best friend's presence.

"Faith, you down, girl?" Sofia raised her eyebrow at me curiously, awaiting my next move. I simply nodded my acceptance since I was too hyped up on nerves to speak. Liquid courage and all. A chorus of *shots, shots, shots* rose from the crowd and we couldn't help but do as we were bid. We downed our shots, feeling the burn of the rye bourbon afterward.

Throwing together a couple of mixed punches with way too much alcohol, we danced along with the music again. People kept showing up and slowly the room became more and more crowded. Like being a sardine shoved into a tiny can. It quickly became the biggest party we'd ever been to together.

Sofia looked over at me, a drink tipping to her lips. "Well, we made it through the second semester of college. Now it's summer. What will you get into?"

"I'll be working at Willow Springs giving lessons to kids. You know, saving up some money."

She rolled her eyes. "Working... gah, that's so boring, Faith. You should live a little, do what you want to do, not get tied down at a boring horse ranch."

I felt defensive, so I snarked at her. "Sof, look, not all of us have rich parents like you do. Besides, there is nothing wrong with a boring horse ranch. I like it there."

She held her hands up, palms out, trying to seem less offensive. "Okay, okay, but think about it. You could hang out with me. My parents rent out this cabin by the lake in Michigan every summer. Me and a bunch of friends are chilling out there- boating on the lake, drinking by the bonfire, hooking up, and most importantly, living life. None of this boring work crap. You're too young to settle down!"

I should have realized this was the moment my night would change for the worst. The one person I thought was my best friend would commit the most heinous of friendship crimes, but we'll get back to that.

The party kicked into gear rather quickly around us, and Sofia disappeared shortly after. The music was way too loud and drinks were flowing freely. Different party-goers were playing drinking games throughout. People congregated out front to dance and out back to smoke and do various other things.

I caught a couple of glances at Sofia in the first hour, but then she completely ghosted me. I'm sure it was to hook up or do something with the people who hung out in the backyards of these parties. The smell of weed wafted up through the windows. It wasn't a new smell to me and certainly occurred regularly with the parties we attended. I had zero desire to try it. The notion of getting high didn't appeal to me.

A few guys hit on me as I moved through the house, waiting for Remington to show up. When it was two hours into the party and he still hadn't shown, I started to worry. Maybe something happened with the colt he mentioned. Maybe there was an accident, and no one remembered to call me: the girlfriend. All possible worst scenarios were flashing through my mind as I paced.

I checked my phone, but there were no new messages or calls. My finger lingered over the call button when I looked up to find the crowd parting like the red sea. My eyes landed on the newest arrival and a sigh of relief leaped from my lips. Remington had finally arrived.

I couldn't help but admire the way people moved out of the way when my boyfriend walked through the middle of the room straight toward me. It was the way he carried himself, a smile he flashed me when he saw me staring.

My eyes followed the lines of his work clothes, down his tattooed arms, bulging with each muscle and movement. Clearly, he had not taken the time to run home and shower first, which was okay with me. I'd grown to love the scent of his post-work, pre-shower musk.

A faint outline of dust clung to his jeans and his boots weren't much cleaner.

I didn't care.

It felt like minutes as I stood there staring at him before Sofia made her way over to me and gasped.

"Damn, girl. Is this the elusive boyfriend you talk about? If so, I see why you hide him away."

I swallowed, finally letting my eyes drift away from Rem. "Mmhmm." Her eyes trailed each line and dip of his body and I wanted to smack her for staring.

"He's fucking sexy. If he wasn't already claimed, you know I'd be tapping him tonight." I rolled my eyes. Remington was sexy as hell and with *me* tonight. A smile tore across my lips at my musing. He'd been getting tattoos for the last couple of years. Full sleeves and across his chest. My favorite was the one he got tattooed right above his heart of my name last Christmas.

He leaned down and kissed my forehead in greeting. "Hey, babe. Sorry, I'm late. Colt's a lot more to handle than we hoped. Finally got 'em calmed down a bit."

I lifted on my toes to kiss his cheek. "I'm glad you're here."

He waggled his eyebrows. "Mmm... you think that'll work in my favor later on tonight. Me showing up to this here party so you can show me off to all your girly friends."

"Uh-huh." I smiled. "I think we can most definitely work something out."

He leaned me back for a little more than a peck on the lips and my heart burst in cataclysmic fashion. A kaleidoscope of love built from years of togetherness. The catcalls behind us didn't help my nervousness over being the center of attention, that's what I'd wanted originally, right?

But being in Rem's arms also made me completely forget.

Forget about the world, if only for a minute.

Thirty seconds to forget about our problems.

To feel his lips against mine.

To feel the weight of his body against mine as we pressed even closer.

He had a way of making me feel safe and protected. It's the illusion of being safe that makes us feel the calmest. Or so I believed...

FAITH

F our Years Later

"Faith, I'm sorry, but we have to let you go. If I had any other option, I would take it. You have to understand. I'm doing what's best for my company." She smiles, but it's was weak. It matches her apologetic tone.

My stomach drops. I knew the company was having some money problems, but I thought they'd worked it out. I was wrong. I listen to her continue to drum on, feeling bad about having to let me go and then saying something about rehiring me if they were able to dig out of the money pit they'd found themselves in.

It isn't the first time my life hadn't gone as I'd planned. Remington had shown me four years ago how plans change.

Putting her out of her misery, I finally respond. "Kate, it's fine. You have to do what's best for you. I hope it all works out."

Briefly closing her eyes, she breathes a sigh of relief. "Thanks for understanding, Faith. Seriously, we're going to miss you."

I nod before leaving to pack up my desk. I've been here for three years now. Starting as an intern my sophomore year of college. It was my longest-held and only job besides Willow Springs Stables. Gazing out the window, I commit the view to memory one last time. My favorite coffee shop sits down the street. The food truck is always parked right outside at lunch for easy access. With a sigh, I drop my badge on the desk, pick up my cardboard box, and make my way to the elevators, hitting the down button. I have no clue what lays ahead now. I'll have to search for another job and explain it to my roommate, Nova. The lobby is busy as I push my way through.

As if my day wasn't going well enough, the rain starts when I step outside of the spinning door. Luckily, the box I am carrying has a lid, but still. By the time I open the door to my car, I am visibly soaked and shaking. The rain was relentless as it pelted me in cold droplets. My shirt is see-through, my hair is stuck to my face, and my eyes hold a black hue like a raccoon. I shut the door before turning on my car. My lights switch on automatically and I crank my windshield wipers to high. Raining cats and dogs is an understatement. It is more like the monsoon taking over my life.

Our home is only two miles from work. I pull into the parking lot, park, and make a run for the front door. Getting out the umbrella is unnecessary, and I know it will be hard to carry with the box. Nova must have been watching me from the window because the door opens automatically when I get to it.

"Faith, you're home early. What's going on?" Her eyebrows draw together, concerned as she scrutinizes me, giving me the once over.

I sigh and shake my head. "I got let go today. I'm so sorry, Nova. I don't know what I'm going to do."

"Hey, hey. It's okay. Get in here, it's pouring. We'll figure it out."

Taking the box from me, she turns and I follow her into our townhouse. It isn't fancy, but we added touches here and there, giving it a homey feel. Throw pillows litter the couch, pictures line the table behind the couch, our slippers are lined up by the front door, and the soft lighting throughout helps it feel more like home than a rental unit.

The first floor consists of a dining room, kitchen, bathroom, and living room, while the second floor houses our bedrooms and another bathroom.

After dropping the box on the table in the kitchen, she swings back around and grabs me in one of her famous bear hugs. "Chin up, Faith. We will figure this out. You know what they say... when one door closes another one opens. So, you have to wait and see what's on the other side of the new door. You are a smart, brilliant woman, and anyone would be stupid not to hire you. Seriously, you'll have no trouble finding a new job and if you want my help searching the job ads, I'm here for you. Gotta pick yourself up and move on, girl!" This is what I love about Nova, her never-ending optimism.

I shake my head. "You should be a motivational speaker."

She chuckles. "I only do my best motivational speaking when it comes to my best friend."

I smile. I never thought I'd find another girl friend to trust after what happened with Sofia in college, but Nova came bounding into my life without giving me the option to say no.

After our hug, I make my way to the kitchen to grab some water. "Anything good in the mail today?"

"He sent another letter." I pick it up, tracing over the letters of my name in his handwriting. I lift it to my nose to catch the scent of his cologne as if some trace of the way he smelled would travel three hours across states on a damn envelope.

Four years later and my heart still cracks open and bleeds out in a trickle every time his name is spoken or I receive one of these damn letters. My body hums as memories assault me like a swarm of killer bees. How could first love sting so deep? Sadness mixes with anger as I regard the letter again. A tear slides down my cheek and I swipe it away like it means nothing. He doesn't deserve my tears anymore. I don't care what he has to say.

Once a cheater, always a cheater.

Like my father.

My parents like to believe I didn't know about what had happened between the two of them. Suzanne Evans was quiet, coy, and even-tempered, but the night she yelled at my father, told him to pack his shit and live with his new little shiny whore, I saw a different side of my mother. Him telling her he wasn't leaving me alone with her because she was crazy. Being there started to change my view on love. The worst part of matrimony. I sat back and took notes of exactly what I didn't want to have. Remington was the final nail in the coffin.

Opening the cabinet drawer, I let the new letter fall onto the others already stacked below it.

Her brows pinch as she opens and closes her mouth twice, as if weighing her words, before finally speaking. "Are you ever going to open one and read it? Maybe it wasn't what it appeared."

I shake my head, closing my eyes. "I know what I saw, Nova." Maybe it was stubborn, but I believe what I saw for years, and somewhere deep down I don't want to know if I was wrong. It is easier to hate him.

"Okay, Faith. Okay." She relents. We've had this fight so many times over the last four years and it never ends well. I end up mad and she ends up apologizing. Pushing away all thoughts of the past, I grab some water and head back to the living room.

Nova eyes me. "I'm sorry Faith."

My voice cracks and I'm startled by how sad it sounds. "I know. It honestly hurts, you know. Four years later and I still need him like I need my next breath. Each time I think about him, I can't breathe, can't think. I'm just here, going through the motions without ever really noticing. What he did left a piece of my heart chipped and I don't think it's mendable."

She walks over and rubs my shoulder. "You had your heart

broken in the worst way imaginable. It's understandable, but maybe it's time to move on. Maybe you need to get back out there and try with someone new."

I wrap my arms around my waist, as if somehow that will protect me from really thinking about my answer. So I brush it off. "I'm not ready yet, Nova."

She raises her eyebrows, crossing her arms over her chest. "Then when Faith? If not now, when?"

"I don't know, okay? I... can't." My voice shakes and unshed tears line my eyes.

Her brows pull in. "Someday you're going to meet a man who sweeps you off your feet and makes you forget all the bad shit between you and Remington. You'll fall in love with him and realize he's the one you were meant to spend the rest of your life with, but until then, let's grab some dinner and job search."

Staring down at my hands, I fiddle with my thumbs. "Maybe we should eat in tonight, Nova. Now that I don't have a job."

She huffs. "You let me worry about dinner, okay? I'm buying. Hitting up our favorite food truck, you want the normal?"

"Sure, sounds great. I'll take a famous burrito with queso and chips on the side, please."

A smile broadens her face. "All right, I'll be back soon!" She grabs her purse and leaves without another word. Even though my day was utter crap, being here was still leaps and bounds better than living with my parents, being around the one person who took my heart out and shredded it to pieces without even a second thought.

It hurt walking away from Remington. Letting go of each memory and thought we'd shared over the years. I've lived in the space in between for the last four years—I hated him for what he did, but I also missed him like a piece of me had disappeared into the atmosphere, forever lost. I couldn't manage to wrap my head around why he'd done it. He'd told me we were meant to be together from the start, so why?

I shove thoughts of him back into the tiny part of my brain labeled *bad memories*.

"I hope you're hungry!" Nova singsongs as she lets herself back into our house, closing the door behind her.

I smile as she sets the food down on the coffee table in front of me. Mmm... a burrito dripping in cheesy goodness and salsa. The perfect thing to shove my face with after a crappy day. As if losing my job wasn't bad enough, coming home and receiving yet another letter from him, drudging up the past where it needs to be left.

Shaking my head, I gaze up at my roommate. Nova is flawless. Not the Sofia kind of flawless, more like the down-to-earth country summer kind of beauty. She's a medium build, not super skinny, but has some curves. With strawberry blonde hair, gray blue eyes covered by goofy black rimmed glasses, and the biggest smile, she's one of those people you want to be around constantly because they make you feel one hundred percent better about life.

Maybe it's a flaw she sees the good in everyone, or how she's always the fixer, but it's also her best quality because no matter how angry I get for her meddling in my drama from the past, I know she has a genuine interest in my feelings. Unlike my relationship with Sofia, Nova and I have a give and take. We share a real friendship, not a flyby when the wind blows my way sort of thing.

We met the summer after I left Moonshine Springs for Ohio. A late-night study sesh at the library turned into a beautiful friendship over the basic principles of economics. On Tuesday nights, we'd hang out at Camille's Pub and play trivia.

She bites the end of her pen as she goes through ads. "Oh! How about a dog walker?"

I roll my eyes. "Nov... I'm a business administration degree..."

She fake scowls. "You're right... but seriously think of all the adorable dogs you could be walking right now..."

I open my mouth to respond, but words elude me, so I shake my head. I take in her chill pose. It must be nice not to live paycheck to paycheck. Her parents are rich, but she doesn't act like it. "How about a tedslist job poster?"

"What in the world?" I quirk an eyebrow.

"Well, according to the ad, they're needing someone with experience who can post ads on tedslist for marketing." She laughs. "This one is hilarious. It says 'help wanted, must be able to dominate the English language like a boss'."

"Wait, are you serious? That's great." She flips the laptop, showing me word for word what she read out loud. They must be desperate.

She snorts, soda flying out of her nose and mouth at the next ad she sees. A hint of mischief lies behind her squinting eyes. "Wait for it... wanted: someone with yard work experience, must also not be opposed to Hoola hooping."

My eyes widen as I shake my head. "Okay, where in the heck are you searching for jobs? Because that seems like a terrible joke."

"In all seriousness, how about this one? Experienced horseback riding lesson instructor. Must be able to work nights and weekends. Will be working with children and their horses to form the ultimate bond. May occasionally be asked to help out around the barn with feeding, turn out, and cleaning stalls."

My ears perk up when she finishes reading. It would be the perfect job for me. I'm familiar with riding lessons already and I'm sure Beau would give me a great recommendation. It's the one thing I miss about back home. Working with horses. The smell of the barn, the sneezing from the sawdust, the nickers and whinnies from horses eager to see you when the day starts. The part about feeling like those animals depended on you. They needed you to survive. They were the first to say hello and the last to say goodbye at night. There's simply something about horses that's golden to a person's soul.

"Where does it say the barn is located?"

Her brows pinch. "Hmm... it doesn't say. It only says to respond to the email address listed for more information."

I hand her a pen and paper. "Will you write down the email for me? I'm going to send a message tomorrow and find out some more information. Watch it be in a different state, you know how those slip in sometimes."

"Got it. Hey, here's another one. Small office looking for a team player to assist in administrative daily functions. Excellent interpersonal and organizational skills are important. Must be a service-oriented individual."

"Okay, I'll bite. Where's this one located?"

"Faith, it's right down the street from here. It says you need to call to set up an interview."

I point to her paper. "Well, add it to the list, then."

We ended up finding a few more jobs throughout the evening while we sat and watched the home and garden network. Two marketing jobs, another administrative assistant, and a waitressing job or two.

REMINGTON

All it took was one night, one drink four years ago, to lose the love of my life.

Faith Evans moved to town when she was fifteen. I remember her as the shy, awkward new kid in school. I'd sit in class and watch her. But not in a mesmerizing sort of way. It was more in a how-is-she-so-clumsy-and-tiny sorta way. I thought short people were supposed to be nimbler. Faith was anything but.

I figured the safest place for her was away from me. I came from trash. My father was an alcoholic who beat his kid and ran my mother out of town. I was the guy everyone condemned. I didn't hold my breath over it. There was no way I'd ever be better than my family name. I was bad, damaged.

Cole's Junk Yard was my father's business.

It's where we lived too. In a shabby little apartment above the garage. It was too small for the two of us, so I spent most nights out under the stars.

Most of my time I spent alone. I wouldn't dare have friends. How could you when you were too ashamed to bring said *"friends"* home with you to meet your alcoholic father? So, the day

Faith Evans peered up at me from her crumpled position against the lockers, my life changed.

I'd tried for months to stay away.

To make the distance to keep her from getting involved with the likes of me.

In one single, solitary moment, the distance was closed.

The gap slammed shut and there we were, eye to eye in the middle of our high school hallway.

I held my hand out to help her stand up, and she took it. Feeling her warm hand glide into mine solidified the fact I wouldn't be able to walk away from her so easily. It was like a hug, warm and solid. Two of the things I'd yet to experience before. It was a seal that cemented and entwined our lives. You see, Cole's didn't give or receive hugs. There was no love in our family.

So, when my warm, sweet, innocent girl with the golden blonde locks gazed up at me with those ocean blue eyes, I was hooked. I was drunk on the way her eyes caressed my face like I could be better than my name. Like I could do whatever I wanted simply because she was in my life. I could no longer let my past or my name define who I was because I wanted to be better for her.

I was transfixed, completely consumed at the moment with her.

My heart pounded, and the world disappeared, all except for the shining angel in front of me. Before she agreed to be my girlfriend, I'd do all I could to not fall into her hypnotic eyes, or even glance her way for too long, hoping she wouldn't notice.

And when she agreed to be my girlfriend, my whole world was rocked. She was perfection, wrapped in a tiny bottle of magic. She had a way of making me feel relaxed. Making me forget my life sucked.

Don't even get me started on her smiles.

I wanted to own every damn one of them, earning them like golden stars for good behavior.

They illuminated her, a bright beacon of joy lighting her already beautiful face.

Faith was way too good for me. I was all too aware of it. Everyone knew it, but she didn't seem to believe it. She saw through the name, through the scars, the black and blue eyes, and the broken ribs to see me.

The real me.

The guy trying to get through school and do the best I could, given the shitty hand I was dealt. I would've done anything for her.

She was the love of my life, still is.

Even four years later.

One night changed us.

One stupid decision.

Something I can't take back.

Twice a month, I write her a letter, but it's been years and I have yet to receive a response. I wonder if she reads them or if she simply throws them away. At least I know she's not returning them to me, so I'm left hanging with a tiny sliver of hope.

"Hey, I wanted to run something by you." Beau walks up behind me and I startle momentarily.

I give him a head nod. "Sure, what's up Beau?"

He holds out a printed job ad to me. "Posted a new ad for a kid riding instructor again."

My eyebrows hit my hairline in confusion. "Okay, not sure why it matters to me?"

"I'm only giving you a heads up. Karen can't keep up with all the new riding clients we're getting, and she needs some help. Plus... there's an email I think you need to see."

He hands me a sheet of paper and I immediately recognize the email address at the top. My heart beats an extra note, but I can't tell if I'm excited about it or not. It's a funny thing how something as silly as an old email address brings back emotions, pushed aside and sitting squandered in the back of your mind.

I shake my head, observing him. "But why?"

He shrugs nonchalantly. "I guess I forgot to put the location of the barn on the posting. You tell me how you want me to handle this one."

I search his eyes. "Why is she interested in a job? I thought she was working at a firm in Ohio. Last I heard she was very happy there."

"Not sure, Rem. Like I said... you tell me..."

I shove the paper back at him harder than I mean to. "Handle it however you want to. She hasn't talked to me in years, Beau. Doubt she'll be running back here once she finds out it's Willow Springs. She's better than this farm, than this life. She was constantly too good for me. Guess I didn't realize it until it was too late."

He tsks. "You don't know, Rem. Fate has a funny way of making us eat our words."

"She ain't planning on running home to me after she has her little life away from all this stuff. She didn't care then; she won't care now. She didn't even give me the chance to explain before she went running off to a new life without me." I ball my hands at my sides, anger ripping through my veins like dynamite.

He searches my face. "Rem..."

"No, Beau. Let it be." I huff and stomp off. Not able to keep my anger hidden. Without another thought, I grab Remy, jump up on a hay bale, and onto his back. There is no need for a saddle. It will only slow me down getting away from here. Remy's been my one constant over the last couple of years. Eternally ready for a ride, not once complaining when we stay out for hours walking every fence of the farm.

We'd rescued him from a kill auction. They said he was untrainable, too damaged, only good for a slaughterhouse. Meaner than a snake and angry, but I could relate to him. I'd spend hours staring at him in the round pen while he snorted and ran, searching for any way to get out. He'd tried to kick me, bite me, everything he could think of, and then one day I screamed at him. Screamed that life wasn't fair, and he needed to get over it because it wasn't going to fix anything.

I knew he didn't understand me, but I swear it changed us. Maybe he'd finally realized when he saw me through his eyes. He was staring at the pain and hurt he felt in himself. Little by little, he learned to trust me and I learned to trust him.

Here we are now, a bonded team. I often wondered how he got his name. He came with it when he was rescued and although we tried several times to change it, he ever held firm to Remy. It was a little weird how my horse had the same name, but it didn't bother me. Plus, it was constantly the barn joke about how I had a horse named Remy.

The wind blows up from behind us on the trail and I have to hold on to my hat, so it doesn't fly away. There's a chilly breeze this morning letting you know fall is around the corner. A few deer creep into our path as we travel through the wooded area at the back of the farm.

I get lost to the sound of his hoof beats, almost melodic in their cadence.

Horses follow along as we make our way back to the springs. It's in the middle of a group of trees, away from the trail. One of my favorite places on this farm. It holds memories, good and bad. Painful and happy.

I stifle a yawn as we get up to the springs. Shadow's cloak most of the area with the sun spotlighting areas where fewer leaves cover the trees.

I slide off Remy and tie him to a tree before walking over to the springs. Reaching down, I grab hold and pull off my boots, rolling up my pant legs to avoid soggy jeans, as I start to slip my feet into the springs. I lower them into the water, the warmth of the water coiling around them, and the feel of the uneven rocks on the bottom under my bare feet.

Moist air is drawn into my lungs, and I inhale deeply as I listen to the sounds of nature surrounding me.

The wind whistles through the leaves on the trees as they sway in the small breeze. The feel of it skittering across my skin is a chilly contrast to the warmth wrapped around my feet. It's peaceful out here, tucked between the trees. Here I could slip away from the realities of my screwed-up life and relieve some tension. It was a moment of escape, my own personal getaway.

When I first started working at Willow Springs, I was in high school. I'd been doing odds and ends at the stables as far back as I can remember. When Faith started college, Beau's dad offered me a job.

Thinking back to the days when I was first hired, I remember it as the last time I was truly happy.

I still had Faith at the time. Life was shaping up. I was out from under my father's thumb and I had a new home at the farm. If only she hadn't asked me to go to the party. If only she hadn't left me alone with her best friend. If only I'd said no when Sofia handed me the drink, it wouldn't have changed everything. But regrets don't matter now, nor can they take back what happened.

Now, I live in the bunkhouse on the ranch. These days I move like a zombie through the hours to get back to the bunkhouse and crash. A large glass of sweet tea, my feet on the coffee table, and the TV set on whatever hits my fancy for the night. Somedays I'll pick up my guitar and strum away.

Now, I'm constantly angry and combative. I lost a piece of my soul four years ago and I'm not sure I'll ever get back.

Most days I can control it.

Most days I push the anger at Faith and myself away and try to move on.

It's a bitter reminder though. I had the world, and I threw it away with one stupid mistake.

Beau had convinced me to start sending her letters when I told him I couldn't even talk about what had happened out loud. I was too embarrassed. It was a moment of weakness and I fell into it headfirst. I'm sure Faith thought the worst of me. I still remember the day she came to school in tears after finding out her father had cheated on her mother, so I knew not telling her the truth would cut deep. The last thing I expected was for her to pack up in the middle of the night and move three hours away from me without a glance or a single goodbye.

I wondered if she'd ever read any of them. Did she know the truth and still refuse to stay away from me or has she shoved them into a box out of sight to sit and collect dust?

I almost hoped Beau would have her stop by the farm, but I knew as soon as she found out it was Willow Springs she'd run for the hills.

A horse whinnies in the distance, and Remy follows suit, sending a reply. The breeze kicks up again, blowing the dry leaves scattered across the ground. My eyes lift upward. The sky is a deep blue today with a little cloud cover. It's hard to enjoy these days. We stay there for a little while longer before time creeps up on me and I have to get back to the farm.

New colts wait for no one when it comes to being gentled.

FAITH

"For fifty points, what U.S. state drinks the most alcohol per person?" the quizmaster asks, and my brain scrambles through the piles of useless knowledge I've gained over the years.

The golden bell on our table dings when she smacks the top. "Nevada!" Nova yells next to me, and I glance over at her. She shrugs her shoulders. "What? I used to live there; they do drink a lot."

I high five her. "You rock, girl." We sit and await the next question, but it doesn't take long to be asked.

"For twenty points, what whiskey brand was advertised with two terrier dogs?"

Nova bumps my shoulder. "Faith, whiskey is your dirty little secret, you should know this one."

I'm leaning forward with my back hunched forward as my fingers tap on the table. "I know. I'm thinking, I'm thinking. Oh. Wait. Bla—"

"Black and White," another team yells out and I bang my fist on the table. "Damnit, I knew the answer!"

"It's okay, we'll get the next one. We're only behind by eighty points." She takes a chug of her beer and wipes the back of her hand across her lips.

"For one hundred points, Pulque is a beer made from what?" My eyes find Nova, and she shrugs. I have no idea either and of course, you can't exactly bring up google on your phone. The team currently beating us shouts out cactus, and Nova nudges me.

I shrug. "Eh, we learned something new tonight. We can still catch up!" I love her cheery vibe and the pub trivia tonight is making me less sad about my lack of a job.

The server swings by, and I ask her for another glass of water. Nova huffs beside me, motioning for the server to swing back after she leaves. "Yes?"

She leans into the server and speaks louder. "Can my friend here get a fun drink? Like a sex on the beach."

"Nova..." I admonish.

She puts her hand over mine on the table. "Let me buy, Faith. You need to loosen up."

I shake my head, sighing. "You can't keep buying my way for things, Nova. Rent is going to be due soon and you shouldn't have to afford it on your own."

"We'll be fine, Faith. I'm not exactly broke. I can afford to pay for both of us until you find a job." I huffed, but it's the only noise I get out before the announcer starts again.

"Okay, ladies and gents. Are you ready for the next question?" A chorus of yes goes up around the room. Nova and I focus intently. "For 10 points, what year did *Game of Thrones* premiere on HBO?"

My hand slams down, ringing the bell. "Oh, yes! 2011!" I yell. Nova laughs beside me.

"Alright, alright. Points to the lady in red in the corner. Apparently, we've got a GOT fan in the house."

I blush, feeling my embarrassment. I may or may not have several bumper stickers on my car.

"For twenty-five points, finish the next line of this Beatles song "Hey Jude." 'Hey Jude, don't make it bad...'"

Nova dings the bell. "Take a sad song and make it better." Nova singsongs next to me. Her eyes catch mine and she keeps singing along. "What, the Beatles are my jam band."

"Next question... For twenty-five points, which famous politician's mother created the Manhattan cocktail?"

A bell dings behind us and my heart sinks. There's no way we'll win now.

"Alright, folks. This team is catching up, they're only forty-five points behind. For fifty points and the lead... On average, how many grapes does it take to make a bottle of wine?"

"400!" Nova shouts beside me and we've won! My chair falls behind me as I jump up in a cheer. We fist bump like the Hall of Famer Stan Musial did in the 1950s as opposed to handshaking.

Nova leaves me for a brief minute to reel in the excitement of finally winning a pub trivia night. We've been doing this for months and it's our first actual win.

When she returns, she's holding a stack of cash. "Winner, winner chicken dinner, Faith. We're getting the prize money tonight."

"How much is it?"

"Only a hundred bucks, but I'll certainly take it." She waves it around wiggling.

"For sure!"

We go back to our table, deciding to stick around for a little while longer. "So," Nova says, picking up her beer. "How'd the job search go today? Any bites?"

"Apparently I'm too qualified to be a dog walker or a secretary. I emailed the tedslist poster ad people only to find out they've already filled the position."

"Okay, so what about the horse barn job?"

"I don't even know where it's at..."

"But... didn't you used to work with horses and give lessons? You'd be perfect for the job."

I nod, trying not to grimace at the pit in my stomach. "I did. I worked at Willow Spring Stables when I was in high school and my first year of college."

Her eyebrows raise above her glasses. "So..."

"Well, fine. I'll email them, but they probably aren't even around here. Large horse farms requiring trainers are normally in the country, not the city."

"Want to job search again tonight?"

I shrug, disheartened. "Yeah, I probably should. I'm bummed, I guess. I thought people would be hiring."

"Faith, have you ever thought about starting your own marketing group?"

"Of course, I've thought about it, but I don't have enough background or experience. I don't want to start up something only for it to fail."

———

The next morning I'm up early. The gurgle of the coffee machine tells me it'll be ready when I get back from my run. The pitter patter of feet behind me lets me know Nova is already awake for the day.

She shakes her head as she walks up to where I'm sitting at the island. "I don't know how you do it."

I feign ignorance. "Do what?"

She gives me a pointed stare. "Get up and run every single day. Haven't you ever heard of sleeping in?" Her hair is sleep ruffled. She laughs as she's grabbing things from the fridge to make for breakfast. Typically, an egg white wrap with fruit and one of those gross green smoothie drinks.

I fake pout. "I've slept in before..."

She folds her hands over her stomach before rolling her eyes. "What... when you were five?"

"Hey, no fair." I chuckle. "You know... you could run with me sometime."

"Nah, I'm good. I'll drink this smoothie instead," she says, holding the puke green drink in my direction.

I fake gag. "Yuck, it appears to be a close relative of vomit..."

She takes a sip, closing her eyes. "Mmm... it's the most delicious thing I've ever had, so what if it's a little green. How about this... I'll try running when you decide to try my morning smoothie."

I scrunch my nose. "Maybe eventually, but I'm not there yet. All right, see you in a little bit."

My feet hit the pavement hard with each step. My lungs feel like they're screaming at the pace I'm setting. The wind whips through my hair, touching each strand before dropping it back to my shoulders. A piece slips into my mouth and I blow it out. I'm sweating. My clothes are sticking to me, but I enjoy the run. The way I push myself. For thirty minutes each morning, it's nothing but me and the outdoors. Plus, some polluted city air. No thoughts, no worries.

My mind drifts back to the one hundred and fourth letter he's sent in four years. I don't understand why he still tries. I've yet to read any of the letters he's sent to me. I should throw them away and forget he exists. Vacate the space blocked out for Remington in my brain.

I can't seem to throw him out, but I also can't let him let me down again. Time and time again, I let thoughts of him invade my brain and get lost in the turmoil of *that* night all over again. A sharp pain tugs on my heart, and I push thoughts of him away.

Focusing on my breathing and my pace, I pick up speed and race back to the house. Meeting me at the door, Nova hands me a cold bottle of water.

"Thanks, Nova."

She eyes my sweat-soaked clothes with a curled lip of disgust. "See, another reason I don't run. Sweat is gross, seriously."

I pause. "Wait, didn't you live in Nevada? Aren't their temps like ninety plus daily?"

She shrugs it off, walking away. "Yeah, but still. It's climate induced, not workout induced. Definitely not the same."

"Whatever you say."

I walk over to the couch to sit down, and she rushes to shoo me away. "You, shower. No sweating on the couches." Getting up, I let her push me towards the stairs. Climbing them slowly, I regain my breath. Today is a new day and I need a job, especially if I'm going to pay rent.

My shower fogs up the mirror and it's hard to see the woman staring back at me. I know her, but I don't recognize her as much as I used to. It's almost like she's a shell of herself. Not even the shy, beautiful girl I used to be. The one who was happy. Don't get me wrong, I'm happy with my life now, but it still feels like there's a piece of it missing. Luckily, I walked away before any more damage was done and it fractured to the point of no return.

It takes me less than twenty minutes to shower and get ready for the day. I had a couple of interviews lined up again today and my goal was to make the best of the situation thrown in my lap. As soon as I was dressed, I sat down at the kitchen island with my laptop, ready to shoot off a few emails, when one grabbed my attention.

It was sent from bmontgomery@willowspringssta-bles.com.

Beau.
Hey Faith,
I've received your email about being interested in the job at

Willow Springs. Although, I'd love to have you back I realized soon after that I'd forgotten to post the location on the ad. I wanted to reach out and let you know the position is still available. You'll have a room in the bunkhouse and paid utilities. It's yours if you want it. I know you've got a past here and coming back would bring up some bad memories. I feel it's my duty to tell you Remington still works at the farm, and if you decide to work here again, you'd be working with him directly. As much as I'd like for you to be here, I feel as though there are some major things you would need to consider first.

As always, it's nice to hear from you. Hope all is well.
Sincerely,
Beau.

Beau Montgomery. Captain, straight, no bullshit, front and center. It's my luck the job would be at Willow Springs Stables.

Even if I consider going home—and I don't want to—it may be my only option. I can't burn this bridge. I wrote a simple note back, thanking him for the response and the courtesy of letting me know where things currently stood at the ranch. He is right; I do have a past there and the very last thing I want to do was work side by side with Remington.

To have to gaze at his gorgeous face and know that underneath his shirt my name was inked against his heart was almost too much to bear.

A wave of emotions hit me, and I could tell my eyes were feeling a little more watery than normal. Damn, I would not cry over him again. He'd already taken too many tears from me.

The problem was... my heart ached for him.

Only him.

I heard Nova walk up behind me, and I frantically swiped under my eyes. She didn't need to see me crying again. She's dealt with it too much over the last couple of years.

"Hey, girl. You getting ready to interview again today?"

"Yeah." I sigh. "That's my plan at least. Here's to hoping today goes better than the last couple of days."

She bumps my shoulder. "Chin up, Faith. Things will work out exactly how they're supposed to."

"How are you constantly so optimistic?"

"Well, someone has to be." She winks at me, and I can't help but grin.

I stood up, grabbed my laptop, and threw it in my bag. "I should get going. First interview is at ten a.m. sharp, one at eleven forty-five a.m., and then I'll probably stop at The Drizzle and get a quick bite for lunch, then I'll be home."

"Okay, good luck. Break a leg." She hugs me, and I head out the door. I walk down the sidewalk toward my car as a breeze picks up tossing my hair around my face. It's a chilly breeze and I can tell the end of summer is here, soon to be followed by fall, my favorite season. I'm sad it'll be another year where I won't be home to witness my West Virginia mountains sprayed in shades of reds, oranges, and yellows, but I need to make this work. I don't have another choice.

The first interview ends up going great. I'm immediately offered a job, but it's minimum wage. A lot less than I was expecting, which means I'd definitely have to get a second job to make up the lost income. The second interview doesn't pan out as successfully as I'd thought it would. The job itself, great. I think I would've liked it. The boss, total creep factor. Not happening. A sigh leaves my throat as I push open the door to The Drizzle. The smell of coffee beans tingles my senses immediately.

A Mediterranean wrap and a soda later, I'm leaving through the front door of the shop. Finally, on my way home from a less than successful day of job interviewing. I know what I have to do even though my head is screaming it'll only end in heartache. I know Nova has been secretly encouraging it all along, but right now there isn't suitable work here for me. I have to move where the money is... and right now it's not in Ohio.

REMINGTON

I splash cold water on my face, hoping it will do anything to clear my head. Closing my eyes, I take a deep breath in and breathe it back out. Faith emailed Beau a couple of days ago to let him know she'd take the job. Which meant Faith was coming home to Willow Springs Stables after four long years.

It's hard to believe it's been so long.

My heart won't stop pounding with a shit load of emotions I don't need right now. Excitement about seeing her again after so many years. Anger and resentment over how things ended. Sadness that she'll be here, in my area, again. Ultimately, it means nothing more than Faith will be working alongside me at the stables. She'll also be living in the bunkhouse under the same roof as me.

My cock perks up at the thought, but I banish it away. *Not going there*, no matter how much I can't deny thinking about it these last couple of years. It's been a while since I've participated in any under-the-covers birthday suit games.

I stare at myself in the mirror, watching as the water drips down my chin, and my eyebrows draw in together in a tight frown. It's a frown permanently marring my face since the last time I saw her, and it's starting to leave a line. Like Michael Jackson's song, I wondered if I'd ever change my ways.

Fuck.

Faith is coming home.

I take a few steps away from the sink and reach over to grab a towel to wipe off my face and hands before exiting the bathroom.

I have a feeling the first week she's here is going to be a shit-show and I desperately want to ignore her, but I'm not sure I'll be able to. She's magnetic - the north pole to my south. It's going to be a battle of wills. Sure, on the outside I may not show any difference, but the complete opposite will be happening on the inside.

Somehow, I need to figure out how to deal with her being back. She's going to be here at Willow Springs, like old times, except different. The farm is laden with so many memories and special spots. But she's not only going to be at the farm, we're going to have to see each other day in and day out. I can handle it. Quite frankly, I don't have another choice.

I quickly finished getting dressed and headed out to the barn. I'm not sure what time she planned to arrive, but I won't be here when she does. A white car rolls up as my left boot hits the door of the double-door barn and I turn to watch as it parks by the bunkhouse.

Faith's gaze meets mine as she steps out of the car before turning toward the barn.

Damnit. She's even more beautiful than she was the last time I saw her. Granted, last time I saw her, she had red-rimmed eyes, blackened with mascara, and burdened with tears. I was shocked, embarrassed, and angry. Angry at myself for being in a position to have her question me, pissed as hell at Sofia for knowing she'd done something but not being able to figure out exactly what that something was.

I need to move, get away. I slip into the barn, determined to find a distraction, anything to keep me away from the bunkhouse. I start walking horses out to their own fields for their daily turnout. Grabbing a wheelbarrow and pitchfork, I get to work mucking out the stalls. Stable hand duties at its finest. Normally I'm delegated to mowing the fields, helping to break colts, mending fences, and other chores, but sometimes it's nice to get back to where it all began. There's something sobering about cleaning up horse shit.

A few hours later, I head into the bunkhouse not even thinking about a certain someone who may be there. As soon as I open the door, I'm hit with the sweet lingering scents of a women's perfume and I know it's not the scent Reagan wears. It's similar to the scent Faith used to wear, but almost aged with time. More defined. Don't ask me how I know, but I do.

Luckily this bunkhouse is set up with separate bedrooms, so it's not traditional ranch hand quarters. I peer into the room I assume she's staying in, and the sight before me makes me stop in my tracks. She's bent over the bed, grabbing Lord knows what, and it's given me the perfect view of her backside.

It's filled out more since the last time I saw her, but it is no less attractive. I barely let a groan escape my lips before I realize I've been caught ogling. Blue eyes stare back at me, framed by blonde hair with dark underneath. It's certainly different, but I can't say I don't like it.

I let my eyes slowly roam over the face I've loved since I was sixteen. The freckles scattered across her nose and cheeks are still as vibrant as they used to be, and my lips tingle, remembering how I used to kiss each one. Which leads to thinking about kissing other parts of her body as well.

No.

I shake away those thoughts. Now is not the time to take a trot down memory lane.

She has the perfectly shaped nose. Not too big, not too small. It fits her face perfectly. Trailing farther down, my eyes find her lips slightly parted in a question as if she doesn't know what to say.

Fuck.

I spent so many hours taking full advantage of losing myself in those lips. Sucking on them. Licking the corners. Biting her bottom lip as it always seemed to stick out when she pouted. I wondered if they still tasted the same as they used to.

Do they feel the same? Or do they feel older, more grown up four years later?

Her head tilts to the side as she gives me a once over. I wait for her lips to crest into a smile, but they remain flat. The air between us is stagnant, but there's a fissure of tension rolling in it too.

Unspoken words and a lie.

Does it make it a lie of omission if you didn't have the chance to tell her the truth?

The connection between us is intense. After all this time, I still feel the pull to her I've felt since high school. It's almost too intense. So much sits on the tip of my tongue to say, but something constricts my words from freely flowing. My throat feels instantly dry. We're locked in a stare down, neither wanting to speak or back down first. The awkward levels are ringing off the charts, but I can't move.

It's like my heart is still tethered to hers. My legs connected to strings like a puppet, only moving when the master tells it to do so. My soul is trying to sync up with the same wavelength as hers.

My first love stands in front of me, completely motionless. Is she breathing? Or are her lungs finding it hard to suck in the air so desperately needed as well? Finally, something breaks. The air between us takes a big gulp, and she speaks. "Hi, Rem."

Fuck, her voice.

It still gives me chills hearing my name whispered across those perfect lips.

"Faith." Her name whispered back is something I'd been imagining saying for years now, but I never believed it'd happen.

At least not in person.

I guess I could say I'm in shock and disbelief. She's actually standing not even ten feet away from me. A ripple of emotions is bombarding my heart, and I'm not entirely sure how to cope.

"It's good to see you." She says it like she's talking to a former coworker. It's cold, emotionless.

My blood boils. "That's all you have to say to me? It's been *four* fucking years, Faith. Four. Not a word, not a peep." I take a step closer, and then another. The distance between us eaten up in a few short steps. The scent I smelled when I first entered the bunkhouse is back. It's fresh and sweet, like she used to be.

Something inside her seems to snap as her lips fall into a thin line, followed by a snort. "You have no right..." She leans in and stabs her finger in my direction, almost touching me, but far enough away there's still a couple inches of air in between.

The reality is I don't have a right, not anymore. Not to her.

"I know, I'm sorry." I break eye contact with her. It's too intense. The feelings are swarming like an angry hornet's nest after you've knocked their home to the ground. I step back, leaning against the doorway, running my hands through my hair like I'm trying to get a hold on whatever is happening inside my body. Or maybe it's the memory of us that's tearing me apart and I hope to hell it isn't showing on the outside.

Fuck.

I close my eyes and inhale. A deep breath might help, but sadly it doesn't. I need to move, to get away for my own sake before we both say something we can't take back, but I'm immobilized.

Why can't my feet work when I need them the most?

What is this spell I'm under?

This can't be happening. I won't allow her to hold the cards. I wrote her over a hundred letters explaining what happened *that* night and every second since then and clearly, she hasn't read a single word of any.

I'd think if she had, the response I'd be getting would be a lot better. I understand the anger, but I also don't.

Yes, what happened looked bad, really bad.

Yes, we were young and stupid, but I'd thought our relationship meant more.

"This isn't easy for me. I'm sorry, I snapped. It's..." she speaks, each word pronounced slowly and measured as if weighing how they'll sound on her tongue, then stops.

"I know." I did know. She's talking about being back here. Being here with me at Willow Springs Stables all over again. I wish somebody would have told me that someday those days we shared would be the good ol' days. I wish somebody would've told me my life would shatter over one night. My life would change for good. I'd lose her, my most important stronghold.

Finally, my feet get the memo and I manage to mobilize myself right into my own room. It smells less like her, less intoxicating to my senses.

Beautiful and serene, like the dangerous blue-ringed octopus. I know it'd only be a matter of time before she struck; powerful enough to kill twenty-six adult humans. Sitting down on my bed, I let my fingers glide through my hair.

How in the ever-living fuck am I going to handle this?

———

Night has fallen and I'm sitting in my room strumming on my guitar when a soft knock lands on my door. I barely hear it.

"Remington."

Hearing my full name from her lips is unusual. She even called me Rem earlier today when she first saw me. Remington sounds so official, so polite and cold. So... disconnected. Like we haven't known square inches of each other's body since we were teenagers.

"Come in," I say and then listen as the door cracks open and she steps inside. "I'm sorry about earlier. I know there are things we need to talk about or else us working together is gonna be hella awkward."

I nod, knowing she's right, but don't respond, allowing my

eyes to graze over her body, top to bottom. She seems different these days. Definitely more athletically built than she was four years ago. I wonder if she works out, but then quickly shake my head to ward off those notions. My heart won't fall for those tricks again.

She quirks her eyebrow, waiting. "Well... aren't you going to say anything?"

I rub the back of my neck. "What did you do with all the letters I sent you?"

I don't miss the slight widening of her eyes before she gets them back under control. "I kept them, but never read them."

"Good, then read the letters. Start from the beginning. Everything you need to know is in those letters. Every. Single. Thing. Once you've read them, we can talk. Until then, I'll stay out of your way and you stay out of mine." My tone is harsh but what the fuck am I supposed to say? Let's hold hands and sing kumbaya?

She stands there, mouth agape, like she's appalled at the words spoken so coldly.

Did she expect me to be pleasant?

Like I'd go along with her, let's forget about everything that's happened and move on with our lives bullshit.

Not a chance in hell.

She juts her hip out to the right and rests her hand on it. A pose I used to find cute, now irritating. "That's how this is going to go? Seriously, Remington?"

I stare up at those ocean-colored eyes as they tell all. She thinks she's been wronged. "It's exactly how this is going to go, Faith. You take the time to actually read the letters and then we can talk. Then I'll answer your questions. I'm not the type to dust shit under the rug and I won't do it this time either. Not even for you."

"If that's what you want." She nods solemnly before slipping back out the door. A part of me feels guilty for being so cruel, but the other part gleams because if she wants this to work, then she has to finally get off her ass and read the things I spent so much time writing.

The door clicks and I get back to playing my guitar. I picked up playing about three years ago. Something to get my mind off life, plus I enjoy sitting and making lyrics. No one will ever hear them, but I can enjoy them. There's a callous on my finger with all the playing I've done, little wear and tear never hurt anyone.

Occasionally, Beau, Jameson, Rhett, and I will sit out by the campfire after work chatting, drinking, listening to the crickets sing, and watching the lightning bugs to pass away the time after a long day of hay hauling. It's a simple life we lead, but it's ours.

This farm is our haven. The four of us have been friends since high school, some longer, which makes us more like brothers than anything else.

When I was growing up, we were poor. Mama left when I was little. I didn't blame her.

Papa had a penchant for drinking a little too much and had been cited multiple times for violence from the police in town. I'd seen the wicked side of his temper one too many times to count. A few days later, I'd be on the mend. Not once stepping foot in the hospital, even if Faith begged me after a bad night of his bender and a few broken ribs, but I still didn't. I confided in Faith only. No one knew my father beat me. I took it and kept my damn mouth shut.

I wasn't about to whine each time life got a little more than I could handle. We Cole's had a bad name. If I told the sheriff about my father's misdeeds, he'd likely laugh in my face before showing me to the door.

Beau's Pop seemed to know when things got bad. During high school, he started offering me the extra room in the bunkhouse in exchange for my helping out around the farm. He was a good man. A true father, unlike the man who donated the sperm to create me. In a way, I was jealous of what Beau and his father shared. Their relationship, I envied it.

My thoughts shift back to Faith. She's home, and it seems as though she'll be here for a while. This can either be a good thing or an awful situation. Hopefully, she gets over her stubborn streak and does as I ask. Only time will tell if she'll read them—if things can ever truly be mended again. Or if I'm to continue on being broken from the girl I've loved since I was sixteen years old.

FAITH

I can't stop thinking about what he said. Tossing and turning all night long so I couldn't find a wink of sleep. It wore on me seeing him again. I knew it would be hard, but each time I glanced at him it was like I was seeing a stranger. Someone I hadn't spent years learning.

Read the letters, start from the beginning.

My stubborn brain wants to refuse his request. To punish him for what happened all those years ago, but a part of me wonders if that's punishing myself as well. Maybe his words are what I need to find closure. To move on.

These thoughts have been pounding my brain over and over again ad nauseam. I worry the words written on those letters will dive into the dormant part of my soul, causing havoc on the things I've kept buried for the last four years. It will resurface feelings I've pushed into the crevices of my mind for safe keeping because some of those memories are my favorite, even if they hurt like hell.

Instinctively, I know I should stop being so bull-headed and simply do as he asks, but thinking about doing something I've put off for so long causes my heart to beat erratically. Maybe I want to hold on to the anger. Hold on to my pain for a little longer, because if I hold onto it, then I won't allow myself to break for him. Being strong against Remington Cole was never possible. He has a way of creeping in and catching hold of my soul.

I pull the box out from below my bed.

The one that holds every message he's ever sent to me.

Each letter.

Every curve of his cursive writing.

The hundreds of tears I've cried when I received each one.

Tiny pieces of my heart scattered over the last four years from one night that ruined what I regarded as the best time in my life.

Sofia was long gone. After that night I swore to her we would in no way speak again. She repulsed me and I wished for bad karma so intensely, hoping she'd regret taking my first love from me.

It's early here. The sun hasn't even breached the earth yet, but I'm awake already. I sit and listen as I hear him walking around the bunkhouse. The bathroom is right across the hallway from my room and the steam from his shower seeps under my door, leaving me with the familiar smell of him. It reminds me of walking through the woods here on the farm - scents of mahogany, wood, and a hint of lavender. It didn't fit him well as a boy, but now he's all man and it suits him extremely well.

Goddammit! I suck in a deep, shuddering breath of air, doing absolutely nothing to rid the familiar scent from my nose. I've been here less than a day and he's already getting to me.

My hands find the box of letters again and I open it. So many thoughts and emotions are sealed within these envelopes. I'm a little shocked Rem even took the time to write them. When we were together, he hadn't taken the time to write me anything.

Although, I suppose if I didn't answer his calls or texts, this was the only way to get a hold of me. How he got his hands on my new address baffles me, but the fact he spent the time to do so cracks a little bit of my shell. Even if I'd never admit it to him.

I flip through the letters in the box, finding the very first one he sent me almost four years ago today. I pull it out and hold it, frozen. It's been four years. Four fucking years. My brain can hardly wrap itself around that thought. Am I finally ready to read this first letter? What does it hold?

A single tear slips down my cheek.

I can't do this. I'm not ready. But when will I be?

I fall back onto my bed and cover my face with my pillow in a pathetic attempt to seal up all the emotions I'm feeling so they don't slip out. I hold the letter to my chest, over what's left of the heart he slowly chipped away at until it shattered.

All the emotions assault me. I'm angry. I'm hurt. Stepping foot back onto this farm is proving to be a lot harder than I thought. It's screwing with me. I'm broken, and if it's possible, still breaking. Seeing him again. Being in the same room. Hearing him say my name again...

How is it possible to break even further? How can a person continue to shatter over an event from the past? How can a man I haven't seen in four years still affect me so deeply that it overwhelms without exception each thought and feeling?

What I want to do is rip up this letter and all its siblings and burn them. But it would only hurt me. I truly believe he'll stick to his word. He won't talk to me until I've read each and every word he's written to me. I'm also curious. I want to know the truth. I want to know why the one person I've loved the most in this lifetime decided to let me down. Maybe he didn't choose to break me; maybe it was simply an unlikely event catapulting the course of our lives together.

I have to know why the boy who was my everything and now my nothing broke me into tiny shards four years ago. Why he committed us to a life lived apart. Lonely. My heart still craves him. My soul still searches for him in the dark of night, asking for the comfort it brought.

Taking a deep breath, I decide it's now or never. If I want to know the truth, this is how I'll do it.

I slide my finger underneath the seal on the envelope and open it. My breath stuttered, my heart thumping so loudly I wonder if it can be heard from down the hall. Tears line my eyes as if they're waiting to fall for me, as if they can predict the outcome of this first letter. Will they tell me exactly what happened? Is this *the* letter?

The tears stubbornly refuse to fall, but obscure my vision all the same. I pull out the letter and run my fingers over the words on the page, as if I could feel him as he wrote them.

Dear Faith,

I miss you. It's been two months since you left me broken, shattered. It doesn't feel right of me to say, but it's what I feel deepest. I want to tell you what happened, but I fear you don't want to hear it. I assume it's why you've avoided my phone calls and texts since that night. So, I'll do something else. I'll tell you about it all, starting from the beginning. You need to know how I feel, how I've always felt about you.

I'll start with the first day I saw you. I remember the first day you walked into Mr. Stephens's classroom. You were nervous, I could tell. Your knees clacked together silently. Your hands shook as you reached up to wave hello to your new classmates. I remember I couldn't take my eyes off you. From the first moment, I knew you would be someone special to me. You would hold a part of my heart no other human would ever have access to.

Your eyes trailed across the classroom until they landed on me. I sat in the back corner of Mr. Stephens's class. I was the loner, the odd man out. No one talked to me, and the girls all ignored me. But when your eyes met mine for the very first time and your beautiful smile crested your face, I was a goner. I was lost to you. You became my world, even if I lacked in telling you.

I'd watch you. I saw when Jimmy Moon tried to flirt with you and you'd ignore him. I saw you when you'd sneak a peek at me in class and smile. You see, I craved those smiles. They kept me going because you were the only one who would give them to me. I lived to see them. You were the reason I showed up at school in the mornings and although I kept away, I still wanted you. Faith Evans wouldn't be with the likes of me. You were good, pure. I was the son of an alcoholic who beat me whenever his fancy hit him or for the fun of it. I'd grown up a punching bag to a man who blamed me for my mother leaving.

But you didn't see that part of me. You saw a boy. Someone who was hurting and lonely. You saw through me, it seemed. You smiled at me and I thought you could see the glimmer of the man I could be. The one underneath all of the scarred flesh and black and blue bruises.

The first time you talked to me, I thought my heart would surely beat out of my chest. I was so nervous. My hands were clammy, my breath short, but it was perfect. Minus Jimmy Moon trying to bully you because you wouldn't reciprocate his feelings. It was unacceptable in my brain. I couldn't stand by and let him treat you like trash. You would never be treated poorly if it was up to me. So, when I saw you with him, I raged. The violent part came out. I wanted to beat him to a pulp, but when you smiled up at me and said thanks, it all vanished. See, you brought out the good in me. Forever have, forever will.

Always yours,

Rem

My eyes clenched shut as a tear finally slipped free, falling to the paper I held, causing a smudge in the ink. His words hitting something deep inside me, causing a small fissure. It feels as though all the air has been sucked from my lungs and I can't breathe. A gasped sob escapes from my throat, unbidden, burning me from the inside out. The first letter has been so much more than I thought it would be. How can I say no to reading the rest now? I'll have to.

One day at a time.

One letter at a time.

It may shatter me, but I have to try. *For closure*, I tell myself. Despite my heart not agreeing. It seems avoiding him and our past is no longer an option. I can't return to Ohio. I cannot expect Nova to pay my way through life when I can't find a job.

I don't know if I'll survive seeing him every day from here on out, but I'll have to try. I'll see him and I'll feel everything I haven't allowed myself to feel for years now. I'll be sucked back into Remington Cole. The boy I fell in love with. The man I lost. The one person my heart wants unequivocally with each breath, no matter how much the brain tells me otherwise.

I shake my head, trying to get back on track. Today is my first official day back and I've got three lessons booked - one this morning and two this afternoon. It's time to wipe up these tears and get on with my day. Fresh air will help too. It'll give my mind some clarity, and the sooner I can get to it and away from the hallway where his scent lingers, the easier it may be.

I clamor out of bed and hurry over to my closet to grab the clothes I'll wear today. I need a shower. I stand by the door for a moment and wait to see if I hear any movement outside. I tried to listen to see if I could tell when he left, but my daydreaming caught me off guard and left me with an unknown. After a few moments of silence, I assume the coast is clear and open my door to walk across the hall and take a shower.

Turning on the shower to hot, I let it warm up while I quickly undress. I peer at the girl in the mirror, and she seems sad. Red-rimmed eyes accompany baggy under eyes and I assume it's from the lack of sleep and tears. A matching soap dispenser and tooth brush holder sit on the sink. There's a holder on the wall for shavers and I imagine one is Remington's. My fingers reach out to touch it, but I refrain.

The scrape of the curtain rings on metal is loud as I pull the shower curtain back. Stepping underneath the hot water, I relish the burn it leaves as it touches the whole surface of my skin.

Searing away the memories I've been dealing with all morning and hopefully rejuvenating me for the day ahead.

I reach up to grab the shampoo I'd put in here yesterday and see his shampoo. The same brand he used to use. Will the memories end today, or am I meant to be tormented for eternity? Shaking my head, I grab my shampoo and it burps as I squeeze out what's left. I'll have to make a run to the store for more. I gently lather it through my hair, followed by conditioner afterward. Some body wash, a quick shave, and I'm finished with my shower.

I turn off the shower and slide the shower curtain again. Reaching for a towel, I find none. My gaze wandered, taking in the rest of the room and finding nothing. I step out and bend down to glimpse in the cabinet under the sink. Nothing there either.

You have got to be kidding me. How did I not think about bringing in a towel with me? I can't believe my errors in judgment.

I stand by the door, listening yet again to make sure the coast was clear. The only place I knew the bunkhouse held towels was in the linen closet down the hall. Slowly, I open the door and glance around. With no voices and no movement, I assume I still occupy the space alone. I creep out of the bathroom and down the hallway to the closet. Upon opening the door, I see a stack of fresh towels. *Jackpot.* Grabbing the one on top I let it fall open and anticipate wrapping it around me but pause when I feel a presence behind me.

As I spin around, I see none other than Remington Cole. One thing clearly hasn't changed; the way he stares at me. The depth of the desire on his face as he gave me a once over had my veins pumping. I shift nervously under his gaze, suddenly hot and filled with something I haven't felt in years—wanted. I have the urge to ask what he thinks now, but it would be asking something I am not sure I am ready to hear the answer to.

His gray-blue eyes roam up and down my body, taking in and categorizing each naked dip and curve of my body. I feel exposed. Hell, I *am* exposed, but I won't let him see me falter. I am not ashamed of my body. I work out on a regular basis and eat the right foods. I am skinny and have some slight curves around my hips. My breasts are kind of small, but still a handful, and they look killer in a push-up bra. I am more in shape now than I was four years ago, so I let him take in his fill.

A few seconds later, I can't handle his stares any longer. It is heating me up in places I don't need to be heated at the moment, and I certainly won't allow it to happen.

Stupid, traitorous body.

I quickly try to wrap the towel around me.

He moves his hand to adjust the bulge in the front of his pants, and my eyes follow. I take a certain pleasure in knowing my naked body still turned him on.

No.

Don't think about any part of him.

It's asking for trouble.

"I'm..." I point to my room behind him and he seems to realize how long we've been standing, caught up in this moment.

"Oh, right. Sorry." He moves to the right side of the hallway, allowing me to pass.

"I didn't realize you were still in the bunkhouse..."

"I wasn't... I came back to grab something and... well, here we are. I'll be on my way now." He moves to walk past me, but his arm still grazes along the side of me, sending tingles up and down my body.

"Okay." I nod, then hurry into my room, shutting the door. I didn't remember the clothes I left in the bathroom when I'd gone in search of a towel, so I grab new ones from the closet. I'll wear those other ones another day.

I hear Remington as he walks down the hall again, immediately followed by the shutting of the front door. Fresh air. I need fresh air. I finish getting ready quickly and head out the same way Rem did just minutes before me.

The morning breeze hits me square in the face as I open the

door, clinging to my wet, freshly washed hair. Dawn has risen and gone and the sun is shining brightly in the sky.

As I survey the expanse of the farm, I listen to the whinnies of horses and different animals as they wake for a new day.

My eyes find him as he walks across the yard, heading toward the barn. I can't help but enjoy the way he strides - all manly, like he owns the ground he walks on. It's as if he knows I'm watching him because he lifts his eyes to meet mine and smiles. A small smile, but a smile nonetheless.

The smile says a million things, but the most prominent is he still cares about me. It's a traitorous thought to have, after how my morning has gone so far. I shut it down. I can't think those thoughts with him in such close proximity. For some reason, it seems my thoughts and emotions are all tangled up in him, which means they don't listen to common sense when he's in my presence. My mind swirls minute by minute, but a car pulls up, finally distracting me from him.

My first student of the day has arrived. I let my feet guide me to the barn, where I greet her. She's barely seven years old and has only been riding for two weeks now with Karen, the stable's other trainer. Her name is Maddie. As I'm introducing myself to her mother, I hear footprints behind me. Two sets. Human and horse.

Turning, I see my old horse, Koko. The white mare I used to ride when Remington and I would hang out at Willow Springs. My eyes try to tear up, but I swallow hard, trying to push them away.

Walking toward her, I reach up to pet her fetlock. "Hey, sweet girl. I've missed you." I whisper it, but it's the truth. Remington's eyes meet mine and I wonder if a part of me thinks the same thing about him. *Does he miss me?*

Get out of your head, I remind myself.

Clearing my throat, I thank him for bringing her in from the pasture. Walking her over to the cross ties in the barn, I slip one hook on each side of her halter.

Looking down at Maddie, I smile. "All right, Maddie. Do you remember what we do from here?"

She smiles up at me and nods. "Yep, we need to curry her first and then use the big brush. It gets all the dust off her fur before we saddle up to ride, so she's not uncomfortable. Then we need to pick out her feet to make sure she hasn't picked up any dirt or stones in the field."

I'm astounded my seven-year-old student has learned this much about Koko in only two weeks of training with Karen. "Okay, then. Let's go ahead and get started."

We make our way to the tack room and she collects the brushes while I grab the tack and the bridle we'll need for today. I hang the saddle over Koko's half open stall door until she's done getting groomed and grab a step ladder so Maddie can reach the top of Koko's back. She seems short for a seven-year-old.

"Ready for me to start brushing, Miss Faith?"

I can't help the smile creasing my lips at her cheerful tone. It's been a few years since anyone called me Miss Faith, and I have to admit I missed it. *This.* Teaching children how to ride and fall in love with horses like I did when I was fifteen.

I remember the giddy feeling of learning something new. Waiting for your next horseback riding lesson and reading all the books you could find on it.

The magic of being able to control a twelve-hundred-pound animal with the twitch of a rein or a flick of the wrist. Maddie starts at the top of Koko's neck, brushing in circles as she brushes down and over Koko's back, stepping down from the ladder to get her side and belly.

"Do you remember why we brush the horse's belly?" I ask her.

"Cause if there's any dirt under there, it doesn't get stuck under her girth, and make Koko angry."

"That's right, Maddie." She gives me a big grin, and I can't help but feel proud of her. My eyes lift over Koko's back and I find movement at the far end of the stable. Remington is moving a wheelbarrow from stall to stall, more than likely cleaning up. I watch as his muscles bunch and bulge under his shirt with each movement of the pitchfork. *Was his body this built back then?* I don't remember him being this muscular. Or maybe I've been trying so hard to block him out. I truly don't remember because I wouldn't allow myself.

His breathtaking gray-blue eyes appraise me, and I quickly glance away, feeling guilty at being caught staring again. I can't help it. My eyes are perpetually drawn back to him whenever he's in my aura. The current of the air feels as if it changes when he's close by, like one magnet drawn to another.

Back to the task at hand, I focus on Maddie's hand as she brushes Koko, who's standing as calm as can be, back leg caulked in a resting pose. She's a bomb proof horse. It's what they've continually said. She's so gentle. If a bomb went off around her, she'd probably eye it once and keep going.

Ten minutes later, Koko is saddled and her girth is tightened. Maddie, although adorable, wouldn't have the strength it takes to fully cinch up a saddle. I slip the bit into Koko's mouth and she accepts it willingly.

I nod at my student. "Okay, Maddie. Grab her reins and let's take her to the arena."

"Okie dokey, Miss Faith." I watch as Maddie gently pulls on Koko's reins and the horse dutifully follows along. She's so slow and cautious when she's being led by children, and I wonder if she knows the difference. Her lowered head tells me a lot. Like somehow, she knows they're more fragile than a full-grown adult.

We walk up to the mounting block and Maddie climbs up to get on as Koko stands quietly waiting for more direction. Patience is a virtue when training children and she has it in stockpiles.

After a few laps around the ring at a walk, I can tell Maddie is itching to speed up, so I suggest a trot. Koko's trot is lazy as she drifts around the ring. I smooch softly to her and she picks up a little speed, but not a lot. "Maddie, give her a little squeeze with your feet. Get her extending out her trot a little bit further. She's being slow and pokey for us today."

She gives her two gentle kicks, and Koko follows the command. Maddie is bumping along as she rides, her arms flailing around like she's grown wings, and I can't help but smile. "Collect your reins a little bit so you have more contact with her mouth. If you give her too much rein, then she may not stop as fast as you want to when you ask. We need to make sure she knows right away."

Brows furrowed and biting her lip, she appears confused. "Miss Faith, what do you mean by collect your reins?"

"Ask her to walk and bring her into the middle here so I can show you." She does as I ask, pulling back on the reins and saying whoa. She doesn't need to direct Koko because the horse consistently walks to the middle of the ring and stops.

"Okay, can you please explain?"

"What I mean when I say collect your reins is to make sure you feel like you have a light connection to her mouth. Here, like this." I pick up the reins and move her hands up them slightly so the reins are more collected and less floppy. "We also want to make sure we're not too collected. If we don't give her head and mouth *enough* rein, then she won't be very happy with us."

I watch as she moves her hand up the reins. "Like this?" she says, her attention on me.

"Perfect, see, you're a fast learner, Maddie."

"My momma says the same thing."

I give her a little wink. "I'd say she knows pretty well then. Okay, let's take her out and try it again."

She leads her back out to the rail and I watch as she squeezes her legs and smooches to get Koko back into a trot. This time her reins are tighter, yet not too tight. "Okay, good, Maddie. Now, try to think about when you're posting. Let Koko guide you into the up and down movement. Don't force it."

Her lesson continues for another fifteen minutes before we call it a day. Little kids only seem to have about thirty-minute attention spans, so I don't push too hard. We take the next five minutes to get her untacked and give her another good brush down, followed by treats of sugar and a carrot or two. Man, this horse is living the life.

REMINGTON

Closure.

She wants to purge me from her memories. From us. I don't want her to have closure. I don't want her to give up on us. I want her to read the damn letters I'd spent months sending her. It will tell her everything she needs to know.

I poured my heart out into those letters and it's a hard thing for a guy like me to do.

To express my feelings.

It was hard to accurately put into words how this girl was my whole world, and still is.

I'm not about to throw in the towel, but I'm also not about to give in and let her have what she wants.

I fought for us.

I'm still fighting for us.

It's her who hasn't given me a chance.

I wanted to tell her I drove out to Ohio. I searched for her and what I found devastated me. I assumed it was the reason for her refusal to read my letters. Maybe she has a boyfriend now. All these maybes are killing me. What ifs and damn maybes.

For four years I've searched for the magical switch to shut off all my feelings for this damn girl.

For. Four. Long. Years.

There was nothing to help me get over her, because the truth is Faith is deep in my bones. She's part of the house that built me. A house has to start with good bones and she's mine.

Our story? It's unfinished, waiting for us to build on it.

But in order to build more she needs to know the truth and forgive me. She needs to let me into her beautiful heart to chip away at it. Let me tap away until I reach the inner bits that were once mine to claim.

She's my one and only. I didn't move on. Hadn't been able to. I can't even tolerate the thought of doing anything with another woman. Faith broke me for any other woman. For four long years I have done nothing but work on this farm, write letters, and pine away over the girl who owns my heart and soul.

I've made myself scarce this morning. I can't bear to be around her because it hurts to be in her vicinity and not be able to talk to her or touch her. My fingers itch to pick up where we left off, but I have no idea where we stand. She's hurt, obviously. Her expression tells all. Join the fucking club because so am I. I'm hurting, angry, miserable. I've been a downright bastard for the last four years and I think Beau is the only one who gets it.

We're both pining over the girls we're in love with and can't have. I know about his past with Cassidy Mae. How he had a crush on her all through high school, yet didn't have the balls to make a move. Now she's married and living in the city with her rich husband. But unlike Beau, my girl is back, and I have a chance to make this right. If she'll let me.

As I make my way back to the barn, I pray she's not in there. Hopeful she'd returned to the bunkhouse or walked up to the main house to talk with Beau or Reagan. But before I even reach the barn door, my chest clenches and a smile trips across the corners of my lips. I can't help it. It's my body's auto response to her presence, even if she doesn't want to look at me. I can tell she's trying desperately to avoid me. And I'll let her do it for now.

A noise from the barn office stirs my attention and I turn to find Beau giving me a wave before he speaks. "Can I talk to you for a second?"

I nod. "Sure, man. What's up?"

"I wanted to check in and see how things were panning out so far."

I shrug, avoiding eye contact, not wanting to talk about this with him, although out of all the guys he's probably the best one to talk to.

"Rem, I can tell it's eating at you. When you aren't working, you're staring at her. When you are working, I can tell your head isn't in the game. So, tell me what's going on."

I swallow hard, the sound audible. "It's weird, I guess. Having her back here again. On one hand I want to wrap her up and hold her close until she forgives me. On the other hand, I'm so pissed at her over how everything happened between us. I know it's not all her fault, but I can't help but want to blame her for not even caring enough to find out the truth before bailing."

I honestly have no idea what the hell I'm doing. There is no damn manual on how to get the girl back after breaking her heart. It's been four years of being alone without her. But the second I saw her standing next to her car outside the bunkhouse, it all came back to me like we hadn't spent time apart. The only difference is she's even more damn beautiful than I remember.

Everything I felt for her came rushing back to me, like it'd been waiting to resurface again. I've never been able to free her. To leave the memories in the past and move on, not from her. She's my endgame.

Beau clears his throat, and I glance over at him again. "Do you need me to move her up to the main house? I know it's close quarters down there in the bunkhouse."

I shake my head. "No, I'm all right. I asked her to read my letters."

He tilts his head to the side. "Do you think she's going to?"

I kick my boot against the floor, my frustration showing. "Hell if I know. She's stubborn, not like I can tell her much. I hope she does. Then we have somewhere to start at least."

A knock on the office door interrupts us and I turn to find Faith standing there, face pale. I wonder how much of our little chat she heard before she actually knocked. Her cheeks are flushed red, as if she's embarrassed. She won't make eye contact with me yet offers Beau a mortified smile. "Hey, can I chat with you a minute?"

Excusing myself from the office, I decide to take off for a ride. I walk out to the pasture and whistle for Remy, who comes running. A whinny announces his approach. "Hey boy, want to go for a ride?"

It's been a couple of days since I walked the fence line and all it takes is a day or two for something to happen to a fence or for an animal to get hurt. I get Remy ready to go in less than ten minutes total, and I can tell he's feeling his oats today. He has some pep in his step and he's been mouthy with the other horses since he left the pasture.

I mount up and we're off, taking the tree line because it's the quietest place on the farm. There's something about being on the back of a horse, fresh air in my face, and a breeze trying to blow the hat off my head. The breeze whistles through the tree leaves, playing its own little tune. The sunlight reflects off the metal pieces on the fence.

The ride is peaceful and sometimes I spend my time talking out loud to Remy. He simply listens quietly, doesn't judge or expect anything in return. So far, the fence still appears fine, but up ahead something catches my eye. A hint of brown against the green grass.

I urge Remy to move faster, and he jumps into a lope. We're up to the corner fence in no time, and I find a small dog tangled in the wire of the fencing. Slowing Remy, I hop off and cautiously approach the fence. The ball of fur sits unmoving and I wonder if for a minute I'm too late. I keep creeping closer, waiting for any signs of life. When I get right on top of the dog, I see its stomach move up and down almost stunted. Its breathing is slow, but gives me hope. It's still alive, for now.

The dog has gotten its foot wrapped up in the wire fencing. I pull out my wire cutters from the saddlebag to break him out of it. The poor thing doesn't even struggle and lets me work, so I do it quickly. Remy munches on some grass nearby, waiting for direction. "It's okay, buddy. We'll get you better." I say softly to the little dog.

Picking him up, I slowly walk over to where Remy stands and grab his reins. I place the lifeless pup down gently in front of the horn on my saddle and then climb up behind. We move at a faster pace on the way back knowing I'll need Beau to call the vet out to exam this little guy.

As Remy trots up to the barn, I holler for Beau, who quickly runs out. "Need to call the vet. Found this little guy about halfway down the fence line. His leg was caught in the wiring and is pretty mangled. Not sure how long he's been out there, but he's not fighting me at all."

Beau pulls out his phone and speed dials the vet, explaining the situation. "Yes, not sure how old the pup is, but I don't believe he's reached maturity." His head nods as the vet talks to him about what to do next. "Okay, we'll bring him right away."

"Rem, we need to run him into town. There's no telling how long he's been out in the field. Given the way his skin is, he's probably dehydrated. Plus, we don't know how extensive the damage to his leg is."

I nod and quickly dismount. Grabbing a horse blanket, I walk over and place it on a bale of hay. I lift the puppy carefully from the front of my saddle and bring him to lie on the blanket while I untack Remy.

I'm walking Remy into the barn when Faith ambles out. "What's all the commotion out here?" Her eyes find the puppy bundle and she runs over. Reaching down, she slips her fingers into the pup's soft fur. The end of his tail tries to wag, and it's the most pathetic thing I've ever seen, but it's also damn cute.

"Hey, little buddy. We'll get you all fixed up. What happened to him?" Her eyes don't leave the dog, not for a minute, but I know she's speaking to me.

"Got caught up in some fencing in the field. A vet trip is in order for this little dude."

"Aww, you poor thing." She leans down and whispers before gently placing a kiss on the top of his head. This dog is dirty and we have no idea what kind of diseases it may have and here's Faith treating it like a family member. My heart threatens to burst from my chest and give her my anger. She'll treat a dog she doesn't know like royalty, but she won't even read the letters I sent her. Without a second thought.

A part of me is bitter. I'll admit it. She's owned my heart for years, yet treats this small animal better than me.

Getting back to the task at hand, I unbridle Remy and connect his halter to the cross ties, followed by pulling the saddle and pad from his back and plopping it down on an empty saddle rack outside of his stall.

He's not breathing heavily, and he's not sweating at all, so I'll take him back out to the pasture.

As my eyes find the end of the barn, Faith comes into view again. Her eyes are shielded beneath bent brows. Almost as if she's trying to figure something out. She's now seated on the bale of hay beside the pup, continuing to pet him.

I untie Remy and lead him out of the barn toward the field. I turn him loose and watch as he runs away, whinnying his return to his friends. I make my way back toward the barn and pick up the puppy from the blanket on the bale of hay. Faith follows me as I lead the way to my truck.

I stop and turn to face her, lifting an eyebrow expectantly. "I'm going with you," she demands.

I raise an eyebrow. Who the fuck does she think she is right now?"Like hell, you are."

Legs spread and arms crossed she looks at me with disdain. "Remington Cole, I am going with you."

There is an edge to my laughter and tone. "No, you ain't."

Putting her hands on her hips, she narrows her eyes. I don't budge and she must realize this isn't working and instead she gives me a small smile that only builds the longer I look at her. Her smile used to melt even my cold, dead heart to her whims.

Lucky for me, her charm doesn't work anymore. Unlucky for me, her pinched brows and pursed lips tell me I won't say no and get away with it. And... we're back to her hands on her hips with a raised eyebrow. "Who will hold him so he doesn't fall off the seat onto the floor? Hmm? Admit it, bringing me along would make him feel more comfortable."

A huff purged itself from my throat. "Fine, get in the damn truck."

"Thank you." She says smugly.

I grind my teeth. "You're not welcome. I ain't about to sit here and fight with you while this little guy needs medical attention. Now, get in the truck. I'm giving him to you while we drive."

Surprisingly, she does as I ask, opening the passenger side door and hopping up into my truck. Opening my door, I jump up into the driver's seat and start the truck. I wonder what she thought of my new truck. Vastly different from the one we used to sneak around in when we were teenagers.

I'd purchased this truck with my own money. With no one to spend the money on I'd been saving, it'd taken no time at all to buy it. I hadn't ever owned a vehicle this nice, let alone ridden in one before buying it. It was brand new, dark sky-blue metallic with black leather seats, and a tricked-out dashboard filled to the brim with bells and whistles.

Did a stable hand need a truck this fancy? The answer was hell no. Did I buy it anyhow? You bet your ass I did.

I watched Faith as her eyes trailed over my most prized possession.

A soft silence befell us as I drove into town. I wondered what she was thinking in this exact moment. Did being in a truck with me bring back familiar, yet unwanted memories? Was she pushing them away too?

"This is a nice truck," she said, breaking the silence as it lingered.

"Thanks, I worked my ass off for two years to buy this thing," I said, suddenly proud of something I'd accomplished. I wasn't about to admit to the fact I couldn't see my old truck and not think of her and the memories it held between us.

Her eyes widen, but she doesn't say anything else. I notice goosebumps crawling up her skin and reach forward to adjust the air. For some reason, I don't want her to be uncomfortable in my truck. In my space.

Gathering herself, she glances at the radio. "You still listen to this silly old country music station you used to listen to when we were young?" She slips a hand to her lips as if the words were spoken unconsciously.

I smile, remembering how she hated the music I used to listen to, but listened anyhow. At the stop sign at Main Street, I plugged my phone into the auxiliary cord and thumbed through my music. I couldn't help but steal glances at her while I was doing it. Her eyes were glued to my forearm, watching the muscle work as I flicked my thumb up.

The upbeat tune of Fishing in the Dark seeps in through the speakers, and I wait to see her reaction. It's a song we both know. We both used to sing along to it all those years ago.

It sums up our love story.

The melody was ours.

We'd sneak down to the river and get lost in each other. A special place no one knew but us. We'd lay on our backs and count the stars on those warm country nights, falling in love over the stroke of midnight and rising with the sun the following morning.

A sharp intake of breath has me inspecting Faith. Her face is easy to read this time. It's filled with sadness and regret. A face I know all too well. One who's been staring back at me for the last four years. I reach for the volume knob to turn it off, but she lays her hand on top of my own, wanting to listen to it anyhow.

I keep my eyes on our hands, not wanting to move. It feels out of this world to have her hand on mine, if only for a minute. It is a comfort of a time lost by years. I wonder what she is thinking. Is she debating, circling, contemplating what happens next between us?

The truck behind us honks, and I look away quickly clearing my throat, the spell between us lifted in the blink of an eye. For the rest of the ride to the vet's office, we didn't say anything else, simply listened to more music as it played from my playlist. It's weird how after four years, it's still comfortable sitting in the silence with her. Words aren't missed as Faith hums along to a song beside me.

When we pull up the office, she smiles, her head still laid back against the headrest as she turns to peer in my direction. "Let's get this little guy all fixed up." The smile is weak at best. Forced. I hated it. I hate the way it curves wrong, not touching those beautiful ocean blue eyes of hers. But she needs time, and I'll give her as much as she needs.

FAITH

It has to get easier, right? Being in his truck less than half an hour brought so many emotions back to the surface. It's hard to keep them from happening. It's his presence. It brings them out in waves, tumbling carelessly and battering my soul from the deep recesses in my brain where I hid them.

How is it possible to need someone so bad I can't breathe, but also hate them so much it hurts? I hate him, but I love him. Loving him is the last thing I want to do, but I can't help it. I'm unconsciously drawn to him.

This is why I ran, but being back here is challenging me. I didn't sleep last night and I wonder how many sleepless nights will happen back-to-back because I can't shut off my brain or the feelings flooding the crevices of my brain each time he materializes.

My body wants him, subconsciously reaching out to him unwarranted. My soul cries out, demanding I read his letters because it misses its best friend, his soul. My heart is black and blue.

The engine turns off and we sit in silence for a moment, unmoving. I'm frozen to my seat, not making eye contact, but then I peer over. I wait for him to move first. Two minutes later, I watch as he gets out. The empty seat beside me where he was sitting is unattended.

He's standing outside my door, his eyes a deep gray blue, touched by the sunlight. For a second, I allow myself to stare at him, the man he's become, before I unclick my seat belt and grab the puppy in my lap. He opens the door and helps me down. My fingers tingle as they slide across his and I am swept up into the dimpled grin now curving the corners of his lips. "Thank you," I say quietly.

He squeezes my hand gently. "Always, Faith."

Chimes jingle as Remington opens the door for me and follows me into the vet's office. The lady at the front desk greets us with a cheery smile as Rem explains the situation.

A few minutes later, we're led to an exam room to await the vet. It's wallpapered in sporting dogs—retrievers, pointers, Weimaraner's—and light colors.

We're only left alone for a few minutes before Dr. Stafford steps in. She does all the normal check-in procedures—weight check, temperature check, physical exam, listening to the puppy's heart and lungs.

"So, tell me everything you know about this little guy?" Dr. Stafford says as she checks over his body.

"Well, we don't know much. I was out doing fence checks at the stables and found him caught up in some barbed wire. Not sure how long he'd been out there, but he wasn't moving much. He was breathing pretty regularly. Noticed a couple of cuts on his leg; may require stitches."

"Yep, it appears he's fairly healthy. Given his physical features and teeth, I'd wager to guess he hasn't reached adulthood yet. So, other than the few cuts needing some attention, I think he's going to be okay. What I'd like to do is give him some general anesthetic to get him clipped and those superficial abrasions cleaned up. I'd also like to keep him over night, to monitor him and make sure everything is okay. He should be able to return home with you tomorrow."

"What about his owner?" I ask.

"I'll check him for a microchip. Until an owner has been located, if he has one, I'd ask you to keep him at the farm. I can give you some food for him and you'll want to monitor him for a couple of days as well."

"When will the stitches need to be taken out?" I ask.

"I'd say in about two weeks, bring him back in for a follow up and we can check his progress then."

I can't help but reach over one last time and run my fingers through the little pups coat. "Okay, I'll be back tomorrow to pick him up."

"Start thinking about a name if you want to. It's better than calling him puppy." Dr. Stafford smiles at us.

I can't help the grin quickly spreading across my face. It'd be fun to own a dog. Unless his owner magically reappears in the next two weeks. *Wouldn't it figure?*

Waving goodbye to Dr. Stafford, we make our exit and head toward Rem's truck. I peek over at him, catching as he sneaks a glance down at my legs. I'd forgotten how short these blue jean shorts were when I put them on this morning. A burst of adrenaline shot through me as I watched him give me a once over. When my eyes find his, he shrugs at me without the least bit of remorse.

I open the door and hop into the truck. Gazing over, I watch as the sunlight streams in after him through the window. A slice of sunshine slid across his face, illuminating the blue-eyed gaze that likes to follow me. Tiny specks of dust dance in and out of the light, proving his truck needed a good dusting.

I realize my breath is stunted. I am suffocating on the smell of him and memories past. He winks at me, and I can't help the fireflies fluttering in my gut. The same wink he used to give when I rode along in his truck. Granted, this truck was nothing compared to the old one, but it is still the same boy who made my heart giddy.

His voice catches me off guard when he clears his throat. "Alrighty, well let's get you back to the farm. I have some other things to do, but they can wait 'til later." The smile no longer lingers on his face, and I wonder when it left.

Is he affected by me as much as I am by him? It was the last reflection I had before he cranked up the engine.

This cannot be good at all.

The trip home was quiet. Almost eerily quiet. Remington didn't speak to me once, and I hated it. I hated the whole damn situation. I wanted to kiss the fuck out of him and beat the shit out of him at the same time. My heart is battered from all the back and forth, the love and hate both radiating over remembrance of him.

I can't help it. My eyes were constantly drawn back to him as we drove home. The memories hummed through me at being alone in a truck with him. We'd spent so much time together, riding around in his truck, going places, exploring things, exploring each other... in the truck bed. I turn slightly and my eyes trail over the bed in his current truck. My mind conjures up the last time we'd been together, and I replay it in my mind, picturing him making love to me over and over again. Waking up the next morning, wondering if this was all a dream.

The way the sunlight hit his chest in the morning light was perfect, illuminating the tattoo he'd gotten etched into his skin. My name is a mark forever, permanent. I wondered if he wished he could take it back now?

It'd been a long time with zero communication; nothing had been easy. Trying to date again, trying to move on, and trying to accept the fact that Remington Cole and I would never be more than a story told in the history book of our life. It wasn't the fact that he hadn't tried to reach out because he had, multiple times. In the amount of over one hundred and four times to be exact. Not once did I make any type of move to respond. Too hurt by his actions to give in and let myself feel.

I wanted closure, sure, who didn't? But I also wanted to know why. Why the love of my life would do such a horrible thing with the girl I called my best friend at the time? I partially blamed myself for what happened. I'd known better than to bring Rem around my friends. For years I had some sort of premonition Sofia was exactly who I feared she was. A liar, master manipulator, and a bitch. I simply didn't want to believe it.

A part of me believed looking him in the eye would give me closure. I would know unequivocally that Remington Cole was a fixture of my past and not meant to be a part of my future. I wished it'd help. Four years is too long to be hung up on the boy who broke your heart, but something still called me to him. Something whispered we weren't finished yet. I gave him everything, each piece of me and he threw it away like it was nothing. Like I meant nothing. But his letters twice a month directly contradicted it. Some part of him did still care.

Remington and I had been friends to start. There was a day, a single solitary moment, I realized I felt more for him than just friendship. I wanted him to be my person. To share more than just the normal friend things. It was something about the way he looked at me, something in his eyes told me he wanted it too —more.

It was how the happiest years of my life started. I was happy with Remington, so happy. Juvenile at times, but happy nonetheless.

———

It'd been a week since I stepped foot back onto the farm and I feel naked, exposed to him. Each morning is the same. I rise at seven a.m., go for a run, and then ready myself to meet my first student at the barn by nine. He brings Koko in for my lessons and I thank him politely.

The days are long and each is different. A new student, a different type of lesson, maybe no lessons for the day. I always find something to occupy my time.

I enjoy lunch and dinner at the main house with Reagan, Beau, Karen, and the other guys. At night, I spend time getting lost in my favorite reads by my unicorn author, while listening to Remington strum away on his guitar in the room next door.

My sleep is restless. I toss and turn until I finally drift off. Sometimes I wake to Rem saying my name as he loses himself to pleasure behind the wall separating us. I have to hold on to my sheets to keep from running to him.

We were young when we first slept together and the sex was subpar, but it was special. I wonder if four years had changed anything. Has he discovered other lovers while we were apart?

One night I'd gotten as far as my hand on his door. My pulse spiked as I pictured all the pros and cons this would have if I made the decision to walk in.

Luckily, movement from inside his room had me fleeing back to my own. My lapse in judgment quickly fixed.

————

My blonde hair was pulled back in a low ponytail today, but the humidity caused flyways to frame my face. The air was hot, sticky, and it made me wish for cooler fall days. My shorts had ridden up my thighs, exposing more of my legs and my tank top was a little lower cut than I normally wear, but the heat was getting to me.

Or maybe it was him getting to me.

For years I've kept to myself. Keeping my head down and working. I didn't party. My only friend these last four years was Nova, and I missed her fiercely. If she were here, she'd know how to handle this situation. She'd know what to do.

My eyes scan the fields and land on Remington. He is a mere man, I know, but to me he is so much more. A savior, a knight in shining armor, the love of my life. He walks around this farm with his hip hugging Levi's and his tight T-shirts, complimented by a backwards ball cap and sexy boots. *How could I not swoon automatically? And why is a backwards ball cap so dang sexy?*

I follow the length of his muscular arm down the leash to the puppy who held a part of my heart. We'd put up flyers in town at Orly's floral shop and Bodine's diner searching for his owner, but so far, no one had come forward to claim him.

We'd started calling him Bandit. Remington and I had started treating him like he was our shared custody child. He'd have him in the mornings and then Bandit would sleep in my room at night.

Shaking my head, I sink back into my job. "Heels down, Elizabeth. Push your weight down into your heel. It'll give you a more relaxed ride and it lets you maintain leg contact with Koko. If she can't feel you asking for more, she won't give it to you."

"Okay, Miss Faith." Her toothy grin makes me smile. I watch as she posts up and down on Koko as she trots around the arena. I teach different disciplines to my students; the hunter jumpers and the kids who want to be cowboys when they grow up. Little boys who admire the guys who work this farm because they are known for their bronc and bull riding at the county fair.

"Chin up. You have to watch where Koko is moving. Okay, let's bring her down to a walk for a cool down."

"Awww..." She sighs, long and drawn out. These little ones certainly hated when lesson time came to an end, and I understand the feeling all too well. I was itching to take a ride, but I wouldn't make Koko work anymore today.

As we finish the lesson, Elizabeth dismounts and takes Koko back to the barn. As I walk behind them, I plan out the rest of my afternoon. Elizabeth is the only lesson slotted for today. So I have the rest of the day to do whatever I want, and I can't help but want to visit the springs. It is my favorite place on the farm.

REMINGTON

I'd spent most of my childhood alone. I wasn't sure I had room in my heart to love another person. My role models weren't stellar with a mother who left me when I was young and a father I tried to avoid like the plague. I wasn't even sure how, but then Faith came along, and it was easy. Easy to love her, to dote on her. We slipped into a pattern, day in and day out we'd spend together. I remembered sneaking out nightly, simply to have her wake up in my arms the next morning. We'd spent plenty of nights under the stars, in the back of my truck, wherever we could find privacy.

I wanted to spend every moment with her I could manage. She was the brightest star in my life. It seemed so simple at the time. There weren't many expectations because we'd built our own bubble.

I had the world at my fingertips and I didn't realize it until it was too late. I shattered along with my heart the evening of the party. Bits of crumpled pieces littered the floor like dust scattered in the sun. They say grown men shouldn't cry, but I cried like a fucking baby the night she walked away from me.

You really don't realize how happy you've been until your light of happiness vacates your life for good.

Not until you're lost in the memories.

The day she walked away from me was one of the greatest mistakes of my life, and I've made my share of them.

It was only the start of my regrets. I shouldered the blame for taking the drink from Sofia. I wasn't a drinker. I didn't want to turn into my father and cringed at the idea. But I'd wanted to let loose and enjoy an evening with my girl. I wanted her to be happy she invited me, but the notion shattered fairly quickly.

I'd started to rely on seeing her daily whenever I wanted and in the blink of an eye it vanished and I was alone again. The hole it left in my heart didn't have a fix. Unless she magically came back to me. But after years it hadn't happened, and I had little hope it would.

Two months after she moved, I drove into the city to see her. I was desperate. I hadn't slept in two months and the guilt was eating at my insides like a parasite taking over my body. I needed to see her, even if she wouldn't talk to me. She'd weaved her way into my veins, providing my own special version of a high.

I drove to the campus of her university and waited. She'd kept in touch with Reagan when she left to give her updates occasionally, so I'd bribed Reagan to tell me whatever she knew. Pulling up to the curb outside her dorm, I'd put the truck in park so as to not draw attention to myself. But there was no way my old rust bucket wouldn't be an eyesore for anyone staring.

I'd rolled down the windows to let the breeze blow through since my truck lacked air conditioning. I was almost surprised she'd made it the whole way here without breaking down. I sat there for a while, waiting before eventually deciding to get out and stretch my legs. Three hours in my hunk o' junk truck was excessive but necessary for my sanity.

I was about to get out of my truck when I noticed Faith walking across campus, but she wasn't alone.

A tall, bulky guy with dark hair, a tight shirt, and loose jeans walked with her across the courtyard toward her dorm, and my stomach dropped. When he moved to drape his arm around her shoulders and she didn't move to brush him off, I fought the bile creeping up the back of my throat.

She'd moved on.

Without me.

I couldn't move, forced to sit and watch as another man held the woman I was in love with so closely.

My woman.

My Faith.

He tucked her into his side as they walked up to the front door of the dorm.

Together.

He didn't release her, even as he opened the door for her. She smiled up at him and mouthed *thank you,* and a curse flew from my lips. It had to be a sick, cruel joke.

Two months.

She'd moved on two months after she'd left me without a word. I could only imagine what was about to happen between them. Anyone could guess.

I couldn't watch anymore, knowing he was with her and I wasn't. Knowing he was touching her body, the same one once mine to cherish.

It was him inside of her instead of me. Jealousy roared through the very heart of me, creeping and weaving into every deep and dark crevice it could find. My fists clenched in my seat as my eyes watered.

How could she do this to me? How could she have moved on? The musing of interest in a woman other than Faith made me feel sick to my stomach. Yet, apparently, it was easy for her. Did she have much apathy for us? He made her smile. One of the smiles only I should have.

In my pros and cons list about coming here, I hadn't realized this is the situation I'd be walking into. I had not pictured her with someone else. As if what was between us wasn't as important to her.

I cursed at myself banging on the steering wheel. I'd done this. My stupidity of taking a drink from someone had given her the chance to find comfort in someone else. Someone who wasn't me.

Starting up the engine again, I put the truck into drive and left. I wouldn't torture myself any further thinking about all the things happening between them in her dorm room this very minute.

I had to release her. I only ever wanted her to be happy and if it was with him, then so be it. I wouldn't stand in her way. I had to force myself to leave. To walk away from the only woman who would hold on to my heart.

I could give up right now. Knowing what I knew, I had every right to move on and forget about Faith and everything we meant to each other. I don't think anyone would've been surprised if I had.

I remembered pulling back up to the farm the same night, lost and empty. Beau was standing waiting for me to get out of my truck. I took one look at him and shook my head. His shoulders sagged a little and I couldn't help the weight that settled in my chest. "What happened?" he'd said.

I rubbed the heel of my palm against my chest. "She's moved on. Faith is no longer interested in me or an us."

He'd invited me into the main house and we had a few drinks. I wasn't a drinker, but it'd gotten me into this mess, so why not continue? She was lost to me. My heavy chest ached for her. My world was spinning. I'd explained the whole situation, and he'd sat back and asked what happened next. I'd told him of my plan to forget her forever.

Slowly shaking his head, he rubbed his temple before calling me a coward. I'd asked him for his advice and he'd stared me straight in the eye and said, "If she won't listen to you then write it down. Tell her everything and let her decide."

I decided that night it wasn't the last time Faith would be hearing from me. She was giving up too easily because this isn't the way we ended. I wouldn't let it be. At some point I needed to get one more chance with her, and I'd patiently wait for it.

One week passed, and my wish was granted to me. A second chance. After four years of solitary, she was finally back in my life again, and I wasn't letting her slip away so easily this time. I wanted to pin her down and demand she read all of the letters I'd sent her now so we could move on, but I also wouldn't rush her.

After I'd brought Koko in for the lesson this morning, I made myself scarce. I wouldn't turn into the creepy guy who can't get over the girl. Even if I had no intentions of letting her go. So, I'd done odds and ends around the farm and taken Bandit for a walk.

A little while later, I'd brought Remy in from the field and saddled him up for a ride. Handing Bandit off to Reagan so she could babysit him like she's been asking to do for weeks. I needed time.

Heading out, no destination in mind, I found my way back to the springs. I came here often when I needed to think and my mind was clogged with so many thoughts and emotions these days.

I dismounted when I reached the clearing in the trees and led Remy over to a tree to tie him. The same tree that held mine and Faith's initials, even after all this time. Through rainstorms, thunder, lightning - it still stood proud. Our heart carved into the tree with the letters FE + RC highlighted in the middle.

Walking back toward the spring, I listen to the water bubble as it heats and gets pushed to the surface. My background noise is Remy as he rips up grass from the hard ground and chews.

I pause to slowly take off my pants, followed by my shirt. No one ever makes their way back here, so my being mostly naked shouldn't be an issue. I dip down into the thermal waters and sigh. It is perfection—with each inch, my worries and stress seemed to slip away. Steam curls up around me as water laps at the stone edges of the springs. The air temperature today is colder than it's been as fall flies in for a landing. Soon the trees will be turning colors and the leaves will start to litter the ground.

Leaning back against the outer edge of the spring, I let my head fall against a rock and close my eyes. The spring is relaxing in its own way, as if it is bringing me back to life slowly. The earth takes and the earth gives back to us and this spring is part of the giving. It renews us, refreshes us.

I stay there for what feels like half an hour before the footsteps of a horse caught my attention. Remy quietly munched on grass near the tree he's tied to so I knew it had to be someone else.

Opening my eyes, I turn my head and find Faith making her way back toward the springs. I watch her approach, waiting to see if she'll notice she has company.

I know the moment she sees Remy because she tenses up, her eyes searching for me. A grin splits my lips as I peer back at her and lift my hand to wave. "Howdy, Faith."

"Rem..."

"Water's perfect today if you'd like to join me." Pulling Elle to a stop, she appears to be weighing her options—her lip caught between her teeth.

"I don't know."

"You didn't ride the whole way out here to turn around and ride back. Don't make my presence cause you to run. I'd think you'd done enough of that in this life." The words fall carelessly from my lips without a second to think it over first. As soon as they are out, I catch the semblance of sadness tinged with anger as it sweeps across her face. It is sudden, but I don't miss a beat of it.

The slight shift in the breeze brings her perfume to the tip of my nose. Sweet, like her. I breathe it in while it lasts.

Her lip is still caught between her teeth as I glance her over. "Well, are you going to sit up there all day or give Elle a break and join me?"

She glances down at her clothes. "I don't have a bathing suit."

"Ain't ever stopped you before, when you'd become so shy? It's not like I haven't seen all your dips and curves before." I wink at her, hoping to ease the tension.

"Fine, but you need to turn around while I get in and no peeking."

Lifting my finger, I cross a line over my heart even though I know I'll break the implied promise. I'd sneak as many peeks as I could to get a glimpse of her gorgeous body again.

She dismounts from Elle and walks her over to the tree to tie her beside Remy. Spinning around, she twirls her finger in a circle to get me to turn and I do as requested, most of the way.

Peering over my shoulder, I catch glimpses as she drops her hands to the hem of her shirt first and pulls her shirt up over her slim stomach, ribs, breasts, neckline, and finally over her head. Slipping her fingers into the corners of her pants, she shimmies out of those as well. She's left standing in a pair of plain panties and bra. It's nothing extraordinary, but on her it's Victoria Secret level sexy. She doesn't need a fancy bra and panty set to interest me. She does it all on her own.

She starts to peek back over my way and I turn again, hoping I wasn't seen in the process. I feel the familiar interest of my cock rise below the water, and I'm glad it's concealed. It would surely give me away.

I feel the water disperse around me as she gets in, and I sneak another glance at her.

"Hey sexy." Her lips parted in a smile, and I couldn't keep my eyes from her.

"Remington Cole, don't you use that naughty tone with me. I came out here to relax my sore muscles after my long ride."

"If you wanted a hard ride, I could've helped. You only had to ask." I watched as she slipped into the water beside me and straddled

my waist. Her fingers strayed through my hair and I'd lose myself to the sensation every time she touched me.

"You're bad." She giggled, shoving my shoulder.

I quirked an eyebrow in question. "Then if I'm so bad, explain to me why we're both naked?"

"I was giving the water better access to my very sore muscles..."

"Uh huh..."

"What? It's true."

I leaned in to kiss her neck and she let out a small moan. "Well, I guess I'll have to enjoy what the water provided for me. You... naked... straddling me like a goddess."

She wiggled her hips and my cock woke up, instantly rising to the challenge in more ways than one.

She winked. "Mmhmm... someone missed me."

"He misses you often."

"Well, he had me this morning..."

I shrugged. "Tomato. Tamato."

Running her hands down my chest, she smiled at me. "Shall we discuss why you're naked?"

My shoulders lifted in a whatcha gonna do pose. "Better chance of getting lucky?"

"Well then... let's make it happen." She rocked her hips against me, causing my erection to reach full potential. My hands lifted from the water and trailed down her chest and around each nipple. I followed it with my mouth caressing first one nipple and then the other - licking, kissing, biting.

"Remy?"

My cock is now officially hard. This is what happens constantly when she is around.

"Remington?" Her voice is spoken with more bite this time bringing me back to the present.

"Do you remember the first time we came here?" A slight blush blossoms up her cheeks as I say it.

"Uh huh."

The barn had been crowded. Another busy Saturday and we wanted somewhere to be alone and hang out.

She nods at me before her eyes widen, shifting toward the water. "Wait, you aren't naked under there, are you?"

I wiggle my eyebrows. "Wanna find out?"

"Remington..." She turns away, and the connection we were sharing breaks apart. Leaving an empty feeling.

"You reading my letters?" I raise my eyebrows and give her a questioning gaze.

Her eyes find mine, her tongue dips out to wet her lips, and she shrugs, so blasé. "Maybe."

"It's not a no."

I lift my hand and drag it along her cheek unconsciously. It is easy, comfortable. And when she lets my hand stay there and leaned into it for a second, a tiny flare of hope lights up my chest like fire in the dark of night.

Hope.

Faith.

My eyes trace her lips as her tongue dips out to lick them subconsciously. I follow the trail it makes, wishing I'd be granted permission to take the same path.

"Remington..." My name leaves her lips on a whisper, a prayer. Begging me almost to do the one thing I want most.

"Faith," I say softly before my lips are on hers. It is a moment right before the first firework happened on the Fourth of July. You're watching the sky, anticipating the boom, anticipating what happens next. I knew this kiss was bound to be magnificent, but this is only the start.

She kisses me back like a woman starved.

Four years starved, needing me to feed the lust.

The passion.

The desire.

I run my tongue along the seam of her lips, begging for entry, and she grants it to me instantly. Her eyes are closed like she's lost in the moment and I want to close mine, but I also don't want to forget another first.

The first kiss of our forever.

I pull the ponytail from her hair, letting her hair hang down over her shoulders so I can run my fingers through it. It's always smelled so good and been so soft.

Her small hands find my chest, and we fall into the kiss.

In the connection.

The spark still ignited brightly between us. It needed to be fanned to flaming.

I pull her onto my lap, letting her legs drape over my own, but as soon as her core finds my cock, she pulls away like she'd been burned. Her eyes are scattering everywhere around us, but not at me. "We can't."

"Why not?"

"I just—"

"Say it, Faith. Don't stop on my account." The words come out gravelly and bitter. Our moment of peace shredded to bits in the blink of an eye.

"You..." She pauses, not sure if she should continue. Looking up from under her lashes, she studies me, weighing the outcome of her words.

"Say it," I demand.

A tear slips down her cheek as she gazes over at me. Pausing briefly before the next words leaving her lips gut me like a knife. "You cheated on me and broke my heart. I can't do this with you. I can't pretend like we're those same people. It's been four years Rem, four fucking years!"

Anger fills me. "Then run, Faith. It's what you do. It's what you're good at." She sends me a long, pained look.

Lifting her chin, she tries to act strong, but her arms wrapped around her torso say something else. "You're not being fair."

"Fuck fair. You think it was fair to ignore the hundred and four letters I wrote to you? You think it was fair to me when I came to find you two months after you ripped my heart out without a single goodbye only to find another guy's arm wrapped around you?! You moved on without a second glance. You didn't even give me the chance to explain. You ran. So, hightail it. Run again. I'll be here when you get back. Right where I always am."

She curls into herself as a tear streams down her cheek, and I fight the urge to wipe it away. Wordlessly she stands up from the hot springs, not even caring that she is half naked now—quickly dresses, grabs Elle, and runs.

My words were harsh. I won't deny it, but she brought out the emotion in me. Guilt laced with anger pours through my veins. I'd carelessly thrown words out without thinking. Without being able to take them back.

Another regret.

Talk about a river of them flooding my brain.

Fuck.

FAITH

My heart slams against my chest the whole way back to the house. I can't believe he said those words to me. Memories from the night in question are coming back to me like it was yesterday, ripping apart the carefully woven pieces of my heart without any remorse.

I almost didn't want to believe them. His words weren't angry, though he sounded almost hurt by them. I didn't understand it.

Urging Elle faster and faster, the gray bunkhouse comes into view quickly. I stopped at the barn long enough to untack and brush her before putting her back in her stall for the evening. Reagan was walking up to the barn with Bandit when I stomped out.

"Faith?" Her voice sounded concerned.

"Hey, Rea." It is the nickname we all called her. Reagan and I had gotten close over the time I worked here, and she was sad when I had to leave. I didn't tell her why I left, but I'm sure she figured it had something to do with Rem and I. They had to know.

Willow Springs was a close-knit group of friends, and I found it hard to believe the gossip didn't spread like wildfire unless Remington shut it down.

As she draws closer, her face grows more concerned. I won't make eye contact, I can't, or I know I'd lose my shit. I won't burden her with it. She'd often asked what happened between Remington and me, but I'd yet to share.

A part of me doesn't want him to get a bad rap in the eyes of his friends.

The other part of me wants to tell the truth, to understand why he'd done it before I blamed him.

Deep down I hoped there had been a reasonable excuse as to why my best friend was straddling the love of my life in a dirty frat house bedroom. Why she didn't have a shirt on and only a bra? A tear slides down my face, and I quickly wipe it away. Gazing down at Bandit, I reach down to lift him. "Thanks for watching him this afternoon, Rea."

Straightening back up, I turn to walk away, but before I can, Reagan's hand reaches out and touches the back of my arm. "Hey, Faith. You know you can talk to me about anything, right?" Her words sound sincere, but I can't deal with that right now.

"I know," I whisper back.

She tilts her head, eyebrows furrowed as she bites her bottom lip. "Okay... well, I'm here."

"Thanks." My smile is weak. I know it. Hell, she probably does too.

In a split second the smile is back and she's bouncing on her toes, like a kid on Christmas morning "Hey, we're all heading over to Bodine's for some drinks and dancing later. You should come with us."

I shake my head. "I don't know..."

"Faith, you've been here a week. You need to live a little. Bust some moves. Drink a little too much alcohol and let loose. Stop acting like you hate being back and start to enjoy it. We aren't all moody, grumpy assholes. He'll come around, give him time."

"How about I think about it?" It isn't exactly a no.

"I'll meet you in front of the bunkhouse at seven. I have the perfect outfit for you."

I shake my head as a small snort comes out. Damn, she is determined. It must be hard being the only lady on a farm full of men. "Fine. I'll see you then."

She squeals, scaring the bejesus out of me, and then laughs. "Damn girl. See, you need to lighten up some."

She'd brought a smile to my face, but as soon as I turned to head back to the bunkhouse the sadness returned. I need to read more of his letters. If he isn't willing to speak to tell me the truth, then I need to read what happened. I am tired of wondering what happened. It is starting to eat at me, and every time I see him, the memories plague me.

I open the door to the bunkhouse and let myself in, Bandit snuggled tight in my arms. I pause in the entryway and let my eyes take in the space. I hadn't hung out here when I was in high school and college, but I like how it is decorated.

I don't think I'd actually consider it a bunkhouse, even though it's what we called it. Typical bunkhouses have rooms with multiple bunks and it did have one large room in the back, but Remington and I both had our own rooms.

The living room area is done in a rustic design. Exposed wooden beam ceilings with evenly spaced lighting. A wooden handmade coffee table with etchings sits in the middle, surrounded by leather couches and a dark clothed recliner. A faux animal rug lines the floor and each side table has a lamp on it - one decorated with metal running horses and the other with horseshoes. The front wall held a stone fireplace and above it is a flatscreen TV hinged to the wall. It is small but quaint.

The kitchen is a decent size for what it is and the appliances are all up to date, indicating it'd recently been remodeled to suit the guests who lived here.

Making my way to my room, I admire the paintings hung along the wall. Most of the time Remington is here, or I was afraid

I'd be caught alone with him without the right words to say, and I didn't have the time to fully take in my surroundings. Not wanting to dawdle too long, I close the door. As I let Bandit down, he scurries off to his bed in the corner.

I grab the box from under my bed and lay it on top of the covers. I need to read another couple of letters before heading out tonight with the crew.

The first letter had been about the first movie we'd ever seen as a couple. Sitting in the dark movie theater, wondering if he wanted to hold my hand as much as I wanted to hold his. Spoiler alert—he did. He was nervous as hell, and so was I.

The movie was horrible. I can't even remember the name of it. But I remember the way his arm felt around my shoulders and the way his hand felt in mine as he asked me to hold his hand for the first time. I remember laying my head on his shoulder and smelling his cologne. I remember the way he made fun of a couple scenes and I couldn't hold in my laughter.

I remember the way he pulled my hair away from my face and kissed my cheek, how I wanted him to kiss me right then and there. I wanted to know what his lips felt like. What the taste of Mountain Dew was like sipping it from his tongue. Feeling his warm breath against my skin. I wore my favorite new shirt and blue jean shorts. It was a warm night, mid-summer.

The second letter was our second date to the bowling alley. We played too many times to count, and he continuously beat me. The bowling shoes smelled awful, and I was pretty sure the guy in the lane next to us was still living in his mom's basement. Not once have I seen someone so excited about a bowling ball and some pins. We'd eaten pizza and had colas. When the bowling alley shut down for the night, we drove around in his truck for the next hour, holding hands and talking about forever.

My eyes are wet with tears. So many good memories, and I can't believe he'd remembered them all. I sniffle as I pull the next envelope from the box. I have an idea what is in this one and although I know it'll make me emotional; I want to read it anyhow.

Dear Faith,

I still miss you. Each day you're far away and I'm starting to wonder if space does make the heart grow fonder. Such a funny saying right, "absence makes the heart grow fonder." I didn't understand it until now. Your absence feels heavier. I'd hoped by now maybe you'd read at least one or two of my letters, but with the lack of response I'm guessing you've either moved on or you're still not ready to talk to me. With time, I hope you change your mind.

Some of those memories I've already shared with you were amazing, but this one is my favorite. Our first kiss. I remember you were incredible and I couldn't take my eyes off you. I'd picked you up in my beat up truck. You'd come running out of your house to meet me. Momma Evans yelling about how you weren't being a lady and how I should come to the door to get you instead of you running out. Let me tell you. I would've come to get you. Every. Single. Time.

I'd have bent over backward if it's what you'd asked of me. Gladly. The dress you wore was a deep burgundy color. We were heading down to Bodine's for food and dancing. I was a shit dancer, but you'd been begging me for weeks. Do you remember? You finally convinced me and I hoped obliging you would be worth one of your kisses.

Shit, I'll admit I was nervous as hell. I remember the whole time I kept wondering if it would happen. If you'd let me kiss you. Me... Remington Cole. The guy from the wrong side of the tracks. I had nothing to offer you, but you treated me like I mattered, overlooking all the gossip.

You had a burger and fries. Insisting on dipping them in ranch instead of ketchup. I thought for sure you would eat a salad. Most girls did. But you weren't afraid to get what you wanted. I liked that about you. Ranch on fries has become one of my new favorite things because of you. You opened my eyes to something I wasn't bold enough to try on my own.

We spent the next hour dancing away to country songs as they lit up the old jukebox. Holding you in my arms was the best feeling. You were warm, comfortable, the perfect fit for me. The way your perfume stuck in my nostrils all night long. The way I kept eating your hair when you laid your head against my chest. I had to discreetly spit it out of my mouth and let me tell you that wasn't easy at all. Your body fit against mine, and I wanted more. More of you dancing against me. More of you in that dress, those gorgeous legs on display.

When you leaned back, I couldn't help it. I peeked down your cleavage. I know, I know... typical guy, but I couldn't help it. You were hot, but not in the "hot I want to tap her way." Well, that way too. But more in the I was the luckiest guy in the world because you were on my arm. And when you walked away from the dance floor to hit the bathroom, I also checked out your ass. I'll admit it. Two words... teenage boy.

We had one hour left until your curfew when you came back from the bathroom, and I wanted to do more than keep dancing with you. I wanted you all to myself. Do you remember what I asked you to do? Sit in the bed of my truck in McCoy's field and watch for shooting stars. I hoped we'd see one. I remember grabbing a blanket and a pillow or two and putting them in the back of the truck, hoping you didn't notice them.

Let's be clear, I didn't think I'd get lucky. I'd hoped, but mainly I wanted to lay there with you in the back of my truck and make memories. We'd driven out to the field and laid there for the next half an hour before we finally did see our shooting star. I remember it like yesterday. I could've sworn the star had some kind of magic because the way your eyes found mine next was a way no one had ever seen me. I remember leaning in and then you leaned in too.

Next thing I knew, my lips were on yours and I remember

thinking how soft they were. How perfectly they fit against mine. You tasted like mint from the gum you were chewing.

It wasn't the first time I'd gotten a boner around you, but it was the first time I didn't care. I wanted our kiss to last for the next half an hour. I remember pressing gently at first, but then begging for more. When I ran my tongue against the seam of your lips, you'd opened for me.

It was the first time you'd let me into your body, and my heart was pounding. My cock was hard. My hands were sweating and all I could think about was you were giving me my very first kiss. The seconds passed and I couldn't think about anything else. I pulled you against me and you lifted your hand to my chest. My hand found your cheek, next turning your head slightly so I could ravage your mouth from a different angle.

I felt like I couldn't breathe. I was gladly willing to die kissing you. If it was the last thing I did, I'd die a happy man. I miss your kisses. Every damn day.

Always yours,

Rem

FAITH

Reagan knocks on my door at seven sharp. With a burgundy outfit in her hands she shoved past me into my room. Here, try this on." A gasp leaves my lips as she lets it fall onto the bed. Deja vu hits hard. This dress reminds me of another one I'd recently remembered.

Granted, this one was a lot sexier, less high school virgin. I shake my head. "Rea... I don't know about this." It is a burgundy swing dress with a keyhole back.

"Girl, wear it. Own it. You have a rockin' bod and it should be shown off."

I don't want to be *that* girl—the prude. I'd been her for most of my life until I fell for Remington and gave him my firsts. I'm not her anymore. Granted, I'd only ever had sexual experiences with one guy. Maybe it was time I changed that. I wasn't ready to forgive him yet, and I still didn't know if I would ever be able to.

"You know what... why not?" Reagan jumped up and down, clapping her hands.

"Yes, Faith! Get it, girl! God, I've so missed having a girl around here to hang out with. These boys are such a damn drag." Thirty minutes later I am dressed, hair done, makeup dolled and ready to let loose as Reagan said. I still don't feel it, but hanging out with my friends sure as hell beats sitting at home feeling sorry for myself.

We all load into the Stable's SUV and head down to Bodine's on Main Street. Well, almost all of us. I hadn't seen Remington since we were at the hot springs earlier, and I wondered if he'd even show after his outburst. A part of me hoped he would, but the other half prayed he wouldn't. If I truly wanted a night out without stress, then I didn't need him there watching me.

Pulling up to Bodine's felt nostalgic. I'd wondered how it had changed over the years and I was about to find out firsthand. The outside still looked like the same ol' hole in the wall joint. The parking lot still had one constantly flicking light in the back, failing to get fixed. I could hear the beat from outside the building, so I knew people were jamming inside.

Beau pulls up to the front door and lets us all get out. I sit there for a minute before Reagan grins at me. "Well, whatcha waiting for? Time to show you and this amazing dress off." She hooks her arm through mine as I slide out of the SUV and we head toward the door. She isn't giving me an out at all.

I expected the same dingy tiled floors and mismatched chairs and tables. Hell, I expected the beer and burgers smell that seemed to linger when I'd visited. I found all of it. But what I also found that I wasn't expecting was a full-blown dance floor and people dancing. Years before, it'd been a small dance floor where only older people or teenagers danced. Tonight, the floor is packed with people of all ages.

They'd added lights and a better sound system. The music blares from the speakers in the far corner of the dance floor and it is deafening. Lights stream across the ceiling, lighting up the people on the floor. It gives the feel of a country line dancing club; except they definitely weren't line dancing. The rest of Bodine's is packed with people eating, drinking at the bar, or playing pool at tables in the back.

"Holy shit," I breathe.

"Yeah, I can imagine this is a little different from the last time you saw it." My mouth slowly drops open as my eyes widen. She glances back at me frozen in place and grabs my hands. "Well, what are we waiting for? We came here to dance, let's get in there."

"What?" I whisper yell. It is hard to hear my own voice over the music, so I lean into her and ask again.

"Oh, I said I bet it's different than the last time you were here," she yells back.

"I'd say..."

She pulls me along to the bar. I'd assumed we were getting drinks first and then dancing. When I glance behind me, I see the guys are finally coming to join us. Beau is dressed in jeans, boots, and a nice button-down shirt. He'd styled his dark hair too. Jameson's blonde hair has that windblown effect as he walks in wearing jeans, boots, and a dark T-shirt. Rhett... well, Rhett has on tight jeans, a belt buckle, a fancy shirt, and boots. He is sporting a beard and his hair is cut short. The man is dressed to impress, even if he had nowhere to go. It makes me smile.

My heart drops when Remington doesn't follow them in. He hadn't ridden with us, so I'm not sure what I was expecting. A sliver of me hoped he'd still show on his own.

Standing at the bar, I do a lot of looking around. I watch as the guys buy their drinks and then fan out to fully enjoy the evening playing pool, dancing, and flirting with women. Everyone except for Beau. He has a pensive face on tonight, and I wonder what is bothering him or why he didn't venture out with anyone else. Why hasn't he mentioned having a girlfriend or doing anything with someone special? He has to be lonely.

Reagan drags me out for a few dances in the middle of the makeshift dance floor, but the music and the heat of the crowd become a little too much for me to handle. It isn't simply me not having fun tonight—because I am—but I need a minute to breathe, a moment of silence away from the moving bodies surrounding me.

Making my way over to Reagan, I tap her on the shoulder. "I'm gonna to step outside for a few minutes. Need a breather!" I scream over the music, and she frowns.

"Do you want me to walk with you?" she yells back.

"No, you enjoy yourself. I'll only be a minute." She nods, and I turn to push my way through the crowd. As soon as I shut the door to Bodine's behind me, it is like shutting off the world. The silence is breathtaking, beautiful.

I sigh, letting out the extra air I'd been holding all night long. I can't help but take in another lungful of air. It is so fresh here, unlike the city. Bodine's is at the end of town, so there isn't much movement this way. The last traffic light is over a block away from here and beyond Bodine's is the McCoy's field.

The moon is bright tonight, shining like a beacon in the sky. Little stars dance around it and I wonder which stars they are or if it is one of those days when a planet or two is close enough in orbit to earth to see. I pull my phone up and open the astrology app. It is one I'd downloaded several months ago to see which stars were which. It is a nerd move, but I don't care.

"Pretty out tonight, isn't it?" His voice is deep and rich like the softest velvet.

I probably should have jumped when I heard his voice, but it was almost as if my body knew it was him. It is buzzing, slightly, like when you feel the presence of something a little supernatural. A ghost or spirit from the past trying to reconnect. I hadn't experienced it myself, but I thought it was probably close to how I felt.

"It is," I answer, not facing him. "I didn't think you'd be here tonight."

I saw him nod out of the corner of my eye. "Didn't plan on it."

"So why did you?" I ask, finally turning to see him. His feet are firmly planted a shoulder width apart and his arms are crossed. A mechanism to save him from getting hurt. He is searching my face for the answer it seems. Maybe he doesn't know why he was drawn here tonight, like me. Something, or more like someone, Reagan, had demanded I be there. The line between his brows vanishes the longer I gaze up at him and I fight the urge to pull up my dress as his eyes dip lower.

He swallows, eyes heated, and I can't help but realize I want him to notice. Maybe it's why I'd said yes to this dress. I wonder if he remembers the last time we were here. The time from his last letter where I'd worn my burgundy dress and he'd danced with me all night. The expression he was giving me gave me such a rush, and I wanted more of it.

"Hey, I'm sorry about earlier," I whispered, my voice failing me in my time of need, but it was enough to snap him out of the cleavage trance he was in.

He sighed. "It's fine, Faith. I get it. I... I wish you'd read those damn letters. Then you'd know. Then we could talk and you could tell me if we had another chance or not."

I hated the conversation we were having. It feels forced, like neither of us wants to have it, but we also couldn't walk away from it either. We'd once shared our deepest, darkest secrets with each other, and now we couldn't even talk like friends.

I let my eyes fall to his face, His broad profile in the moonlight. He was beautiful and at one time he'd been mine. My heart waged with my head. I wanted him but my brain held me back.

"Are you enjoying being home? Not the farm specifically, but I'm sure it's nice to see your mom again. Have you seen all the improvements around town?"

I hesitated before speaking. "It's weird, I suppose. I... I didn't think I'd be back here jobless and homeless."

He frowned. "You have a job..."

My head shifted from left to right, figuring out how to say what I wanted without coming off like an asshole. Because there was nothing wrong with Moonshine Springs, I just thought I'd gotten out.

"I didn't see my life panning out like it has at all. I miss the city. The cars honking, the noise of the city alive at night. My roommate, Nova. Tuesday night bar trivia."

"Bar trivia?" He quirks an eyebrow in question.

"I'm pretty skilled at it and I've made a little money these last couple of years..." I smile before remembering he wasn't there those last couple of years. It was my fault.

"It's okay, Faith. I realize you've had a life without me."

Remington is now standing close enough. I feel his breath whisper across my lips as he said it.

The door opens behind me and I hear Reagan say my name. Remy and I both turn to her voice. "I wanted to check..." Her words stopped as she peered at me and then at Remington. "You okay out here?" I nod, smile softly, and turn back to Remington. "Another time?"

"I don't play fair, Faith. Fair warning." I don't know what he is referencing, but I don't have the chance before Reagan is dragging me back into Bodine's. His eyes darken as he watches me walk away, and I can't shake the feeling Remington had plans for me.

Walking back into the bar, my gut swarms with mixed feelings. My eyes flicker back to him all night as I danced it away with Reagan. I don't know what is coming, but cautionary tales told me to be wary. Whatever he is planning includes me, and the last thing I want is for my heart to get broken in the process. I don't think I could handle another Remington heartbreak, but if I was going to be anybody's heartbreak, I'd rather be his.

REMINGTON

I hadn't planned on coming tonight, but I knew she'd be here and as much as it killed me, I couldn't be away from her. She didn't see me at first, and I took a few stolen moments to shamelessly ogle her burgundy dress.

I wondered if she'd read my letter finally. The one of our first kiss where I told her about the burgundy dress. I wondered if she'd worn it for a reason. Maybe she was giving me a sign. Telling me she was reading them without actually verbalizing it. Not much had changed over the years. She is a little taller, maybe, with a few more curves. She is definitely more toned than she used to be.

I'd yet to see her work out at the farm, but it didn't mean she wasn't. I've tried to keep my distance. I expected her to jump when she heard my voice tonight, but she surprised me. Maybe she is as in tune to me now as she had been four years ago, but I'm not sure what to think.

I wish she'd said yes to reading my letters earlier. It'd put me out of my misery. Maybe then I could relax and wait for her to gravitate to me once she knew the truth, but I can't wait. Because what if she isn't reading them? What if they are still sitting in the box under her bed? Don't ask me how I know where they are, but I do.

I blame Bandit. He'd snuck under there one day when she was out giving a lesson and I'd found them. I'd noticed there wasn't dust on the box, but I didn't dare open it to see if she'd been reading. It was too much of an invasion of privacy. More so than I'd already done.

She'd walked with Reagan to the bar for a glass of water, but now they are headed back to the dance floor. I can't help how my eyes follow her motions. I keep myself firmly planted at the edge of the dance floor, being her quiet protector in case someone worked up the nerve to be handsy.

Guys have definitely been checking her out tonight. It seemed she'd caught the attention of everyone in here with the little number she was wearing. It sure as hell caught my attention. She is stunning in it. My hands itch to touch her. My feet pleaded to run to her, but I stood frozen. She was enjoying tonight, and I wouldn't ruin it for her.

I made my way to the bar, pushing past the crowd to get a drink. Knocking on the bar, I grabbed the attention of the bartender. "I'll take a Coke, please."

The bartender lifts his brow in question but moves to grab it for me. I hadn't had a drink since the night Beau and I sat down. I knew it messed with my emotions, and I needed a clear head. The girls were drinking, so someone needed to watch out for them. Beau, Jameson, and Rhett were all doing shots with Reagan and Faith, so I was going to be the sober one.

Resuming my post by the dance floor, I watch as Faith throws her hands into the air, seemingly lost in the rhythm of the song. What I hadn't noticed was the guy slowly moving toward her as she danced. She must not have seen him either. When he places his hands on her hips from behind, she halts. Is she thinking it's me? Her eyes filled with hope for just a moment before they found me.

She knew I was staring; she must have. I can't figure out why in the hell she would allow him to keep his hands on her if for no other reason than to make me jealous. And fuck was I jealous. I want to run to her and beat the shit out of him for daring to touch what was mine. But she isn't mine anymore.

Her eyes stay on me as she grinds against him. I grit my teeth watching them. My eyes are hard on him, but he doesn't see me. I rip them away to glance down at her again. Her eyes still find me. I mouth the word *stop* to her, but she shakes her head.

She doesn't want to do this.

Not tonight when I am barely hanging on by a thread.

Not when I don't know where we stand.

Not when there is a chance for someone who wasn't me to swoop in and grab her attention away.

Fuck no, I think to myself.

Before I know what is happening, I am halfway across the dance floor, hands empty. I am gunning for him. If she planned to tease and antagonize me, then she'd find out the hard way what happened to men who tried to touch what was mine. And she is mine. Always had been, forever would be.

Her eyes widen as she tracks me approaching her. She shakes her head. But I am determined. The guy behind her doesn't realize what was about to happen as I stalked toward them. She moves away from him, but the bastard grabs her to keep her in place. My anger grows.

"I'm cutting in," I say gruffly when I reached her.

"Rem..." Her voice is nervous.

He shoves me, but I don't move. "She's dancing with me, buddy. You can have her next dance."

"You're done." He comes at me again and I about lose my shit but manage to keep the last strand of self-respect attached. "You don't want to start this. Walk away man." I puff up my chest, making my shoulders seem broader. Rule number one of fights, make yourself more intimidating than your competitor.

Backing away, he puts his hands up in defeat. "Okay, she's all yours."

"Good."

"Damn it, Remington. I was enjoying dancing," she says as I drag her away from the dance floor.

Turning, I lean down so I was eye level with her. "I told you, Faith. I don't fight fair."

"I hate you right now!" she yells at me.

I scoff. "Hate me. At least you're feeling something toward me." She storms off and heads toward Reagan. I'm sure telling her all about how terrible a person I am for ruining her dancing and her night by showing up. I don't give a damn. I won't watch her with another man.

I spend the rest of the night watching her take shot after shot with Reagan. The guys had all paired off with other women. Even Beau was chatting with someone.

It is getting late, and I know last call will be soon. I am ready to be home, sitting in front of the fire and strumming on my old guitar. But I can't leave without her. She isn't in the best mind set after drinking for so long and I wasn't about to leave something bad happening to chance.

I knew something was off about her. Because as my eyes scaled the bar, I realized for the first time since she stepped back on Willow Springs land that she's smiling at me. The smile I haven't seen in four years, filled with flirt worthy notes and seduction.

The smile known to get me naked in two minutes flat. And as much as I wanted her in a sexual way, I can't. It's not the right time. Plus, I don't fuck drunk girls. Never have. Never will. It's a moral thing.

Beau, Reagan, Faith and I are the only ones in the car on the way home. Jameson and Rhett choose to stay behind and get their dicks wet instead. I'd have Beau drive me out to pick up my truck from Bodine's tomorrow. I need to make sure all of them arrived home safely, especially Faith.

I clambered into the drivers seat with Beau in the passenger seat while the girls fumbled into the back seat. Giggling and laughing about lord knows what. "Rea... isn't Remington smoking hot tonight?" She says it like she's whispering, but the whole damn car can hear whatever she says.

Beau looks my way, his eyebrows bunch and a frown mars his mouth. I shrug it off. This is not the first, nor will it be the last time I've been forced to deal with a drunken Faith. This time will just be the first time we aren't together while doing it.

I turn left into Willow Springs, onto the paved path to the farm. It's dark out now so you can't see the horses in the field, but there are some out there. Sometimes in the summer months it's too hot during the day to turn them out, so we do night turn out. We don't get many predators on the farm, but we tend to keep the horses in the pastures closer to the house.

I pull up to the bunkhouse and park. Beau gets out first, walking back to open Reagan's door and help her out. I follow suit with Faith, opening her door and offering my hand for her to step down. She takes it willingly.

I feel the spark of electricity tingling up my arm at her touch. I knew it was still there, but it's nice to have confirmation. Peering down at Faith's face, it is apparent she felt it too.

"All right. I'm taking Reagan to the house. You all right here?" Beau's words are directed to me. His stare is point blank.

I'm not worried about my actions. I have self-control. She is too drunk, so all she needs was to be put to bed, no matter how much my cock protests.

Remembering I hadn't responded, I glanced back at him. "Yeah, we're good. Thanks, man." He nods and turns toward the main house.

I slide my arm around Faith's waist to keep her upright, and she leans into me. The strawberry citrus of her perfume lingers right at nose level, and I inhale deeply. It'd been too long since I smelled it and I want to roll around in it.

No rolling around in anything involving Faith, I remind myself.

I unlock the door on the bunkhouse before pushing it open. I shuffle us through the door and pause long enough to shut and lock it behind us. We're clearly in for the night.

"I've missed you," she says quietly. The words spoken so soft I almost miss it all together.

"There's not a day that passes by where I don't miss you, Faith. It's the God's honest truth." I reply automatically, and her eyes find mine. She smiles at me and I want to melt into her. Give her whatever she wants from me.

Faith is smart, kind, and gorgeous. She's worthy of so much more than I have to offer her, but at this moment I'll accept her words. I've been waiting years to hear them. It doesn't matter that she's drunk and won't remember them in the morning.

I've found, sometimes, the most truths are located in the bottom of a liquor bottle. It's when people are the most honest because they have no inhibitions holding them back. No voice in the back of their brain telling them not to say it.

As I'm standing here mulling it over in my brain, I miss seeing Faith stripping right in front of me. She's trying to pull off her dress, and here I am trying to pull it down for once.

"Why are you trying to take your clothes off? I ask.

"Why are you trying to stop me?" she retorts.

"We need to take things slow and when you haven't been drinking all night. You're not thinking clearly right now."

"But you still want me?" Her eyes meet mine and the question kills me because it's true. I want her more than the air I breathe, but I don't want her bad enough for her to wake up with regrets the next morning.

"You hate me, remember?" I say, repeating the words she spewed my way earlier.

"I do." She whispers it like she is reminding herself.

I run my hand through my hair. "Faith, I've done my share of fucked up things in this life. The worst one happened four years ago. So, if you're willing to give me a chance, I want it too, but it's not a decision you can make while drunk. I want to do right by you this time."

"Slow?"

I nod. "Yes, I want to take it slow."

Even though my dick is protesting like an angry toddler, I know it's for the best. He keeps reminding me of all the places he'd like to see her bent over around the room. God, I would too, but not like this.

"Okay, we can move slow..."

"Good."

"Rem..."

"Yeah?"

"I may not remember any of this tomorrow, but will you at least kiss me? It's been so long since I've been kissed and I miss how it feels."

"We kissed in the springs not too long ago."

"I know, I don't care."

"You want me to kiss you now anyhow, even if you hate me?" I ask.

"Especially if I hate you."

I'm standing there weighing my options like a goddamn loser. The love of my life is asking for something simple, for a single kiss, and I'm sweating bullets like I'm going off to war.

She smells like strawberries, citrus, whiskey, and sweat. It's a deadly combination. I'm putting so much pressure on this kiss as if somehow it's going to erase the bad memories.

I know it won't, but I fucking wish it would.

I pull her in close to me, no longer weighing the options. I'm taking the opportunity given- kissing my girl. My thumbs trail up the soft fabric covering her back until I find skin. It's as smooth as I remember.

She sucks in a surprised breath, and her skin prickles beneath my touch. My hands trail back down her sides until I'm outside of her ribcage. I can feel each inhale and exhale.

"Kiss me, Rem." She breathes almost a plea.

My one hand reaches up and I grab her chin between my thumb and forefinger. "You sure about this?"

This unsung need is static between us. The chemistry is still strong after all these years. Our bodies yearn to be together, even when we try to control it.

She's peering up at me, waiting for an answer, when I finally nod. It all sinks in. I'm about to kiss Faith Evans. She rubs her lips together and my eyes trail the movement.

At this moment, it's what I've wanted for years. Faith's blue eyes stare up at me in anticipation. Those waiting lips part as if she's predicting my next move and I want to take all of it in first. I wish it wasn't like this. I wish her heart was open and she wasn't drunk, likely to forget this tomorrow.

But I'll take what I can get, right?

I lean down slowly, and she closes her eyes, preparing for it. The longing is so strong I slam my eyes closed when our lips finally meet in the middle of this battleground. Love is war, and I'm taking this kiss as a prisoner.

I wince as the feelings of anger, hurt, and then love course through my body. She opens for me beautifully as I beg for entrance. My tongue glides in without preamble and slips alongside hers, and I moan as her sweetness tingles on my tongue.

Our kiss takes a heated turn, and she moans into my mouth, her resolve slipping. My cock protests against its blue jean cage. He knows what it's like to be inside her and he's begging on his hands and knees to have her again.

This isn't any normal kiss. It's one of those kisses that completely sears into every part of your soul, leaving a burn mark on your memories. One that snowballs into other things. It's not only a single kiss. It's a kiss proving the heart wants what it wants no matter how much you deny it.

She moans into my mouth and I get off on the sound. There's just something about the tone of it, or the way her eyes squeeze shut even tighter as if she doesn't want to believe this is happening.

It tells me something I already knew. There is no getting over Faith Evans. Or this kiss. There's only finding out how to make sure it keeps happening.

Breaking away, I try to catch my breath. Her heart pounds in her chest as it's pressed to mine. I rest my head against her forehead, breathing in her warm air. Somewhere I find the words to speak. "This kiss didn't taste like hate, Faith, it tasted like unfinished business."

"I know," she whispers, her eyes closed. "I know."

Faith

My heart was pounding, trying to free itself from the cavity in my chest. Each breath came in one burst after the next. His body was pressed so hard to mine I worried I might slip into a state of numbness. Like how your arm falls asleep if you lay on it too long.

We were in a tangle—lip locked, hands all over, and searching fingers. Somehow, between being turned down last night, I'd decided there was no more holding back. I knew I should stop him because it was wrong.

What we were doing was wrong, even if nothing about it felt sinful.

It felt fucking heavenly.

I also couldn't find it in me to care. I'd wondered if he'd improved over the years. Starting from a bundle of fumbling hands and ending up a fucking God in a mere couple of years.

I didn't care about a goddamn thing other than the way his fingers trailed up and down my skin, leaving fiery kisses with each stroke.

Whatever he was doing, I didn't want him to stop. I hadn't felt this amazing in years. It was euphoric the way he could bring sparks behind my eyes so easily with just the press of his lips to my skin.

I opened my eyes when his lips left the place he'd been kissing on my neck and watched as he pulled the shirt up and over his head. I let my fingers trail down his tattooed chest, hovering over my inked name before lowering over his abs, and fanning out right above his happy trail. My eyes took in the single pieces of work painting his body. Holy fuck, grown up Remington is in a whole other league.

The tattoos were hot. I couldn't deny it. Especially the one over his heart of my name. I let my fingers trail over it, wondering if the skin had left a bump where the ink bled in, but it was smooth beneath my fingers.

Puzzle pieces of ink had a story to tell - some good, some bad, some heartbreak and then love. So much love. A chronological story of his lifetime worn proudly on his body.

I'd missed the sight of him like this. Turned on and wanting me as much as I wanted him.

I couldn't understand my complete mind flip from last night, but I wasn't complaining. I was begging for more. Silly heart, I thought.

He bent to kiss me; his shirt banished to the corner of my room. His lips on me were frantic, fevered. He stole the breath from my mouth. We were sharing the same air between us.

My heart was lodged in my throat. His tongue flicked against my top lip and I reminisced in the feel of it.

I closed my eyes as he stole me away - my heart, the bad memories. I wanted our single kiss to erase all the shitty things that'd happened between us. As if it hadn't happened in the first place.

I sucked in a gulp of air when his lips finally left mine, heading in a downward pattern leading to ecstasy. When his hand slipped up my thigh, I begged him for more, moaning as I twisted the sheets in my hands. He was so close to where I wanted him to be.

So damn close.

Only a few more inches.

He kissed down my neck, over my collarbone, breasts, ribs, stomach, until his head disappeared between my legs. His warm tongue slipped out to taste me, and I lost my shit. Reaching down, I ran my fingers through his hair, grabbing on and urging him to keep doing whatever he was doing with his tongue so well.

All the pent up sexual frustration was playing out and dissipating in front of us. It'd come to a crushing head, a need to blow steam.

I sighed. *When did he get so skilled at this?*

Something jumps up on the bed and licks my face. Turning to find Bandit, I mumble, "What the hell?"

I leaned up, opening my eyes. The piercing morning sunlight streamed through the window making me cringe. I groan. "Fuck it, I'm dreaming." I let myself fall back to my pillow, my arm covering my eyes.

Remington is no longer here, and I am left with the face licker, Bandit. Pushing him away, I frown. "How could you ruin such an epic dream, little buddy?" My clothes, although sweat drenched, are still intact. *How unfortunate.* Maybe I need to get laid.

They do say the best way to get over someone is to get under someone else, right? I have zero clue how I'd accomplish it in this small town. Maybe I'd have to Tinder a town or two over. I'm sure it would still get back to the gossip mill here.

"Fuck my life," I huffed, heart still hammering against its cage.

I wanted to fall back asleep, but one glance at my clock told me it was already time to get up. *Damn him.* I peeled myself out of bed and stretched.

Let's get this over with.

I open my door and shuffled across the hallway to the bathroom, not even realizing I am still in a pair of pink panties and a "bite me" camisole. I rubbed my face as a yawn crept out and I gazed back at my warm bed longingly, thinking about how wrong it felt to leave it so early. I wasn't thinking about all of the deliciously delightful things Remington had done to me in my dream, with his hands, lips, tongue.

Stupid fucking dreams...

Moving back here might have been the worst damn decision I've ever made, but dammit, it makes me smile to see him in the mornings. It also doesn't help when he stares at me like he's going to devour me the first chance I break down and let him in. All I'd have to do was ask.

Remington and I have a past, a history. It can't be removed, no matter how much those lips of his tried to tell me otherwise. No matter how many sexy as fuck dreams I had about what would happen if we became a couple again reminding me of all the naughty things we'd get into. God, a part of me wants it again. Wants *him*. But I don't know if I can survive his type of heartbreak again. I don't know if I'll come out as unscathed the next time. But am I really unscathed? My heart is definitely black and blue.

I glance up at myself in the mirror. Ocean blue eyes filled with sleep stare back at me. I pull my blonde hair back into a ponytail before leaning down to splash water on my face.

I want to wear something warmer. Fall is no longer around the corner, it is here. Sweatshirts and pumpkin spice were upon us, and I am excited at the idea. Bonfires slipping late into the night. Kissing in the dark... if you have someone to kiss. I quickly brush my teeth and open the door to walk back to my room. My pulse explodes when I run into Remington in the hallway.

I stand frozen in the bathroom door, not sure whether to run or cover myself up.

He sneaks a glance down at my naked legs. I'd forgotten how almost naked I am. My pulse speeds up, adrenaline pumping harder, as I watch his eyes trail over my body.

Thank God, I am not wearing old white granny panties. I don't think I could live it down if I tried. When my eyes find his face again, a smirk covers it.

Ass.

His eyes on me feel like lasers burning into my skin.

A little tingle of attraction feeds into my brain like an unwanted parasite and I can't decide if I want to let him do what his eyes are promising or if I will keep all those dirty little pieces tucked into the back part of my brain where they would be banished from the light of day.

"Morning, Faith," he drawls. A smirk dances at the corners of his mouth and he winks. I'm at a loss for words, but damn. Talk about panty melting, wet dream vibes. My eyes find his again, and I felt an all too familiar pull to him. It was one of those moments we've had for years. His baby blues do it for me—I swear if he searched deep enough, he could see each single emotion and feeling flowing through me.

He points at my shirt. "You name the time and the place."

"Huh?" Glancing down, I see the reference. "You wish... last time I checked you had the opportunity last night, and you said no."

"You're right I did. Because the next time I'm inside you, Faith Evans, I'll make damn sure you remember all of the ways it makes you feel."

A blush burns up my cheeks. I gaze everywhere but at him because damn it, he was right. I don't want to miss a second of it.

"Come on, Faith. Don't pretend like you don't think about it. I seem to recall a pretty interesting dream you were having this morning. And if I remember correctly, you said my name... twice."

Fear paralyzes me as I stand frozen, replaying all of the dream from earlier. I don't remember saying his name, but what if I did subconsciously, and what if he was walking right past my door when it happened? Fuck. My. Life.

I shake my head, non-guiltily, of course. "Did not."

The corners of his lips crinkle into a smirk and I want to smack it right off his magically delicious face. "Uh huh. I'm pretty sure it was something to the effect of... Oh, Remy. Yes, Remy. Right there. Yes, yes, yes." His eyes were closed as he made a fake "O" face.

Holy horror takes over my mind. It sounds like something I'd definitely say, and now I have no clue what the fuck to believe.

"Fine. I'll admit it. I've pictured it." I pause, giving him time to soak in my words, and his eyes take a turn into needy.

"Yeah?" His voice sounds hopeful and I can't help the extra beat my heart takes thinking about being naked with him again.

I nervously twiddle my fingers in front of me and look down. "I have a proposal."

He clears his throat, his swallow audible. "Okay..."

Building some courage I look back up at him and thrust out my chest. "I say we have a no strings, mutually beneficial, friendly get it out of our system fuck. No feelings, no talking, simply two naked bodies pressed together in a twisted tangle of limbs."

His jaw has dropped like he's preparing to catch flies. I watch him swallow so I know he's still breathing.

"Rem..."

"Hold on... I'm processing the words coming out of your mouth. W... when were you thinking you wanna do this?"

My lips pinched together, my brows furrowing. "I'm thinking this weekend. And don't think for a second this is an I forgive you fuck. It's two people who are friendly helping each other out with a little horizontal tango. A release, if you will."

A fluttery feeling overtakes my stomach waiting for his response. My heart has gone zero to eighty in two point five seconds and I'm starting to wonder if this is a really, really bad idea. "Fuck, Faith. I'm speechless."

I breathe out a sigh of relief and warmth radiates through my body. "Well, fucking is the main objective."

REMINGTON

Fuck.

She wants me to fuck her. No feelings. No talking. *What in the actual fuck?* Can I say fuck again because...? *Fuck.*

My brain is flying down a highway, speeding zero to ninety in six seconds. It's in a mind spin. I had to get out of the bunkhouse before I made a major fool of myself. Tiny molecules in my body begged me to say yes. My cock was fully on board and ready for action at the drop of a hat.

I practically run to the barn to occupy my brain with something... anything else. Beau pops out from the office as I walked in, a smile across his face. "Hey, man. How's are ya?"

"I honestly have no fucking clue." I don't have any desire to tell him about the conversation we recently had because I'm not even sure how to process it right now.

"Faith will come around," he says, taking a seat at his desk.

I raise a brow. "Sometimes I doubt it."

Beau does his best to stifle a smile in a conspiratorial way. "Where is your optimism?"

"Buried. Sometimes I think we're getting somewhere closer to being friends and she shuts down."

"You do realize the only thing in the way of you two getting back together is the two of you, right?"

"Well, you seem to have all the answers."

His brows draw closer while his lips formed a straight line. "Only for other people. I can't seem to find them for myself."

I raised my eyebrows. "Want to talk about it?"

He flashed a lopsided grin. "Nah, I'd rather talk about your problems. I was convinced bunking together wasn't an issue when she first showed up, but maybe it's a blessing in disguise. Maybe you can find a way to work through this and find out what happens on the other side."

I wish it was true with each fiber of my being. "I think it's a little more complicated, Beau."

He tilts his head to the side. "She reading your letters?"

I shake my head and shrug. "Honestly, I have no fucking clue. I mean... the box under her bed is no longer dusty, which gives me hope, but I didn't open it to find out if the letters were open. Figured it was crossing the line."

He raises a curious eyebrow. "What were you doing under her bed?"

I put my hands up in defense. "Look...Bandit... he went under there one day and wouldn't get out."

He makes a face but doesn't say anything else about it. "Any news on his owner?"

I shake my head. "None. Dr. Stafford said there hasn't been a peep since the flyers went up."

"So, back to the letters. Have you ever asked her if she's reading them?"

"Yep, and I get varied answers."

It only took a couple of minutes to figure out this was more of an interrogation than a check-in. If giving him what he wants to hear gets him off my back, so be it.

I grind my teeth, my body tense. "She won't forgive me, Beau. She straight up told me last night she hates me."

His dark brow arched. "Ouch... hate is a pretty strong word to use. It's almost as strong as love. Maybe she's confusing the two?"

"I thought the same thing, but I try to bring stuff up and she shuts me down."

Beau grimaced. "Damn."

I shake my head. "She's either going to forgive me or she isn't. She's the only one who can decide. All I know is how I feel." I let a sigh slip from my lips. "Here's the thing. Faith isn't just my high school sweetheart. She isn't only the first girl I loved or the first chick I boned. She's my everything. Being with her..." I glance away before continuing. "It was like seeing a color television after only having black and white movies for the first sixteen years of my life. Loving her was terrifying. It still is, but I don't regret it for a minute. Do I regret what happened? Fuck yes. Day in and day out. But I can't take it back. So now I'm dealin' with the consequences."

He gives me a disapproving frown. "Sounds to me like you're being a pussy and giving up."

A scoff slips from my mouth as I run a hand through my hair. "I'm not giving up. I'm being realistic."

He folds his arms over his stomach in disbelief. "I think you're smart enough to realize you could break her down and win her back if you tried hard enough."

"Uh huh..."

He raises his hands in defense. "Look, all I'm saying is give it time. A tree doesn't grow over night. Love isn't cultivated with the flip of the wrist. It takes time, patience, and the courage to put your balls out there even if there's a chance she'll say no and walk away again."

"My balls are in a comfortable position right now and I'd rather not rock the boat. I'm counting on those letters getting through to her." My mind rewinds back to the other night at

Bodine's when she wore a burgundy dress. No way in hell she'd know to wear burgundy without reading the letter I wrote. Or maybe it was a coincidence.

"All right, enough of this. There's a fence to fix. Grab Remy, we're heading out." Walking out of the office, I follow him. He stalks off to the tack room to grab Apache's stuff and some tools. I grab Remy's rack and we are off a couple of minutes later.

The fence needing mendin' isn't far from the house, but far enough to give me space to think through the things that'd occurred in the last half hour.

I still couldn't piece together where Faith had decided on such a crazy damn idea, but I wasn't complaining. A night with no talking I could do. A night with zero feelings was the part I was having an issue with because there would forever be feelings with Faith; it is a guarantee.

Even when I pretended to hate her, my heart still bled for only her. Still bleeds for her. My heart was trained to love her before it even knew what it meant to love. And yeah, it's probably not manly to say, but it's the Goddamn truth.

Beau rode back to the barn to grab the necessary materials while I stood there dismantling the rotten boards from the fence that needed replacing. He was back with multiple boards laid across the front of his saddle in less than fifteen minutes.

We started to work on finishing up removing the old part of the fence and putting in new pieces. It didn't take long at all—five rails in total needing to be replaced. We worked in companionable silence.

The work was mundane, and we did it in silence, which was a much-needed reprieve. I knew he wanted to ask me questions or talk about the situation with Faith. It's who Beau is, a fixer. He is the guy who ran around putting us all back together again.

I think a part of him felt like if he could fix Faith and I, then maybe he could fix his own life. He'd been in love with the same girl for years, but now she lived in the city with some rich husband.

The chances of her returning to small town life were fading as each year passed, and I figure he was finally realizing he'd lost his chance.

I can relate, but fate gave me a second chance and I wasn't going to let it slip through my fingers. I allow my eyes to drift across the field toward the barn and catch sight of her. The air is colder today so she isn't showing as much skin as usual. It is a blessing and a curse.

Blessing because it'd cause my eyes to stray less from her face and curse because I know what hides underneath those clothes.

Her hair was pulled up on the top of her head in a bun. She was wearing a long sleeved Henley and jeans not meant for general eye consumption.

She must have felt my gaze as it lingered on her because she turned my way. She tucked a strand that had fallen from her pony-tail behind her ear before offering me a small wave. I smile, tipping my ball cap to her. I can't wave. It would seem entirely too desperate. But isn't it what I am... thinking about sleeping with my ex-girlfriend for the sake of being close to her again?

Beau's phone rings, catching my attention as he pulls it from his back pocket to answer. "Willow Springs Stables, Beau speaking" There was a long pregnant pause. "Yeah, sure. Remington and I can check him out this afternoon." I arch my eyebrow. He mouths, *new colt this afternoon*, before finishing the conversation. "All right, see you in an hour." He hits the end button on the call and turns to me. "Well, we have plans today."

"So, I heard. How old?"

"Two-year-old colt. Owner says he's meaner than a hornet's nest. Bitten the last few trainers who tried to tangle with him."

"Damn, so he's trouble."

He nods. "Sounds like it."

A grin spread across my lips. "My favorite kind. I reckon I know a thing or two about hell raising colts full of fury."

"You're the best at what you do, Remington. Anyone can settle him down, you sure can. Have you met Remy? He's tamed as a kitten now."

I laugh; a hearty noise bellowed from my throat. "I don't know if I'd go that far..."

"All right, let's get back to the house. I want a full stomach before I deal with Devil's kin."

"Sounds like a plan." We both put our tool belts back on, load the dead wood onto Beau's saddle and walk back to the farm. I took both horses, untacked, brushed, and put them away before heading to the main house for lunch.

The main house is loud as we all clamber in for food. Word of the new colt coming in spread like wildfire. Dark hardwood covered the floor beneath me as I make my way into the kitchen. We redid this kitchen last summer and I still can't believe the difference it made.

The original kitchen had a 1950s vibe, and it's moved into the 20th century. I remember the tedious placement of mosaic tile on the backsplash and how much of a hassle it was to install the new stove and dishwasher.

I pull open the fridge door, rummaging around the drawer for sandwich meat and cheese. I grabbed the mayo from the door and the bread from the pantry and make my way to the table.

The guys are making their way to the table to make their own food when I see Faith and Bandit step through the front door. My world freezes. *How do you move on when she's the only thing in your life that's always ever felt right?*

We're starting to feel like a fucking yo-yo. Longing one day, hate the next, and it was never the same as the day before.

She is back home at Willow Springs. Down the hall from my room. Across the pasture from where I work and across the table at meals. She lives in my head, occupies my dreams, and still takes my breath away. I felt her presence wherever I went and it didn't bother me a damn. I didn't want to escape her. Being there with her felt right after so many years of wrong.

Maybe this is how it was supposed to be. She was supposed to leave and grow up. I was supposed to realize she's the only person in my life who matters to me. Maybe in the long run she knew taking a chance on the broken man I was would be a penance she had to pay. Maybe it's why she stayed away.

Or maybe it is a chance. To prove to her I can be the man she needed me to be. The offer of silent sex was a second chance. I wouldn't waste it. The fibers of my soul told me to run with what I could get, and if it was her body for right now, I'd take it all. As long as she'd let me.

I eat my sandwich slowly, sneaking glances at Faith. I couldn't help the way my eyes searched her out like a beacon in the night. Occasionally I'll tease a smile from those perfect pink lips and I'll call it a win.

————

Half an hour later we watch as Mr. Johnson backs his diesel and trailer up to the round pen so he can release the colt needing our help. The vast number of snorts and kicking coming from the trailer sides told us we were in for an interesting time. He finally stops backing up and Beau opens the round pen as Mr. Johnson opened the trailer. A jet-black colt comes flying out of the trailer like he was out for blood, snapping and kicking at us the whole time.

Beau walked up to me after shutting the gate and clapped me on the shoulder, smiling. "Our work is cut out for us."

"How long will you take to break this one, Beau?" Mr. Johnson asked haughtily as we stood and watched the colt charge us from inside the pen.

"Been a while since I've seen one this hateful. You know I ain't about breaking them. I'm about trust and the way he's running around like he lost his damn mind tells me it'll be a little bit longer than normal."

He scoffed. "I ain't paying you to be nice to 'em. I'm paying ya to break him."

Beau shrugged. "You know my deal. You want me to gentle this horse, you need to give me the time to do so. You want it quick and dirty with a horse who doesn't trust ya more than he can toss ya, pack 'em up now and take him elsewhere. Guarantee no one else'll wanna work with him after what I've seen so far."

He sighed. "Fine, but I ain't paying extra for any extra time needed." I can't help but chuckle. Mr. Johnson is a stingy fuck.

He was forty-two. If I didn't know better, I'd peg him much closer to eighty with the way he grumped about shit. His hair was buzz cut, and he had a beard scattered with grey hairs. He'd gained a few pounds in the last couple years. My guess is it had to do with all the beer he drank. It still lingered on his breath as he swore and headed back to get in his truck. "Call me when he's ready."

We worked with the colt for a few hours, making him run in the round pen earning his trust. It wasn't much, but a little progress was better than nothing. Tried to put a halter on him and like most colts he refused it. This little demon was headstrong and believed he was in charge. He'd learn soon enough how things went around here.

May seem like he has the upper hand now, but things would change in the next few days. Eventually he'd have to give into us.

We left him in the round pen overnight and brought him some hay to munch on once he was cooled down from his workout.

Rhett found us on the way back from the pen. "Y'all down for a little night fishing tonight?"

Beau smirked. "For sure."

He raised an eyebrow in question at me. "Rem?"

I shrugged. "Yeah, sure, whatever. I'm down to catch some fish."

He bumped my shoulder. "Good. Ya need to let some steam off. Faith came back and you're bottled up tighter than a jar of unopened salsa. I'm waiting for you to explode."

I'd like to explode for damn sure, all over Faith.

No. I shook my head to wipe away the notion. Maybe fishing is exactly what I needed. A night out with the guys. No feelings. No bullshit. No drama. A lake, some fish, a bottle of cola, and the stars sounded relaxing.

"Great! We'll hit up the lake after it gets dark out. I'll run home and grab the boat." Turning to me, he smirks. "Don't think I didn't remember your birthday."

"Fuck," I mumble under my breath. I was hoping the guys had forgotten what today was. Faith hadn't mentioned it, and neither had anyone else. I'd almost survived the whole day without celebrating it.

He lets out a full gut laugh. "Thought I'd forget, didn't you?"

My lips went flat. "I'd sure as hell hoped so."

"No worries, Rem. We plan to make sure you enjoy your birthday to the fullest." He pats me on the back before laughing at my discomfort.

I sigh. "Can't wait." There was only one thing I wanted for my birthday and tonight I planned on cashing in on it. When I arrive home. I hadn't given Faith an answer yet. I should change that.

He turns his attention to Beau. "Now that I think about it. Maybe we should lock him and Faith in a room together so she can fulfill all of his birthday wishes. Or at least until they make up."

A growl escapes my mouth. He was starting to piss me off. The last thing I need is them fucking meddling in my shit.

———

The sun had set for the evening, and we were getting ready to head out to the lake. I knocked on Faith's door to let her know we'd be out for a while. I didn't want her to have to hole up in her room on my account. This bunkhouse belonged to both of us for the moment. Seeing me shouldn't be a reason for her not to enjoy all the benefits of the bunkhouse.

I heard scratching at the door after I knocked, and I knew Bandit was there.

"Come in," she yelled, and I opened the door as Bandit scurried out. There she sits in the middle of her bed, trying hard and failing to hide the letter she'd been holding. She must assume I didn't see her tuck it under her thigh when I entered.

My heart soars with hope. She'd been reading my letters all along.

I clear my throat, swallowing the thump over the knowledge I'd acquired with a simple knock. "Um, I wanted to let you know the guys and I are heading out for some night fishing on the lake. No need to stay holed up in here all night. I'll start a fire before I leave if you want. So, you can curl up in front of it and read or watch TV."

The smile this time sparkles as it grazes her eyes. "Oh, it'd be nice of you, Rem."

"It's no problem. I want you to feel comfortable here. You may keep fighting this, avoiding me, pretending the inevitable won't happen. But I think it's all a sign. I don't believe in fate, but sometimes things work out for a reason and maybe I can convince you of it too."

"I don't think proposing sex is exactly avoiding you."

"Sex, no. Sex with no talking and no feelings. It seems like a whole lot of avoiding to me."

"You need to stop, Rem."

I feigned ignorance. "Stop doing what?"

Her look said a whole bunch of *really*. "Being nice and sweet. Making me swoon."

"Why, is it working?"

She shakes her head, but she can't help the grin that spread her lips.

FAITH

To say this was one of the most uncomfortable days I've had in a while would be an understatement.

I can't believe I'd paraded in front of him in my cami and panties this morning, followed by my embarrassing proposition to fuck each other without feelings or talking. How the fuck we would accomplish it was beyond me because Remington and I had nothing but feelings littered between us?

I didn't know what I'd do if he followed through and did what I asked. A part of me hoped he did.

I tried not to think about the spark lighting up his eyes when I mentioned being together again. Those gray-blue eyes searing into me as he pictures what this means for us. He was slowly setting fire to the barrier I'd held up to shield my heart from him. The flames licked between us like they always did, only this time they weren't extinguishing.

I remembered the words coming out of my mouth.

"I say we have a no strings, mutually beneficial, friendly get it out of our system fuck. No feelings, no talking, only two naked bodies pressed together in a twisted tangle of limbs."

The more I think about it the more confident I am. I can leave all feelings and thoughts aside while we do our tangled twist of sex.

Probably.

Most likely.

Maybe.

Then I remembered watching him working, without his shirt on the other day in the barn. I watched each bead of sweat as it pooled and ran down his chest, over his pecs, eight abs, and down his happy little hair trail leading down under. I wanted to trace along the line it took with my finger and then my tongue. I wanted to lick the dips and curves of him, but it was totally beside the point. Right?

It didn't matter if he was covered in sawdust and caked mud. I wanted to take back the memories of us all those years ago covered in sawdust and in love with the idea of forever.

I think about him sleeping less than ten feet away from me on the other side of the wall. So close, in fact, I can hear each time he uses my name to grasp at a modicum of pleasure.

I reach under my bed and pull out another letter. I wonder which memory this one held. Between the naked chest sightings, the letters, and the way he's been acting, he is wearing me down. It wasn't the first time I wanted so badly to forgive him and let my heart be happy with Rem. But then one notion slipped free. And then another.

Can I trust him with my heart?

Can I trust myself with him?

It is also hard to move past the very real fact he'd cheated on me.

I'll want everything again. I'll want to be all in.

Because the truth is, I miss the fuck out of him. I miss my friend. I miss my lover—my first, last, and the in between. His hugs when I am feeling down. His sloppy kisses when he is horny. The way life was so easy when we were together.

This letter held smeared ink, and I wondered if it had some

significance. Did it get caught in a rainstorm or was he emotional
as he wrote it?

Dear Faith,

*At this point I have little hope of you returning a letter, but my wish
is you're reading them even if you choose not to respond.*

*If you're reading these in order, then you've read about our first
date at Bodine's, our first kiss under the star covered night, the weird
bowling experience with smelly shoes, and various other things.*

*If you're reading this... you've made it to the part where we gave
ourselves to each other. Our first time. The perfect gift you gave me of
fumbling hands, wanton kisses, and awkward moves. I can't even
say I would've picked a better setting because any setting with you is
the best it could've been.*

*So many firsts happened. I remember needing to tell you I loved
you before we did anything serious. I didn't want you to think I loved
you only because I wanted to have sex. I wanted you to know, because
I was falling madly in love with you and I couldn't keep it in any
longer. I wanted to shout it from the damn rooftops.*

*Our first time is why I had to get rid of that old rusty pickup. I
couldn't stare at the bed of my truck and think about you naked,
covered up in blankets as we spelled out the word love between us.*

*I was so afraid of you. Afraid of hurting you. Afraid of going too
fast and missing things in between. Afraid of shooting my load
before even ten seconds was up. That's how much out of this world our
first time for me was. I may seem like less of a man for telling you
these things, but it's the God's honest truth. I want you to know it all.*

*Being inside you was like renting space in heaven for a little
while. The warmth as you surrounded me. The pleasure of getting
lost in you. The feel of your breasts beneath my hands. Your tongue in
my mouth. Your fingers in my hair. The moans as they slipped past*

*your lips. The way you called out my name the first time you came.
It's something forever burned into my soul for as long as I live. Hopefully longer.*

*You see... right now things seem far away. You're mad at me and
rightfully so, but someday I'll get my second chance to feel all of these
things with you again and, quite frankly, I cannot wait.*

*I missed you then. I miss you now. I'll miss you always. Until I
see you again.*

Always yours,
Rem

Yet again, the tears fall from my eyes. It is hard remembering all
those magical things. A memory takes up the place of one before it.
Each one with its own sort of old school charm. Each one of him
and I together.

I remember the night in his letter vividly. We'd snuck out late
night fishing to avoid our families. We spent the night sipping
moonshine, making plans, and thinking about our future together.
It was romantic. He'd packed us a late-night snack on the boat -
nothing fancy but most of my favorites.

He'd sung me song after song since there was no way to bring a
radio out on the boat, not to mention it'd scare away the fish. We
didn't catch a damn thing, but it wasn't about how many fish we
caught. It never was. It was about the two of us enjoying time
spent together whenever we could.

I remember the promises he'd made *that* night. The first time
he'd told me he loved me. It didn't make sense why he told me
before we had sex that he loved me until I read the specific part of
his letter. He wanted me to know he loved me, but not for the sex
I'd give him - it was for me.

We didn't drink to get drunk. He'd wanted me to have a sip or two of moonshine, so it'd be easier on me for my first time. It was Rem to a tee; taking care of me first, making sure I was the priority.

I think it's why I'm reading the letters. I want to know why someone who claimed to put me first didn't seem to think about my feelings for a second before jumping into bed with my best friend.

Something didn't add up.

A knock on my door makes me jump, and I scramble to hide the letter I'd been reading. Bandit runs to the door and started scratching. He knows who's standing on the other side of that slab of wood.

Hoping I'd covered up the letter enough, I yelled to come in, but it was too late. I watched his eyes as they traveled across my bed. He'd seen it. The cards were on the table now. I had to toe the line to see how things panned out going forward.

Once the door opened fully, Bandit took off like a flash down the hall and left me alone with Remington.

He'd simply wanted to let me know him and the guys were heading out for the night. My heart dropped a little, thinking he'd been coming in for me. To tell me something, anything. I'd interact with him and he'd practically begged me for another chance. To see him. The real him. To see whatever he'd been hiding this whole time.

I wanted him to tell me why, but I also didn't have the heart to ask. What if I didn't like his answer?

My heart yearned to give him another chance and sooner or later, the caving bitch would decide it was all or nothing and I'd give in. But I wanted more time before that happened.

He'd offered to build a fire in the fireplace in our shared living room before he left, and I took him up on it. I listened as he left to get wood for the fireplace. The scent of smoke and rustling of the grate caught my attention through the crack in the door.

Dressing in my most comfortable sweatpants, I'd thrown my

hair into a messy bun and donned my extra fluffy slippers before heading to the living room to sit down. Bandit circled in my lap until he was the proper amount of comfortable.

It'd be nice to cuddle under a blanket and get lost in one of my favorite tv shows—*The Vampire Diaries*. Because who wouldn't want to be in an imaginary love triangle with Damon and Stefan? Plus, there was drama, but it wasn't real life. If it was too much, I could get up and walk away, but it wasn't my style. I was much more of a fake it til' you make it type of binger.

Until, of course, Netflix asked me if I was still watching. Like bitch... I know I haven't moved in three hours, but could you judge less, please?

I didn't even notice how late it had become when I hear the truck brakes squeak as they pulled up to the bunkhouse. The guys aren't shy about being quiet as their heavy boots tramp across the gravel, and I take it as my cue to head back to my room. I quickly turn off the TV, pick up the blanket and Bandit, then creep down the hallway and close the door softly.

I'd changed into my sleep cami and slipped into bed when I heard the door on the bunkhouse close. Remington clomps down the hall, the bathroom door shutting behind him as he steps inside. The water turned on and off and my brain conjured images of him brushing his teeth and washing his face like he did nightly. It wasn't even weird. His nightly routine had remained the same after all these years. He used to tell me he couldn't fall sleep with dust on his face.

A few minutes later, I listen as the hinge on his door squeaks like it is signaling the end of another night. A sigh escapes my lips. My heart pounded against my chest cavity, wondering what happened next. Was he going to bed?

If he came to my door tonight, all bets were off. I wasn't sure I'd have the self-control to tell him to leave, nor did I want to. I was so tired of skating around each other. The tension between us was reaching an unfavorable pitch, and there was only a matter of time before we cracked. Before our bodies subconsciously gave into the craving, the need to be with one another.

At the end of the day, Remington Cole and I are much more than a girl and a boy who fell in love a long time ago. We are two souls woven and tethered into a past and a forever together. Not caring what came before, during, or after, with the infinite wisdom, we would eternally end up together. It is deep and it rocks me to the core. Goosebumps light up my skin in an awakening unlike anything I'd felt before.

My eyes are heavy with sleep when my bedroom door cracks open slowly, the hallway light piercing the darkness surrounding me. I should be afraid, thinking someone was sneaking into my room. But the fear doesn't rattle me like it did when I walked down a dark alley in the city. It was as if subconsciously I knew it was him. If I lay very still, I can hear his whispered breathing and his footsteps. My heart pounds out a staccato beat in anticipation of what might happen as he creeps across my bedroom.

I can tell he isn't naked but for the top half. The light from the door spotlighted slivers of his broad tattooed chest and my eyes strained, hoping to see my favorite one branded over his heart.

The bed dips as he cautiously crawls up the end of it between my legs. I wait for him to say something, anything, but he never does. The scent of his cologne wafts my way with each small movement, surrounding me in a cloud of him. It was the way his breath sounded against the absolute silence of the room around us. The deeper pitch he had when his mind was full of lust and love.

His body slides against mine as he inches closer; our skin touching in more than one place. I'm cocooned in the mixture of my perfume and his cologne.

My heart threatens to break loose of my chest, and I can feel my breath coming quicker than usual. I wonder if he can feel it too. *Is his heart pounding infinitely faster like mine?* I finally broke down and whispered. "Remington, what are you doing?"

But he never responds, simply lifting a finger to my lips to hush me. His breath caresses the contour of my neck as he leans in and whispers the words, "Do you want this?" Without hesitation, I nod my agreement.

The truth is, I do want him, and like I told myself earlier, I wouldn't turn him away. It wasn't even a question; it was a decision. Give in to him or hold back and keep fighting it.

His firm lips pressed softly against my cheek, followed the line of my chin, slipping down my neck and over my collarbone. The sensations lose me in a wave of emotions as I remember the first time his lips touched me all those years ago. Deja vu creeps in and I drift away.

His fingers inch down my body slowly, as if he might miss something going too fast. He pauses as he reaches the hem of my shirt, begging me for permission he no longer needed. I am in this as much as he is.

I rise up enough to let him slip the cami over my head. Skin on skin sensation was something I'd been picturing since I'd been home but having it in person is so much better. His hands are rough against my soft skin, and I love the contrasting difference.

I was sure it'd feel awkward being this naked with him again, but the tingly sensations of being with someone new never come. Maybe it's because our bodies remembered each other after all these years. Subconsciously telling us the familiarity is because it was meant to be.

I lift my hand to press it to his heart. I have to know if his was pounding as much as mine.

He lowers down onto his elbows as he makes love to my mouth with his. Our tongues aren't dueling for power. They are simply dancing to a swan song, beautiful and poetic. Electricity dances on the tip of my tongue as it slides against his, caressing it.

His lips skim again, trailing lower. My breasts are fair game, bared to his pleasure. He takes one nipple into his mouth and his forefinger and thumb find the other. Sucking and kissing it as he moved along, it is a direct shot to my core I hadn't felt it in years.

Each kiss elicits a parade of goosebumps up and down my skin.

His toned chest is pressed against my skin, a touch memory. It's like being able to feel something after you've been numb for too long.

His hard-on digs into the side of my leg, but I can't find it in me to care. I want him as much as he wants me. This is proof of his desire for the things happening between us. I keep finding it harder and harder not to remember all the times we'd been together.

He slid himself down the bed as he lowered yet again to my stomach and even closer to the place I craved him most. I am on fire, burning up from the inside out for him. He warm breath against my belly button tickled, but I held back the laughter.

Memories flashed through my mind in brilliant detail, a slideshow of our love affair with each blink. I try to hide the tears as each one hit more brutally than the last, but a sob tore from my throat before I could stop it.

His head lifts, eyes finding mine in the darkness. Trying to read through the emotions I knew were plaguing my face. For once, I am thankful for the lack of lighting in my room. He may have known I was crying, but it helped he couldn't see it.

"You okay, Faith?" he whispers softly, peppering kisses to the inside of my thigh.

"Yes, perfect," I responded. At the moment, it is perfect. I am getting lost in him like I had all those years ago. Remington and I against the world. I wanted it to last forever. Pushing away those nagging feelings about the things happening between us, I focus on him and his lips as they travel to the apex of my thighs, kissing gently, one after another.

He tortures me slowly with each kiss as if photographing it to memory and I can't help but do the same. If tonight is all we have, then I damn sure want the memories for the next time I felt alone.

I tug gently on his hair, trying to get his lips to the spot I needed him most, and he obliges.

All mind space diminishes when his lips suck around my bundle of nerves. It is something I hadn't liked when I was young, but all of a sudden it felt enlightening. I'd gladly take his lips anywhere on my body.

I can feel his breath against me, warm yet rapid.

I moan as his tongue slips down to taste me; the place vacant for many years now. An alarming picture of cobwebs came to mind, but I push it away as soon as it pops up.

I will not think about cobwebs while Remington is doing this thing with his tongue. It must've been something new he'd picked up since we'd broken up and I can't say I don't like it, but a part of me wondered where he'd learned it.

I didn't notice myself cringe, but Remington whispered against me to stop. As if he knew I was in my own head about things. "Don't think, just feel, Faith," he says before going back to making me delirious with need.

I squirm beneath him, needing more, needing him, but he doesn't seem to notice at first. "More," I whisper on a prayer, hoping he'd hear it.

"You need more, babe?" he says, slipping a finger, followed by a second inside me. It felt good, but it still isn't enough. I needed him, all of him, inside me.

The nickname fell from his lips so easily. He used to call me babe all the time, so it felt normal, comfortable. Remington was like your favorite pair of boots—comforting and dependable. He was like coming home in the middle of a rainstorm—the guy who'd get soaked running to your car with an umbrella so you didn't get wet. He is also the danger I craved—I know if I asked him for anything, he'd do it without any regard. He was my ride or die.

"Rem, I need you." This time I said it loud enough he wouldn't miss it.

He slid off the bed to shed his pants and pulled a square from his back pocket like he'd anticipated exactly what would happen. "You sure?" he asks.

"Positive." There are no take backs. I'd asked him for sex and instead of answering me, he was showing me. Actions spoke louder than words to me, he'd known it.

I sneak a peek as he stands beside the bed, pants around his ankles, boxers following suit. My eyes roam up and down the shadows on his body created by the light creeping through the door. Broad shoulders, slim waist, rippling abs, and a V-line slipping in a sexy way down to his package.

They caught on the shaft, standing proudly between his legs. I didn't remember him being big, but maybe I'd forgotten in four years. Surely muscle memory would wake up and remember him. Goosebumps crawl over my arms. I am nervous. I shouldn't be, but I am regardless. My body has changed since I was sixteen.

"Holy shit," I whisper, without thinking.

"It's nothing you haven't seen before." He said like he was smirking.

"Well, it seems bigger than it used to."

"Well, I am a bit bigger all around than I used to be. Don't worry, I'll go slow. It'll still fit." I know he'd be winking if I could see him. Another reason I am glad for the darkness.

It offers an extra layer of protection against the heartbreak, inevitable from happening the next day. For now, I'll enjoy him.

Live in the moment.

I watch as he pumps a couple of times before he climbs back into bed. He positions himself over me, between my legs, and I spread them more to accommodate him. This time he doesn't ask again if I am ready. His lips find mine again as he directs his tip to my entrance, teasing me.

His finger fins my nub and rubs as he presses himself inside me slowly—the distraction almost working. There was an initial pressure when he was finally seated within me, but soon it amps into pleasure. He feels good. We feel right together. As he starts to move within me, I revel in the significance of this moment.

Remington Cole and I are having sex after four long years of twisted emotions and love sick heartbreak. It is something I didn't see happening again, but it changes things for me.

It is the moment where I realize no matter what happened before today, or four years ago, we were meant to be. To exist as one. It didn't matter how many love letters he wrote apologizing. It didn't matter how many times he brought back old memories and made me relive them. Nothing mattered - only us and what happened from now on.

He must have known my brain was flying at the speed of light. It's probably why he whispered *no thinking* before taking my breath away with another kiss. His mouth is making love to me as much as the rest of him. My hands find his back and slide down over pure muscle to grip his ass as I asked for more. A sheen of sweat covers his skin. I probably have the same sheen, but I don't have it in me to care.

Damn feelings. As much as I told myself no talking and no feelings, I can't help but feel every single thing as it slices through me. Anger, hurt, pain, but mostly love. I loved this man with every fiber of my being, and nothing could take it away. Maybe I couldn't get over Remington because I wasn't supposed to.

Increasing his speed, he finds my magic spot and lives there until I feel the wave of my first orgasm trying to break free. Our hearts start beating the same melody as our breaths turn into pants and moans. A chorus of pleasure bellowing from our lips.

He starts pounding into me harder and harder, as if he knows I need this as much as he does. Because maybe when we get sex out of the way, the rest will fall into place. He won't be the guy who cheated on me, and I won't be the girl who ran. We'll be us. The Remington and Faith trying to figure out our forever, whatever forever means to us.

His hands crawl down my arm and entwine with mine. I let

him take me to the edge before I drop. My body seizes and I'm lost in the sensation of the first orgasm I've had in years.

It's better than I imagined and I can't help it as a tear slides down my face. Perfection, pure and simple.

He releases a few minutes later, breathing out my name like I'm a song he'd like to sing for the rest of his life. "I love you," he whispers before collapsing on top of me.

I'm frozen beneath him. His weight heavy on me, cocooning me so I can't run from the three words he whispered in my ear.

I want to say it back to him so badly, but I can't.

There's so much between us left unsaid.

My heart feels like it's in the middle of a war, getting shot from one side while being blown to bits on the other. At this point, it's definitely black and blue. If you pulled it from my body, I bet it would be a swirl of colors and shades.

A part of me thinks I have all these emotions from the serotonin in my body from the best and only sex I've had in years. The other part thinks it's too soon to be this hopeful about there being an *us* again. I'd like to think we've hit rock bottom and there's no way but up from here, but how do you know for sure?

Now, the emotions of having sex were behind us and the self-doubt started to seep into my brain. I saw what cheating did to my parents. It destroyed them and I'm not sure Remington and I have what it takes to survive it. I don't think I'm strong enough.

Once our breathing has returned to its normal pace, Remington stands up and pulls the condom off, tying it in a knot. A few seconds after he left my room, I heard the sink turn on in the bathroom, and I wondered if he was repeating the same ritual as before.

I knew I should probably get up, shower, and then get some much-needed sleep before tomorrow, but I am not ready for tonight to end. I'm not ready to wash him from my body. I want to hold on for a few more minutes or hours, however long he'd give me.

As he turned off the water in the bathroom and walks into the hallway, I wait with bated breath to see where he'd go. Would he return to his own room? Was it honestly a get-sex- out-of-our-system bang or would he return and cuddle like he used to do? Thousands of questions ping through my mind and I can't get them to shut off. He creeps back into my bedroom and sits down gently on the side of the bed. He leans over to kiss me on the lips again and waits to see what I'd do.

When I lift the covers for him, he slips beneath them with me. I am giving him an in and he was taking it.

I opened my mouth to say something and he kissed me again. Once his lips release mine, he speaks gently. "No thinking, Faith. Tomorrow, we can talk. Tonight, let me hold you, okay?"

I nod, not wanting to ruin the moment. I roll onto my side and he tucks me into his body closer. His arm slips over my hip and down my stomach. I could feel his breath slow down, and I knew he was finally asleep. I ran my finger gently over his arm like I used to do when we were together. This moment felt perfect in its own way.

A certain serenity seemed to always pass before the storm hit. I had to brace myself and hope the tide didn't pull me under this time. If I kept my head above water, maybe I could survive whatever came next.

REMINGTON AND FAITH

The sun slips through the curtains of her window as it breached the horizon, bathing us in rays. I lay there staring at the ceiling, trying to figure out what to do now. The start of a new day brought all types of unknown into play.

Last night Faith and I made love for the first time in four years. No bullshit, no talking, and all the fucking feelings I could handle.

What would happen when she woke for the day? Would she be happy with the events of the night prior, or would I see the regret pasted across her face?

The pillow under my head is entirely too comfortable, like something at a fancy hotel. The sheets we slept on were definitely a higher thread count than I was used to.

How could she ever want simple me?

I laid perfectly still; afraid I'd wake her. I didn't want this dream to end, but like all good things, it must end eventually. I didn't deserve her. I was Remington Cole, a nobody with a deadbeat dad. The truths came at me in a hailstorm of fury.

Faith is better than me, no matter which way you looked at it. She didn't grow up with shit parents like I did, even with a cheating father. She had a college degree. She'd seen life outside of this little town. She was made for better things, bigger dreams than I could ever help her to achieve.

I wonder if Willow Springs is a steppingstone before she was called for another job opportunity somewhere else.

A swarm of questions pound my brain, and I find myself questioning if maybe I should get up and leave now before she wakes up. Leave on a happy ending before our love became complicated. Because it's who Coles were. There for a fun time, but absent when shit hit the fan.

She rolls over, her head on my chest, her arms curled against my side. I can smell her perfume from here and I inhale it like a drunk craving whiskey. Slowly I reach up to brush the hair away from her face, and she smiles. She isn't awake yet, but her damn smile made my heart beat a little funky.

Faith is gorgeous, like a painting, each part intricately put together to make a full masterpiece.

Her eyes are closed, but I can vividly picture how blue they are and how they light up when she smiles. The tips of her eyelids are darkened with black to match her lashes fanning out over her cheeks. I notice how long her lashes were, like she'd been handed an extra set at birth. My eyes trace over the freckles dabbled across her nose and cheeks.

When she was younger, her hair was a light blonde color. The woman now laying beside me has long, dark, dirty blonde hair, giving her an edgy look. She's bold, confident, and beautiful.

Faith used to tell me she was overlooked and nothing special, but I could see the truth. Guys in school stared at her like she hung the damn moon and stars. Jimmy Moon bullied her because she turned him down, plain and simple.

Her skin under my fingers is still as smooth as an overly expensive alcohol sliding down your throat. I remember how it felt under my hands last night and again early this morning when she asked me for more. I couldn't deny her anything. I didn't want to.

And as much as I don't want to move, I need to. I need something to kill these nerves. I'd never been this nervous with anyone but Faith Evans. I am afraid she'll realize she is too good for us here. I am afraid the big city will call to her and she'd forget about me. I'd be a distant memory of the past to her, before her future started.

She would forever be a memory I didn't mess with. I couldn't shake her. I replay each movement of our bodies last night, saving it like the best story book.

The fight-or-flight urge kicks in and I take it as a sign to leave. I can't bear the disappointment pasted across people's faces when it came to me. Sliding her off of me gently, I put the pillow beneath her head.

Sitting on the side of the bed, I lean down to kiss her forehead. All the rustling around I was doing roused Bandit from a dead sleep. I'd been amazed he slept through the night, but where would he have gone? One glance at me, a tail wag, and he is up, ready to do his business.

Standing, I turn around for one last glance at the love of my life. Leaving her naked was the last thing I wanted to do, but nature was calling. I had to help break a colt today. Bandit needed walked and taken out to do his business. I have chores at the barn, but before all that happens, I needed Faith to know it was more than a one-night stand.

I went to the bathroom and showered, dressing in my own room, then spent half an hour in the kitchen making breakfast, followed by writing her a note. It's something I'd become familiar with, so I let all the words in my head slip out onto paper. I want to give her the time to read it and to form an opinion about what happened last night without me hovering.

Bacon, eggs, and pancakes I left on the table with a plate and silverware. I snuck back down the hall to leave the note I'd written on her nightstand so she'd find it when she woke up.

I knocked twice to give her time to fully wake up and then I left. I can't be there any longer. As much as I wanted to climb back into bed with the woman I loved, I couldn't bring myself to do it. She'd need space and as much as it killed me, I would give it to her.

The longing her eyes carried for me last night, followed by the way she moaned my name, told me it wasn't a onetime thing. Maybe I am overthinking things and getting ahead of myself, but seeing her lost in us told me what I needed to know. She is still mine after all these years. She had to realize it herself and I'd be here when she did. There's a certain chemistry between two people meant to be together, blinding you to truly seeing any other individual for the remainder of your life.

We had chemistry in spades. The kind not easily extinguished. It pours out like a rainstorm and floods without warning. We were made for each other a long time ago. Kind of like trees are made for initials of love carved into them. Early curfews are made for sneaking out.

Being without Faith these last four years has been like a song without a melody. A ship without a sail. A boat without an anchor.

The sound of footsteps is my hint to leave. I want to get out of the bunkhouse before she wakes up and started moving. Plus, I have a colt to work with to get my mind off her. I was flying right now. High on Faith and the love we'd made last night. I feel like I could soar, like I could do anything. I am invincible with one glance, one kiss, one touch.

Grabbing my ball cap and boots, I slip out of the house and head toward the barn. The morning is cool, a breeze blowing through the trees. The air is filled with snorts and whinnies as the new colt threw himself around the round pen.

Beau comes from the barn, a big grin draped across his face. "You ready to tame the beast today?"

I snort. "Not sure it's possible, but I think we try anyhow."

He wrinkles an eyebrow. "You're chipper this morning. Why are you in such a good mood?"

"Had a real good night of thinking."

He exchanges a knowing look with me. "Thinking, huh?"

I nod with a smirk. "Lots and lots of thinking happening."

He claps me on the back as we walk to the round pen. "Well, it sounds like progress to me. I hope it continues for you. But right now, I need your head in the round ring, not the clouds. This colt is so fired up. It'll be tougher than normal."

"I'm not worried," I say, but in the back of my mind a part of me is afraid. Not of the colt necessarily. Of whatever happened today. Okay... and maybe it was partially the colt too. I'd never seen one spit fire so easily. He has a temper a mile high. This colt put Remy to shame.

He charged us as we approached the round pen that he was currently trying to turn into firewood. He lashed out with his mouth and his feet, both ends taking up the unknown fight in his flight or fight reflex.

A part of me feels for him, this unknown fear unleashing within his body. Afraid we're taking his freedom from him. The purpose of all of this is to train him to know we aren't the enemy. We're here to help him, but until he understands it, he'll fight tooth and nail to the end.

I climb up the fence and throw a leg over, watching him as he runs around and around in a circle. His fiery eyes find mine and he charges the fence, but I don't move. Moving would give him the upper hand. I want to show dominance. His fight may scare me shitless on the inside, but I don't flinch outwardly.

He does it again, and I glance over at Beau. His face is a shade of white I haven't seen before, but it matches how I feel inside. This colt is fucking nuts. As I turn back to the colt in the pen, I lose my balance and fall to the ground. What happens next moves faster than the speed of light. I don't see the kick he launches at my head. I don't see the anger in his eyes as he tries again. I don't hear the screams and shouting. I only see darkness.

My world turns black.

Nothing.

It's peaceful. I wasn't thinking about anything, it was like I was floating emotionless.

People have often wondered what death feels like, and now I'm here. Floating in the space in between.

Faith

I woke up slowly this morning and rolled over. My hand moved across to an empty, cold spot beside me. My heart dropped. I'd hoped he would still be there after our night together; it brought my fears I'd pushed to the back of my mind to front and center. I was officially wrecked for him. There was no going back now.

I wanted to tell him today. I am all in.

Nothing mattered anymore—what happened four years ago, the letters, the past.

The only thing that matters now is where we go from here.

The scent of breakfast drifts down the hallway from the kitchen and I find my feet taking me to the kitchen. Pancakes, eggs, bacon, all on a hot pad in the middle of the table waiting for me. There's a flower in a vase in the middle of the table. The whole thing makes me smile and hope spreads through my veins like wildfire.

I inhale the food. It's slightly cold, but still delicious. I head back down the hall to hop into the shower, but notice a note on my nightstand. It's in his handwriting and I run my fingers along it, wanting to see if the ink lifts off the page like the way seeing it lifted my heart.

I pull it off the stand and walk in to sit on the bed to read it.

The smell of his cologne wafts into my nose as I open the note and I breathe it in headily. Taking a deep breath, I prepare for whatever he's written in this letter. I wish Remington could say these things to me out loud, but I understand his need to only write them down.

Dear Faith,

I'm finding it very hard to put last night into words so it makes sense. My brain is running sixty miles a minute. You told me no talking and no emotions, but it's like my head is no longer in charge and my heart has taken over again.

Memories of you fill my mind, and it's something I don't ever want to mess with because it's perfection. You are perfect and I won't measure up, but I'll spend the days for the rest of my life sure as hell fighting for it. For you, for us.

I remember the first time I held your hand in the middle of December because it was so damn cold out. I remember laying a blanket down by the crick in the middle of summer so I could make love to you all night long with the crickets in the background. I remember the nights we spent beneath the stars. I remember the first time you told me you loved me and I couldn't figure out how in the world someone as gorgeous as you would be interested in such a loser like me.

I remember the time we covered my truck bed with a tarp and turned it into a jacuzzi because we were too broke to buy a damn pool. You complained the bright red bikini you had on was too small, but I wasn't complaining. As I recall, I couldn't take my damn eyes off you.

I remember the first time I saw you in your red sundress in the middle of a field, dancing around a bonfire to Springsteen, while sipping on apple pie moonshine. You winked at me, and I was a damn goner. Still am. I think somewhere along the line you stopped being Faith and became my girl. You see, you and me, we're meant to be together. Even if it takes me years to convince you, I will do my damn best.

Last night was one of the best nights of my life and it's not because we had sex, it's because it was you. I believed I knew what love was at sixteen years old, but nothing would've prepared me for love as an adult. I didn't know it was possible to love another human as much as I love you. I feel it in my soul, in my bones. You're a part of me and will be until my dying breath. One smile and I was ready to start wars for you.

These last four years I've been a ghost. Moving from day to day, time to time, without even feeling it. One continuous motion without ever truly living. It's like watching a movie on an old black and white box television until someone upgrades you to a sixty-five-inch flatscreen. You make me see life in vivid, brilliant colors.

I was the best with you because you make me a better man. I fall back into you, into the memories, into loving you as easy as the snap of my fingers. I'll admit I was obsessed with you back then, but now it's a whole different type of obsession—a full body one.

Loving you isn't only for the good days, it's for the Mondays when you don't want to work, the Tuesdays when you look longingly for Friday. The Saturdays when you get to sleep in. The Sundays spent making love.

It's the fights, the love made in between, and the living happening along the way. And I want all of it with you. So tonight, I want to do things the proper way. Tonight, I want you to dress up in something special. I'll pick you up at 7pm, we'll go on an adult date - out to dinner, then dancing because although I don't dance, I know you love it and you make me want to for you.

I want to give you the world and it might start with a kiss or a dance, but it'll be another memory of us. I'm not needing an answer right now, but I'm hoping you say yes. I know this is a lot to take in, but tell me you'll think about it, about us. Loving you is the best decision I've ever made, and I don't want to wait another day longer to show you.

In the meantime, breakfast is in the kitchen and I picked you flowers. Don't say no, okay. Say yes because I've already set my mind to winning you back and you know how I get when I put my mind to something. You're my girl. Always have been, always will be.

I love you. I know it doesn't seem like enough, but I'm not sure how to say it better, so let me show you.

Always yours,
Rem

I wipe the tears from my face. How does this man make me swoon so damn much? I sniffle because I'm a blubbering mess of snot and tears. My arms are covered in goosebumps and my hearts beating a mile a minute with exquisite joy.

I can picture each of those moments, almost like a movie. Tears stream down my cheeks onto the paper, smearing the ink. But I don't care. He told me he wants this, us. I need to find him, tell him how I feel.

That's when I hear them.

The sirens.

The screaming.

Running out of the bunkhouse, I go toward the noise. Beau's waving his hands and Jameson is running his hands through his hair like he's scared. I'm taking note of each person standing outside the round pen, except the one I desperately need to see right now.

Where the fuck is Remington?

As I approach, I see a body lying in the round pen. I get to the fence and it hits me all at once. The body is the man I love. Remington is laying in a pool of his own blood on the ground and he's not moving.

"Remington! Remington! Remington!" I hear myself

screaming as I slide through the fence and hit the ground, crawling toward him.

I hear Jameson tell Rhett to get me out of there, but I won't leave him, not like this. I can't leave him. His face is covered in blood, the gash on his forehead is about an inch deep and I can see tissue. The bridge of his nose is bruised and his eyes are already swollen. Glancing down, I notice his left leg is turned the wrong way, and I wonder if it's broken too.

If I didn't know who it was, I probably wouldn't have recognized him. My heart is pounding in rapid succession. I feel like I'm choking, like someone has their hands around my throat and my airway is constricted. I suck in breath after breath, trying not to deprive my brain of the oxygen it desperately requires. I'm fucking helpless as I sit and watch him bleeding out. All I can do is watch the love of my life as he lays lifeless in front of me. My eyes flood with tears and I can't hold it back anymore. Leaning down to Remington, I tell him he's too young to die, to fight because I need him, to fight because I'm all in. This can't be where it ends.

A part of me is struggling with the fact he's blacked out, but the other part thinks maybe this is best to heal him. Maybe it's what he needs right now to fight.

Rhett bends down, trying to pull me away, and I beat him away with all my might, shaking my head. "No! No! I need to be with him!" I scream at him. "What happened? He was fine this morning!" I grab for the dirt beneath me to hang on and with the other hand, I grab him. I'm not letting him slip away, I can't. I won't. We need more time.

It's an out of body experience, almost as if I'm floating above myself watching it all happen and not being able to do a damn thing. I'm crying over him, drenching his clothes, hoping with my heart these waterworks will flood him with life again.

Rhett pulls at me again, and I curse at him. He's not giving up. He shakes me, holding my shoulders so I'd pull my eyes away from Rem. He grabbed eye contact. His voice is dead serious and for a man who's rarely serious, it's eerie. "Faith, the paramedics are here. They need to take care of him."

I'm still screaming incoherent things. They don't understand. I can't lose him, I just got him back. The sirens are right outside the round pen now and EMTs are running in with a stretcher, yelling to each other, but all of it sounds like garbled words.

Rhett finally grabs me around the waist and hauls me away from Remington so the EMTs can get in to assess the damage. Tears are streaming down my face and blurring my vision. I keep seeing him in my mind, lying lifeless on the ground.

My mind keeps bringing up worst scenarios, one worse than the next. Rhett still has his arms around me, as if I might try to make another break for it. They get Remington loaded into the ambulance and one of the EMTs asks if anyone wants to come along. I'm moving before I say yes; I'll be by his side, no matter what happens.

A hand lands on my shoulder, and I find Beau as I swipe under my eyes again. "Faith..." He says in a low voice.

"I'm riding along, Beau. I have to." I almost whine it out loud.

He simply nods and climbs into the ambulance behind me. The rest of the crew wants to come, but the EMT says only two people are allowed in the ambulance with Rem. They agreed to meet us at the hospital. The doors close and we're off, flying down the backroads to the hospital at breakneck speeds.

I feel like I can't breathe again. There's a lump in my throat I can't swallow. Tears fell from my eyes without a pause button. A warm hand wraps around me and my eyes find Beau. "He'll be okay, Faith. He has to be."

I'm shaking my head. "You don't know. You can't promise it'll be okay. He's... really fucked up, Beau."

"I'll be here with you the whole time. We'll get through this and he'll come out on the other side. He's a fighter, Faith. He's the strongest man I know." He pulls me into him, and I let my head fall on his shoulder. I believe him.

"I didn't tell him..." my words trail off.

"You will." He smiled, but it didn't reach his eyes. It's a sympathetic smile to make me feel better, but it doesn't.

This is what you do when you're in love. You fight for it. I know he'd fight for his life, for us, because I'm not giving up on him. It's the exact moment where our past falls away—the fights, the break up, the cheating, the sleepless nights, the snarky comments.

For a short few minutes, I saw a future with him. Our future—the one we'd talked about all those years ago. Tears fill my eyes again and it feels heartbreakingly poetic how this happened now. Were we forever doomed, our own Romeo and Juliet tale? I need him.

If he makes it through this, I'll give him everything.

FAITH

The ride to the hospital is so quiet I swear I can hear my heart beating out loud. If I didn't know better, I'd say it was coming through the speakers in the ambulance. I keep thinking over what he said in the letter and my hope falls all over again because the man I'm seeing now is not the same one who wrote the letter.

I don't even realize how much time has flown by when we arrive at the hospital. Remington is put onto a gurney and carted into the emergency room. We're told the doctors need to assess him and then they'll give us an update as to his condition.

I pace in the room as we wait. I can't stop. I need to keep moving because if I stop then I'll think about him and seeing him like that and I'll lose it. I have one arm braced across my chest, the other arm perpendicular, fingertips pressed to my lips. I can't stop crying.

My old nail biting habit from high school creeps out and I worry my nail to death.

After the doctors finish assessing his injuries, he's transported to the intensive care unit. We're told he has minor brain swelling, a fractured skull, a broken nose, and a crushed sinus bone. He also has a sprained knee. The nurse leads us to his room so we can see the post clean-up of his wounds. I'm anxious to see him awake again and functioning, but as soon as we enter his room, it's a different story.

Seeing six foot Remington Cole covered in wires and hooked up to machines is one of the scariest things I've ever witnessed. A man so strong brought to this by one kick to the head. My lips tremble as I ask the next question. "Why isn't he awake?"

The nurse peers back at Remington before turning back to us. "The doctor will be in shortly to talk with you both."

We nod simultaneously as she turns to leave. My nerves are rattled to the core and too much more waiting may tip me over the edge. The doctor takes mercy on us when he knocks on the door a couple of minutes later. He appears too young to be a doctor, like freshly washed and right out of med school. Remington needs the best physician he can get, so I'm skeptical about the hot shot standing in front of me. Even his smile makes him seem cocky.

"Hello, I'm Dr. Thomas, the physician in charge of Remington's care." He holds his hand out to shake both of ours. I'm sure trying to give us some modicum of security over him, appearing like he's twelve years old.

Beau shakes it and introduces himself. But I don't care about shaking hands, I want to know about Rem.

"I'm Faith, Remington's girlfriend." The words slip out of my mouth and they don't sound a bit wrong. In fact, they sound so right. "Why isn't he awake yet?" I ask the same question as before.

He glances at Remington briefly before facing me again. "We've put him into a medically induced coma so his brain can rest."

A tear slips down my face, and I cross my arms to brace for my next question. "How long will he be like this?"

"Only time will tell." His expression is somber as he speaks the words. This has to be hard for him, giving people bad news. "We will be monitoring him day and night. He needs to have surgery to fix the gash on his forehead, his skull, nose, and leg."

"When will that happen?"

"We'll give him a couple days of recovery before we do anything. Like I said, we'll monitor his progress and work from there."

I peek over my shoulder again, my eyes trailing all of the lines attached. "Can he hear us if we talk to him?"

He nods with a small smile. There's a warm hand on my shoulder and I know who it is without even checking. Beau. My eyes find his and I'm surprised there's as much sheen to his eyes as there is on mine.

The doctor leaves us alone. I'm sure to attend to other patients and I can't stop peering over at Remington, so helpless in his hospital bed. Sadness wrecks me over and over again with each glance. "What will happen with the colt?"

"I don't know. Let's focus on helping Remington, okay? The colt is the least of my priorities."

A sob slips past my lips. A confessional without words. "If he dies, Beau. I need you to promise me something."

He grabs me by the shoulders, turning me, and eyes me head on. "He's not going to die, Faith."

I reach up to swipe away another tear. It hurts to speak the words, but I need to say them. "If he dies, I need you to promise me something. I need you to shoot the colt yourself. I will buy him if I have to, but if Remington Cole dies, it'll be both of their lives."

"Okay, okay, I promise." He pulls a chair over beside the bed for me and I sit down, slipping my hand into Rem's. Beau puts his hand on my shoulder. "I'm heading back to the farm to grab some things. What do you need?"

"Clothes, Reagan knows what I like, my bathroom stuff, and... a pen and paper."

He nods, "Okay, I'll grab those." He turns to leave, but I stop him again.

"Beau?"

"Yeah?"

"There's a box under my bed. It's teal with a brown checkered pattern on it. Can you grab it for me too?"

He smiles. It's small, but hopeful. "You want to read his letters?"

I cock my head at him. "You know about the letters?"

"He didn't shut up about them, Faith. He's been dying for you to read them."

"Do you know what happened?" His eyes fall to the floor before he nods. "Will you tell me?"

He shakes his head. "It's not my place, Faith. I'll bring the letters to you."

He walks to the door, reaching out to turn the knob, and I speak again. "Beau..." He turns around, his eyes finding mine. "Thanks."

"Read the letters, all of them, Faith. The day you left him was the worst day of his life. It's been four long years of insufferable assholish tendencies and moping. The day you walked back onto this farm you brought back the old Rem. The one who's moderately tolerable being around. So, if you want to do this, be all in. He'll need someone when he comes out of this thing and I'd really like it to be you. But if you decide you can't stick it out. If you decide whatever is in those letters is unforgivable, then you leave before he wakes up. I'd rather you do it now, instead of drag him along."

He doesn't say anything else before he leaves and I let the words sink in. I could get mad about the fact he thinks I'd walk away now, but I understand the concern he has for his friend. I'd want someone in my corner too if I was in Rem's condition.

It's all so unknown and terrifying. All we can do is wait.

A few hours later, I wake to the sound of a knock on the door. Beau came back with a bag and the box as requested. "Hey, sorry, I didn't mean to wake you up."

I stand up to grab the stuff. "No, it's okay. I must've been tired." I turn my neck back and forth to alleviate the kink sleeping in the chair left behind.

Beau seems tired today, it's the first time I've truly taken the time to scan him over. Black bags rest beneath his eyes. He's handsome for a man, but he isn't as handsome as Remington is, even with all these wires and a busted-up face.

I think it's how I knew it would be with Remington. I've never felt this way about another man, and no one has ever caught my eye like Rem. I used to think it was a crush. The hormones telling me I loved him, but I think deep down I knew I would love him forever.

Our souls speak to each other like long lost lovers and best friends, to be parted nevermore.

I've had four years of not liking him, but the love for him remains. It's steady and constant, like a heartbeat.

Silence lingers in the space between us as we both stood over our friend. "I still can't believe it's him in this bed. It should've been me. I took on the colt." I can tells he's beating himself up.

My hand finds his upper arm and I squeeze. "You know it was an accident, Beau. How were you supposed to know Remington would fall into the ring and get kicked?"

He shakes his head adamantly. "I should've said no. I knew he was bad news, but the farm could use the money. Mr. Johnson pays very well. I..."

I slide my hand up his arm. "Hey, look at me." His eyes are wet as he turns to me. "You did not do this. You did not put him in the hospital, okay? The colt did this. Not you."

He runs his hand through his hair, leaving a trail. "Fuck, Faith, what happens if he doesn't wake up?"

"I don't know," I whisper. I can't think about it or I'll lose my composure. The little I was holding onto at the moment, but my eyes find the box of his letters and I knew what I wanted to do. I would read the remaining one hundred letters until he came back to me.

When he woke up again, there would be nothing between us. I'd know the truth, and we'd be together. I am not allowing myself time to wallow or to lose hope, because the second I lost hope, the war my brain was fighting would win.

Losing him again would wreck me.

I set the bag and box down by my chair, dropped my toiletries in the bathroom, and returned to my chair to sit down. It'll be a long night.

Beau pulls a chair over to the bed beside me, and I gaze over at him. "You don't have to stay. You're exhausted. Head home, get some sleep, and come back tomorrow. I'll stay with him tonight. We have some catching up to do."

I was tired too, emotionally exhausted.

"You sure?"

I nodded, "Yes."

"Okay then." He leans down to kiss me on the forehead. It feels nice. It isn't a sexy kiss at all, it was more of a familial kiss. Like a father would bestow upon a child. It is comforting in this moment of unknowingness. He leaves with a quick goodbye, a promise to watch Bandit, and a promise he'll be back in the morning.

The nurses came and went over the next couple of hours. They'd hooked me up with a comfy chair, a pillow, and extra blankets. I am thankful because I hadn't planned on leaving anytime soon. I was happy he was in a single room. We wouldn't have to share it.

Snuggling in under the blankets, I pull the next letter from the box and dig in.

Dear Faith,

. . .

Do you remember the night we carved our initials into the tree out by the hot springs? Do you remember me saying why I picked the specific hot springs tree?

I remember it like it was yesterday. I'd spent the day examining trees all over the farm. This was the biggest, the strongest, and I knew it could withhold our love carved into the side of it the best. It'd been in the same spot for years and it would be there for years to come, reminding us this thing we had was forever.

I wanted to do something crazy, something to bring us back to solid ground if we ever headed toward unsolid footing. A symbol tying us forever.

That night was the third time we'd had sex, and I still couldn't believe it. You still wanted me. You wanted the loser. The guy no one would come within six feet of and not because of any reason other than you didn't mess around with a Cole. I wanted to memorialize our love.

We'd grown accustomed to using the bed of my truck for our love-making sessions and I'd finally used the right number of blankets so you didn't feel the hard metal of the truck digging into your back as I made love to you, missionary style. Call me weird, but I liked watching you. I liked knowing you saw me, the real me, and you wanted me anyhow. I loved the faces you made as my body gave yours pleasure.

It was such a weird feeling of connection, two separate body parts coming together as one to give a euphoric sense of feeling and plea-sure. For sixteen years I'd pictured it, but the moment it happened was like an explosion of color. You were my first and only. You see, I decided I would only give myself to one girl in this lifetime and I trusted you with it all - soul, body, heart. It was yours for the taking and eventual breaking.

Love seems so easy in the movies, like it's flawless. Hollywood lies to you and makes you believe in fairy tales and happily ever afters. You think about love with the perception of what do I have to lose, but the truth is, you have everything to lose. In the end, heart-

break comes in many forms - lies, cheating, manipulation, lost love.

But at sixteen, you don't know any better. I was falling head over heels in love with you and I wanted to get lost in the feeling of it. You made me feel alive. You made me want to be a better person for you. To rise above the Cole name and not get sucked into the same shit hole my father found himself in daily. So, I vowed to be the best I could for you.

I guess you could say it was the day I realized I couldn't let you slip away, and I'd do whatever I could to keep you. My brain seems scattered tonight. Maybe it explains why I keep jumping from one thought to another, but I want to get it all out.

I remember after we made love; we stared at the stars under our blanket until the cold crept in and forced us to get dressed. I wasn't ready to leave you so I brought you to the hot springs. Two birds, one stone. We'd get warm and we could carve our names on the tree that stood guard.

We'd spent another half an hour in the springs making out because we could. Heavy petting followed after, followed by more love making. When it started to sprinkle, you ran for the tree. The one I'd picked out earlier the same day. I pulled out my knife and asked which spot you wanted to do it in.

So, we stood there and carved the initials FE and RC into the side of the tree in the middle of a rainstorm. Our clothes were soaked. Your hair hung in drenched curls. You'd wrapped my arms around you afterward as we stood staring at the forever mark we'd left. Turning, you'd put your lips to mine and I was lost in the magic of our kiss.

My heart beat like crazy and I wanted to get down on one knee right then and there, but we were so young, too young. So, I didn't. I decided I'd wait. Not a day passes by where I regret not asking. I'd ask you right now if I could. Because no matter what happens, I want you and only you.

You don't know this, but I visit it each Thursday to run my

fingers over our initials and remember all the good times it's seen. Somehow the initials carved into the tree helped me stay close to you, even if you lived three hours away. It was like the tree embodied our souls, even if they weren't in the same state. Maybe someday we can revisit our spot together. I hope so.

This is all for now. I love you.
   Always yours,
   Rem

My eyes raise from the letter and I whisper at him. "You wake up from this thing and I promise to visit our tree with you anytime you want."

I wait for a response, but I know it wouldn't come. My purse vibrates beneath me and I grab my phone. "Hello."

"Faith, oh thank God. Are you okay? I've been trying to reach you all day."

"Nova?" My voice had more questions than I intended. It'd been a couple of days since we'd talked, and I hadn't even remembered to check my phone today.

"Yeah, babe." Concern leaked through her voice, and I knew she'd been worried about me. I hated myself for putting her in the situation where she had to.

"Oh, Nova. It's Rem... he's been in an accident." I choke on the last word. "He's... in the ICU."

She starts moving around while talking to me. "I'm coming. Tell me which hospital you're at."

I shake my head. "You don't have to, Nov. I'll be okay."

"Faith, I'm coming, now tell me where I'm going or I'll call the farm." It's how Nova is, had your back to a fault with or without your consent. The type of friend who dropped whatever they were doing if you needed them.

"Okay, okay, we're at Moonshine Springs Memorial Hospital." I sniffle, barely holding back the breakdown rushing through me.

"We can talk when I get there. I'm leaving here in a couple of minutes once I get things packed and call the boss. Do you need anything?"

"I need him to be okay," I say honestly.

"He'll be okay, Faith. The man loves you. Dying would be giving up. I'll see you soon."

The call clicks off, and she is gone. I am once again in silence except for the machinery around me, keeping him functioning.

I cried myself to sleep the first night. All of the emotions from the day came rushing back, and I cried them out one single tear drop at a time—death of a painful memory and birth of a new memory, tear by tear.

FAITH

T he beep of the machine woke me up slowly the next morning. I blinked open my eyes and stretched out a bit. The room was bright, but the sun was absent from the sky, reminding me life was a little duller without him.

My gaze trailed the length of the room until I found Remington. My heart dipped when I saw him attached to all those machines. I hated it. Seeing him like this, lifeless. As if the life was sucked out of him and he was hanging on by a thread.

I clear my throat and shake my head. *No negativity today,* I remind myself. I reach over for his hand and hold it before standing to press a kiss to his cheek. His skin is warm to the touch, and it reminded me he was still in there somewhere. "I love you, Remington Cole, and I don't know if you can hear me or not, but know this, I'm not going anywhere. No matter what those letters say, you're stuck with me. I'll be right here when you wake back up. Now, I need to get dressed, no peeking."

I shake my head at myself. *Of course, he won't peek, you idiot.* He is in a coma. I grab my bag and make my way to the bathroom, where I change, run a brush through my hair, and brush my teeth.

I glanced at myself in the mirror. At least I seemed somewhat presentable - minus the blood-shot eyes and bags under my eyes.

The sound of voices carries into the room outside, and I rush to finish. Pulling the door open, I find two sets of eyes staring back at me—Beau and Nova.

"Faith, girl. Come here." Nova opens her arms and I can't help but run into them. Her hugs are some of the best around. I still can't believe she'd literally dropped work and life to be here. "How are you doing?"

"I'm hanging in there. When did you get here?"

"Last night, around ten. I ended up staying in your room at the farm. Oh, and I met Jameson... talk about interesting..." Her cheeks lit up with a light shade of pink and I know her expression all too well. Someone had a thing for our Jameson.

"You'll have to tell me all about it," I whisper in her ear.

"Later..." I knew she wouldn't talk about it in front of Beau. Nova is shy around men. She'd kick loose with me later on and spill all the details of what went down. Pulling away from me, she glances over to where Remington lays. "Oh man, this is definitely not how I imagined meeting him, but I guess it'll have to do." I smiled. Nova was awkward, but that's what I loved most about her. "Any updates today?" Her eyes found me again, and I shake my head.

"Nope, I only woke up a little bit before y'all showed up. I was getting ready to head to the farm for my nine o'clock lesson with Maddie."

"Karen will be taking over lessons for now." It was Beau speaking this time.

"But..."

"No, you have enough happening right now. I don't need you worried about giving lessons. I want you to focus on taking care of you, reading those letters, and being here for Remington."

"Thank you." He nods at me. I am grateful to him. I wasn't

sure how I'd survive any lessons without having Rem there to help me with Koko.

"Guess it means you get to show me around this small little town of yours." Nova smiles at me, and I can't help but smile back. It's nice having her back after only a couple of phone calls back and forth.

"Um..."

Beau looks at the both of us. "Head out, I'll stay with him." I bite my bottom lip, still unsure if I should be leaving Remington right now. "Look, I'll update you if they say anything. Go get some rest and relax."

He cocks his head toward the door. I knew he'd call if there was news, so I let Nova pull me out of the room and down the hall. My heart cracks a little leaving him, but Beau is right. I need rest if I will be staying with him.

When we walk to her car, Nova asked where to first. I asked to go to the farm, and she hit the GPS on her dash. The drive back doesn't seem as harrowing as the drive away yesterday had been. There was one place I wanted to visit before I started showing Nova around town. I need to see it again.

Our tree.

She pulls up to the bunkhouse and parked. I unbuckled my seatbelt, opened the door, and ran. I could hear her footsteps behind me, but I didn't slow down. It felt like if I didn't get there right now, every little thing would disappear in the blink of an eye. My legs threaten to buckle below me, but I pushed on until it came into view.

Slowing when I reached the springs, I give Nova time to catch up. "Jeez wildcat, a little warning next time you decide we're sprinting please." She bends over, trying to catch her breath, but I keep moving. I finally reach the tree and let my fingers run over the love letters we'd carved. I closed my eyes, locking in the memories he'd written in the letter. I needed to remember a time when we were both here, making love like teenagers without a care in the world.

It's clear as day on a slideshow in my mind, playing to a soundtrack of a July Saturday night.

Crickets chirped along to the wind as it blew through the tall grass in the field. Lee Brice sang through the speakers of his old pickup truck. The bull frogs from the crick ribbeted to their heart's content. The stars shined so brightly overhead they sparkled like diamonds. The stack of blankets spread out in the bed of his pickup truck beneath us was soft to the touch. The feel of his bare skin so close to mine felt like we were on fire together. The brush of his lips against mine as he kissed me again and again. The heat of the springs as we got frisky a second time.

The smell of rain as it came pouring in on a summer afternoon.

Our damp clothes.

Holding hands.

Tasting sky water as it pours down in waves around us. The way those grey-blue eyes had found mine and held on for dear life, entrancing me. The way he'd pulled me closer at the last minute to save me from the majority of the downpour.

The way he'd whispered to pick the spot we'd carve our initials for the rest of our lives. The story he'd told me about why it was this tree he'd picked out of all the others.

The lyrics of Thompson Square's "Are You Gonna Kiss Me or Not" come to mind and I hummed along. God, how I wish he could kiss me now.

Opening my eyes again, I turn back to Nova. "This is the exact spot Remington and I promised to love each other forever. We carved our initials. If it's not written down, it's not legit. Wasn't that how it felt back in high school? What was it they used to say, it's not official until it's social media official?"

———

Over the last five days I've read about half of the letters, each different from the last. They're filled with most emotions known to man.

Love.

Desire.

Passion.

Anger.

Hurt.

Sadness.

Withdrawal.

I know I'm coming up on the one letter I've been expecting since I finally decided to read them. The one explaining what happened the night of the party. The night I ran. The moment that changed my forever with Remington.

I'm scared of what it'll change. Terrified those words will make me feel things I've been pushing aside for too long, but I need to do this. I need to read it so we can move on with our lives.

Each day I visit the place he told me about in his letters the day before.

The first morning I spent time at our tree and at the hot springs with Nova. In the evening I'd talked to Remington all about the day—the visit to our tree and the springs. His lashes fluttered when I told him about it. As if it was his way of telling me he knew I was there and he was happy I was finding my way back to him.

On day two, I swipe the keys to his truck from his hook in the bunkhouse and made the drive out to the old place we'd slip off to in the middle of the night. Nova rode along with me as I gave her the tour.

The third afternoon I visited the crick where he used to take me fishing. The crick we drove to at three a.m. because no one else knew it was our make out spot.

The fourth day I went to Bodine's and sat at the same table we did on our first date. I ordered a burger and fries with ranch and remembered how he made fun of me for it until I had him try it.

Yesterday I visited the Springs again on the farm. It's the place I feel closest to him. I lay back in the water and picture him sitting beside me, running his fingers over the top of my back like he used to do. It's an automatic reflex. I picture him holding his arm up so I can sneak under and cuddle in close to him.

I've been sitting here all morning talking to him, and I swear he knows I'm here with him. Nova left two days ago, so it's only been Remington and I getting to know each other over again. Well, mostly just me, cause he's yet to respond.

Beau shows up to check on me and sometimes sends me home to sleep, but for the most part it's simply us.

Beau has some other things happening in his life right now, occupying most of his time.

My time with Remington is quiet, but I enjoy it. The silence drowns out the rest of the world while I let myself reminisce and recapture the years of Rem and I.

I don't remember him being such a charmer. It seemed like giving him a pen and paper gave him an outlet to express himself the way he couldn't in real life. I wonder if this accident will leave him without his memories. If it does, I'm hoping he only loses the recent ones and keeps the best ones.

Taking a piece of paper and a pen, I start to write him back. It's not a response to his letters, more like written memories since I've been back. In case he forgets.

The first one is short and sweet. First impressions after seeing him four years later. The way my heart still skipped a beat when he smiled at me.

I decided to write him one letter a day, it's the least I can do. One hundred and four letters show a dedication not many people know in this lifetime and I won't let him slip through my fingers so easily.

. . .

Dear Rem,

I bet you never imagined I'd be writing these letters back to you, huh? Well, here we are and I want to write about what's happening because I don't want you to miss a thing. Mr. Johnson came back to get the colt today. He's selling him to someone else. I have a feeling it means slaughterhouse, but I didn't ask because I didn't want to know.

To be honest, I don't give a damn what he does with the colt as long as it isn't anywhere close to you again. Seeing you lying there lifeless in the middle of the round pen tore me apart. I believed the worst... guess I still do. The night before the accident was one of the best I've had with you and it's not only because of the sex, it's because of how close I felt to you in those few brief hours. It felt like the old us and I want it again with you.

I've read 80 of the letters you've written to me. I guess you could say I had a little bit of time to catch up. I'm glad I waited to read them. I think if I had read them when you sent them, then I wouldn't have processed the words as easily. I was mad at you for a very long time after what happened. Seeing you with her shattered me into a million pieces, and all the string and duct tape in Moonshine Springs couldn't have kept it together.

I miss you, babe. The night before the accident, I realized all the love and forgiveness I've been holding back. I was pissed at you for cheating, and even more so because it was with Sofia. I was hurt because I truly believed you were it for me. My heart felt like you were taking a razor blade to it, cutting around each vein and artery to get to the main part before you tore it out with your bare hand and squeezed it until all of the blood pooled on the floor below you. I'd have been dead after then, but you get what I mean.

Have you ever wanted something so bad that the moment it slips away you feel like there's nothing left? This probably sounds dramatic at this point, but four years ago I was a lot more immature than I am now. I've had time to grieve us, but I couldn't move on.

I wanted closure, or so I believed, but it's the last thing I want. Today is the day I'll get to read the letter. The one from that night and I know for a fact whatever I read won't change how I feel about you. I've decided I want this regardless.

Maybe you'll be mad at me for running without cause. Without you having the chance to tell me what happened. Maybe you have the right to be pissed off at me. Hell, maybe when you wake up from this thing you won't remember a damn thing.

All that matters is you and me and fixing us. You, Remington Cole, are stuck with me until you tell me to leave.

Always yours,
Faith

I sit the pen and paper down, tucking away the envelope into the front of the box. Taking his hand in mine, I feel comfort and warmth. I wonder how long he'll be like this and pray it's not months. Looking at his hand, I wonder if it'll lose muscle mass while he's in the coma. I've read about people who have muscle atrophy after coming out of a coma for a month or months. I can't picture his hand as frail.

His hands are big and full; a real man's hand, calloused and rough. Squeezing his hand with one of mine, I allow the other to run along his cheek over the stubble growing in a little under a week. The hair on his head is longer on top than he normally keeps it. I didn't realize how curly it gets when it's long and I wonder if it's why he continually kept it shorter.

"Okay," I whisper. "I'm about to read the letter, Rem. No matter what, I'm not running this time." I squeeze his hand again before leaning down to grab it from the box.

My heart is battering my chest with anticipation of what I've been waiting to find out for the last four years. A part of me wants to keep running, but I need to know so we can move on together.

I slip open the envelope and take a deep breath. *Here goes nothing.*

Dear Faith,

It's taken me months to figure out how to write this letter to you. I still don't know if I'll fuck it up or not, but you deserve to know the truth about what happened.

Promise me one thing—read it all, the whole way to the end before you pass judgment. I know the events of the night led to the demise of our relationship and I know this letter won't fix things between us, but I hope it at least explains why what happened, happened.

I remember it like it was yesterday. My gut was so filled with nerves. I wanted it to be a perfect night for you because I knew it meant something to you. Inviting me to meet your friends for the first time and the last thing I wanted to do was screw it up.

I didn't want to let you down, and it's exactly what I did. I shouldn't have accepted the drink from Sofia, but I perceived turning it down would make me look bad. The next thing I knew, the room was getting foggy, and I remember what I rationalized was you suggesting we find a room. All I wanted to do was find a room and sleep with you.

The second her lips were on mine, I knew something wasn't right. They weren't the same supple lips you give me; they were thin and unpleasant. I was groggy, and my body didn't seem to want to move. I felt like I'd been drugged.

My brain said push her off, get away, but my hands simply wouldn't compute the command. I was so damn tired all of a sudden. Closing my eyes gave me the briefest sense of peace, but I had no idea what she would do if I let myself slip into an in-between state of mind.

To be paralyzed was a fear I hadn't known, even with an abusive father. I wanted to yell at her for putting me in such a vulnerable position, but my mouth wouldn't form the words. All I could do was lay there and watch as she did what she wanted without my permission.

All I could think about was her doing things to me I couldn't control, and it pissed me off. Contrary to some cocky guys, not all of us liked the idea of nonconsensual sex with women. My body was yours and she was trying to take it away from you in a vile manner. It was low to have to drug a guy to get him out of it enough to do what you wanted.

So, I guess a thank you is in order. Thank you for storming in when you did. Thanks to you, she didn't get further than removing my shirt. We never had sex. It was all a huge misunderstanding, and I paid for it dearly, but in the end, you stopped something shitty from happening to me. It's you, Faith. No one else ever measured up.

I hope you're reading this and you can find it in your heart to forgive a fucked-up situation. To forgive me for letting you believe I cheated, because it was too embarrassing to tell you I was almost raped by someone half my size. A lie of omission was easier than the truth for me. I'm sorry your heart shattered while I watched and couldn't do a damn thing.

I remember watching her leave right after you did. I don't know what happened next, but I woke up the next morning wondering what the hell happened. Why my head felt like someone was beating the shit out of it. Why my mouth felt clogged to the brim with this dry cotton feeling.

Slowly throughout the day, it came back to me. One thing after the next, I cried myself to sleep thinking I'd lost you forever. I was mad at you, hell I was pissed. You didn't even give me the damn chance to explain or to tell you the truth. Hell, I don't even know if I *would have, but you didn't stick around to find out. By the time I arrived at your house the next day, your mom said you'd moved out, off to the college they'd picked for you.*

Maybe in a way I knew you were better than this town for me. I remember thinking it was a sign. Ending things this way was for the best, even though I felt like I'd been sliced open by an unclean knife and was dying from infection. I drank way too much, came back to the farm, and drank more until I couldn't see straight. I wouldn't be better than the Cole name, right?

Beau found me passed out in the driveway in a pool of my own vomit. He stayed up with me all night to make sure I didn't vomit in my sleep and die. Each day since has been hard.

I can't help but wonder what had happened if you'd stayed. If you'd trusted me enough to find out the truth instead of running. If I'd been brave enough to tell you.

Well... now you know. The whole story of the night that wrecked us. I know you may not read this letter, but it feels better putting it to paper. Like somehow, it's freeing. No longer only my secret to keep.

I love you.
Always yours,
Rem

Tears drop onto the page, leaving smeared ink and blotched spots where they once held his words. Words that shattered each little thing I believed and felt over these last four years apart. I was completely stunned, speechless. My eyes drifted to him before they landed on the letter in my hands once again.

I re-read the same line, once, twice, three times, but it's all the same each time. He didn't cheat on me. Four years of hate and misery based on an omission of the truth. But I had the letters for years, so maybe some of the blame falls on me too.

I sit down on the edge of the bed slowly; almost afraid I'd wake him. The pit in my stomach over all of these truths forces more tears to slip out. I take his big hand in mine. "I'm so sorry, I didn't know Rem. All these years I've hated you and blamed you for cheating on me and you hadn't. In fact, you'd almost been..." With a jagged swallow my words fail as I choke back the sob threatening to break free.

How could I have believed Remington Cole would cheat on me that easily?

FAITH

Light escapes the room as day turns to dusk. I've been sitting holding Remington's hand since this afternoon and I can't stop thinking about the letter. I feel like a shell of myself, unable to cope with the truth. My running had damaged him more than I realized. My soul healed in the four years since I'd seen Remington, but his continued to shatter after my departure. I was to blame fully.

I miss his deep gravelly voice, masculine in its own right, as it used to wrap around me like a warm blanket.

I'd called Beau about thirty minutes ago to see if he could come sit with Remington while I went out. Some time out of this stuffy, lifeless hospital room would do me well.

I was sitting, talking mindlessly about anything as it came to mind, when all of a sudden Remington's hand twitched. I hit the nurse's button and a couple of minutes later, she entered the room. "His hand twitched. Does he know I'm here? Can he hear what I'm saying?"

All hope fled on a whim when I saw the expression as it crossed her face before she shook her head. "Don't think anything of it. It's only his muscle spasming while he's in the coma."

"Oh, okay." My voice is a low whisper, exuding disappointment.

"Was there anything else?" Her lips form into a smile, but it was one of pity written in her eyes. Glancing down at Rem, I shake my head and listen to her footsteps as she crosses the room and closes the door behind her.

A tear slides down my cheek onto his face as I lean up to kiss him. He's been on the receiving end of so many of these tear-soaked kisses lately. I'm starting to wonder if he feels flooded with them yet. I feel like I've literally cried him a river.

Ten minutes later, Beau knocks on the door and then enters. "Hey, how's he doing?" He said softly, his eyes finding where Rem lays lifeless on the bed.

I shook my head. "He twitched his fingers earlier, but the nurse said it was a muscle spasm. God, it's so hard to see him like this. He's such a strong, broody dude. My heart breaks over the knowledge his father doesn't even know he's here."

His eyes dropped as a sigh slipped from between his lips. "Not to sound like an ass, Faith, but I don't think he'd care even if you told him. He hasn't had an easy life. He was more my brother than he was ever their son."

"I know... it's..." My voice trailed off as my heart broke for him.

"I know. I'll stay with him for a little while. Get some space from here for a bit." I lean down to Rem and whispered I'd be back before I thanked Beau and took my leave.

On the way home, I call in an order to Bodine's; a meatloaf melt with fries and a strawberry banana milkshake. It was greasy, but I knew it'd be amazing. I wanted their hometown breakfast meal of buttery biscuits and gravy, double cut bacon, and brown sugar grits, but it is almost dinner time so I knew it wasn't available.

Stopping briefly at the diner, I pay and tip my normal waitress, Patty, before continuing on my way home.

"Memory I Don't Mess With" by Lee Brice streams through the radio on my drive home and I couldn't help but sing along with the lyrics. Remington Cole is a memory I'd never mess with.

I slow the car as I approach the entrance to the stables. Two willow trees stand proudly by the road beckoning you in to enjoy the willow tree lined drive. These trees were planted before I started coming to Willow Springs, but they've grown like crazy since then.

I watch as Titan and Remy run along beside the car, only a fence dividing us. Their whinnies carry on the wind; a response from horses in a nearby field. I see Karen in the big arena working with a student, probably Alison, at this time of day.

She is one of my newer kids. I'd told Karen I could start doing lessons for my students again, but she'd told me to take a few more days first. She could handle them for a little while longer. I remember her laughing when she said it. Joy was an easy expression on her face when she spoke about teaching children.

A warmth spreads through my chest thinking about all the times Remington and I had driven up this same driveway. The illusion of a perfect life hanging right in front of us, simply waiting for us to reach out and grab it.

My heart pangs thinking back to the letter I read earlier today. I still could hardly wrap my head around it. I'm pissed at myself for believing a lie and not even giving him a chance to explain, but then again maybe four years apart is what we needed to find our way back to each other again.

I see Reagan walk out of the barn with Bandit as I pull up, and a smile creeps across my face. It is nice to see the little fluff ball. Reagan runs up and gives me a hug as I get out from the driver's seat. "How are you doing, babe? How's Remington?"

"I guess as good as expected. He's still in the coma for now. I've seen some hand and eye twitches, but the nurse assures me it's only his muscles spasming. But Rea—I feel like he knows I'm there."

Her lips turn up into a genuine smile. "Oh, I'm sure he does."

"I hope so. They say they'll give him another week or two before they try to reverse the coma."

"Well, that's good news."

"Yeah, I guess I needed a little bit of time away from there today. I think it's all getting to me."

"Hey, can I ask whatever happened between the two of you?"

A sadness curled my lips into a frown. "Turns out, I was an idiot. I saw something and instead of sticking around for the whole story, I ran."

"Excuse me if I'm being too forward, but was it because he cheated on you?"

"Is that the story spread around town?" I asked.

She nodded. "Unfortunately, small town gossip is some of the worst. Things weren't very easy for Remington after you left. Being labeled as a cheater gave people the opportunity to look down on him and treat him like garbage. It was nothing new, but it seemed like this news inflamed it. Remington's been frowned upon sheerly for being the son to his father all of his life. This didn't help matters."

A tear slides down my cheek, thinking about the shit storm that hit the fan after I left for Ohio. I may have hated Remington at the time, but I never wanted him to be outcast and treated cruelly for something when he wasn't even to blame. I didn't know at the time how much not his fault it was. Nope, this laid squarely in the hands of Sofia.

"He didn't say anything about what really happened? He could've explained what happened at least."

"Faith, who would've believed him? You know the Cole reputation."

I nod my head. "I do..."

Reagan clears her throat. "I made dinner. Are you hungry?" I duck back into my car, pull out the bag from Bodine's, and wave it at her. "Well then, let's head in and eat some grub."

Quickly shutting the car door, I then follow her and Bandit

into the main house. He ran straight to me once Reagan took off his leash. I stoop down to pet my wiggly friend and he jumps into my arms; his excitement evident. "Hey Bandit, you miss me bud?"

He smothers my face in kisses as his butt shakes uncontrollably with delight. I haven't seen him in a week, and it's nice to hold him. I rub him all over and gush over how cute he's being. He begged to get down, so I let him down. Reagan slid a chair out from the table for me, and I sat down and unwrapped my meal.

A few minutes later, the rest of the crew drags in—Jameson, Rhett, and Karen. They asked about Remington, and I told them the same message I had relayed to Reagan minutes earlier.

Voices carried through the kitchen and dining room as we chattered about the happenings in their lives, on the farm, and around town. Finished with my food, I stood up and headed toward the kitchen to throw it away. I'd brought more of the letters because I was so close to getting the whole way through the box.

As I made my way over to Reagan, I told the guys goodbye. Bandit had been staying with Reagan, so I asked if I could borrow him for an hour or two. She nodded and squeezed my arm before turning back to continue the conversation she was having with Karen.

The leash hooked onto Bandit's collar easily, and he walked with me as we left and headed toward the bunkhouse. I made a quick stop at my car and grabbed the box of letters I'd brought along with me. About twenty something more letters to read, and I would have finally read them all. Walking toward Remington's room, I stop and grab his pillow, a few throw blankets from the couch, and made my way out to his truck. My destination is the back part of McCoy's field, our field.

His truck rumbles to a start as I turn the key in the ignition. Before I'd helped Bandit into the truck, I'd grabbed Rem's cologne from his center console and gave the truck a brief spray. Now all I could smell was his masculine scent of mahogany, wood, and lavender.

I inhale deeply, with each breath almost believing he was actually there sitting in the seat beside me. Isn't it funny how a smell brings a life event or a certain memory to life? I read studies on it in school about how a certain smell can bring back a childhood memory.

It's the same feeling I get when I open a new paperback and remember myself reading them in the dorm room. I can still picture the bean bag chair I sat in with the soft outer layer and sense the quiet in the middle of the day when other kids are out running about their business.

For me, Remington's cologne gives me those same feelings. My nostrils devouring his scent as his body pressed so close to me when we made love. It's now embedded into my memory, and I associate it with happy feelings. So, each time I smell it, I think of him and my warm feelings surrounding him.

Bandit is in the passenger's seat, nose pressed against the window making nose art, his tail wagging as we watch the scenery pass us by. I'll softly say his name occasionally, and he'll glance back, bark, and then revert to sightseeing.

I slow down as I approach the McCoy's field. Taking a back trail, I slip behind the fence to the part in the tree line where the crick was accessible. I didn't want to be in it, but I wanted to be close enough so I could hear the water trickle down the stream over rocks and under, bubbling as it traveled.

I turn off the truck and grabbed my blankets from the back before hopping out, leaving Bandit barking like a crazy man in the front seat. I could see him bouncing up and down with each bark, annoyed I'd left him.

Lowering the tailgate on the bed of the truck, I set up the blankets and pillow I'd brought with me. I open the back door of the cab, grab the box of letters, the lunchbox of drinks I'd packed, and Bandit.

I shut the tailgate so Bandit can't escape, then set him down in the bed. Climbing in, I settle into the blankets, grab my box, and pull out the next letter. Bandit burrows into the blankets beside me and curled into ball. I needed some time alone with Remington. Although this next letter was the last thing I was expecting...

Dear Faith,

Fuck you. I'm pissed at you for leaving me like you did. Without an explanation. Do you have any idea what the gossip rags are spilling about right now? Me. Me cheating to be specific. Except now you know I didn't actually cheat, but I couldn't say a damn thing about it until you knew. I promised myself I'd come clean to you first.

I hoped the gossip would pass. They'd move on to someone else's sordid affair, but for years I've still been the subject of the townies. You know how this town is, Faith. You knew what leaving would tell them and you fucking left anyhow.

Right now, I'm feeling hurt and angry. You shredded my heart and my reputation in this town all in one night. Granted, being a Cole, my reputation couldn't have been any worse, but it still cut pretty deep.

Word went back to my pops I was a cheater, and he told me the apple didn't fall far from the tree. In fact, it's like he was proud of it, which made me sick to my stomach. The last person I wanted to be like was him. It was also before he beat me for cheating. I mean, how fucked up, being proud of your child for cheating and then turning around and beating the shit out of him?

Knowing my father, the two probably didn't even go hand in hand. He probably wanted to beat me because it was his favorite pastime when he was drunk.

You don't know this, but I came to see you, to explain everything in person while you were at college. Reagan had your address, so I decided to take a day trip.

I remember my hands being sweaty, waiting for you to stroll out of your last class for the day. I parked in front of your dorm and hoped no one said anything about my junker pickup truck. My heart leapt when I first saw you again, but then quickly crashed when I saw the guy who ran after you and threw his arm around your shoulder.

I wanted to jump out of my truck and punch the fuck out of him, but I knew how it would appear. You were probably still pissed at me, so I didn't want to risk you telling me to never contact you again or something worse. So, I white knuckled the steering wheel the whole way back to the farm, and then I drank all night long. Chased away my emotions with straight liquor as it burned on its way down the back of my throat. I ended up passing out on the couch at Beaus. I couldn't even walk straight enough to make it to the bunkhouse. Talk about royally fucked up, right?

Beau is the reason I've written all these letters. He told me not to give up. He said, even if you hated me after you found out the truth you deserved to know. I didn't keep my promise, I told Beau. It's hard to keep secrets when the alcohol flows so freely.

So... that's it for this letter. No sweet words, only sadness.

Still always yours (even if you don't want me anymore),
Rem

Laying down on the pillow, I cuddle Bandit into me and cry. His words were so hateful. I could feel the pain clearly written across the page. I sit there watching the lightning bugs lighting up the night sky. I listen to the crick make its own lullaby. A breeze blows through the tall grass, and it almost whistles along adding to the melody of the night around us.

Bandit kept finding different things to keep his interest, but I wanted to sit and think. I'd brought paper and pen with me to write Remington a letter, but right now I simply can't bring myself to think about what I'd even say.

It was a long two hours before I packed us back into the truck and headed to the barn. I needed to get back to the hospital. I'd promised him I wouldn't run, even if all I wanted to do was run.

This evening, I kissed Remington on the lips and begged him to return to me because we had so many things not completed yet. I begged him to love me enough to open his eyes. I told him about the kids we would have and how I couldn't wait to be his wife someday.

"Love me, Rem. Love me, please."

———

It's been almost three weeks since the accident. Eight days after he came into the emergency room, Remington had the surgery to put a plate in his head, fix his nose and sinus cavity, plus repair his strained knee. I've been by his side for each step of this journey. The nurses and physicians have been so kind and knowledgeable throughout his time here. Some days were hard, sitting here with the man I loved not knowing if he would wake up again, but today's the day.

The day they reverse the coma. The day I find out if Remington is still in there, or if this brain injury has changed him. I've read all the articles I could find on brain and skull injuries from a horse kick, and it terrifies me to think he may have to deal with horrible headaches and memory loss for the rest of his life. But regardless of what happens, I'm sticking with him.

We're told people generally take between six hours to a day to fully wake up, and we're all prepared to be with him. Beau and I are the only ones that have been visiting his actual room. The others show up to the hospital, but they don't want to see him like this. I wonder if it'll change if he doesn't wake up from this.

The anesthesiologist came in earlier and reversed the meds, so now we're waiting. His fingers have moved slightly, but we don't know if it is muscle reflex or him waking up. I'm almost afraid to breathe or gaze away in case I miss it. I haven't slept since.

———

Today marks ten days, four hours, and twenty-two minutes since they reversed the coma. The room is lifeless, and I'm starting to lose hope over him waking up. The doctor assures me this is normal for brain injury patients because we never know how much trauma the brain has sustained. It's why they put him into a coma so his brain could rest.

I'd run out quickly for lunch when Beau stopped by. I was standing in line at the deli when my phone rings. It's Beau.

His voice sounds weird as he says his next words. "He's awake. He opened his eyes, Faith. I ran to tell the doctors and we're waiting for them to see him. Can you come back?"

I don't even respond. I toss the phone back into my purse and race back to the hospital.

He's awake.

He came back to me.

I slap my hand frantically against the buttons once I get into the elevator. I'm pacing and mad that I left in the first place. I didn't know it would be today. The day he woke up and I wasn't even there to see it.

The doctor is walking into Remington's room when I almost fall out of the elevator. I run to Beau, and he wraps me in a tight hug. I whisper, "See, he's a fighter. I told you he'd be okay. This is good right?" I say to the doctor.

"We won't know exactly what we're dealing with until he's

fully conscious, but he's awake and breathing on his own. So, it's progress."

If it's the only thing he can do on his own, I'll still be here. I made him a promise, and I won't take it back. I planned on in sickness and in health a long time ago and I'll stand by it.

"Hey," Beau says softly from beside me. "Breathe and we'll take this one step at a time. It's all we can do."

It may be the doctor and nurse in the room with us now, but I swear it feels the most alive it's felt in over a month. There's life here that didn't exist even this morning. His lashes flutter as I give him a once over before gray-blue eyes peer back at me. I close the distance between us as quickly as I can without running.

The doctor is checking his vitals and taking notes, but my eyes don't leave Rem's. I see a wave of emotions flash behind them—confusion, hurt, pain, and anger. Seeing him without all the tubes and wires, I notice he's lost weight in his face. It's not as full as it was before he came here over a month ago. A chill creeps up my spine, and I shiver.

He opens his mouth like he wants to say something, but the only thing escaping is air. I worry maybe he doesn't remember me, or what's happened since I came home. The doctor said he may have short term memory loss.

It's why I've been writing him the letters, so he remembers.

For the last week, I've been worried sick thinking maybe I was starting to grieve him, even if he was still alive. It was plain torture. Not knowing if he would wake up again. If he'd remember who I am. If he would remember anything.

Remington lets out a small groan, and our eyes shift to him. My heart rate is jumping up at the speed of light. He tries to mumble something, but his throat must be sore and dry from the machines. I pat his hand to tell him it's okay. He doesn't need to speak yet, but he shakes his head.

"He's trying to say something," Beau says from behind me.

The doctor leans over, so close to Remington's mouth he could hear a whisper. "Say it again?" He asks Rem.

Gray-blue eyes find mine again, and I'm lost to the onslaught of tears. He's awake and trying to talk. It means something, right? It has to. But what he says is not at all what I'm expecting. "Why is she here?"

His voice breaks and it's weaker than normal, but the words are clear. I hold my breath, unsure what to think. My heart pounding out a staccato against my ribcage.

I reach down to squeeze his hand. "I'm here for you, Rem. Don't you remember?"

He coughs, his throat still dry. "Leave."

"What?" My voice breaks on a sob. His heart rate monitors start beeping as his heart rate increases and the doctor motions for Beau to get me out of there.

He grabs me by my shoulders and tries to lead me out into the hallway. Tears are streaming down my face, and I can't understand why he wants me to leave. After all of this he wants me to go away?

I feel broken inside. I've waited for weeks for him to wake up and be okay, and I'm the last person he wants to see. I guess I should've known, but I didn't know it'd hurt this bad.

"Grab Reagan, Rhett, and Jameson and head back to the farm. I'll stay with him. Give him a little time, okay? We knew it was a possibility he may have some memory issues."

I nod, because I can't form words. *When was the last time I was this speechless?*

"It'll be okay. Did you write the letters like I suggested?" I nod again. "I'll make sure he gets them, but in the meantime, I think it's best for you to stay away for now."

Reagan, Rhett, and Jameson are in the waiting room when I walk out. They all know he's awake because Beau probably called them too, but they're more concerned about me right now. I must have a haggard appearance because the concern is multiplied across all of their faces.

"All right, sweets. Let's get you home, okay?" Reagan says, and I nod again because it's all my brain is managing to handle at the moment.

Jameson speaks up next. "Nova is on her way. She'll be here in an hour or two."

How these guys already know is beyond me, but I'm sure the click and text of a cell phone has kept them up to date.

Putting her arm around my shoulders, Reagan leads me out of the hospital. Rhett has my bag by the time we get to Reagan's truck, and I don't know how he has it, but I simply cannot manage to care right now.

I'm broken. Shattered. At this point, I'm not sure the pieces can be melted back together. A part of me feels like this is all a dream. Like I'll wake up and Remington will know it's me. It's like I'm watching the whole thing in third person. My heart drops to the floor as flames engulf it, singeing it until it's fully blackened and unusable.

REMINGTON

Waking up in the hospital was no Cinderella moment for sure. It felt like I was in a nightmare. My brain felt like a fog machine on Halloween night. There were people talking above me, but I couldn't focus on who was speaking specifically.

One of the voices sounded familiar, but I couldn't put my finger on who it was—a soft and sweet tone. The other voice belongs to Beau, and he's asking something to the doctor, but it's all a little fuzzy.

Opening my eyes, I'm met with a dull light as it seeps in through the open blinds. The sky outside is full of clouds. A dreary day.

I feel like I'm in one of those movies where people are flying past you increasingly quick while you're seemingly standing still when I open my eyes. It's like the world was on fast forward while I'd been here for who knows how long.

My eyes finally focus on Beau as he talks quietly with the physician. I try to listen in, but I only gather bits and pieces. Ocean blue eyes find mine as I scan the room.

What is she doing here? I haven't seen her in four long years.

She walks over to me and slips her hand into mine, but I don't squeeze it.

I stare up at her. Her blonde hair is now darker. It's darker than it was when I last saw her. Definitely different.

How long have I been here? Glancing down I see all the tubes and wires coming off my body. The dots don't connect. *When did I end up in the hospital?*

Is it her fault? Maybe it's why she seems like she's about to cry?

A groan slides past my lips, and their eyes find mine. The doctor is taking my vitals and I open my mouth to say something, but only air forms. My throat is scratchy, and I try to clear it.

Faith pats my hand, telling me it's okay not to speak, but I need to know. Why is she here? Why after four years has she come back to torment me? Wasn't it enough to shatter me and walk away the first time?

I heard Beau tell the doctor I'm trying to speak, and he leaned down closer, trying to hear me.

I open my mouth again and words slip out in a whisper. "Why is she here?" I say nodding to Faith. She's the last person I want to see right now. She needs to leave.

She quirks an eye at me confused. "I'm here for you, Rem. Don't you remember?"

I obviously have no clue what she's talking about, so I cock my head in concern. What don't I remember and why?

I cough, trying to get the lump in my throat to swallow. "Leave," I say, looking directly at her as her eyes fill with unshed tears.

It's harsh, but I'm still trying to put the pieces together. I watch as Beau grabs her by the shoulders and walks her to the hallway. He's whispering something to her, but I can't make out the words. She's at a full out cry now.

A part of me feels like a dick for making her cry, but I obviously have my own shit happening right now. There's a tingling sensation over most of my body like it's been asleep for too long before finally waking. I can't remember how I got here. It's hard to pinpoint the last memory I do have.

My eyes find Beau as he walks back into the room. "Why was she here?" I demand.

"She's been back at Willow Springs for months, what is the last thing you remember, man?"

I wrack my brain, unable to conjure the last memory. "I have no idea."

"You don't remember Mr. Johnson's colt coming in? Needing to be fixed?"

"Nope."

"Well it'll return to you. For now, focus on the present."

I try to flex my muscles and stretch, but for some reason it feels harder for my brain to process the request. "How long have I been here?" I ask glancing over at Beau.

The expression on his face tells me I didn't want to know the answer to my question, but he enlightened me anyway. "It's been over a month, Rem. There was an accident at the farm with a colt. They had to induce a coma to help your brain heal."

As soon as he said it my brain flickered a tiny flashback. The colt flying at me teeth bared, prepared to do some damage with his hooves. Apparently, he'd succeeded.

When I close my eyes, sleep reminds me it's not finished with me yet. Only this time, it feels like less of a black hole and more of a dreamland. I let it take me away. Tomorrow, I'll deal with this when I wake. For now, I'll get lost a little longer with my musings.

———

The sun is beaming in through the windows as I open my eyes the following day. I try to sit up, but it's hard given the fact that my muscles have atrophied slightly since I've been in this bed.

My eyes trail over the flowers and balloons littering the room.

It's as if people cared I was here. Like I was legitimately missed while I was out.

I wonder if it's true, or if people felt obligated because it's the thing to do when someone you know ends up in the hospital for an extended period of time.

My brain is a mist in a deep valley.

"Why was she here?" I say, my voice box scratchy. I've had a couple of sips of water since last night, and my throat still feels like it's clogged with sawdust.

Beau's eyes meet the floor. "You two have been getting back together for the last couple of months, Rem. She was here and has been here since the day of the accident. She was worried about you."

"Together?" Confusion laces my brain. There's no way we've been together. I mean, I haven't seen Faith in years. It doesn't add up.

"Yeah, it's my understanding you two were *together*, together the night before the accident. You were planning on convincing her to give it another try. Something about a letter you left with the breakfast you cooked her."

The marbles are rolling around in my brain but still not connecting. "I don't remember any of this."

"Wait, let me grab something. I'll be right back." He leaves the side of the bed and pulls a small box from below a chair in the corner. *Why does that box seem so familiar?* I can't seem to put my finger on it. He comes back to the bed and lays it down. "We knew this may happen, so Faith has been writing you letters. She was hopeful it'd help you to remember."

"Thanks." I glance down at the box filled with about thirty letters, if I had to guess. I'm not sure I'll actually read them, but maybe it'll help me to figure out why she appeared so hopeful when I woke up. Why was she standing here waiting for me? Why is she back and why in the hell does Beau think we were getting back together?

I push the letters away and try to sit up. It's clear my muscles haven't worked in a while because they shake as I try to straighten myself up farther in bed. I could call the nurse and ask her to lift up the bed for me, but I don't want to appear weak.

"Here, let me help you," Beau says once he notices I am struggling.

"No, I can do it. It's not like I'm paralyzed," I say too sharply.

"All right, all right," he says putting his hands up in defense. "There anything I can help you with?"

"Nah, I'm sorry. It's a lot to process. Life is all fine and dandy then boom I wake up in a hospital bed one month later, and I'm apparently getting back together with the girl who walked away from me four years ago. It's..." I'm breathing heavily as my lungs seem to take in less oxygen than I remember.

"I get it."

Rhett and Jameson were here earlier this morning before Beau showed up. They left when the doctors came in to do a myriad of tests. The doctor says physically I'm fine, but mentally I appear to have some memory loss.

No fucking kidding.

The urge to piss takes me by storm, like I haven't pissed in ages. They must've taken the catheter out because I don't feel it in my dick anymore. Beau stares at me as I use my arms to move my legs to the side of the bed. It's also when I realize there's a brace on my left leg, but I don't have time to worry about it right now. "Rem, maybe you should call for a nurse."

"I can do this," I reassure him against my better judgment. He's right, I probably should. I have no clue what'll happen when I try to stand. Moving my damn legs takes way more effort than it ever has before, leaving me breathless. *Fuck.*

"Damn it. Here, I'm helping your dumb ass before you fall and hurt yourself." He bends down, and I throw an arm around his shoulder as he grabs me and helps me stand.

I grunt. "So, we're clear, this is only to the can. Once I get there, I don't need you standing there watching me piss. It's fucking weird."

He shakes his head, chuckling. "Brother, never had the urge to watch you piss before, today ain't the day it changes. Now, let's do this."

We move slowly on the way to the toilet. A wave of dizziness hits and I silently curse each foul word known to man because damn, this shit is intense. The pain in my leg is intense too, but no turning back at this point.

"Hey, you're not supposed to be out of bed yet without my assistance," the nurse says from behind us, but I don't stop. The urge to piss wears more on my brain than her disappointment over me not in bed like a little boy doing as he's told. Instead, I call over my shoulder.

"The hose needs a leak lady, and I prefer to do it standing up holding it like a damn man."

Ten minutes later, I'm relieved and back in my damn bed. The nurse keeps giving me mean mugs, but I don't care.

Glancing at his phone, Beau turns back to me. "I gotta get back to something on the farm. You want me to call someone for you?"

"Nope, I'll be fine."

"You sure? I can call Faith. She will sit with you. Has been here basically nonstop since the accident. Maybe it'd give you two time to catch up."

"Nope, still fine," I mumble.

"Fine, have it your way. There's a physical therapist coming later this afternoon to check you out. I'll be back in a couple of hours."

"Well, I'll be here... clearly not going anywhere." Without anything else to waste away my time, I picked out the first letter from the box.

Might as well do something to occupy my time.

. . .

Dear Rem,

If you're reading this, it means you're finally back in the land of the living. Welcome back! I, for one, am glad you came back to us.

There's a chance right now you're pissed at me. The doctor said you may have memory loss, and I'm guessing it's true if you're reading this letter instead of letting me say it to your face.

If you're pissed at me, I'm sorry. I don't know what to say. I've been back at Willow Springs for a couple of months now. I'm giving lessons to the kids because Karen was so swamped.

My job in the city didn't have the money to keep me, and I had no other option but to head here. I couldn't live with my mom knowing what's happened between her and dad. So, I took Beau up on his job offer even though I knew it would be hard to see you daily. I wanted to try anyhow.

The first couple of days, you were an absolute asshole. Instead of being a polite adult, you acted like a child. I'm sorry, but it's the truth. You all out demanded I read your letters before you'd talk to me. I get it now. I know why.

I've gone through almost 95 letters, and I plan to keep reading because I want the whole story. Reading these letters made me feel closer to you while you were in the coma, but it also told me exactly how you felt, and although I hated reading some of them, I needed to.

So, hopefully this answers the question as to why I'm home. Don't worry, I'll write more so you know what all has happened since the accident. I didn't want to throw you too much at once.

Always and forever,
  Faith

. . .

The next couple of days I tore through those letters, one by one. Each more intense than the last.

Her words poured onto the page as if she'd rehearsed each one. As if they were spoken from her heart. It wasn't something you could pull out of everyday life. It was spoken from down deep within you. She breathed life into each word and punctuation mark as they flowed effortlessly across the paper.

It was hard to believe her words because my brain still couldn't put them with memories. I knew Faith wasn't a liar, she was a runner. Besides, what was there to gain from her saying things falsely?

It seemed her world had been shaken as badly as mine had. We were two people dealing with the cards we were dealt. No matter how unfortunate they were.

I am finally returning home today with the promise I'd keep up with my physical therapist on a weekly basis. We'd done some exercises he wanted me to practice daily, so I could regain my strength.

Jameson had shown up to give me a ride home from the hospital. My brain was a whirlwind of what would happen the next time I ran into Faith, seeing as how twice now, we'd left on unhappy terms. I hadn't seen or heard about her since the day she left my room at the hospital crying. No one brought it up either. A part of me still feels guilty for it.

I wanted to trust her, to believe each word she'd written was true. Maybe we'd truly made it past all of this and found a way to ourselves again on the other side, but life never seemed to work out so easily for me; hence, the caution I proceeded with. Maybe I would give it a couple of days and feel it out.

My heart and head grapple for control, fighting against each other for supremacy. One part of me lived in a fantasy land and wants the girl I'd pined over for years. The other wants to sit back and let the cards fall as they may, one by one.

Trust—it was something we hadn't fully formed between us.

She states in her letters we have, but again my brain doesn't know any better. I've lost my faith in Faith. Four years ago, she promised me forever and then walked away without another glance back. Now, she's back and telling me she isn't running anywhere, and I don't know what to believe.

Do I lay myself on the line again and hope the memories suddenly make a reappearance, or do I guard myself against her potentially walking away and breaking me again? It was a fine line. How quickly hate could turn to love or the opposite.

The old back road feels familiar beneath me. Jameson's SUV bounced and dipped with each curve and bump in the road. He turns at the old familiar rock, pulling down the willow tree entrance to Willow Spring Stables. I watch as a herd of horses runs beside us along the fence line.

My eyes trail Remy, his whinny carrying on the wind as it breezes through the windows of the vehicle. It is like he was calling out to an old friend.

I have no idea if he knew it was me, but I could imagine he'd missed me. He ran with his pasture mates—Koko, Jet, and Cash. Seeing Koko brought a pang to my heart, but I can't put my finger on why.

Is it a memory trying to slip in and consume me? I don't know, and I am having trouble trying to pull it from the dark crevice of my mind.

Faith's small car is parked outside of the bunkhouse. My heart pounds with anticipation. I hoped she wasn't there when I walked in because I needed a minute to compose myself. I am not exactly prepared for the awkwardness.

I pause, taking a breath, before opening the door to the SUV. I slide down to the ground slowly and open the back door to grab my cane, bag, and the box of letters from the backseat before rounding the front of the SUV and heading toward the bunkhouse.

The house is quiet as I enter, the only sound is the fridge

making more ice. I attune my ears, listening to any small sounds indicating another presence.

Walking down the hallway, I pause outside of the room beside mine. I'm assuming it's the one she's staying in since Beau mentioned she lived in the bunkhouse with me. The door is open, and the bed is made, but she's not in there. The bathroom on the other side of the hallway has her lingering perfume essence, and I breathe it in. It's a similar scent to the one she used to wear all those years ago, but it's aged with time like a fine wine.

My masochistic heart still beats strongly for her. Love and pain fit hand in hand, it seems.

I continue on my way to my own room and unpack from the hospital. It is the same as it always is. The bed sits against the largest wall in the room across from the closet. My old guitar sits on a rack beside my desk, lyrics and music spread across the top. There's a pair of dirty Levi's lying on the floor in the corner, more than likely from a toss across the room aimed at the laundry basket.

The urge to pick up my guitar and string some words hits me, but I need to check in with Beau first. Don't want him to think I'm not pulling my weight around here.

A knock on the door catches me off guard. "Hey, I'm out here in case you need anything," Jameson's voice finds me through the door.

I roll my eyes before I open the door and find my way to the bathroom, ignoring Jameson. Quickly disrobing, I heat up the shower and dip under the water. Washing slowly, I remember how nice it feels to simply stand under hot water while it pours over me from above. It's almost soothing. I don't put too much pressure on my left leg with the strain.

Fifteen minutes later, I'm back in my room getting dressed. Socks first, then boxers, followed by my Levi's, a T-shirt, and the leg brace.

I run my hand through my hair and wipe the excess water on

the side of my pants before making my way to the front of the bunkhouse. The door creaks as I hobble through on my cane, squinting into the bright sunlight beating down upon me. My eyes roam the stable area, seeking her out, but choosing not to think too hard into why.

I see horses grazing in the pasture behind the bunkhouse and make a quick pass toward the fence when I realize it's the band Remy runs with in the morning. A shrill whistle leaves my lips as I call for him and wait as he comes galloping over, a cloud of dust kicking up behind him.

He neighs as he gets closer, his signature hello. "Hey Boy," I say, holding my hand out as he rubs his forehead against it. "You miss me?" He snuffles down my shirt, searching for the treats or sugar cubes in the pocket of my jeans where I keep them. "All right, all right. I grabbed a few."

Pulling two out of my pocket, I hold them flat on my hand for him to take from me. He munches happily before searching for more. His eyes pleading to give in and let him have one more. "Hey now, too many and it'll rot your teeth, bud." He has no idea what I'm saying, but he seems to listen quietly anyhow.

I hear Faith's voice coming from the arena as I sit there whispering with Remy. His attention is drawn to her too. I'm not surprised, not many people aren't drawn to her. I shake my head, still finding it hard to believe we've done a 180-degree flip. I guess I'll find out eventually. As if it's a secret between the two of us, I lean into Remy's face and whisper. "How's she doing, buddy?"

I don't know why I expect him to answer. He's a horse and they don't exactly talk back, but he's someone who won't judge my question as to her wellbeing. Anyone else in this place would definitely think more into it.

REMINGTON

"Man, great to see you back with us. Up and around and all." I turn to find Rhett walking my way. He works here at Willow Springs part time. The rest of the time he's an EMT in town. There aren't many emergencies in this small town, but when there are, he's there to help.

"Nice to be back," I say, patting him on the back as he shuffles up beside me.

"How's the leg?" He nods down to the brace strapped to my leg.

"It's only a sprain." I shrug.

"You've signed up for physical therapy to strengthen it back up and get walking better again, right?"

"Yep, twice a week. I'll have to find someone to give me a lift since I can't exactly drive with this thing." I eye the bulky mass covering my pant leg with disdain.

"Well, there's a bunch of us hanging around here at any point in time. I'm sure no one would mind giving you a lift."

My mind drifts to Faith, and I wonder if she would even offer after the way I treated her at the hospital. A part of me feels like a total dick for telling her to leave. In the heat of the moment, I was confused, my brain scattered, and my fight or flight kicked in. With me in the hospital bed, I couldn't leave, so I'd made her do it for me. Call it a gut reaction, and I hated I'd treated her that way.

He stands beside me for a minute, before excusing himself to check on something else before lunch rolls around. I nod him farewell.

Now this didn't mean I believed anything she'd said so far. No, she needed to prove those words to me.

There was a letter on my bed when I arrived home today in her handwriting. I haven't opened it yet because I have a feeling I'll need to take a breather after reading it. I'm assuming it's one of two things. Either she still thinks we deserve another chance, or she's telling me to fuck off like she should've done a long ass time ago and she's finally realized I'm not good for her.

I'm hoping it's the first, but no one has ever fought for me before, so it didn't seem like a likely outcome. I head toward the barn in search of Beau. He wasn't able to pick me up from the hospital today because he had to deal with the guy who brings our horse's hay.

He sees me and smiles. "Nice to see you home, brother. Hasn't been the same around here without ya."

I nod. "Happy to be back. Where can I start?"

His eyebrows pinch and he's avoiding a lot of eye contact. This isn't good. "Rem... I need you to relax for a while. Heal up your leg and focus on your physical therapy."

I harrumph. "You know, I can't sit around on my ass all day and do nothing, Beau."

He nods. "I know, but you're gonna have to try. If something happens to your leg it'll be a bigger issue than it is now. One wrong twist or one wrong fall and you could break something. I know it may not mean a lot right now, but it's something my conscience won't allow. You wanna help around here, I can use you for helping with feedings, but that's about all."

I sigh. "It makes sense, but doesn't mean I like it." The last thing I want to be is a liability, but I'd take what was given. I need to help in any way I could around the stables because I take pride in doing a great job.

"Sorry, man. Give me a couple minutes and you can help me get lunch together for the crew."

I laugh, but it's lacking in oomph. "Delegated to sandwich boy, I see how it is."

He pats me on the shoulder before walking away. I see Rhett and Jameson head toward the main house, and I start the same direction myself. It'll take me a few minutes with this bum leg and cane, so I start early.

Lunches around here consist of quick and easy meals, generally sandwiches. I unload all the sandwich fixings from the fridge, grab chips from the pantry, and fry up some bacon for those interested.

Reagan and Beau pop in a couple of minutes later and start making up their plates to take to the table. My eyes fall to the door, waiting.

Where is she?

The front door opens again, and my heart pounds out a solid beat as I hold my breath waiting for her blonde hair to appear, but it's not her. Karen breezes through with a smile headed toward the kitchen. "Mmm... someone made bacon." She inhales dramatically.

Minutes pass, and the whole crew is now seated at the table shoving food into their faces and making small talk like no one is missing.

I haven't seen her yet. Not since the day I told her to leave. The urge to take care of her overwhelms me, and it's a notion I haven't felt in years. *So, why am I feeling it now?* I push it away and get back to the group of people in front of me. I fix myself a sandwich and sit at the table. I can't focus on the conversations around me because I find myself thinking about the one person who isn't here.

As they get up to head back to their prospective jobs, I stay behind to clean up. I place the plate I washed on the rack beside the sink, watching as the water glides down its side and onto the draining board below. Once finished with all the plates, I pull the plug on the drain in the sink and listen to the gurgling noise as water is sucked down the pipes.

———

My memories prior to the accident still haven't returned. The anger I felt toward her when I first woke up is no longer as strong, but still lingers in the back of my mind. How does someone who claims to love you simply walk away?

The morning progresses slowly. Beau is treating me like a child and not allowing me to do anything majorly weight bearing. I'm delegated to feeding and watering the horses.

I understand his concern. The atrophy in my limbs was much worse than expected. I can still do most things; however, I find quite a few ordinary things difficult. I walk with a cane right now to support myself.

Unfortunately, the one thing that does still work is my dick, and it hasn't forgotten her. It seems especially interested in Faith. He keeps begging and I keep telling him to get the fuck over it.

She must be having nightmares when she sleeps. Only last night I woke up to her screaming, and I felt the pull to comfort her, but we haven't spoken since I returned to the stables. Hell, most days she's up and out before I even wake up. It's like she's afraid of running into me.

Her letter still sits on the desk in my room, unopened. Maybe today will be the day.

Today slips by in a flash, another blip in the scale of my life.

We all had dinner a while ago, a Willow Springs favorite prepared by Reagan. My stomach is so full, I'm bloated.

I have no idea how long I've been sitting in this chair. The little voice in the back of my head said it was probably time to head to bed, also confirmed by the lack of sunshine outside my window.

I can't bring myself to slide into bed yet.

I have too many things weighing on my mind.

My eyes scan my desk again, over the sheets of lyrics to the letter standing prominently in the middle.

Calling to me, whispering to open and read the truth as it spills across the page.

Telling me to find out why the girl who used to be the love of my life is now avoiding me like a contagious strain of the plague. Other than the glaringly obvious cause of me telling her to leave at the hospital.

Not yet, I whisper to myself.

Lifting my guitar from where it sits against the wall, I strum out the same tune I'd been working on a while ago. It's an unfinished song and I can't seem to figure out where to run with it, but tonight I feel the words flowing through me.

A picture of Faith lights up in my mind. The first time I saw her. The soft curves of her body. The slight tip of her lips as she smiled at me. The swoosh of her hair.

The first time we kissed in the back of my truck in the middle of a star lit night. As she lay in the truck bed next to me on our first morning together. When she found Sofia and I in the room together. She cared so damn much she ran from me. She didn't fight for me then, but her last letter said otherwise, for now. It wasn't her fault what had happened between us. I was angry at her, but had things been different I would've done the same thing, run.

And now, after things shattered between us, we're bunking under the same roof. What a twist of fate.

Sitting the guitar back down, I decide it's time. I'm opening the letter tonight.

I wonder if she sprayed her perfume on the letter because the scent hits my nose immediately as I opened up the flaps. I take a deep breath in and prepare myself for whatever I'm about to read. I stare at her handwriting as it daintily drifts across the page, making words and letters with each swirl. Her handwriting hasn't changed over the years, it's always been overly girly and simply her.

Dear Rem,

By now I'm hoping we're on the same page, at least where the letters are concerned. I've read them all. Every single word you needed me to know, spoken within 104 letters. My mere 30 letters may seem small in comparison, but hopefully you feel like you haven't missed much in the month you were under the coma's influence.

The doctor warned us multiple times of the possibility you may not remember things when you woke up, but I guess I didn't take it to heart. When you opened those gorgeous grey-blue eyes and peered up at me with anger and confusion, I knew gut deep you couldn't figure out why I was there. Obviously, the pieces hadn't formed into a cohesive memory.

You told me to leave, and I was hurt, crushed. My heart shattered like broken glass against the floor in your room, and I had to fight the air in my lungs simply to breath. To take a step back. To walk away like I knew you needed me to do. But God, did it suck. Does it crush me daily knowing in a couple days you'll be home again, living under the same roof as me only remembering we ended years ago and finding out you hate me now? Every fucking day.

My guess is you've read them, but don't know what to believe. It's hard, I get it. I'm not sure if I was in your situation, I wouldn't be feeling the same way you feel right now. I would probably be as confused as you are about things.

Here's the thing, Rem. We've known each other for years. For the longest time, I felt like you were the other part of my soul. So, I hope deep down you realize I meant what I said. I want this again. I want us. The past can stay where it belongs because the here and now with you is what matters.

I'll give you space, all the space you want for now, but I'm here the second you decide you want this. I won't give up on us. I knew on our first date we were more than a passing affair; we were forever. It's been written in more than 104 letters now. Each word, another part to the story of our love, our life, our story.

If you need me, I'll be there. Each step of the way. I hope something sparks a flame that lights a memory blazing across the night sky. I hope you remember us. Either the way we used to be before it fell apart, or think about how amazing we could be now that we're older and more mature. Now it's all been laid out before us.

We've both suffered these last few years with the unknown and the truths hidden from view, but I promise to you I'm not running this time. I'll only stay away from you a little longer before I start fighting for us. We are a memory you can't run away from and somewhere in there it's playing over and over again, you just have to reach inside and find it. I don't play fair, Rem. Fair warning.

Always and forever,
Faith

I go in search of Beau. I need someone to talk to, and he is the closest friend I have these days. It's dark out, probably late but I don't care. I knock on the office door before opening it. Beau sits behind his desk with a stack of paperwork in front of him. The only light streaming from an overhead fixture.

"Hey, man. Have a minute to talk?"

He glanced up from whatever he was doing. "Sure, have a seat. What's up?"

"Faith... I... I don't know what to do about her. It's been almost two months, and nothing has come back to me. I still can't remember."

He looked pensive. "You read the letters she wrote?"

I nod. "Yeah, I did, but it's hard to believe what she wrote when I don't remember any of it actually happening."

"So, you don't trust her?"

I rubbed a hand over my chest. "I don't trust myself I suppose. The last time I saw her, she left me for four years, Beau. How do I move on? What she did cut deep, I..." I shook my head, unable to articulate exactly how I was feeling.

His lips formed into a slight grimace. "You're afraid she'll leave you again? You're afraid to get hurt."

I scoff. *Fuck yes, that's what I'm afraid of.* "No..."

"Rem... you can talk to me. You gotta remember I was here with you when she wasn't. I saw your pain, the hurt in your eyes. I watched you mope around here for months. But do you know what happened the minute she stepped back onto this farm?"

"No?"

"You had this expression of hope on your face again. You started smiling again. For the first couple of weeks, granted, it wasn't pretty. You guys fought like cats and dogs, but you figured it out, you made it work. I could tell the moment she realized she wanted to give it another try. The morning of your accident... You were fucking smiling so big. And it had to do with her."

I sighed, disheartened, "I wish I could remember it."

Eyebrows raised, he reached up to scratch his jaw. "Rem, you have her name tattooed on your chest. For a guy who's claiming to not still be in love with his high school sweetheart, you're doing a shit job of convincing me."

"I don't know what I want. A part of me says walk away, it'll be easier in the long run. The other part of me says fight, because it sucks to not have her in my life."

"I think there's your answer."

I shrugged. "But how do I know?"

"Guess you don't. No one does. Life plays out how it's meant to without our approval or acceptance, it seems."

"Something on your mind, Beau?"

"You remember Cassidy Mae from high school?"

My eyes widen. I remember exactly who she was. Left for school, ended up marrying some big shot, and moved to the city. "Yeah?"

"She's back in town again... Reagan offered her a groom job here."

"Oh..."

"Yeah..."

"And how do you feel about it?"

"To be honest, I haven't wrapped my head around it yet. I spent years infatuated with the girl, and I believed she was gone. So... I guess I don't understand why she's back. She was married."

"Women..."

"I'll drink to that." Pulling two bottled waters from the fridge behind him, I can't help but chuckle.

"What? I have bills I need to pay and shit to work out, doing it drunk don't seem right."

"All right, well I'll leave you to it." I get up to leave, but halt when he speaks again.

Turning to look back at him I see his downturned facial features. "Hey, Remington. You may not remember the last couple of months, but I can tell you one thing. When Faith saw you lying there lifeless on the ground the day of the accident, she broke. When she sat in that damn hospital room day in and day out waiting for you to wake up, she cracked a little further. When you woke up and told her to leave... I watched her shatter. I don't think I've ever seen someone stare at you the way Faith does. She lights up time and time again when she sees you. If I were you, I wouldn't let her slip away. I would hold onto it with both hands, memory be damned. Because if you don't... she'll be gone, and you'll be filled with regret. I don't want to see it come to that, so fix this, Rem."

I nod before turning to leave. "Thanks for the advice, Beau. Let me know when I can return the favor."

I have a lot to think about and work through. Is it worth risking the love of my life a second time simply because I can't remember us getting back together? I still wasn't sure. If she left me again, I'd break. If she stayed, I could still lose her. What happened next, I never saw coming...

FAITH

The days drum on, yet nothing changes. It's been two months since Remington came home from the hospital, and the hope I had of him remembering us has dwindled. My heartbeat slows with time waiting for him to find his way home to me.

He's back to helping me with Koko for lessons.

Occasionally, he jokes with me, and it'll feel like old times and damn my hopeful little heart, but it beats a little harder in those few instances. The tilt of his lips with a smile gives me a giddy feeling, one I haven't felt in a while.

Other days, I'll catch him staring at me like he's trying to conjure up an old memory.

Earlier today, I was in town grabbing some groceries at Moonshine Springs Grocer and I ran into Colton. We'd been standing in line together when he asked me to have dinner sometime.

Initially my first instinct was to say no, call it a gut reaction, but I didn't. A part of me still felt like I belonged to Remington. Even musing about dating with someone else makes me feel like I'm cheating, but Rem has made it pretty clear we aren't together.

I'd accepted his invitation for a date. And now, I was standing here wondering how I could get out of it. The only first date I'd ever had was with Remington, and I'd known him for a while. I was nervous, ringing my hands out about how seeing someone new would go. I had a rock in my gut, a lump in my throat, and I felt like I'd lose my breakfast at any second.

Colton had been nice to me whenever we'd see each other at the same town functions over the years. He went to the same high school as Remington and I, but we managed to run with a different crowd. He'd been popular back then. Hell, he still was now.

Peering over at him now, I realized he was missing the handsome features Remington possesses. He definitely lacked the tattoos Rem had painted across his body, but he was kind and wanted to settle down.

Colton was a little taller than me at around five foot nine. He has wavy blonde hair and deep jade-colored eyes. He'd recently shaved, and I can smell his cologne. It is a light, musky fresh scent that made me feel like I was drifting at the edge of an ocean.

He didn't have the past or the baggage Rem and I had acquired, and for once I truly believed it'd be nice to not have our past hanging in between us like an elephant in the room.

A chance to move on, to let my heart love. To stop torturing myself with the what-ifs.

I am standing in the kitchen, cooking up some taco meat for a salad, something quick and easy when I hear the bunkhouse door open and close. I knew who it was without even turning around these days. I could feel his presence before I saw him.

Today is no different. I peer over my shoulder at him, and he smiled before heading down the hallway to his room. "You want some lunch?" I holler after him.

A few minutes later he was back, walking into the kitchen like he owned the place. His Levi's hung to his hips, showing off the powerful muscles of the legs encased within. His shirt was tight again, and I could see the outline of his pec muscles and eight pack.

His boots were covered in dust, and he had his hat on backward like he always did. "Whatcha making, Faith?"

"Heating up some taco meat for a salad, but there's tortillas in the pantry if you'd rather have a taco."

"Sounds good." He heads toward the panty and grabbed the tortillas. From the fridge he grabs salsa, sour cream, cheese, lettuce, and tomatoes. After putting all the supplies on the table, he walks back over to me. "What do you want to drink? I'll grab it while you finish cooking."

"Water's fine for me." Making a second trip to the fridge he pulls out a water for me and a beer for himself.

We eat lunch with silence dangling between us. Too busy eating and too scared to say anything. I wanted him to say anything so many times, but I'd finally given up on hearing it. I'd given him all the letters he wrote me back except for the one the morning of the accident. I kept hoping something would jog his memory, but so far nothing.

I cleared my throat, determined to talk about something, anything. "I heard the guys talking about their plans tonight. You going with them?"

He shrugged, his focus solely on the taco in his hand. "Don't know yet. Depends on what they're planning on doing and I don't even think they've decided yet."

"I have a date tonight," I say, turning to glance at Remington. I don't know why I expected him to show any type of reaction. I'd hoped maybe I'd see anger or even sadness, but I found nothing.

"Oh, well who's the lucky guy?" He smiled, but it never reached his eyes.

"Colton."

"Huh... good guy."

Why didn't the idea of me dating someone else make him angry?

This is it. The end of our conversation.

A couple of minutes later, he stood up, took his plate to the dishwasher, and left the bunkhouse. I remained there stunned, glued to my seat.

How could he not even care?

It is... nothing

Surprisingly, I felt relief. If he doesn't care, then I'm free to go out on a date. I am tired of being alone, feeling lonely. Maybe it is time to move on with someone new.

The afternoon passed by in a flash and the night rolled in. I was finishing up getting ready when Remington came into the bunkhouse again. It was supposed to be cold tonight, so I was wearing blue jeans, a cute pair of boots, a dressy blouse, and a cardigan with a scarf.

He stops in my door as I stood in front of the mirror gazing at my outfit. "You're beautiful, by the way."

"Thanks, Rem," I respond back, my eyes catching his in the mirror. His signature stare made me feel a little heated. Somewhere between a burn and a shiver. My stomach dropped when he walked away without another word.

"Why are you doing this?" He stepped back into the doorway a few minutes later and asked.

I raise one eyebrow. "Doing what?"

"Dating... you said in the letters you would wait for me." He walks toward me until we are face to face, only an arm's length separating us.

My eyes fell to the floor, my lower lip threatening to tremble at the emotions flooding me. Why did he have to wait until right before my date to bring this up?

"I was waiting. I told you I'd stay away until you were ready and you..." I bit my lip. "You have barely spoken a whole sentence to me in months, Remington. I don't know how to fight for something that seems like an impossibility."

He swallows, his eyes holding mine before traveling down to my mouth and back. "You don't understand what this is like. This being told, but having no firsthand knowledge. My brain is a constant battle, Faith."

"What do you want, Rem?"

"I don't know..." He glances away, a certain sadness filling his features.

"Then I need to do this. If you can't look me in the eye and tell me you want me and you want this, then I need to go."

His tongue slipped out to wet his lips before he spoke the next words. "I was trying to stop myself from doing this..."

He pulled me into his solid form. Before I can register what is happening, his lips are on mine, devouring me. All the things I'd been thinking suddenly flipped on its end, tilting my whole axis.

I hold my breath as he attacks my mouth. I have to lift up on my toes to kiss him back, but it's exactly what I did. I wasn't holding back. It'd been months since I'd been able to feel his lips pressed so tightly against mine, and I couldn't help but melt into how it felt. I fisted my hands in his shirt to pull his body even closer to mine as we both fought for the next breath of air. Remington sucked my bottom lip into his mouth, letting it slip away with a groan after kissing me full force.

His tongue slips gently against my lips, and I open, no questions asked. I give him whatever he wants because it's been too long, and I wanted this more than I'd consciously allowed myself to believe.

I am teetering, losing my grip on the edge of reality with him and I wanted to fall, if only he would catch me. I love the way he feels—his strong arms wrapped around my waist, the taste of his tongue, his kissing skills. He kisses me like it's been four years and for him, it probably has in a way. My knees started to go weak at the way he took control and owned the kiss and me.

"Damn it," he groans, pulling back so his forehead rested against mine. Our breaths are heavy, rushed as we stood there so close.

"Rem..." I whisper.

"I know, I know. You have a date." He backs away from me and I immediately feel the distance. He spun, running his hands through his hair like he wasn't sure what to do next. I wasn't really either. I wanted him to kiss me again. I wanted to not go on the date with Colton, but I needed to because I said I would. I wasn't the kind of girl to back out of something.

He ran his hands through his hair again. "Fuck, Faith. I don't know what we're doing here. I'm sorry. I don't know what I'm doing..."

My heart had soared in his kiss, in the moment. But as soon as those words left his mouth, they dropped to the floor like a pile of concrete, heavy and powerful. He was sorry about the kiss. Which meant, he is regretting it already.

It was the best kiss Remington and I had ever shared, and there he was regretting and apologizing for it. The best kiss of my entire life and it vanished in an instant. That happy feeling, fleeting.

He left my room without another word. I wanted to curl up into a ball on my bed and cry, but I couldn't because I had a date... with Colton.

A few minutes later, my phone vibrated with a text from Colton. He was outside waiting for me. Wiping away the tears that had fallen, I square my shoulders and leave my room. Remington's door must be closed because I can't see any light coming from his direction.

Heading toward the front door, I practice putting on my smile when smiling was the last thing I felt like doing right now. I'd made this date and I intend to keep it.

Pulling open the door, I see Colton standing outside, a bundle of flowers in his hand and a smile spread across his face. "Wow," he said, eyes trailing up my outfit. "You look amazing. Are you ready?"

I smile back at him. "Definitely." Not an ounce of my body agreed with my answer, but I had to try. I didn't want to be alone, especially when the one person I wanted didn't seem to feel the same way about me.

"These are for you," he said, handing over a bundle of daisies.

"Thank you, they're beautiful. Let me put them in some water and then we can leave. Want to step in for a minute?"

"Sure." I turn away and listened to the cadence of his footsteps as he follows me into the kitchen. It is definitely a different gait than the one I am used to hearing in this house. It doesn't sound right.

I grab a vase from below the sink and fill it with tap water, depositing the flowers and putting them on the table. "There, ready?" I ask, turning to Colton.

"After you," he says, waving toward the front door. I swallowed the lump in my throat and smiled. I would get through this date, maybe even enjoy it. If only the little part of my heart nagging me to just stay home would stop it's whispering.

He holds the door open for me as we exit the bunkhouse. *Men and their trucks.* I smirk as we approached his vehicle. It is a white jacked up Ford F-150 pickup truck saturated with chrome detailing.

Colton speeds up to get to the passenger side of the truck before me and opens the door. "Thank you," I say politely.

"Of course," he replies with the biggest grin.

He runs around the front of the truck before opening his door and jumping in. "You ready?" His eyes find mine and I nod, but my heart said no.

I sit there waiting for Remington to run out of the bunkhouse.

For him to stand dramatically in front of the truck and demand that I get out.

That I don't leave on this date.

None of it happened.

It didn't happen when he started the truck.

It didn't happen when he backed away from the bunkhouse.

It didn't happen when we started pulling away.

But why would he stop me when he can't even remember what we mean to each other?

My heart sinks a little, but I am determined to brush it off. I need tonight to feel something, anything other than the broken shell of a girl who loved a boy who couldn't remember her.

I plastered on my fake smile when he peered over my way in the truck, but I was shattering on the inside.

We pulled up to Cindy's Sweets and Treats. It is another shop along Main Street—one of my favorites. Cindy's was the place to hang out anytime you needed a sweet fix. She made an assortment of chocolate delights, multiple flavors of hot chocolate, and specialty coffees.

It's the perfect place for a date with a sweet tooth. This time of year, she makes fudge, chocolate dipped bananas, and marshmallows. During the summer months she does more baked items and ice cream.

Yet again, Colton makes his way in front of the truck after shutting it off and getting out. He opened my door and offered me his hand to help me down. "Thank you," I say softly.

"My pleasure." His words made me giggle. Each time I heard the phrase my mind went back to ordering food at Chick-fil-A. "What'd I say?"

"Oh nothing..." They didn't have those here, so I wasn't sure he'd understand the context behind it.

I slipped my hand into his and allowed him to help me out of the truck. It was a chilly evening tonight, and I was glad for the cardigan I'd worn.

Entering the store, a bell dings above us. Cindy has a smile for me from behind the counter. It's fairly busy in here tonight, but I'm not surprised. This time of year is always busy. That's what happens when you make the best chocolate delights in town.

We order chocolate goodies and head toward a booth in the corner.

"So, I haven't seen you since high school, what's new?"

"Well, I was in Ohio for a while. Decided to come home a couple months ago. What about you?" I feel bad. I don't want to be here making small talk. My mind keeps going back to Rem's kiss, and I find myself wondering what the question is I'd asked.

"Working for my dad's construction company. We have a big job out there, building a brand-new house out by McCoy's. Wasn't expecting Remington Cole to ever build, but there's a first for everything I suppose."

I try to hide my reaction. *Why was Rem building a house?* Colton mentioned a couple months ago it started. Is he officially done with me? He obviously is if he is moving out of the bunkhouse, and why didn't he tell me? I feel crestfallen at the news. Maybe he is done. It was the moment my mood slanted from decent to sour.

I feel the cement hardening in my stomach. W*hy wouldn't he have told me?*

I survive the next couple of minutes before I can't anymore. There isn't anything wrong with Colton, he is great. The whole evening felt wrong—the date, him touching me, him smiling at me like this was more than friends. I feel sick to my stomach. The only thing that'd been right about this evening was the kiss with Remington. At the end of the day, I could date all the men in town, but my heart would still long for him.

Colton must have noticed my mood change. "Hey," he says, reaching across to touch my hand. "Are you okay?"

I shake my head from side to side. "Honestly, I'm not feeling so great. Would you mind if we called it a night?"

His face says he is disappointed, but I can't continue on like this. "Sure, no problem."

We both get up at the same time and head to the trash can to discard what we didn't eat. The atmosphere is morose as we head outside and walk toward his truck. The last thing I want him to feel is like this is his fault.

Colton is perfect. I should be swept off my feet because he's handsome and sweet. But he will never be anything more, even if he'd fill the space Remington left hanging open like a bleeding wound.

I should've cancelled after our kiss happened.

I should've never said yes in the first place.

The drive back to the farm was soundless. So many things were hanging between us, but I didn't know what to say without throwing up. I still felt sick. The faster I jumped out of this truck, the sooner I could be done with this whole night.

He pulled up to the bunkhouse and turned off the truck. "Was it something I did?" he asks, turning to face me in his seat.

"No, you've been the perfect gentleman. I don't feel well and didn't want you to have to hang out with me not feeling well."

"That's it?"

"Yeah, why do you ask?"

"Honestly, I was kind of shocked you even said yes. When Remington approached me a couple of months ago, I assumed he was building a house for the two of you. You came back to town and I think we all assumed you'd be back together by now. You were always connected at the hip."

"I don't know what we are, Colt. I'm sorry you were dragged into this."

"I had to try," he says with a shy smile. "You never know what'll happen unless you step out of the bubble. For what it's worth, I hope you two figure it out."

I bite my bottom lip. "I'm sorry, Colton."

He leans over and kissed me on the forehead. "Take care of yourself, Faith. If he doesn't see how great you are, then he doesn't deserve you. If you ever decide you want to give this a go again, you give me a holler."

I smile back, but it's weak. "Okay," I whisper.

He left the engine running as he exited the truck and ran around the front to open my door. Lifting his hand to me for the second time tonight, I took it and allowed him to help me down.

He started to follow behind me as I made my way to the door of the bunkhouse. I stopped and turned. "You don't have to."

"Just because you turned me down doesn't mean I won't stop being a gentleman."

I nod, giving him permission to walk me to the door. He kisses me on the cheek when we reached the entrance and told me to have a good night. I watch him as he walks away from me. I can't help but admire the fine ass below those Levi jeans.

I still felt guilty for dragging him along, but he was right, Remington and I needed to figure out whatever the hell this was between us.

I waved as he backed up and drove off before heading into the house. Emotions swarmed my brain like a bunch of angry bees.

How could he keep this from me?

Or was it not meant for me at all?

I'd been hoping he'd be sitting on the couch waiting for me to come home. Waiting to tell me the kiss meant something, to yell at me for dating another man, but it was eerily dark and silent as I walked through the front door. Hanging my keys on the hook by the door, I made my way down the hall and turned into the bathroom.

Standing at the sink, I stared at myself in the mirror.

Where did this all slip away from me?

Would it ever go back to the way it'd been?

I turn on the water and cupped my hands together to collect and splash some on my face. I needed to wash off all the makeup before bed. Taking the time to finish washing my face, I then move on to brushing my teeth.

Five minutes later, I am in my pajamas and ready for bed. I knew tonight there would be a lack of sleep. I'd already prepared for it. Tomorrow is a new day, but right now I am terrified of it.

REMINGTON

I am angry, there was no way around it. She'd told me countless times in her letters she'd wait for me and there she was parading off with Colton of all people. Colton. Captain of the football team, bully of many in high school, drunken contractor Colton. If that's what she wants to do, I won't stop her.

Maybe I am angry in general. I want so badly to believe Faith and I would get our chance, but I have so many doubts.

Had we truly moved past it all without a backward glance?

Will I ever get the memories back of her from before the accident?

I am sitting on my bed, the morning light streaming through my window as I strum on my guitar. I keep singing this same melody in my head, and I want to write it down on paper. I hum along with the tune one more time before getting up to grab lyric paper from my desk. When I was shuffling things around, I noticed some papers on top.

Turner & Son Construction was written in script across the top of the paper along with an address and phone number.

As I scan over the paperwork, I realize this is a contract to build a house. *When had I signed to build my own home?*

It took a minute to skim over the words. It appears I'd signed a written contract four months ago authorizing Turner and Son Construction to build me a house from the ground up. There is a big field next to McCoy's property and I'd snatched it up when it came up for sale. I wondered if I'd told anyone else about my idea to build a house, so I left the bunkhouse and make my way to the barn.

My eyes took a while to adjust from sunny to dim as I walked through the double doors. I find Beau in the office again tending to some paperwork. I swear, some days it's all he did. I knocked on the door. "Hey Beau, mind if I bother you?"

"Not at all. I'd welcome it." He laughs, putting down the paperwork he'd been staring at like it was the devil. "What's up?"

"You know anything about this?" I said, handing over the paperwork I'd found in my room.

He quirked an eyebrow as he read through it. "When'd the hell you decide to sign a contract to build a damn house?"

"About four months ago. I didn't happen to mention this at all, did I?"

"Nah, man. Sure didn't. Where you building?"

"Out by old man McCoy's place. Guess I bought up a piece of land for a great deal and decided to build."

"Honestly, Remington, it doesn't surprise me. This was around the same time you and Faith started getting together. Think it has anything to do with her?"

"I have no idea what to think."

"Still no memories?"

"Not a one. I hate it. I fucking hate myself for not being able to remember anything the two of you have told me. I want to believe her. You have no idea how badly because Faith is all I've ever wanted, there's simply a lack of memories standing in the damn way."

"Well, I'll say this. Give me an hour or two and we can drive out to see your new house if you'd like? It's been a couple months, I'm sure you're curious how it's going."

"Yeah, man, thanks. Sounds like a plan. Well, I'll let you get back to whatever you were doing. Come find me when you're ready."

"Sure thing."

I hadn't been cleared for riding yet, but I want to spend some time away from the bunkhouse. So, I decide to leave on a walk to clear my mind and end up at the hot springs. I'd hoped maybe it would bring on some memories... and it did, but not the ones I was desperately craving.

I remembered our first time here, and I walked over and noticed our initials carved into the tree. FE+RC forever... but what was under it baffled me. There was a date, a newer date, exactly four months ago. I don't remember putting it there, and I wondered if Faith had. Or maybe this was yet another thing I'd done and couldn't remember.

After stripping off my clothes, I wade into the hot springs and lean back to relax. I let the steam enclose me in its midst. The heat of the water wraps around my joints and muscles with a warming touch. A sigh slips from my lips as I rest my head back against a rock on the outer edge. It is continually peaceful here.

I was drawn here thinking I could clear my mind, but clearly it isn't working. I was so confused on why I'd decided to build a house. It'd been a dream to own my own house. I didn't see myself living in the bunkhouse for the rest of my life, but this all felt too soon. Or was it too soon? Was my brain planning ahead knowing it would all work out in the end with Faith? Maybe building a house would tell Faith I was serious about us and our future. Whatever the reason, I was sure I wouldn't figure it out today, possibly ever if my memories had anything to do with it.

I lowered into the water, letting it rush over my shoulders, the cold breeze blowing through the trees leaving a chill on any exposed skin available for the taking.

I sit there for what feels like hours, listening to my surroundings—the peace and quiet. The animals living in the woods around me went on about their day without a care in the world.

A woodpecker tapping on a tree.

A squirrel making an alarm call to a fellow squirrel.

A rabbit rustling through leaves on the wood floor.

I heard her footsteps before I see her. She stops in her tracks when she sees me, but she doesn't say anything. She stands there facing me, while I faced away from her waiting for her next step.

Her voice sounds soft, broken as she spoke. "Hey, Rem."

I turn in the water, creating a small wave. "Hey, Faith."

"How are you?" she asks, tentatively.

"I don't know," I respond back. I honestly have no idea. I want her, madly. My soul burns to be with her, but I still hold back. My emotions are an amalgamation of fear, uncertainty, and anger.

"Fair enough. You mind if I join you?"

"I don't think it's a good idea, Faith."

"But why, Rem? Why is it a bad idea now?" There is a dash of desperation behind her words, and some part of them reached deep inside me.

I blow out a long breath trying to figure out how to say this without crushing her feelings too badly. "Because I don't trust myself to stay away from you. Proven farther by last night."

"Then don't stay away from me. Give this a chance. Give us a chance."

"I don't know."

"I wish you remembered. I wish there was something I could do or say that would spark a memory."

"I'm sorry..." I mean it. I am sorry. I could wish for a memory til' the cows came home, but I don't trust my heart to let her in again without being certain this time. What if I let her in and then she leaves again? She's already proven she's a runner, what will stop her the next time?"

As if she could read my mind, she spoke again. "I'm not running anywhere, Rem. I'm here."

"You're lying, Faith... If you were here and all in like you claim, then you wouldn't be going on a date with Colton Turner."

"It was a mistake. It meant nothing."

"Well, it meant something to me. It means something when the words you speak don't match the actions you take."

"I'm sorry, Rem. I want you. It's been you forever. I just... feel so alone."

I stand up in the water, not caring I was essentially naked and stepped out. Reaching down, I pick up my clothes and put them on one by one. "I need to go. Beau and I have plans." I can't stand there any longer looking at the hopeless expression on her face. It is breaking me in two.

"Okay," she whispers as a tear slips down her cheek. My heart begs to comfort her somehow, but I know doing so will only make it worse, so I walk away. I head toward the bunkhouse hoping she doesn't follow me.

My phone rings halfway to my destination. "Hey, man."

"Are you ready to see this house you're building?"

"More than anything."

"All right, let me head up to the house and let Reagan know we're leaving."

I changed directions and headed toward the main house. Ten minutes later, we were in Beau's truck heading toward McCoy's farm.

He turned off onto the dirt road and headed toward the newly constructed house. From the road I could tell the foundation had been laid, as well as roof, and walls were done. It'd only been a couple of months according to the paperwork, and I was shocked to see how much progress had happened since then.

Beau sucked in a breath as we pulled up to the house and stopped. "Damn."

"Yeah."

"Well, let's check out your new home." Beau parks the truck in front of the house and we both slide out. It is a two-story farm-house plan with a wraparound front porch. "Damn, Rem. I can't believe you don't remember this. This is a house you'll get married and raise kids in. I think deep down you had Faith in mind when you planned this out. I guess I don't understand what's holding you back. You were so gung-ho about winning her over when she came home and now it's like you've given up."

"I haven't given up…"

"Easy to say, but your actions prove otherwise. She's hurting, Remington. Maybe you didn't see the light as it left her eyes or the way she stares at you like she can't look away, but I do. She's lonely."

"She went on a date last night." The words part from my lips without thinking.

His eyes widened. "She what?"

"You heard me right. She had a date with Colton Tucker last night."

"Damn."

"Then I kissed her…"

"When?"

"Last night before she left for the date."

"Did she still leave?"

I shrugged. "Yep, but she came home pretty early."

"Did she say anything else about it?"

I lifted my eyes to his. "She said it was a mistake."

"Remington, great to see you again!" I turn to see Tom Turner walking toward us. "I wondered when you'd be out to visit us. Glad to see you up and about again." He holds out his hand as he stops by us, and I shake it.

"Glad to be here."

"Shall we get started?"

"Lead the way," I say pointing toward the front door.

"So, out front here is the wraparound porch as requested." We walk up the two steps to the porch area and I can picture a swing in the corner and some chairs. He opens the door for Beau and I to walk through. Windows line the sides of the door giving the foyer area natural light.

"Here is the first floor. Right now, it's only walls and flooring, but when it's done, you'll have a great room, kitchen, breakfast, and dining nooks, a master suite, and a utility room. Upstairs you'll have three bedrooms and two baths."

"Wow." It is all I could think of to say. It is confusing as to why I would build such a big house unless I was planning exactly what Beau said—marriage and kids. Four bedrooms?

As we walked through the house all of the talks I'd had with Faith came flying back. We wanted two kids and she'd have an office for her business. The three bedrooms made sense from her point of view.

Tom droned on about what the plans were from here on out, but I only caught half of what he said. I can't believe this would to be my home. I wish I could remember the conversation prior to me signing the contract. I wish I could remember literally anything from before the accident.

Faith's words come back to me like a boomerang. "I wish you could remember."

I shake my head. *I wish I could remember too.*

"Any other questions for me?" His question brings me back to the present.

"Not right now. It's fantastic."

"Glad to hear you're happy with the progress."

Beau and I said our goodbyes and turned to leave. Once outside on the porch I took a moment to envision life here. I imagined it would be peaceful and the scary thing was how I could see Faith and I living here, having two kids and our goat named Elvis. We'd build a barn out back for the horses and have a bunch of cats to fend off the mice.

The memory made me wonder why protecting myself from a

potentially broken heart again was more important than the dreams Faith and I had created when we were younger. How did I think this was easier than fighting for love with the girl of my dreams?

I need to know. I need some sign I wasn't imagining things. We could have this simple life together and be happy. I need her to reassure me she was in this all the way.

———

Winter had seemed to blink and then disappeared. It'd been a while since I'd seen the house for the first time after the accident. It is hard to believe spring is almost here.

The house is nearing completion and I can finally picture myself living there, but it still feels like there's something missing. I moved out of the bunkhouse three weeks ago and started moving all my stuff in here. The furniture arrived this week. They're finishing up final touches and the yard out front.

The holidays swept past in a flurry and weaved us into another year. I have a feeling it'll be a great one. Faith and I haven't talked other than the occasional hello or thank you. We're rupturing and bleeding out and I don't know how to fix it.

Cassidy Mae is back in town and Beau is occupied with her. Apparently, some shit happened with her husband, so her being here is a secret for now. She's jumpy and nervous around most of us. I'd seen this behavior in my mom before she left us. Her husband had been abusive, it was something I could see.

We're having one of those family dinners tonight at the ranch, and Reagan threatened my head if I didn't show up tonight. I've seen Faith in passing a couple times, and there's been an occasional hello, but that's about it.

———

Faith takes a seat beside Reagan as we all sit down at the table. Reagan had prepared meatloaf, potatoes, and green beans. It is one of my favorites. She wasn't as good a cook as Faith, but I'd still ask for seconds. We discussed the new colt Beau had taken on from Mr. Johnson. It was the first one of his colts we'd worked with since the accident.

We joked about how he expected us to throw Miracle Grow at them, so they'd magically be broken. It was like old times. Since I'd moved, my dinners had become lonely and it was only then I realized how much I'd missed these guys.

Midway through dinner the conversation ended abruptly, all eyes on Cassidy Mae. Her face was white like she'd seen a ghost. Something had happened.

Dinner finished quickly afterward, and we all left. It was obvious Reagan and Beau wanted to speak with Cassidy Mae alone, so we gave them the space.

The rain had started to pour down steadily as I walked outside, but it didn't bother me. The rain brought me peace.

It washed away the old, making room for the new and maybe it's what I needed.

Or what I believed I needed.

Until I glanced across the driveway and saw her standing there staring at me in the rain.

Her hair is soaked and sticking to her face and neck. Black streaks run down her cheeks, and I can't tell if she was crying or if it was mascara running. The longing in her eyes makes my knees want to buckle below me though.

I don't know what compels me to walk toward her, but I do.

I don't know what compels me to lean in, wrap my arms around her, and pull her close, but I do.

I'm definitely not sure what I am thinking as my lips found hers in the rain under a pitch-black sky.

She melts into the kiss as it sizzles between us, begging for more as my arms tightened around her waist. Water runs down our faces and in between us. We are soaked, but nothing matters at the moment. It feels so right. My lips go on a journey along her jaw with kisses as my fingers trail through her soaking wet hair. A moan slips past her lips as I devoured her mouth like I was desperate.

She jumps at the noise and shoves me away. "Did you always mean to break my heart or was this some sort of payback?"

I instantly tense up. "What does that mean?"

"I've known about the house since the date with Colton, but not once did you tell me you were leaving and you were done. You moved on like it was no consequence to my feelings."

"Faith. I didn't even know about the house until the day we talked at the springs and to be honest, we weren't exactly on speaking terms."

"So, this is it? You're moving on?"

"Isn't it easier?"

"Nothing has ever been easy for us, Rem. I never thought you to be a coward that runs from his feelings and put us aside because he can't remember."

"Faith..."

"No, Rem. We work together here. Clearly, you don't want us since you're making decisions without me. So, don't talk to me. Don't look at me like you miss me and sure as hell don't kiss me. I'm tired of being tossed around like a rag doll. Pulled one way because you say you can't stop, then immediately tossed away like I mean nothing. You can't keep being a heartbreaker. I'd say we've had enough heartbreak for one lifetime."

"What if I said it didn't matter anymore if I remember or not? I want you anyhow."

"I'd say it's too little, too late. Love is a you-know-sorta-thing and if you need memories to remember you're in love with me then maybe it's not love at all."

"I love you."

"Rem... I can't..."

"You can."

"Go home to the house you built without me. I can't stand you being so close and not being with you."

"Then be with me."

"No. You once said you would fight for me, Rem. Do you remember? You said you were a fighter, and you didn't play fair. Breaking my heart like this is not fair and it fucking hurts."

"I will fight for your heart, Faith. It's been mine for years, I simply need to remind it who it belongs to."

She turns to leave, and the space between us as she moves away grows. I hate the seconds it took. I wanted to run to her, throw her over my shoulder, drive her to our house, and make love. But now she'll make me work for it, and I don't mind at all.

FAITH

Once I am inside the bunkhouse, I lean back against the door and take a long, slow, shaky breath. My body is screaming to run after him. To tell him I still love him, but I hold back. My cheeks heat with a faint blush as I remembered the passionate way he'd kissed me in the middle of the rainstorm. I'd always pictured a kiss as magical, but not like this.

My hair drips water onto my shoulders, and I realize I am soaked from head to toe. I imagine my makeup has run down my face and resembles a panda at this point. I wish I felt more confident. Remington told me he loved me, but how can you love someone you keep pushing away? So many conflicts whirl in my brain trying to piece together the conversation we had.

I slide my shoes off my feet and place them on the rug inside the door before heading toward the bathroom. I want to shower and wash these feelings all down the drain. The rain had been cold, and a chill started to spread over my skin.

I'd planned to see him tonight, but I didn't expect any of the things that happened afterward. Ugh. I expected him to get in his truck and drive away after dinner without speaking to me. It's been months since we've even held a conversation that didn't consist of one or both of us upset. I pull my wet shirt over my head and my pants stick to me as I slide them down. Both socks slop to the floor as I pull them off as well.

I turn on the shower and let it heat up and steam the bathroom. Stepping under the water, I let the hot water pour over me, washing away the tears that had fallen. Closing my eyes, I take a deep breath in and a deep breath out and continue to do it for many minutes after. I stand there for half an hour thinking things over before I realize I am letting him control my emotions and my feelings. Maybe I need to let it all drift away and see what happens?

A few days prior, Cassidy Mae had returned to live with Beau and Reagan in the main house. He was very protective of her. I watched as Remington and Jameson had helped her unload the car and take in the boxes. My heart banged at the reminder that Remington and I would never be moving boxes into a place of our own. He'd taken the chance away from me.

Tears cloud my eyes before they started to fall one by one. I swipe at them harshly. I want to scream, yell, and beat my fists against his chest as he holds me close and tells me it would be okay, but I don't believe it.

I am back to hating him, but loving him, and hating what he did to me, and how he made me feel. I hate myself for loving him, but I can't seem to stop. Love shouldn't hurt this bad, so why do I continue to let it affect me this way?

Each hurtful thing he's said in the past few months was true. I'd run from him without pausing to ask what truly happened. I'd been angry when he woke up from a coma and he couldn't remember. I'd tried to push him into wanting something when he wasn't sure about it. Now, he's decided he wants me again, and I'm not sure if my heart can take it.

I feel so selfish. So, fucking selfish.

I turn off the shower after my skin has become pruny. I grab a towel from the rack outside and towel off my body and wrap it around my hair.

I leave the bathroom and walk back into my room. There is no one here, so I am perfectly in my own right to walk around the damn place naked if I so chose to. I walk to the dresser and bend down to open the bottom drawer, retrieving my favorite shirt of Remington's. I'd stolen a couple shirts of his before he left. I was shameless, but I wanted the comfort of them.

The cologne on his shirt is starting to fade, but it still gives me comfort. I slip it on over my head, and it reaches down mid-thigh. I grab a sweatshirt too and walk over to the bed to lay down. I lay there with his sweatshirt against my nose, picturing him instead of this silly sweatshirt. God, I miss him so damn much. I am tired of fighting with him. I am tired of all the broken promises and emptiness taking over my gut.

I spend the next two days locked in the bunkhouse. I cancelled my lessons. I needed a couple days away from the outside world to think without anything else persuading my opinions. I let myself get swept up in thinking about my job here at the farm, about the current Rem situation, and about my parents and how it's affected my life.

The one thing I couldn't stop thinking about, it landed forefront in my mind, was Remington and I. What we were, what I wanted us to be, if anything. I called Nova on the phone, and we talked for what seemed like hours. I ate a whole carton of ice cream while we talked. I knew I'd have a stomachache, but it was worth it if I could eat my feelings away.

I cried myself to sleep, while listening to our favorite songs. I took bubble baths to try and make myself feel better. I felt like an addict trying to survive my withdrawal from him.

The second day, I drank like a fish. As much alcohol as I could before I ended up sloppy drunk and texting Nova about how I missed Remington, and had messed up by telling him to leave me alone. I didn't want that. I wanted the Remington who fought for my heart, who fought for me. I wanted the Remington Cole I had once, but I didn't know if he was still in there.

There was so much hate and pain between us, and I wasn't sure if it could ever be mended. Later in the afternoon, there was a knock on the bunkhouse. On the ground in front of the door was a bouquet of daisies and a letter. I knelt down to pick up the letter, and my heart skipped a beat and pounded in my ears at the writing on the outside.

It was from *him*.

I should've been surprised, but I wasn't.

Letters were our way of communicating. Opening the envelope, I find the letter is not the normal length. In fact, there are only two words on the paper.

I'm sorry.

Across the driveway, I see Beau and Cassidy Mae in the round pen with Zeus. He waved but I didn't wave back. I wasn't ready to emerge out of my bubble yet. I wasn't ready to do anything. Tonight, I found myself searching for jobs online. I wanted to travel anywhere away from here.

There was only so long I could sit by and work with him when he wasn't mine. When I wasn't sure he ever would be mine. The truth is we both said we'd fight for each other, but when it came down to actually doing anything, we were too afraid to try.

It seemed like a rollercoaster ride. Getting to the top only to zoom back down to the bottom again. It guts me to wonder if he'd move on, marry someone else, and settle down.

I knew I wouldn't because there would only be him for me. Even if I couldn't trust him. Even if he kept breaking my heart over and over again. Even if I spent the rest of my life alone.

———

The lunch table today is filled with talk of who would be competing this year and in what category for the county fair.

Rhett and Jameson were talking about the bronc riding when Remington piped in. "Either of you knuckleheads ever been on a bronc? It ain't like riding Jet or Remy. These horses get damn determined you ain't to be on their backs. They're likely to throw you off faster than you can blink."

Jameson smirks. "Aww, Rhett. He's worried about us. I feel touched, how 'bout you?"

Rhett smacks him on the shoulder. "Yeah, Jame, warming the cockles of my tiny little heart over here."

I choke down a sob, my mouth opening before I had a chance to think about what I was about to say. "Don't be an ass, Remington. I don't think they should do it any more than you do. I wouldn't let you ride and get hurt either." All eyes turn to me, and I can't help the blush as it crept up my cheeks. My mind flutters back to all those months ago when he ended up in the hospital from an erratic colt. I couldn't live through it again. I wouldn't make it through to the other side.

Remington rolls his eyes and scoffed. "Uh oh, Faith. Am I detecting emotions? Feelings? I don't know if it's the weird sensation that makes me almost, almost feel like you care..." His words are venomous as they slip from between his lips.

I sigh heavily, glancing away from his dark gaze. I couldn't make eye contact with him. "Never said I didn't, Rem," I whisper softly.

My throat tries to close up as I peer over at him. He tried to seem unaffected by my response, but he was anything but. The crease in his brow, the thin line of his jaw as he grinds his teeth. Instead of responding to me, he turns back to Rhett and Jameson, "Fine, get yourselves hurt. Can't say I didn't warn ya."

Luckily, the others seemed to move on soon enough to Cassidy Mae. I'd forgotten how big of a deal the fair was to the town. I'd always had good memories, but unfortunately, those memories were also part of him. Everything I did, thought about, or happened in this town reminded me of him if I was honest with myself. He is all around me. The old us is hanging over my head.

After a while, they finally convince Cassidy Mae to run barrels with Oakley. And so it continued day after day, week following week. We barely spoke other than to spew hate at each other. I wanted to call a truce or anything to get it to stop.

Remington was like the air I breathed, and if I cut myself off from him completely, I may suffocate to death.

I stand up from the table and take my dishes to the sink before leaving to head over to the barn for the next lesson.

Koko was in her stall waiting for me, so Remington must have brought her in before he came to lunch. I tried not to read too much into it because it is his job, right?

I watch as Beau saddles Titan and Remington saddles Remy. They are headed out to ride out somewhere, destination unknown to me.

My mouth grows dry, and my heart pounds in my ears as I sneak a peek at Remington from head to toe. He is in his usual white tee and Levi jeans. He has his ballcap on backwards today and his boots are covered in dust like normal. I watch his arm and leg muscles as he pulls himself into the saddle, and my damn heart swoons a little. How is he still so attractive?

Back to work, I tell myself.

Reagan catches my eye walking toward the main house with Bandit, and I wave.

As they ride away, I open Koko's stall door, halter her, and lead her out to stand in the cross ties and await my next student. Five minutes later, Madison shows up.

"Miss Faith, Miss Faith," she yells running up to me in the barn.

"Madison, remember we shouldn't run around the horses. It'll spook them and you could get hurt."

She was bouncing from foot to foot, trying hard to seem apologetic. "I'm sorry, Miss Faith. I just... was so excited about my new boots."

Glancing down to her sparkly boots, I smiled. "Oh, those are super cool, Mads. Did your mom buy those for you?"

Her eyes lit up with excitement. "Yep! I got 'em for my birthday."

"How cool. When was your birthday?"

"Three days ago!"

"Well, happy belated birthday. Are you ready to tack up Koko?"

"Yes!" I wish I had half of the enthusiasm she possessed today. I want carefree joy again.

"Okay, well she's ready for you. Let's grab your brushes and hoof pick."

I watch as she runs to the tack room and grabs her brushes and hoof pick. First, she uses the curry brush on what she could reach and then pulled over the step ladder to get Koko's neck and back. I help her pick out Koko's feet because although she was bullet-proof, I am not taking a chance with a kid around her feet by herself.

Saddling and bridling Koko, I lead her out to the arena. Madison grabs her helmet from her mom and climbs up the mounting block. Once she is in the saddle, I hand her the reins and instruct her to walk out to the rail.

I lost track of time as the lesson continued on. Most of it consisted of telling Madison to put her heels down, to sit up straight, and to watch where she was going instead of down at the ground.

Reagan brought Bandit out after I was done with the lesson. He's become her dog since the accident. We didn't have the time to spend with him that he needed, and Reagan was there. I missed him like crazy, but seeing Bandit brought up all the bad memories.

REMINGTON

"So, you told her everything, did ya? Finally confessed you were in love with her, but now you aren't sure if she could ever give herself over to you and truly love again? Is that what I'm hearing?" I say.

Beau glares over at me as we were digging holes for the fencing. His shoulders, neck, and arms are visibly tense. We'd been needing some new fencing for a while now and were waiting for the lumber to arrive.

"That's about the whole of it. I can tell she wants to be with me. But there's also a part of her scared to death to be tied to anyone again after what happened with her bastard of a husband. I don't blame her. She's damn brave to leave like she did. She's been letting me in slowly, but other times she clams up and shuts down like I'd use her words against her."

I grind my teeth. "Yeah, well, that's a woman for you. You make one mistake and it haunts you for the rest of your life, making you feel as confused as a field mouse in an ocean. One minute she likes me, the next she hates my guts again." I jammed the shovel into the hole a little harder than last time, taking my frustration out on the ground.

His eyebrow tilts. "You thinking about Faith?"

I snort, refusing to answer. I don't feel like chit chatting about my personal feelings at the moment.

"Can I ask something?"

"I suppose. No one else out here to ask."

"Okay, smart ass. If Faith decided to give you another chance, would you take it?"

"Yeah, I would. Why'd you ask?"

"Because all you do is mope around and grouch at people. I miss my friend, man. You'd pick on us, but at least we'd know you're okay. This person you've become. Standoffish. Rude. This ain't you, man. This girl has you so frazzled you don't know what to do with yourself."

I stop working and run my hand through my hair in frustration. "I know, Beau. I don't know what to do about her."

He gives me a knowing look. "You still love her."

I snort. "You asking a question or making a statement?"

"Statement."

"I do love her. I've tried to talk to her, but we seem to continually end up in a lip lock, and then we fight. I want her back, but I'm not sure what else to do. So, I'm not doing anything."

"You're giving up?"

I turn my back and start walking toward the truck. After we'd arrived to the ragged parts of fencing, we'd figured out the horses couldn't carry the lumber needed like a truck did.

As I was walking, I notice her immediately. Across the field, my eyes find Faith as she works with Madison. I'd brought Koko in for her earlier today and sent her flowers, but she didn't say anything about either.

Sometimes actions speak louder than words. We'd had so many uphill battles in the last couple of months, and it would take more than a few words on paper to win her back.

Beau must've noticed. "Whatcha lookin' for buddy?"

"Nothing," I say, shaking my head. His eyes told me whatever he didn't say out loud. I have it bad.

———

I'd returned home and made dinner when a knock sounded on my door. I wasn't expecting anyone, so I was cautious about opening the door. Peering through the peephole, I find Nova standing on my front porch. She seems pissed.

I open the door, and she storms past me, not even waiting for me to invite her in. "You and I need to have a talk."

"Well, hello to you too." I say after her.

She narrows her eyes at me and crosses her arms over her chest. "I'm not here for small talk, Remington Cole. I'm here to find out what you intend to do about our girl."

"She doesn't—" I don't even get the words out before she cuts me off.

Nova walked right up to me and poked her finger into my chest. "No, I'm talking and I need you to listen."

"Okay."

"Sit." I show her into the great room and take a seat on the couch, assuming she would sit too, but she doesn't. She stares at me like I'm the bad guy. I wonder how much Faith has told her.

"I don't know what she told you, but she doesn't want this, me, us anymore."

With curled lips and a raised voice, she shoved her finger at me again. "You're an idiot then, and quite frankly, you need to figure your shit out because I'm tired of getting phone calls with my girl crying because you fucked up again."

I sigh, finally admitting something I'd been holding back. "I don't know how to fix things..."

"She loves you. This tough exterior she's showing is a facade. You weren't there in college with her. You didn't have to see her cry all the times you sent her a letter. You didn't see her turn down good guy after good guy because they weren't you. You couldn't see the torment she went through because she lost her job and had to move home. You weren't the one on the other side of the phone listening to her cry again because she's confused or hurt by something you did. I was."

She shakes her head. "Faith was the one who sat by you daily while you were in a coma. She's the one who stopped her life to make sure she was there for you. You were the one who told her to leave. All you've done is break her further and quite frankly, I'm sick of it. Either love her or leave her be."

It guts me, listening to Nova. I feel sick to my stomach thinking about all I'd done to Faith over the last couple of years. I didn't realize how hard it was for her. I'd been selfish.

"What's your fear?" I scowl at her, but don't answer. She taps her foot on the ground, fidgeting. "Well?" She raises her eyebrows, waiting for a response.

I shrug. "Honestly, I'm scared she'll run again. I mean, why wouldn't she? She's too smart for this place, too beautiful for me."

"See, that's a shit kind of attitude to have. You are enough, Remington. If you weren't then Faith wouldn't believe in you like she does. She would have given up on you years ago and never looked back, but she didn't, which is why I'm here giving a shit about you too. I'm tired of seeing her hurt and you're the only one who can fix it before she's too far gone."

"I don't know how."

"Put on your big boy pants and figure it out. You managed to win her back before the accident. I'm quite certain that pretty brain of yours can figure out how to swing it again. I suggest a grand gesture. Take her to one of those special places you both know or do something she likes to do. You know Faith. Hell, you dated her for how many years…"

"Nova…"

"Nope, not done. Last but not least, I am pissed at you. I'm not helping you because I like you because quite frankly you've let my friend down one too many times and she should've given up on your ass a long, long time ago. But for some reason, she still loves the fuck out of you. So here we are. I'll say this one more time... Do. Not. Fuck. This. Up!" Her nostrils flared as her gaze seared into me.

Hands up, palms toward her, I hoped she would stand down. "Can I speak now?"

Her arms are still crossed, but she nods. "You may."

"I admit things were messed up. I'll be the first to admit I hate having no memories of us before the accident."

Her arms are swinging here and there while she talks. "So, you don't love her enough to try and win her back even without the memories? Is that what you're saying? I want to make sure I'm hearing this right."

"It's not... Nova, have you ever woken up from a coma and the last thing you remember is the love of your life walking out your door?" She shook her head. "Well, imagine waking up from who knows how long and finding her standing beside your bed, crying. Then you're told you've been in a coma for the last month. How do you think you'd react?"

"Remington, I get it. Obviously, it would have been difficult, but Faith wrote you notes. Beau confirmed everything with you about before the accident, yet you didn't believe either of them. That's a level of stupid I'm not sure can be remedied."

I sigh, looking down. "Look, I know."

She shakes her head, her expression tight. "No, you don't know. Do you know how many times over the last couple of months she's called me with hope only to end up in tears? You can't keep kissing her and then walking away. Relationships take work and if you don't want it with Faith, then leave her alone."

"I can't leave her alone. I'm not willing to live without her anymore." The truth pours from my lips automatically. I almost surprise myself.

"Then you have a long road ahead of you..."

I nod, running my hands through my hair as I sit on the couch. Nova staring me down. "I know."

She reaches into her back pocket and pulls out a square piece of paper. "Here, I think you should read this. Maybe it'll help you remember something."

"What is it?" I say, reaching for the piece of paper in her hand.

"The letter you wrote Faith the morning of the accident. She doesn't know I have it. I found it in her trashcan the last time I came to visit and I believe you may want to read it."

"Thank you." A smile starts to part my lips, until I see the look Nova is giving me.

"Don't thank me yet, we're not on friend level yet. Not until you make my girl happy again."

"That's the plan," I say with a smile and a wink.

"Well, I think we're done here. I'll leave you to read the letter. If you need help, here's my number, but I think you have this under control." She handed me a second slip of paper with a phone number.

"Okay." She turned to walk toward my front door. "Thank you for this," I call after her.

She shoots a wave over her shoulder at me before leaving.

Squeezing my eyes shut, I take a few minutes to breathe. I should try to slow down my rapidly beating heart before opening the letter Nova dropped on me. I don't remember writing it, but maybe it's the key.

I open the letter and start from the top. Some of the letters were smudged as if she'd cried tears and I prayed to God they were happy tears.

Dear Faith,

. . .

*I'm finding it very hard to put last night into words so it makes
sense. My brain is running sixty miles a minute. You told me no
talking and no emotions, but it's like my head is no longer in charge
and my heart has taken over again.*

*Memories of you fill my mind, and it's something I don't ever
want to mess with because it's perfection. You are perfect and I won't
measure up, but I'll spend the days for the rest of my life sure as hell
fighting for it. For you, for us.*

*I remember the first time I held your hand in the middle of
December because it was so damn cold out. I remember laying a
blanket down by the crick in the middle of summer so I could make
love to you all night long with the crickets in the background. I
remember the nights we spent beneath the stars. I remember the first
time you told me you loved me, and I couldn't figure out how in the
world someone as gorgeous as you would be interested in such a loser
like me.*

*I remember the time we covered my truck bed with a tarp and
turned it into a jacuzzi because we were too broke to buy a damn
pool. You complained the bright red bikini you had on was too small,
but I wasn't complaining. As I recall, I couldn't take my damn eyes
off you.*

*I remember the first time I saw you in your red sundress in the
middle of a field, dancing around a bonfire to Springsteen, while
sipping on apple pie moonshine. You winked at me, and I was a
damn goner. Still am. I think somewhere along the line you stopped
being Faith and became my girl. You see, you and me, we're meant to
be together. Even if it takes me years to convince you, I will do my
damn best.*

*Last night was one of the best nights of my damn life and it's not
because we had sex, it's because it was you. I believed I knew what
love was at sixteen years old, but nothing would've prepared me for
love as an adult. I didn't know it was possible to love another human*

as much as I love you. I feel it in my soul, in my bones. You're a part of me and will be until my dying breath. One smile and I was ready to start wars for you.

These last four years I've been a ghost. Moving from day to day, time to time, without even feeling it. One continuous motion without ever truly living. It's like watching a movie on an old black and white box television until someone upgrades you to a sixty-five-inch flatscreen. You make me see the world in vivid, brilliant colors.

I was the best with you because you make me a better man. I fall back into you, into the memories, into loving you as easy as the snap of my fingers. I'll admit I was obsessed with you back then, but now it's a whole different type of obsession—a full body one.

Loving you isn't only for the good days, it's for the Mondays when you don't want to work, the Tuesdays when you wish it was Friday. The Saturdays when you get to sleep in. The Sundays spent making love.

It's the fights, the love made in between, and the living happening along the way. And I want all of it with you. So tonight, I want to do things the proper way. Tonight, I want you to dress up in something special. I'll pick you up at 7pm, we'll venture out on an adult date - out to dinner, then dancing because although I don't dance, I know you love it and you make me want to for you.

I want to give you the world and it might start with a kiss or a dance, but it'll be another memory of us. I'm not needing for an answer right now but I'm hoping you say yes. I know this is a lot to take in, but tell me you'll think about it, about us. Loving you is the best decision I've ever made, and I don't want to wait another day longer to show you.

In the meantime, breakfast is in the kitchen and I picked you flowers. Don't say no, okay. Say yes because I've already set my mind to winning you back and you know how I get when I put my mind to something. You're my girl. Always have been, always will be.

I love you. I know it doesn't seem like enough, but I'm not sure how to say it better, so let me show you.

. . .

Always yours,
Rem

Seeing my words on paper confirmed what Beau and Faith had already told me. I can't believe it. I drop my chin to my chest and run my hands through my hair, pulling on the ends. I was ashamed I'd been so cruel.

I sat there for a while after Nova left, thinking about how I'd win her back. Soon, my eyelids started to fall shut, and I decided it was time to hit the sack for the night. I'd need to deal with this in the morning, and I needed Beau's help.

My lips peppered kisses against her silky-smooth legs as I made my way up to the apex of her thighs. She squirmed below me in protest at how slowly I was moving, but I was mentally photographing each single moment. I wanted to remember the details about tonight. The way her body curved in all the right places. The way she smelled. The way she peered at me in the darkness, the only hint of light peeking in between the curtains. The way she moaned my name in desire.

It may have been four years since we were together, but damn if it still feels like always, only more exquisite.

Her breath came heavily as she begged me for more. I found the paradise between her legs and wrapped my lips around her bundle of nerves. I worked my tongue around and around, nibbling and licking up and down her slit. Her hips undulated upward, silently asking me for more, and I gave it to her. Slipping my fingers into her core, I found the spot on the inside that drove her crazy and rubbed it while still circling her clit with my tongue. She screamed as she came on my face, and I lapped at her eagerly.

Pulling away, I trailed up her body and found her eyes with mine. I couldn't see her well, but I heard her audible breaths as her body shook from release.

"More," she crooned.

"You need more of me, babe?" I said, my voice husky with need before my lips found hers again briefly.

"Rem, I need you," she said, her voice filtered with lust. I raised up from the bed and let my pants fall to the floor.

"You sure?" I asked her one more time. She was giving me this one night, and I wanted to take whatever she'd willingly offer, but I wouldn't do it without permission first.

"Positive."

I slid down my boxers, standing in front of her naked as the day I was born. My cock a solid ridge of steely flesh between my legs. Ready to win over her pussy in a battle like none before. Climbing back onto the bed, she spread her legs for me, and I couldn't help but take in the view. I couldn't get enough of her.

Leaning down on my elbows, I captured her lips with mine as my tip kissed her entrance. I gritted my teeth as I slid inside her, trying to make sure I didn't reach release before it was all over. She was tight, so fucking tight and glorious.

I could tell her brain was speeding along with so many questions, so I leaned into her ear and whispered. "No thinking."

Our breaths were short and ragged, my heart pounding as I pressed her into the bed. She squeezed my cock, and I almost lost it. I was so close. I lifted her hands above her head and entwined them with mine as I bent to kiss her. I picked up pace, shoving my cock into her over and over again. My hand found her clit and worked her until she came screaming my name. I roared my release shortly after.

"I love you," I whisper, kissing the outer shell of her ear.

The alarm on my phone starts blaring, and I sit straight up, gasping. *Fuck.* I slap my hand on the side table until my alarm shuts off. It was only a dream, but it felt so damn real. I am shaken to the core because suddenly it all fell into place.

Holding up my phone, I open my eyes slightly to scan the time. Ten in the morning. I slept for twelve hours straight. I never slept in this late. *Shit*, I'm late for work. Throwing the blankets off me, I stumble out of bed and head toward the bathroom.

The dream confirmed my plans. Faith had been right all along. Now I had to make her believe we were meant to be, and she'd be mine again, no questions asked.

———

I pull into the driveway for Willow Springs, my mind decided. I know exactly what I needed to do to win Faith back, and my heart-beat anxiously against my chest. I hoped it would work.

Remy ran along the fence with my truck as I pulled in, and it brought a smile to my face. Today, there were no more questions, I felt settled finally.

I'd texted Nova this morning to ask for her help, and she'd told me it was the perfect plan. Now, I needed to get Beau involved.

Nova was in town to have a girl's weekend with Faith at the bed and breakfast on Main Street, so I had a couple of days to get it all worked out. I park the truck by the bunkhouse like always and open the door to get out.

As I walk toward the barn, I notice Beau is in the round pen working with his new rescue horse, Zeus, and Cassidy Mae is in the arena with Oakley working the barrels.

The state fair is coming up and everyone is excited because it's the thing you do in these small towns once a year. It was the *it* place, and this year I planned to have the perfect girl on my arm. I hoped so at least.

Beau glances my way and tips his hat to me in the way he said hello. I wasn't traipsing over to bug him. Instead, I walk up to the gate at the fence line and whistled. I keep fidgeting as my hands rolled my keys back and forth, waiting for Remy to come. A couple of minutes later, the thunder of hooves hit my ears and I see him running at a gallop.

Dust flies around him as he comes sliding to a stop in front of me with a nicker. You'd think he was a reining horse instead of a cow pony with the way he slid. "Hey, bud. Interested in a ride?" He waits patiently as I hook a lead line to his halter and open the gate, moving him around so I could get the gate closed back up without any of the other horses escaping.

The click clack of his hooves against the ground as we made our way across the gravel is one of my favorite things. I line him up in the middle of the aisle and put him in cross ties so I could get the saddle and brushes from the tack room. I do a quick brush and tack him up. I didn't bother with a bridle and decided to use his halter and lead rope.

Five minutes later, I'm leading Remy out and getting on his back. I turn him toward the wooded area around the hot springs. It's a peaceful place to relax and think. I knew Beau would probably be a little bit before he was back around. I'd missed riding since my accident.

The drumming of a woodpecker on a nearby tree catches my attention as a small brown rabbit runs out in front of Remy on the trail. He doesn't spook at it, only watches with curiosity as we keep on our way. I spoke to him, telling him my plan about Faith, knowing he couldn't talk back. I needed to prepare myself for how to ask Beau to do something with the potential to definitely piss off Faith.

He isn't the type of guy who liked to piss off a lady, so I knew he wouldn't like it, but he'd most likely do it. The slight breeze whistles through the trees, picking up strands of Remy's mane on his neck. He shakes his head and blows out a breath. When we reach the springs, I hop off and tie him to my favorite tree.

Our initials stand there prominently, and I run my hand over them. Soon, we'd be adding another date, hopefully the final, to this tree. I spend the next half an hour relaxing in the springs. It is so quiet with simply the sound of Remy munching on some grass. Occasionally a horse would whinny from a nearby field and Remy would respond with one of his own. I envisioned the whole plan in my head and by the time I saddled up, I knew exactly what I had to do.

———

Remy trots back up to the barn, right as Beau is leading Zeus into his stall. "You done with him for now? Need to talk to you about something."

He nods. "Sure, get untacked, and I'll meet you in the office. Sound all right?"

"Works for me."

I quickly untack Remy and take him back out to the field, turning him loose.

I nod toward the arena. "Saw Cassidy working with Oakley. how are things?"

"Good, she's doing really well. I wish she'd let me help her."

"She's working through some stuff, give it some time."

His brows hit his hairline. "Isn't that the pot calling the kettle black... So, what's up?"

Rubbing my hands together, I smile. "I'll coerce her into giving me another shot and I have a plan, but I'll need your help."

His eyebrows raise. "Why do I have a feeling I won't like what you're about to ask me?"

I lift my hand and rubbed the back of my neck. "Because you're probably not."

We spent the next hour discussing all the details of my plan, and he finally agreed to help me. Nova was in as well. Let's hope all the cards fall into place and I won my girl back.

Memories are starting to come back to me ever since last night and I was getting more and more hopeful, but I know it's been months since Faith and I sat down and had an actual conversation. I didn't know where her head was at and it scared me the most. What if I'd done enough this time to truly push her away?

The way she watched me when I saw her daily made me believe I still had a chance. She gave me a glimmer of hope, no matter how small it was.

FAITH

"I don't know what to do, Nova," I say to my best friend as she sits across from me. She'd driven in this morning and was staying at the bed and breakfast in town.

My thoughts turned back to Rem. I was in the same position now Remington had been in for years. Unsure if he'd read the letters, but hoping he had. He hadn't given me any indication it was the case.

Nova's brow furrowed as she turned to me. "Give him time, Faith. You have to realize he's been through an ordeal and he needs to work his way through this. As much as you want things to go back to the way they were, he needs to be the one to remember on his own. Don't... try and force things."

"I've been avoiding him. It sucks." She lifts a shirt out of her suitcase before her eyes cut back to me, examining my face.

"It's for the best. Let him work his way back to you."

I huff. She is right, although I won't admit it to her. Changing the subject, I ask about how things are going between her and a certain someone I know. "So... when will you spill about how things are going with Jameson?"

She giggles and a light flush spread up her cheeks. "Oh, I don't know, Faith. He's so..." She trails off like she's lost in reflection.

"Somebody has it bad, huh?" I chide her.

"Well, he's different, I suppose. He comes off as this overly confident guy, but he's so sweet. I'm always weary of those types. Normally the sweet is a facade."

"Jameson is one of the good ones. He's soft spoken, but he has the best heart and the humor to go with it. Are you hanging out with him while you're here?"

"He definitely wants to, but I hadn't decided yet." She gazes over at me demurely. "You honestly think he'd be interested in me. Captain of the nerd squad with a little extra to love?"

"Nova, babe, you have curves. You rock them. Do not put yourself down, you're a very pretty lady!"

Nova's cheeks are rosy, as if she were embarrassed. "I know. I'm skinnier than I was, yes, but I still feel like the fat teenager who was bullied in school."

I smile at her. "You are perfect the way you are. You are a smart, beautiful, intelligent lady and if Jameson doesn't see it and immediately drop to his knees and beg you to marry him, then he's not worth your time."

"Thanks, Faith." She comes over and gave me one of her famous bear hugs.

"I missed you, girl." I couldn't help but say it out loud. Since I've been home, I haven't felt the same. I've been walking on eggshells around Remington and I talked to Reagan and the others, but no one gets me like Nova. With her, I felt like I could be myself.

"Aww, I've missed you too Faith. So... tell me what we're getting into today?"

"Well, I hope you don't mind, but I may crash here for the next couple of days while you're in town. I told Beau this morning I needed a couple days off and I didn't have anyone on the books either. He said it was completely okay. I think he's starting to feel bad for me."

She bumps my shoulder. "No worries, girl. We'll turn your frown upside down while I'm here. So... I want to see this famous Bodine's diner while we're here, and maybe let's catch a movie at the old theatre this afternoon?"

My fist bumps into the air. "Done and done. I'm excited about having a straightforward day to hang out and chill. Nothing to worry about, no one to run into except you, me, and this small little town."

I'd brought a bag with me to the bed and breakfast and decided I wanted to change into something else before heading out. The clothes I currently had on were covered in dirt and dust from my morning chores.

I quickly change into blue jeans, a tee, and my chucks. We grab our bags and leave the room, heading down the stairs to the first floor and out onto Main Street.

It's a beautiful day outside, slightly warm, but I'm not complaining. I'd take a warm summer day over a cold winter blizzard any day of the week.

A small robin sits in one of the trees, singing away to its own little melody. The sky is a cornflower blue with few clouds and it's nice to be able to take a minute to enjoy the simplicity of a beautiful day and forget the rest of crap happening in my life.

Nova and I chatted as we walked along Main Street, passing Orly's flower shop, an old-fashioned candy store where we stopped to load up on penny candies, and several other little boutiques that had moved in over the years.

"I love this little town. People smile or wave at you as they pass. You smile or wave in the city and people are likely to shoot first, ask questions later."

I gape at her. "I know, right? I missed it while I was away."

My eyes found the sky again, and it reminded me of the color of Remington's eyes.

No, I shake my head. I wasn't thinking about him right now. *Not today.*

Today was my day with Nova and I wouldn't waste it.

I had to admit, it was nice having her around today. I hadn't realized how alone I'd felt these last couple months, even though I was surrounded by the Willow Springs crew.

I hoped Remington and I would get back to the *us* I wanted. The one I knew we could eventually be, and we wouldn't simply end up as another shitty chapter in the story of our love life. Things weren't too hopeful right now, but I refused to give up.

The bell rings over our head as we enter Bodine's. Like usual, Patty is our waitress. She comes over with a smile and a hello, dropped off the menus, and said she'd be back in a few minutes to take our order.

"Oh, my gawd, everything here sounds fantastic. What's your favorite?"

Pointing to a couple of options on the menu, I reply, "I love the hometown breakfast meal, personally, but the patty melt is pretty tasty too."

Our food arrives twenty minutes later. I ordered my usual and had to blow on the gravy because it was steaming hot. Nova ended up getting a bacon patty melt with extra Bodine's sauce. "Mmm... Faith, why have you been holding out on me? This is amazing," she says, taking a bite. The cheese dangles from the sandwich as she pulls away from the bite. They don't call it a melt for nothing, right?

Her eyes peruse Bodine's and she spots the dance floor. "Wait, you guys dance here?"

"Yep. Remington and I used to hang out here when we were younger. It's had some improvements over the years."

My mind replayed the last night Remington and I were here. I was drunk off my ass, flirting with whoever would pay attention. A blush crept up my face at the memories of what happened when we got back to the bunkhouse. The way I'd shamelessly thrown myself at him without a second guess. I'd ambushed him like a bonafide hussy.

I couldn't believe how out of control I felt when I was around Remington these days. It felt like it was slowly slipping from my grasp and gravity was pulling it down.

I wanted Rem. Maybe it was reckless to feel this way at this point.

I mean, what if he never regained his memories or learned he could trust me again? This whole situation hit a new level of complexity, but it couldn't be rushed. If I rushed Remington, he'd shut down. I'd finally healed from past hurts and now this...

We finished our lunch and decided to split a piece of cherry pie with extra whipped topping. A little sweet to mix with the saltiness of our meals, the perfect compliment. Music played, filling the space between us as we happily munched. It was the comfort of simply hanging out with my best friend.

Earlier today we'd stocked our bags full of penny candy so we wouldn't need to buy anything at the movie. Finding our seats, we pulled out our goodies. We were totally breaking movie theatre law by bringing in outside food, but we didn't care.

"So..." Nova says as soon as we find our seats and get settled.

"Yeah?"

"What do you think I should do? Jameson asked me out on a date again via text while I'm in town."

"What'd you say?" I ask, excited for her.

She bites her bottom lip like she's always done when she's nervous. "Um... I don't know."

"Why? You should totally do it! What's the worst that can happen? You have a bad time? Then say no the next time. Live a little, fall a little, the possibilities are endless." Nova hasn't dated in a while. I've only ever seen her with one guy and it was a rocky ending. I understand the hesitation. I felt the same way when Remington was attempting to woo me after I moved back.

Why did my mind continually run back to him?

"Oh, you should totally do it. It'll be fun. You won't know unless you say yes and I think you should totally say yes."

The previews started, and we quieted down. We had the whole room to ourselves. The movie we were watching we'd seen hundreds of times, but it didn't matter. It's one of those movies you can't say no to every time it's on tv. Or you need a super awesome ugly cry movie.

I wanted a guy like Carter. A little screwed up, but willing to change for the girl he loved.

It reminded me a little of Remington and I, only I wasn't dying.

It'd been days since I'd seen him last and each one is worse than the next. It's like a withdrawal of the drug that's kept you moving for the last couple of months is finally leaving your body.

You're itchy, irritable, and searching for the next high to fix the need. I needed to talk to him regardless. We needed to either make the conscious decision to fight for what we had, or walk away and let the pieces fall apart so we can finally start mending them back together.

I knew it'd break me if he walked away. I'd shatter like last time, only this time there would be no crack to fuse back together. It'd be an open wound, and I was pretty sure I'd have a scar to go with it.

Pulling my phone from my purse, I send him a text.

Me: We need to talk.

He didn't respond immediately, and I hadn't expected him to. Knowing Rem, he was probably trying to figure out my angle first.

Ten minutes later, three little bubbles popped up and then disappeared four times before a response finally came through.

Remington: Ok.

It was all he said back.

Me: I'm away from Willow Springs until the weekend. So, I'm thinking Saturday night?

Remington: Ok.

I knew I wouldn't get more than the simple one or two word responses. He was never one for texting, so one word responses weren't unusual for him. I'd wondered if calling him would've been easier, but I knew we needed to do this face to face.

Sitting across from someone gave all the tells of the real answers behind the spoken ones. I wanted to see what he was saying out loud and with his eyes. I'd hoped he'd read my letters. I meant what I said when I told him I'd fight for him and I didn't play fair.

I planned on reminding him Saturday night.

The rest of the day passed us by in the blink of an eye and when we crashed at night, we slept for a full twelve hours straight.

We woke up to the sound of horns blaring on Main Street. We planned the rest of the day around basking in the sun at the lake and meeting up with Reagan a little later on for some food and dancing. Ladies' night out, she'd called it when we invited her. The night blended into the next day.

My head is spinning as I squint my eyes open this morning. I remember hanging out at Bodine's last night and drinking way too much. Rhett and Beau ended up coming out and taking us back to the bed and breakfast before dragging Reagan home. It felt amazing to simply relax and let loose.

Nova had accepted the invite to dinner with Jameson and he had it all planned out for tonight, which meant I'd have the room all to myself. Earlier today we'd headed down to Daisy's book nook, and I'd grabbed two romance novels - one contemporary and one shifter. It would definitely pass the time away.

We'd spent the afternoon getting our nails and toes done. I wanted her to feel special. To enjoy this evening out.

I am happy for her, but regardless I am sad for myself. I don't want to be the girl who stands in the way of her friend finding her potential happily ever after. Jameson is a decent guy who'd been raised with manners, much like the rest of the guys at Willow Springs.

The sun is still shining when we finally return from the little boutique down the street. I'd helped Nova pick out the perfect first date dress for their evening out. A blue paisley halter top dress, low cut between her breasts in the front, but still modest, with enough flow to create an impressive twirl if they went dancing the night away. We'd also picked out a cute cardigan and a pair of sandals to match in case the chill seeped in over the evening.

An hour later, she was waving at me as she left the room. I'd wished her luck and settled onto the bed with my romance novel. My phone pinged half an hour later. I wasn't expecting to hear from anyone and my heart sank thinking it was Nova already and she had a bad time on her date.

Quickly grabbing it from the nightstand, I pull up the message. It's him.

Remington: I have a physical therapy appointment at the hospital in an hour and no one here is free. I hate to ask, but would you mind giving me a lift? I can drive there, but I always ask someone else to drive me home. My knee gives me too much pain to drive afterward.

Me: I'll be there in fifteen.

Remington: I do appreciate it.

I don't respond to the last text.

I quickly grab my keys from the table, pause at the mirror long enough to check my hair, face, and clothes, then left. Locking the door behind me, I take the stairs at a jog. Scurrying through the front lobby, I didn't bother to see if anyone was sitting around, then unlocked my car on the street as I stopped by it and hopped in.

Cranking the engine, I pulled the shifter into drive and headed to the stables on autopilot. I could navigate the road in my sleep if I had to. Pulling down the entrance sixteen minutes later, I see him standing outside of the bunkhouse.

I pull up and rolled down the window. "All right, let's get to it," I say, waiting for him to open the door and get in. He doesn't and instead stood there staring at me. "You coming or what?" The annoyance slipping out into my words as my fingers drummed on the steering wheel.

"We'll have to take my truck." It clicked then. Remington was six foot, and I highly doubted he'd be able to fit his tall frame into my small Toyota Corolla.

"Right," I mumble back to him. Pulling into the spot beside his truck, I parked and got out. "Keys?"

He holds them up and unlocks his truck. Opening the door, I grab onto the handle to pull myself up. Why do trucks have to be this high up from the ground? Don't they realize short girls aren't all acrobats?

"You all right?" he says from already inside the truck. I don't miss the smirk as it slowly spread his lips as he watched me try, and fail, to compose myself.

"All good." I cranked up the engine, and the truck came to life below us. I backed out slowly, making sure not to hit my car on the way by. "Hospital?"

"Yep. Thanks for doing this." The way he said it sounded genuine.

His scent fills up the inside of the cab as we drive, and I suck it in like a bad habit.

How does he manage to continuously smell so damn yummy?

The man smells like musky cologne, good memories, and... dirty intentions.

It melts my insides and makes me want to crawl over to him and put my head in the crease of his neck so I can get closer to the source. *No,* I shake away the reminders and focus back on the road. My fingers felt their way to the radio, and I turned it on, trying to fill the obvious silence with the void of music.

Country music had the speakers coming to life. It isn't a song I am familiar with so I just listen along as we drive. The only other noise in the cab are the breaths we take along the way.

Silence hangs like a dead weight between us. A few times I

catch him staring my way, but he turns away when my eyes meet his. I want to say something, anything, but we'd already decided on Saturday and I don't want to ruin today with any kind of talk. So I remain silent.

Twenty minutes passed, and I pulled up to the hospital. Parking the truck, I opened the door and slid out, following Remington. Seemingly confused, he opened his mouth. "Where are you going?"

"Well, I'm coming with you."

"No need."

"Remington Cole. If you think for a second, I'll sit in your truck alone when dusk is falling you have another thing coming. I'll sit and be quiet. Please... don't make me sit all alone in the dark." It is almost a demand and a plea.

I'd spent enough time alone waiting for Remington lately.

Maybe the physical therapist could walk through his routines with me so I can help him.

We sign in at the front desk and wait patiently to be called back. Remington and I sit yet again in awkward silence, his silver cane sitting beside him. Most of the people here are in wheelchairs, crutches, or walkers. I mean, it is physical therapy.

Five minutes later a tall, dark-haired guy comes our way with a big hello for Remington. "Hey, man. How are you doing today?"

"I've been worse, I suppose," Rem responds.

He was attractive, with dark chocolate brown eyes and a smile pronounced by an adorable pair of dimples. His lips quirk up at the side when he notices me, and I can't help but smile back. "Well, hello there. I'm Theo, and you are..." he holds out his hand, and I take it.

"Faith. Nice to meet you." His eyes ran between us. "And what's your relation? You two dating, married..." I believed at first it was an odd question to ask, but I suppose if I was the one helping him at home they'd want to know. But before I have a chance to respond, Rem answers for me.

"She's a…" his eyes met mine as if he was searching for the right thing to say, "friend."

"All right, well glad you could join us today. Probably a better idea to have someone else know the exercises we talk about here in case you need help at home."

"That won't be necessary."

He didn't even blink at Remington's blunt response. If they'd been working together, he probably understood Remington was a man of few words. "Right this way." He leads us back through the workout areas.

A lot of the people in the facility seemed high school age, and I realized this was a sports therapy center too.

Walking toward the back of the building, we headed to where tables lined up against the wall. "Okay, Remington, let's start with our normal stretches and leg lifts. Get up and lie on your back on the table there."

Remington's eyes meet mine. It is almost as if he was waiting to see if I was leaving before doing as he was told.

A minute later he is lying back on the table, and I let my eyes trail the length of his body. Perusal at its finest. He has on a black tee today, and his tattoos peek out from below the sleeves. His washed-out jeans have tears in them, but not the kind you'd find in store. Genuine holes from working them so much doing hard manual labor.

A flashback of Remington standing in the sun, sweat dripping down his body with a backward hat on as he fixes a fence, attacks my brain and I can't help but gulp at the way it makes me feel all tingly. *How is it he makes me feel so weak? So desperate?*

My heart pulses in my chest, sadness breaking it apart as I realize this could be our new normal; silenced car rides, awkward moments, and distance between us. A lump forms in my throat and I can't seem to choke it down, so I walk away. I can't break down here. Not in front of people I don't know. I scan briefly to where Remington is doing leg exercises.

He hasn't noticed I'm no longer right beside him, so I make my way out to the front of the building and breathe in the air deeply. The sky is dark as nighttime closes in around me. A small breeze stirs the hair on the back of my head, leaving behind a chill. It smells like rain is coming. My nose keen to the change in the air temp and wind. Shortly after, I hear the all too familiar tink tink tink of raindrops on the roof above me. It's a slow drizzle.

I find my way back inside and find Remington still working on his leg. There's a slight sheen of sweat brimming his forehead, and I have the crazy urge to wipe it away with my fingers. How is it he looks sexy as hell any time I get a glimpse of him?

His eyes met mine as I walked back into the room, but he didn't smile. Although the smile across Theo's face was broad. The sad part was it did nothing for me.

The rest of the therapy session flies by in a heated streak of exercises and stretches. I was exhausted by the time Theo said we were done. Between the therapy session and the drive back to the stables, the car was bathed in utter silence. So quiet you could probably hear a pin drop or the soft echo of my heartbeat. My heart urged me to talk, to say anything, but my brain said no. So, there I sat, completely numb and silent.

I expected him to get out of the truck and leave tonight without even a thank you, but to my surprise he did say it. My heart soared for two point five seconds before it dropped back to reality. Remington still didn't remember, and I hated it.

I wanted to do something, anything, to flicker a tiny blip in his brain. Something to shatter us wide open so we could mend back together again.

Before I knew it, it was after nine when I showed back up at the bed and breakfast. I opened the door to a wide-eyed Nova. "Girl, where have you been? I texted you like ten times."

"Nova... I didn't expect for you to be back so soon. Was it bad?"

"It was perfect. Jameson and I had a great time. He said a simple kiss and a perfect date was the best way to end the night."

"What'd you do? Wait, you said kiss... how was the kiss?"

I watched as her cheeks flushed. "It was the perfect amount of soft and firm. Gentle and needy. Grade A material."

I reminisced about the first time Remington and I had kissed. I remember I was nervous from all the butterflies swarming in my belly. I had started to sweat, and I was so worried I would be a bad kisser and he wouldn't want to do it again. He was my first crush, my first love and even if our first kiss was a bunch of fumbling nonsense, I wanted it to be the first one of forever.

It's been how many years and I can still remember the way he felt against my lips. The way his tongue swept into my mouth and took control. The way he tasted. The biggest smile, followed by the fresh blush as it slowly spread up his cheeks. We were only babies then. We've grown so much since then.

Shaking my head, I get back to Nova. "So... stop stalling. Tell me, what did you do?"

"He took me to Maggie's, a town over. It wasn't super fancy, but it was such a nice night. River views, music in the background, pork chops and clams, and a bottle of wine. It was perfect."

"Oh man, it seems like the sweetest date. A perfect first date. So, are you seeing him again?"

She smiles shyly. "He already asked to see me again before I leave."

"Aww, babe, I'm so excited for you. When is this happening?"

"He wanted to do a date again on Saturday but I'm not sure how he's going to possibly top this date."

"Hunny, he's a country boy. They tend to plan the best dates. I remember when Remington used to plan dates for us. When we were kids, we were so broke, but he still made the best of it. Whether it be a picnic in the back of his truck under the stars, fishing in the creek, or hanging out in the hot springs, it was special. But I guess it was always special because it was with him, now that I think about it."

"You totally miss him, don't you?"

"How can you tell?"

"Oh, I don't know. Maybe it's the sad eyes and the hopeful expression you get each time you think about him."

"I wish there was something I could do, ya know? Something that'd catch his attention. Something to make him say, wait, I remember or a phrase he'd pick up and... lightbulb."

"Give him time, girl. It'll work out. Hey, wait... have you two been back to the springs since he was released from the hospital?"

"Yeah," I say, remembering the last time we were there and fought.

"What about going somewhere that holds good memories?"

"I guess I hadn't thought about it."

"Has he said anything to you since he's been home?"

"Yeah, we're meeting to talk on Saturday. I need to know where we stand. I need to know if he's willing to try or not. I don't like this situation. I can't control the outcome, and it scares me almost as much as him walking away. I don't want him to walk away again." A tear slips down my cheek, one emotion letting loose without permission. I've cried a river's worth over Remington Cole, what's another few drops?

"Aww, Faith, if he knows what's good for him, he'll give it a try. I mean, you can't hold a grudge against someone forever, right? Or maybe... you may not want to hear this, but maybe it's time to get closure and move on."

Friday came and went, and before I knew it, Saturday had crept up on us. Nova was giddy with excitement over her second date with Jameson, while I had a lump in my gut over how my conversation with Remington would pan out later in the day.

Yet again, I helped Nova get ready for her date this afternoon. It is colder out today as autumn set in, so she chose blue jeans with a cami and cardigan. I'd allowed her to borrow my pearl necklace, and she sported Tom shoes with her outfit.

She left her hair down this time, curled it, and used a light layer of makeup to give away a flawless appearance. I couldn't get over how phenomenal my friend was when she wore more than old sweatpants and a messy bun. If Jameson didn't see it, he damn sure didn't deserve her. They were spending the late afternoon and evening together, so I wished her farewell halfway through the day.

Remington had sent me a text earlier today asking what time I was coming over to talk, and I hadn't responded for half an hour. I didn't want to talk; in fact, I was scared. I have a bad feeling in my gut he is going to speak the words I didn't want to hear. I knew, whatever happened today, I would still move on, either with or without him. If it was with him, it may simply be harder the second time around.

The willow trees lining the stables entrance have changed from green to yellowish or blue color. It's funny how they're the last trees to drop their leaves in autumn. How hadn't I noticed the change in the trees?

The sky is filled with clouds today, and I wonder how it shadowed what was about to happen.

A part of me worried how I'd react tonight when we finally talked. This was the accumulation of over a month of not talking, worrying, and dreading.

I'd driven back into my self-imposed cage, where I'd once felt so free. Where once I'd found peace and quiet with the love of my life, but now I was about to find out what happened from here out, and I wasn't sure I was ready for the answer on the other side.

I smile at Reagan as I pull up to the bunkhouse, shut off the car, and grab the bag from my back seat.

"Welcome back, girl! It's been overflowing with testosterone since you left. Did you two have a fun?" she asked, grinning widely at me, her hair sticking to her head like she'd been sweating.

I nod. "Hey, Rea. We did. Nova has another date with Jameson tonight."

She squeals. "No way, how awesome. He deserves a love life."

My brow furrows. "Hey, you said testosterone, but isn't Cassidy Mae here too?"

She nods. "Yeah, but she's working through her own stuff right now. That or hanging out with my brother." She rolls her eyes and I can't stop the laugh that freely falls from my mouth.

We stand there for a few seconds before I nod my head toward the bunkhouse. "Have you seen him recently?"

She bites her lip. "Yep, he's been here for a couple hours. Not sure what he's doing. You two are finally willing to sit down and talk it out?"

"Yeah, I think it's about time."

"Right on. All the luck."

I walked toward the bunkhouse, dread pulling down deep to my toes. So in I walked, heart in my throat, sweaty palms, and hope in my soul.

REMINGTON

The day before Faith left to spend a couple of days with Nova, I'd been given the letter I'd written her the morning of my accident. Ever since, I've been having some memories and flashbacks. Granted, they haven't all returned, but they've slowly revealed glimpses of her and I back together since she left me over four years ago.

I'm confused.

I'm angry I can't remember them all.

I wish the accident hadn't happened and wrecked my life again.

I feel helpless, but a tiny flicker of hope once fleeting has now returned, and I choose to believe if I let it smolder long enough, a slow flame will ignite.

The doorknob to the bunkhouse turns and my breath halts in my chest, waiting to see if it's her. The chime on the clock dings letting me know it's the top of the hour. I sit and listen to the click, click, click it makes my heart in my throat.

Blonde hair sweeps over her shoulder as she turns to push the door closed slowly, so it doesn't slam. It still needs a coat of WD40 because the squeak is unmistakable. I'm sitting on the couch in the living room as the tv drones on in front of me. Some cooking show I stopped watching about ten minutes ago.

Her eyes find mine and silence hangs like a cold friend between us before she starts moving my way. A small smile graces her beautiful face, but it never reaches out to touch her eyes. There's a hesitation in the way she holds herself, the way she walks. She's afraid. I can tell by her unsure posture.

Earlier today, I felt the same way. Maybe saying no to all of this would be easier. To stop it before it gets started again. To let us both down easy so we can move on and live our own separate lives, allowed to lick our wounds in private. But fuck me, I've forever been a little selfish and seeing her now reminds me why.

She's engraved herself so far into my soul I couldn't say no to her without giving it one more chance. I've only ever seen her. I've only ever wanted her and even when I couldn't remember these last few months, I still felt a pull to her unlike anything I've ever felt toward anyone else.

But before I break down and tell her I'll fight; I want to know what she's thinking. Right now, we're both open books. All the truths have been brought to light, what will she say about the night I lost her the first time? About the memories made since she returned home?

"Evenin' Rem." Her smile was small and nervous. I felt the same way.

"Hey, Faith." I try to give her back a smile, thinking it would make her feel a little more comfortable. But who was I kidding? It was awkward all the way around. "You ready to talk?"

"No..." She shakes her head, "but yes?" It's almost a question asking how I feel about it.

I scoot over and pat the spot next to me on the couch. I don't want her to be too far away when we talk. The feeling she'll run overwhelms me, and I push it down. This conversation has been on my mind all day and I'm still not sure I have the right words to say to her, but I'll try because it's what she deserves.

It's weird how I feel like I've lost years of my life, yet it's only been a couple of months. Her letters kept me caught up on the happenings since then. Cassidy Mae came back into Beau's life and it's a whole lotta crazy. Apparently, she's divorcing her husband and running home. I'll be catching up in real time now too, hopefully remembering more as time passes because I want to remember each moment with her. Every. Single. Moment.

I open my mouth to speak, but she silences me. "Let me start, please? I have a lot to say and I want to get it off my chest."

I nod and smile, encouraging her to continue. "I want to talk about that night. The night," she says, sighing. I nod again. She tells me all about how she felt walking in to see her best friend straddling me shirtless on the bed. Lipstick on my face, my hands on her ass. The shock. The anger. The sadness. The times I told her it was only ever her and then seeing me with Sofia. It breaks my heart listening to her as she tells me about every emotion she felt.

She then continues on to tell me how she felt reading my letter and how if she had known she wouldn't have run. I didn't blame her for running. After a while, I understood how it appeared, although I hated her for it.

I remain silent as she talks, letting her voice lull me into a peace only she can fully give me. As far as I remember, this is the first time we've sat for this long and simply talked. It's nice, comfortable and reminds me of all the times we did this when we were dating. Staying up all night long talking about whatever suited our fancy.

There's a tension between us I can't shake, but I need to keep responding. "When you didn't respond to any of my letters, I figured you'd finally moved on. Decided you were bigger than this little town and me. You were better than this place, Faith. It's never been a question in my mind. I didn't want to hold you back, but I wanted you to know the truth, so I did the only thing I could think of, I wrote it down and sent it to you."

Her eyes filled with sadness. "Oh, Rem."

"Did you know I came to see you?"

She nods slowly. "I remember you yelling at me about it in one of our fights before the accident."

"Yeah, it was about two months after you left, I came to find you. I wanted to apologize and talk in person. Drove to your dorm and watched as some other guy threw his arm over your shoulder and walked back inside with you. You seemed so chummy. You were smiling. My brain fled to all the wrong scenarios. I couldn't think about you or him or what the two of you were doing together. It was too hard, so I left. Started up my old beat-up truck and drove away without a second glance in the rearview mirror."

"I wasn't with him, Rem. It was my roommate's boyfriend at the time."

"I didn't know. All I knew was the girl I'd loved for most of my life wasn't mine anymore and it cut pretty deep."

"You're breaking my heart, Rem," she whispers softly, meeting my gaze.

"You broke mine first." My voice cracks without my permission, but it's the truth. Her eyes widen as if in surprise. Maybe when she thought I cheated, she assumed her heart was the only one that broke. I wanted her to know.

We sit in silence for a couple of minutes, not knowing what to say next. My heart feels like it's been sliced open and is sitting there waiting for her to sew it back together.

"I'm sorry one wrong decision led to us being separated for years. If I could take it all back, I would. I'd give us our second chance. I'd give you all my heartbreaks knowing you'd be there to pick me up afterward. Four years is too long to feel broken, to miss the other half of my soul." She says it softly.

I swallow. "I guess I can't help the way my heart wants you. I want you in any way I can have you. Because I may have been in major like with a scrawny little girl, but I fell, hardcore in love with the woman she became and is becoming. I'm so proud of you. You left for college, received a degree, worked in the real world, outside the walls of this little town, and you thrived."

She shakes her head, biting her lip. "I'm sorry for not responding to the letters. You can't help who your heart wants, who you fall in love with and I fell in love with a six-foot tall, sixteen-year-old boy with a Kid Rock shirt and funky hair do."

I can't help the chuckle as it falls from my mouth. "Hey, now. I believed I was pretty suave back then."

She reaches up and lets her fingers slip through my hair. I memorize how it feels. "Rem. You have perfect *dude* hair, why did you have to highlight the tips blonde? Promise me you'll never do it again."

I nod. "Promise."

Her eyes shine as she waits to ask the next question, and I wonder if she's holding back tears. "So, you remember?"

I glance down, but my eyes continually drift back to her after a few seconds. "Not all of them. Nova left me the note before she headed to the bed and breakfast; all of a sudden, the light switch flipped. I started to remember things, but they weren't from the *us* back then, it was recent. As the day continued on, a few more things clicked into place. Hell, I dreamed about us. I wanted to believe what you said so badly. In my heart, I knew it was true, but my brain took a little while to catch up."

She focuses on me now, a tear streaking down her face. "I love you, Remington Cole. I will forever and until the end of time. Heartbreak after heartbreak, it's still been you. I wouldn't pick a heartbreak with anyone else."

"I didn't realize when I was young how truly and wholly, I could love you, but now I do. I get it... what I didn't know then. We could be a million miles apart, in different time zones, and I would still love you better than it's possible to love another person. You are my person. I want to love you in a way the world longs for, a love true and lasting."

"I'm not leaving you this time, Rem. I want to fight for us."

"In case you haven't noticed, I'm a fighter. I've been fighting for us for years. You had to figure it out. Some days may be shit. We may fight, we may get angry. I've fucked up things, Lord knows it. I'm a Cole for Christ's sake, but I promise to you I'll be whatever you need me to be. I would give up my world to be with you."

She smiles and this time it reaches her eyes, but I don't stop yet. "I'm all in. All fucking in with you this time. No take backs. No walking away. Our story has been written in letters for years and I say it's about time we stop writing about it and start living it. What do you think?"

"I think it sounds about perfect. And Rem..."

"Yeah?"

A sob escapes her throat. "I won't run again, Rem. I'm all in too."

Wetness leaks from my eyes and I'm man enough to cry, but these tears aren't sadness this time, they're joy for all the possibilities.

Without saying another word, I swoop in and capture her lips. I've missed these lips, these kisses. Her kisses. Once I run my tongue along her lips, she parts immediately, allowing me a taste of her. "I love you too, Faith. Always yours."

I will never stop being there to love and protect her, it's a strong sense. Stronger than the one I had all those years ago. This time it feels real, stemming from deep inside my heart and stretching outward. I love this woman.

We hang out for a little while before she tells me she needs to head back to the bed and breakfast. Nova is leaving in the morning and she wants to spend more time with her best friend. What she doesn't know is Nova will be helping me with my little plan tomorrow, and she won't be leaving in the morning.

She stands to leave, and I stand with her. I pull her into me and kiss her on the forehead like I used to do when we were younger. For the first time in months my heart doesn't hurt. There's no longer a pressure sitting on my chest making it hard to breathe. My eyes find her lips and her pink tongue slips out to wet them, knowing I'll bend down to kiss her one last time before she leaves.

I don't want her to leave, but it will be the last time she has to leave me.

As if all the pieces have finally snapped into place, I complete the song I've been unable to finish for the last couple of months, too in my own head. My heart soars. All it took was finding my way back to her to finish the notes. She was my muse. A beautiful array of notes and lyrics spread out across the page. Always has been, always will be.

I lean down and devour her mouth. She tastes like sunshine and sugar and I can't get enough. I bite her bottom lip and she moans, her body pressing into me further. I skim her lips with my tongue, begging for entrance, and she opens willingly. My tongue entwines with hers and does a dance of love. This isn't the searing, passionate kiss like the night she left on the date with Colton. No, this is a promise—a kiss of forever.

I could kiss her forever and I don't want to stop, but I know I should. She feels perfect in my arms, and I don't want to release her yet. So, I squeeze a little tighter, kiss her a little longer, make love to her mouth, leaving her with a promise of forever. I have a surprise tomorrow and I'm hoping she loves it. It may scare her, but I need to do it. It's the perfect *all-in* grand gesture.

She pulls away, and I let my forehead press against hers. Our breaths are short and ragged. She laughs lightly and I chuckle along. "I've missed you so damn much."

I breathe her in. "You sure you have to leave tonight?"

A small smile crosses her lips. "Yes, I want to see Nova before she leaves. Who knows when she'll visit again."

I pull back and wink at her. "Oh, I think she'll be back before you know it if Jameson has anything to say about it. He's pretty smitten with her."

Her smile broadens, reaching her eyes this time. "Yeah? It's awesome because I'm pretty sure she's in the same love boat."

"Okay," I pout. "If you must."

"Don't worry, I'll be seeing you tomorrow."

"You bet your cute ass you will." *If only you knew how much.* I want to say it, but refrain.

———

I couldn't sleep. All night long I tossed and turned, my heart in my throat. Today was the start of my new forever, one with Faith hopefully by my side. My plan was a little crazy, but I was hoping she saw it as more endearing than crazy.

I'd woken up early and cleaned up around the house—picking up laundry, washing dishes, sweeping, and dusting. I glance at the clock, eight in the morning. Two hours until my plan starts. My phone pings in the other room and I run over to grab it.

Beau: I'm about to head into town. Are you sure about both tires?

Me: Yes, she can fix one by herself, not two.

Beau: All right, makes sense. Hope she forgives me.

Me: She will. I promise it'll all work out.

Beau: Well, best of luck.

I had to run into town and hit Orly's flower shop, the grocery store to make dinner for us later, and to get some other essentials. I stripped my clothes in the bathroom before turning on the water to take a shower. Stepping under the stream, I let the water rush over me as I think about my plan of events today. I'm restless, yet riddled with nerves. It's like they've been dosed with drugs because my body is on fire.

I turned off the shower and opened the curtain to grab a towel to dry off. Steam is covering the mirror and I wipe it away so I can see my face.

Taking a deep breath to prepare myself, I realize I can do this. I take the time to towel off and then walk into my room to get dressed. One more glance in the mirror, a quick brush of my teeth, and I leave the house to drive into town, my heart pounding out a staccato against the cage it's being held in.

FAITH

Nova came in from the date super late last night, so I can only assume things went well. She's still sleeping in the bed beside me and I don't want to bother her, so I'm extra quiet as I make my way to the bathroom to shower. Memories from my chat with Rem seep into my brain and I get all tingly thinking about seeing him again today. The butterflies are finally back. The lion previously situated on my chest is no longer there.

I'm finally seeing the light at the end of the tunnel. I gaze at myself in the mirror and for the first time in months there's less baggage under my eyes and I dare say I'm happy. I turned on the water and let the room start to steam up before I dropped my clothes off in a pool on the floor. The water wasn't hot enough, and I cranked the heat a little more. I liked my showers scalding. I wash my hair and body quickly, not wanting to use all the hot water.

I grab a towel from the rack beside the shower, then reach up and turn the knob. The water stops, and I step out to dry off. Grabbing my clothes from the toilet seat, I put them on. I'm wearing a plain navy tee, Levi jean shorts, some sexy underthings for later, and some cute booties. The blue jean shorts stick to me since I'm still a little sticky from the steam in the bathroom. I hit the fan and hope it takes care of the steam bath happening.

Nova is sitting on the bed, smiling at me. "Morning, Faith."

"Good morning, you. How was your date last night?"

She shook her head. "Nuh uh, you tell me how yours was first."

A flush bloomed across my cheek, bathing my skin in a light red color. "It was amazing. He asked me to stay over last night, but I told him I wanted to see my best friend off this morning."

"Well, that was nice of you, but you could've stayed."

I can't help the corners of my lips as they tip up in a smile again. My mouth is starting to hurt from all the smiling I've done in the last twelve hours. "I'll see him again today."

She winked at me. "Yep, you will. All right, let me get a shower and then I'll need to start packing up my stuff. Wanna grab breakfast before I head out?"

"Sure, I like this idea."

I get myself together as she hits the bathroom for a shower. It takes her fifteen minutes to shower before we're both back in the room packing up our clothes. She stops and turns to me. "So, how about Bodine's and you can tell me all about last night?"

"Yeah, let's do it. I'll take my car so we can both leave right from Bodine's."

She smiles, but there's something off about it. She's been extra fidgety this morning and I want to ask her what's up, but I'm worried it's about something that happened with Jameson last night and I don't want to push it. "Okay, that'll work."

We head out to the car and I realize automatically my back two tires are flat. "You're kidding me!" I run my hands through my hair and pull.

"What? What's wrong?" Nova hurries over, concerned.

"My back tires are flat and I only have one spare. How did I not notice it last night?"

"Oh, man. Well, we can take my car to breakfast and then I'll drive you home afterward. Maybe Rem can swing by and fix it."

I sigh. "Okay, this is the last thing I wanted to deal with today."

"Hey," she says, patting my shoulder. "It'll be all right; I promise. Let's grab a bite to eat and get your mind off it."

"Yeah, let's do it." She slips her phone from her pocket and sends a text message.

Odd.

The smell of bacon hits us as we walk through the front door of Bodine's. Patty walks past carrying a tray and hollers to pick a seat wherever and she'll be right over. We make our way to a booth near the back.

She swings by our booth and sets down some menus and says she'll be back in a minute. The diner is hopping this morning as everyone enjoys their breakfast feasts. From pancakes, to hash browns, to grits, and anything in between people, young and old, are happily munching away. I smile as a little boy waves at me from a table across the way and I wave back.

"Okie dokey, man busy morning today," Patty says as she stops back, a writing pad in her hand. "Hey, welcome back! What can I get for you ladies?"

Nova speaks first, "I don't know about y'all but I'm starving so I'm diving in with the hearty breakfast plate - buttermilk pancakes, eggs sunny side up, bacon, and a fruit cup - please."

"One of our favorites, you made an excellent choice." Patty replies. "And for you, Faith?"

"Oooo, I love how y'all are on a first name basis!" Nova laughs.

"Small town life, don't you love it?" I say and Patty nods.

I speak up. "I'll have the stuffed biscuits and gravy and a mimosa."

"Sounds good too. Damn, I'd like a mimosa, but I have to drive..." Nova says, peering back down at the menu.

"All right, ladies, this should be out shortly."

"Stay a little while longer," I pout at her. I forgot how much I loved hanging out with Nova. I almost don't want her to leave, but I also want her to leave so I can have Remington all to myself for the rest of the day. I have big plans for him.

I'm gazing out the window when a familiar truck passes by. "Huh, wonder what Rem is doing in town today?" I say out loud.

Nova shrugs. "Maybe he needs to stop by the grocery store or something. Ohhhh, maybe he's making you dinner tonight."

"Ahh, sounds fantastic!" I whisper-shout. I'm so giddy. Electricity lights up my veins and I haven't felt this alive since the night before Remington ended up in the hospital for a month. We're finally getting back to us and I'm so damn excited.

My nosey self watches as he pulls into Moonshine Springs Grocer parking lot and gets out.

"Hey, so tell me about your date with Jameson last night." I say, taking a sip of the mimosa Patty dropped off at the table.

"It was amazing. We stopped at this hole in the wall barbecue joint in the next town over and ate way too much food, but damn it was the most delicious thing I've ever had in my life."

"Yum, I love barbecue. And then..."

"Well, when we were done, I told him I didn't feel like heading home yet, so we visited the outlook."

"Oooo, you went to *the spot* on your second date. Isn't it magical out there? Sitting in the back of the truck, his arms around you, underneath the midnight sky littered with stars, with the sound of crickets and frogs from the crick setting the background mood. Ahhh, those were some of my favorite nights."

She blushes a little. "Yeah, it was a lot of fun."

"Did you kiss him again?"

"Yeah..." She wasn't trying to give up any extra information, but I can tell her blush is spreading. She'd done a little more than only kissing, but Nova always seemed embarrassed talking about doing stuff with guys, so I didn't want to push her into telling me if she didn't want to. "We got to second base last night."

"What?!" I exclaimed. "You naughty little minx."

She glances around, "Shhh... Faith."

"I'm sorry, I'm so excited for you."

"All right, now dish. What happened with you and Remington last night?"

"A lot of I'm sorry, some tears, some kissing. We pretty much talked about our past, the letters, to the accident, to how I felt, to how he felt. We've decided to give this a full shot. We're both all in."

"Babe! I'm so incredibly happy for you. You deserve your happily ever after."

Emotions clog my brain and unshed tears line my eyes. "I do deserve it and I'm so glad it's with Rem. I mean, I know we have a long road ahead of us, but I can't wait for it to start."

Our food shows up and conversation quiets down while we eat breakfast. It's a comfortable silence. As I'm eating, I notice Remington's truck heads back down the road toward home, and I can't help but wonder what he's up to. I'll find out later.

I pull out my phone to text him.

Me: Hey, you.

Remington: Hey, babe. How's your day so far?

Me: Kind of weird. Both of my back tires were flat when I walked out to get in my car and head to breakfast with Nova at Bodine's.

Remington: Do I need to come get you?

Me: No, Nova said, she'll drop me back at the bunkhouse when we're done.

Remington: Okay, I can help with it later today.

Me: Thank you. You still all in after last night? No cold feet?

Remington: My feet are nice and toasty today. I have plans for you tonight.

Me: I saw you at the grocer earlier, you making dinner?

Remington: Don't ruin my surprise, woman.

Me: Never...

Remington: Uh huh. So, how's Nova this morning? How was her date?

Nova is scrutinizing me, a grin plastered across her face when I glance over. "What?" I say.

"Oh nothing. You must be talking to captain swoon cause your face is all lit up right now like you've won the jackpot."

"It's Rem."

"I figured."

Focusing back down at my phone, I type out my next message.

Me: They got to second base. *Wink emoji*

Remington: Well, I won't lie. I'm hoping for a damn home run this evening.

Me: Since when do you play baseball?

Remington: Oh baby, you can play with my bat and balls any time you want.

Me: Naughty.

Remington: Wait til later.

Me: Can't wait.

Remington: See you later, babe.

I couldn't help but swallow at his perverse words. I closed my legs, trying to control the things his naughty words were doing to my lady bits. It'd been way too damn long since I'd gotten laid, and I needed a bit of vitamin D tonight.

Peering back at the texts, I grinned again. Gone was the broody Remington I'd seen for the last several months and in came this charming, cheeky man whom I couldn't get enough of.

Patty brought us the check as we were finishing our meals, and I paid. "You didn't have to pay, I could've paid." Nova tightened her eyes at me.

"It's my treat. You've done so much for me this week, it's the least I could do."

"Well, thank you."

"You're welcome. You ready to head out?"

"For sure."

We leave a tip on the table for Patty and head out of the restaurant. She waves goodbye and we pass her taking care of another customer. I circle around the front of Nova's car and hop in the passenger's side.

"So," I ask as she pulls onto Main Street. "When are you seeing Jameson again? You guys doing long distance?"

"Yeah, I think so. It's only a three-hour drive so I think I'll visit him some weekends and then he'll visit me in the city some weekends."

"Wouldn't I love to be a fly on the wall. Can you imagine any of these guys dealing with the city and the traffic?"

She laughs. "I know, right?"

"You'll have to take all the pictures of Jameson enjoying city life."

"Oh, I will."

"I think you like him; you seriously like him." I sing song and laugh.

She grins over at me. "I do. Jameson is different, ya know? He's a true gentleman, one of the good ones. And I know it's only been two dates, but it feels like I've known him my whole life. I feel comfortable with him."

I understand the feeling completely and nod along. "I'm happy for you, Nov."

"I am too. I hope it continues. After last time, I've shied away from dating and men in general."

"You can't shell up for the rest of your life. Jameson may be the guy who makes you believe in forever."

Her eyes found mine briefly before returning to the road. "Like Rem has been for you?"

A smile creased the corners of my lips as I reminisced about Rem. "Yeah, I guess so. Rem is cooking me dinner and maybe visiting our favorite spot. He texted me earlier."

"You guys are seriously perfect for each other. I can't wait to see what happens next."

I smiled to myself. I happened to think so too. A part of me worried last night had been a dream, and I'd imagined Remington saying it, but maybe it hadn't happened. I'd worried as soon as I woke up it'd slip away and I'd still be missing him. But I had a text message waiting for me this morning when I woke up saying I love you from Rem.

It soothed me in a way I wasn't fully expecting and left a warm, happy feeling lingering behind it.

Nova's phone rang from its place on her console. She grabbed it and hit the answer button. "Hello?" She watched me for a brief second as she answered her phone. "Oh, hi Rem. What can I do for you?"

I furrowed my brows. Why was he calling her? Wait, and how did he get her phone number? I don't remember giving it to him.

I shrugged it off. Maybe they'd exchanged phone numbers at some point, so I guess I shouldn't be too surprised.

"Sure, Remington. We were on our way to the bunkhouse, but I guess I can stop and grab it for you. How many, only one?" She listened, nodding along. "Okie dokey. See you soon."

I was staring at her when she hung up. "What's he calling about?"

"Oh, Remington needs me to stop at the grocer. He forgot something for y'alls dinner later on tonight."

"Why can't he run out?"

"I don't know. He's probably working on something and can't pull himself away." I nod. I mean, it made sense.

A couple of minutes later, we were back at the grocer and I sat in the car while Nova ran inside. I thumped out a beat on the dash with my fingers as I listened to the sweet sound of Niko Moon coming through the speakers.

Her face was flushed as she came back to the car and she was breathing heavily like she'd been rushing. "Sorry, it took me forever to find exactly what I needed and then I had to call him to verify and...ugh."

"No worries. The longer you're here the more time I get to spend with you." We head toward McCoy's farm, and my heart started skipping beats. I hadn't been to Rem's house, and this would be my first time seeing it. The anticipation was killing me.

As she slows down, she turns onto a gravel road, the car dipping with each bump and spewing dust all around us. "Hey, do you want to run it in for him? I'll wait in the car in case you two feel like sucking face or anything." She thumps her fingers on the steering wheel, an anxious tick I'd picked up on over the years.

"Sure, I can," I say, a smile plastered across my face.

"Okay, awesome. I'll wait in the car and once you're done, we'll get you squared away at the bunkhouse. Last time I checked you have a dinner date tonight and my girl needs all the help getting ready for it."

"Okay." I rub my hands up and down my thighs as I wondered how the inside of the house was designed.

The sun beat down on the car as the gravel crackled under its tires. Wooden rail fences lined the driveway and new grass was finally starting to grow again. The house was a two-story farmhouse with a wraparound front porch. It was all of my dreams come to life about us growing up and a part of me was still upset Remington had built it without me.

Dust kicks up around us as the car came to a stop in front of the house. The front lacks color and I envision a few flowerbeds which would add a nice touch. I'd mention it to Rem.

Nova shuts off the car, and I unbuckle my seat belt, excited to see the house I'd only ever heard about. My feet meet ground as I step out of her car. I walk around the front of the car and head toward the porch, and take the steps one at a time. Glancing right, I see a hanging swing at the end, and I can picture us sitting there swinging while we talk about our day. Or maybe swinging trying to put a baby to sleep. A tear threatens to fall, but I quickly wipe it away. I hoped it was in our future.

Turning back to the car, my eyes find Nova waving at me, essentially shooing me in.

I knock on the door twice with no answer, so I cracked the door and spoke inside. "Rem..."

I am still met by silence, so I open the door a little wider and stepped inside. "Hey, Rem, you here?"

"Hey, Faith! I'm back here!" he yells from somewhere deeper inside the house.

The foyer is bright and airy, light shining in through the windows to the sides of the door. It was beautiful.

There are pictures lining the light gray wall as I walk back toward Remington's voice. Pictures of us from high school and from college hung in wooden picture frames. It brings special memories to me as I walked. I also notice several pictures I had at the bunkhouse.

Why are they here?

The farther I walked into the house; the more trinkets I see. My life seemed to fall into place here and it gave my heart life. I wanted them to stay here forever. Hell, I wanted to be here.

As I peer into the living room, I see Remington passing in front of a stone fireplace. He grins at me as he watches me walk into the room and winks at me nervously. I can't help but stare at the twinkle in his eyes as he saw me.

"Hey, here's the stuff you needed."

"Thank you." He walks over and takes the bag from me before placing it down on the coffee table.

The dress pants he is wearing hug his muscular thighs and where I expected to see boots, he wears dress shoes all complimented by a dark blue button down that complimented the blue in his eyes. The arms of his shirt, pulling around his biceps, made my mouth water. His hair is gelled, and he shaved today.

Fuck, my guy is hot, even with clothes on.

My insides tingle, thinking about what happens when all those fancy clothes come off. I knew what he looked like naked, and I am anxious to see it again.

But why was he dressed up? I am confused. I also feel way underdressed.

He walks over, leaned in to hug me, and pressed a soft kiss to my cheek. "Hey, babe. I'm so glad you're here."

"Rem, what's going on? Why is my stuff here? What..."

He cuts me off before I can continue. "I feel like I may puke, can you... let me get it all out first?" I nod, standing there awkwardly. "Here, have a seat on the couch." He presses his hand slightly to my back as he helps me sit, and I can feel the warmth.

"Okay, Rem, you have my attention." My foot bounces against the floor as I waited for him to speak.

Licking his lips, he finally breaks the silence. "Last night, we made some promises. We decided we were doing this, and we were all in, right? So today, I drove over to the stables and packed up your stuff. I wanted to move you in and surprise you. If we're doing this, then I want to jump in with both feet. These past months have been some of the worst in my life and I know the one constant is I wouldn't want to do this with anyone else. I love you, Faith, and instead of dragging this out any further, I want to make us a permanent thing. You deserve more than love letters from me.

"You need a home where we can build a life.

A home we can raise children in.

A starting point for the rest of forever."

My eyes started to tear up as I listen to the words I'd been waiting to hear for years.

Slowly lowering himself to one knee in front of the couch, he appraises me with unshed tears in his eyes.

"Faith Evans. I have loved you since the moment my eyes first saw you. I loved you still when you left. I loved you when I didn't know I did. I will love you for the rest of my life. So, today, here, I want to start living it. I want you to move in with me. I want you to wear my ring." He pulls out a velvet blue box from his pocket and opens it.

I clasped my hands to my chest as he opened the ring box. An emerald cut blue sapphire ring with a diamond halo sat in the middle, and I let a tear finally slide down my cheek. *This wasn't happening, was it?*

"Rem..." I whispered.

He gives me a big grin. "Will you marry me and make our love story outlast the hundreds of love letters spelling it out?"

"Yes!" I whisper through tears, holding my arms out to hug him. I can't believe it. I knew he wanted to be with me, but this was an all-in moment.

He hugs me before pulling the ring from the box and putting it on my finger. "When did you..." I asked him.

"When you saw me in town this morning, I was getting the final touches." My eyes finally scanned the living room, noticing all the flower bouquets on the side tables. He followed my gaze. "I had to get your favorites."

I squinted my eyes. "So, you didn't actually need Nova to stop back to the store?"

The dimples showed brilliantly in his face as he shrugged mischievously.

Tears were streaming down my face, only this time they were happy tears, not sadness. Things were finally coming together like I'd always dreamed about.

"So... when did you decide to build the house?"

"I built it for us when we were finally getting back together before my accident. I found the papers on my desk a little while after I got home from the hospital. When Nova gave me the letter, I'd written you the day of the accident. It all started coming back to me. Faith, I'm so sorry for not believing you. I should've known."

"Are you sure about all of this?" I ask, waiting to see any sign of hesitation in his face. All I saw was the dimpled smile of the boy I fell in love with in high school.

"I'm all in, Faith. You're stuck with my ass." My stomach flutters with butterflies. He could tell me daily and I wouldn't get enough.

"It's about damn time your ass figured it out." I laughed happily.

"See, I told you it'd be worth it." Nova says, sauntering over to us. "It's all on film, like you asked." She hands over the camera to Remington and I raised an eyebrow.

"Working with the enemy, huh?" I say to Nova with a laugh. "Let me guess, you had something to do with this morning, too?"

"Nope, I didn't do it. I'm pretty sure it was someone else."

My eyes narrowed at Remington. "You?"

He put his hands up in a non-defensive manner. "Nope. I was sworn to secrecy. I can't disclose the accomplices."

"Uh huh... So, why the camera?"

"I wanted us to remember this exact moment, so instead of writing about it I decided to ask Nova to film it, so in case something happens again you can show it to me instead of waiting for me to get my shit together."

"No more crazy colts for you."

"I can't promise that, but I may limit our daze-inducing sex to after I work with colts for the day instead of before."

"Rem," I said, jabbing his shoulder lightly, a slight flush creeping up my face.

Nova squirmed behind him. "And... there's my cue to leave. You can take it from here, Remington?"

He winked at me. "You betcha."

My eyes found Nova. "But..."

"Don't worry, I'll be hanging out with Jameson for a while. Let me know when the two of you are done celebrating. I'll be in town a couple more days."

"Sneaky, sneaky." I shake my head, but mouth *thank you*.

She winks at me and then turns to leave. I can't express how I am feeling. It is a lot, but I can't complain. My mind was swirling, but I was on cloud fucking nine.

REMINGTON

F aith is all mine at last. It'd been a long time coming and my nerves were frayed. I couldn't make up my mind about what I wanted to do to her first, needing all parts of her at once.

Leaning down, my breath melding with hers, our lips caressing each other, sending sparks down my spine. I'd forgotten how soft and supple they felt against my own.

Her taste is sweet and I couldn't get enough of it. She moaned into my mouth, but it was muffled by the kiss. I devoured her lips, biting her bottom lip and sucking it into my mouth. I bit lightly and felt the shiver as it crept up her skin. I don't want to close my eyes, because I am afraid I'd miss something.

"Open your eyes," I whisper, pulling away slightly, and she does as I requested. Bright blue eyes found mine, and I could see the intricately woven little bits of silver in her irises.

Those ocean blue eyes could hold my gaze forever, but I was burning for something more. Desperate to have all of her under me, with me. To be inside her again. To show her the love I've been waiting to pour over her for years.

Finally, free to express all the things I've been holding back, I want to set them loose like a beautiful kaleidoscope of butterflies.

Whispered kisses are pressed against her jawline and down the perfect curve of her neck. She tilts her head, giving me all the access to her I want, and I take advantage. My lips pause against the vein in her neck, feeling how fast her blood was pumping.

My body heated with lust and desire for the woman I love. I wanted to woo her, to seduce my girl. To speak in body language what I'd only ever spoken in words on paper.

Her eyes fall shut again as I made my way down her body, over her neckline. Each breath more rushed than the last. "I want you, Rem."

I tilt her chin up to me with my thumb and forefinger. I needed verbal confirmation after what I'd thrown at her. "You sure?"

Her eyes were half lidded with desire as she appraised me. "Fuck yes, I'm sure. I need you."

I kiss her one final time. It's rough, passionate, and extremely intimate, but what we're about to do will be so much more intimate. A solidifying of two souls, two bodies tangled together in a weave of finding our way back to each other.

"I love you," I whisper into her mouth, realizing my body is shaking with need.

"I love you too," she whispers back. My hands run down and skirt up her thighs, slowly traveling the length to her waist, grateful I can feel her soft skin against me. The shorts are in the way, but it'll be an easily remedied situation.

She curls her fingers into my shirt and tries to pull me closer as I lift her leg and drape it over my thigh. I want her to rub against me. I want her to be as needy for me as I am for her. "Rem."

"I know, baby. I feel it too." Putting my hands under her ass, I lift her off the ground, winding both of her legs around my waist. Her core is warm against me. I'd like to take her to the bedroom and make this special, but I won't last long. I need her now.

Finding an open wall, I walk her up against it, my mouth on hers again. I can't stop tasting her. My fingers skim the top of her shorts and find her button, popping it open gently and sliding down the zipper. I don't want to, but I need to set her down to get her out of these shorts and underwear.

I groan, "Killing me, baby." I grab the waistline of her shorts and glide my fingers below the waistline, grabbing her panties as well and push them down as far as I can before I drop her legs back down the floor so they can fall down.

My desire to fuck her hard up against this wall is slowly passing, and I throw a blanket from the back of the couch onto the floor by the fireplace. I bend down and pick her up, only to slowly lay her on top of the blanket. I want to feast on her properly.

I see emotions pass in her expression as her eyes find mine again. The pain vanishes, the sadness recedes, and I'm left with love.

Lowering myself on top of her, I start to kiss my way down her body again. My hands find the hemline of her shirt and she raises so I can lift it over her head. Reaching around her back, I unclasp her bra with one hand while the other finds her breast - her nipples peaked and needy. Throwing the bra behind me, my mouth finds her nipple unattended and ravishes it with licks and nips.

Her skin is perfect, blemish free. I can't think of anything else except for the beauty in front of me. My fingers skim down her body, running along the moisture seeping between the apex of her thighs. She cries out as I touch her there. I can't think straight, my blood pooling below the waist, fastly escaping from my brain.

My blood heats as I tease her most intimate parts with my fingers. I skim up and down her seam, feeling as she gets more aroused by the minute.

"Remington," she whispers, writhing beneath me. It's all I imagined and more. I slide myself down her body, peppering her flat stomach and mound with kisses before parting her legs, finding the source of my want. My mouth is there moments later. I need to taste her. I can't wait any longer. She screams and I know this is exactly what she wants. I suck, nibble, and lick at the lips of her pussy. Her beautiful pink little pussy.

It's been so damn long, and I can finally feel the familiar tingle I get when I'm so aroused. My cock is rock hard in my pants, begging me for release, the heat rising more with each lick and nibble. I haven't felt this in so long and there's no stopping now. I'll have all of her.

She pushes against me, riding my face as she takes what she needs without shame. I wrap her legs around my shoulders, giving me more access to devour her properly. I suck on her, pulling all the arousal I can from her body.

I pull away for a moment and she whimpers from the loss. Her body protests as mine does. I have her exactly where I want her, good.

Her eyes find mine and there's a hint of fury there. I stopped her from releasing. I planned to build her up. She can do better, and I'll give it to her.

Finding her pussy again, I get back to work, nipping, sucking, and licking. I pull her clit into my mouth and suck. Her hands find purchase on the blanket and for a split second I wish she was grabbing onto me as intensely.

I allow my tongue to slide back into her seam and into her warmth. I've never done this before with her, but I'm definitely enjoying this new experience. She's my fiancé now and we're about to start making a whole bunch of firsts. She holds the rest of mine, what's another one?

Her walls clamp down around me as her climax hits hard. The buildup was worth it. I drink her in and lick my lips as I pull away. "Damn, that was..."

"God, Rem. I swear it's better now than it's ever been."

I wink at her. "You're saying exactly what I want to hear from my fiancé."

Her breathing is rapid, her chest rising and falling in quick succession as she lays there panting on the floor. I get it. I feel the same damn way, but I'm not finished with her yet.

Sitting up, I crawl up her body and kiss her lips, hoping she tastes herself on my mouth. She moans into my mouth, and it gets swallowed by our kiss. I love her. My heart is pounding in my chest, beating for only her.

"Are you ready for more?" I ask, kissing her behind the ear where she likes it most.

"Born ready." She smiles lazily at me. "What are you waiting for then? I need you inside me, Rem."

"Hold on then, baby. I can't guarantee it'll be sweet. Later I'll take my time with you, but right now I can't wait any longer to make you scream my name."

I reach between us, anchoring the tip of my cock at her entrance. I'm hanging on the end of gravity, waiting to remember what ecstasy feels like within her.

"Make love to me," she says it with a shy smile.

"With pleasure, but not now. Now, I need to fuck you. Later, I'll make all the love you want. I need to feel your warmth wrapped around me."

"Then what are you waiting for?" I don't wait a second longer, plunging into her heat and almost losing my breath in the process. It's better than I remember. Each thrust in and out, and I feel like I'm already about to lose myself. I won't last long. It feels too phenomenal, too right.

I get lost in the feel of her, of us coming back together for the first of many times. "Harder," she pants, squirming below me, and I give it to her. The all too familiar tingle in my balls tells me I don't have much time left. I'm about to blow my load, but I'll make it up to her later. Reaching between us, I find her clit and rub in small circles exactly how I know she likes it. With my other hand, I skim up her body, finding her hand and raising it above her head. My fingers entwine with hers as we squeeze the blanket together.

I watch as her toes curl and her hips raise to meet me thrust for thrust. I'm pumping faster, working her clit like my life depends on it when her wet core finally clamps down on my cock and showers me with arousal. She screams my name, and a smile broadens my face. God, I've missed her so much. I can't hold off any longer. I let loose into her body, and it feels like an out of body experience. I black out for a second, it's how powerful the sex is between us.

Our breathing is ragged as my eyes find her face. Her eyes are closed and there's a smile on her lips. I lean down and brush my lips against hers, and she grabs me by the back of my neck and crushes my face into her further. Her fingers trailing the bottom of the hair on the back of my head. I love the way her fingers move through my hair.

We're still holding hands and my dick, although slowly deflating, is still within her. I don't want to move. I don't want to lose this moment.

I roll to her side and wrap my arms around her, kissing her yet again. These kisses are dangerous and addicting. My cock is already springing back to action, and I want her again.

Her giggles reach my ears. "Ready again?"

"Always ready for you, Faith. I'm forever yours, which means this cock only raises for you."

We spent the next couple of hours getting reacquainted—in the living room, bedroom, shower. Not an inch of Faith was untouched by my lips, hands, or cock.

———

I'm seated on the couch watching Faith admiring her ring. The diamonds sparkle and shine with each shift of her hand in the light. I surprised her with the exact ring she told me about when we were eighteen.

I can't help but love the smile as it lights up her face each time her eyes find it.

In the last three days I've been revived from heartbroken to whole.

Sad to happy.

It's crazy after the worst of things, how we've seemingly fallen right back into how we were. I'm sure it won't be like this forever. Relationships are hard, but I'm in this now.

The big screen over the fireplace is on, and we've been binge watching house shows. She's curled into my side, and I have my arm around the back of the couch, my fingers drifting across her neck.

I told her this place was now our place and she could decorate it however she wanted to. I don't care as long as she's here. She's all I ever wanted.

It's all I've ever wanted. I only had to remember.

Her stomach growls loudly in protest of not eating since the morning, and I immediately feel bad. I haven't fed my girl yet. Blue eyes find mine and a burst of laughter falls from her lips. "Are you hungry?" I asked her.

"My stomach says yes, apparently."

"Well, let's get you fed then, babe." I start to get up from my couch, but wait until she's righted herself so she doesn't fall when I leave.

"Sounds fabulous to me. How can I help?"

"Want to sit in the kitchen and talk to me as I cook?"

She teases me light heartedly. "Remington Cole... cooking dinner for me. I never believed I'd see the day."

Her lips part on a sigh before I leaned in for a chaste kiss. Anything more would lead to more sex and less food making. "I wanted it to be perfect for you. The perfect day for the perfect fiancé."

I help her up from the couch, leading her by the hand to the kitchen. It is by far my favorite room in the house, and I couldn't wait to share it with her. I can picture us here, cooking together, dirtying the counters, ice cream sharing late at night followed by naughty whispered nothings. Maybe in a couple years I could see Faith barefoot and pregnant, dancing around in my t-shirt and singing into a spatula.

Things are finally aligning right.

My kitchen is decked out in stainless steel appliances. A hanging rack with pots and pans hangs above the island, making them easily accessible from the stove.

A silver handled kettle sits on the stove. I even upgraded for a touchless water faucet for the big sink. I grab ingredients from the fridge and pantry for dinner and put them on the counter.

I'd planned to make Faith Marry Me Chicken for dinner to accompany my proposal. Later tonight I was planning on driving my truck out to the crick to sit under the stars and just enjoy an old favorite of ours. Who knows, maybe I'll get lucky again. Not that it was about the sex at all, but sex was hot and I'd take whatever I could get.

I reached up and grabbed a skillet from the hanging rack above the island and turned it on to heat up. I needed to sear the chicken before adding the rest of the ingredients. Six minutes later, I am pulling the chicken from the stove, pouring off half of the fat and then returning the chicken to the skillet with garlic, thyme, and red pepper flakes. A minute or so later, I'm also adding heavy cream, broth, sun-dried tomatoes, salt, and parmesan.

Once it seems heated through, I throw the skillet in the oven and let it cook. Gazing over at Faith, she's watching me with rapt attention. "So, we have seventeen to twenty minutes to wait. You want to grab us some wine from the fridge?"

"Yes, sure." I had the wine fridge installed in the corner of the kitchen. I hoped that Faith liked a little wine with her meals.

The smell of garlic teased my senses as our food cooked in the oven. I grabbed some green beans from the fridge and cooked them up in a pan with a little garlic and butter.

Faith pulled a chardonnay to pair with our food, and the cabinet above the counter squeaked as I grabbed two glasses to pour. I was much more of a beer drinker, but tonight we were celebrating.

———

I turned on music in the background as we enjoyed our meal. Each moan from Faith's mouth and eye roll confirmed my meal was indeed perfect.

The garlic and thyme made me salivate, and I couldn't wait to dig in. "This is so delicious, Rem. The way the spices play with the sauce, combined with the chicken. Mmm."

"I'm glad you liked it. I've been practicing this specific dish for the last couple of nights."

Her eyebrow raised in curiosity. "Oh really? What's it called?"

I grinned at her. "Marry Me Chicken."

She laughed, and it was music to my ears. "How appropriate."

I winked over at her. "I happened to think so."

She yawned, covering her mouth with her hand, and I smiled. "Not getting tired on me yet, are you? Our day isn't over yet."

Her cheeks glowed as she beamed at me. "What else do you have up your sleeve?"

I shake my head, not willing to give anything away. "It's a surprise, but I promise you'll love it."

She furrows her brow, her eyes trained downward. "Okay, do I need to change clothes or anything?"

"Nope, you're perfect as is. Unless you want to grab a sweater in case it gets chilly."

"Hmm..."

I winked. "All right, I'll be back in a couple of minutes. Feel free to make yourself at home, since it is technically yours now too."

I'd snuck a bag full of blankets and pillows along with a picnic basket into the hallway closet when she excused herself to run to the bathroom earlier today. She made it almost too easy to do nice things for her. I wanted to end tonight with a boom. The perfect way to remember us.

I turned to see where she was before opening the closet and pulling my supplies. Once I'd confirmed she couldn't see me from her seat in the kitchen, I made a beeline to the truck out front. I threw my bags in the back seat and shut the door quickly behind me.

The front door to the house glided quietly as I opened it again. I found Faith inspecting the pictures on the mantle over the fireplace. "Where did you find all these photos, Rem?"

"I kept them over the years."

"Oh, you're so sweet."

"I simply couldn't let you slip away that easily."

"Charmer."

"Only for my beautiful girl." Her cheeks flushed whenever I called her beautiful, and a part of me wished I'd said it more when she was younger. When she was a girl, she was pretty, beautiful even, but now she was a showstopper, gorgeous.

FAITH

D usk turned to night as darkness settles in around us. He'd led me to his truck and helped me get in, followed by quickly blindfolding me. I have no clue where he's headed, and he clearly wants to keep it a surprise. I don't mind too much.

His calloused hand squeezes mine as we sit side by side in the truck on the way, and I squeeze back. I'm so close I can feel his body heat. The truck bumps and dips over the ground as we make our way to the destination. "Love you, Faith."

My heart flips and flutters. It will never get over hearing those words from his lips. "Love you, too. How much longer?"

He tsks, "We're almost there."

My brows raise until they hit my hairline. "And... where is there?"

"Patience..."

I huff, but I love the fact he won't tell me. It's sweet the way he wants to do something nice for me. Like making me dinner earlier. I wasn't lying when I told Nova country boys planned the best dates.

The truck slows to a halt five minutes later and I hold my

breath, listening for any hints as to where we are. His voice is deep as he speaks next. "Stay here, I'll be right back."

"Can I take off the blindfold?"

"Not yet, babe."

"Okay," I say, disappointed. He leans over, his lips finding mine, leaving me begging for more. I follow him as he pulls away. It's like I'm a sex crazy teenager and I can't get enough. A pout forms and he boops my nose. "I have more kisses to divulge, you just have to wait a little longer."

He shuts off the engine and opens his door. His keys jingle as he slides out of the truck. The sounds of evening hit my ears briefly before the door shuts again and I'm alone with my thoughts in the silence as it flows around me. I wonder what he's planning, but if now is any indication, I don't mind a bit. A minute later he opens the truck door again and grabs something from the back seat. Is it a bag or a box? I can't tell.

I hear bumping and moving in the bed of the truck and I turn my head trying to see under or around the blindfold, but he'd made it secure enough I can't see anything else. *Jerk.*

The passenger side door opens and my eyes find the sound, but I still can't see him. "Okay, let me help you out." He grabs my hand to help me down and I slide down the seat to the ground.

"Can I take this thing off yet?"

"Yep, you sure can. Here, let me help you." He reaches up to the back of my head and slowly, without pulling my hair, unties the back of the blindfold. My eyes quickly adjust to the night, and I hear the sound of running water nearby. A breeze shushes through the grass around us as a small animal scampers on his journey to wherever he's headed.

The sky is completely clear, allowing the stars to shine like illuminated diamonds twinkling here and there. "Where are we?"

"This is the pasture behind our house, babe. I figure we can either leave it as is or buy some horses. Maybe bring Remy over and let him have a field to himself. Maybe buy him a little filly to fawn over. Get his bad boy self on."

"Rem... is your mind permanently stuck in the gutter tonight?"

"Faith... it's been months since I've had sex with you. You and I made love all afternoon and I swear to God it's still not enough. I need to be inside you again, like yesterday. But first..."

His fingers lace with mine as he pulls me toward the bed of the truck. I peek over the side, and it's lined with blankets and pillows. There's a picnic basket in there too.

For some reason it makes me emotional, and I can't help the unshed tears lining my eyes. It's a replica of the first time he took me out in the back of his truck, only this time we're older and we're getting married.

The breeze blows around my shirt and a few loose hairs on my neck. It's a cool breeze and I'm thankful it's chilling the heat flowing between Remington and I. The longer grass slides against my bare legs as I make my way to the tailgate. Sitting on the tailgate is another bouquet of my favorite flowers. *This man.*

My tears streak my cheeks, happiness flowing in abundance. I'm sure the moonlight will show them off if I stand just right.

"Rem, this is perfect."

"You're perfect. I wanted to bring us a happy memory from long ago. The smile on your face says I've succeeded in my goal and that's priceless. Want to get up there?"

"Yes!"

"Come here." I walk over to where he stands, his arms outstretched. His hands find my waist and heat seeps through my top. A flush creeps up my face and my skin tingles as I remember how gifted those hands were a little earlier today. He lifts me without resistance onto the tailgate of the truck. It makes me feel like I'm weightless.

I step into the bed and kneel down to sit in the middle of the blankets. The truck dips as he climbs in behind me, and I can't help the way my eyes watch his shirt bunch over his muscles. Slivers of moonlight light up his face and I take it all in. I love the way his face is highlighted in the glimmer of the moon.

He crawls up beside me, pulling me into his side. The rest of the world slips away as his lips find mine. What starts out as a slow kiss quickly turns into more, and soon enough, I feel the brush of his fingertips along the underside of my breast. My hand slides up his chest into his dark brown hair and I pull him into me closer, asking for more.

His hand trails to my hemline and sneaks underneath my shirt, finding my skin. Fingertips are on a mission to drive me to need, to crave. He unclasps my bra with one hand, then pulls my shirt up and over my head. My nipples are exposed to the cool breeze and pebble up.

Laying me back, he continues to kiss me. His lips making a journey peppering kisses down my jaw, neck, and my chest. He's on a mission to make sure my breast is on edge from his attention. He swirls his tongue around my tight bud before sucking it into his mouth again. I can't help the groan as it slips out.

He's making me feel like a lust filled hussy simply with all the nipple play currently happening. Each time his teeth graze and nip me, my pussy flutters, begging for more. He kisses each curve and dip of my exposed flesh from my shoulders to the waistline of my shorts. A man on a pleasure mission and dare I say, he's exceeded very well.

I'm becoming a mess of need and want, begging him for more with my writhing and pleading.

He edges my shorts and then my panties down, kissing more of my exposed skin, and I squirm. He needs to take off these clothes so he can get where I want him, but a part of me also wants to satisfy something for him as well.

I want to taste him on my tongue.

To drive him to the edge with my ministrations on his cock.

My pussy clenches at the emptiness, wanting to be filled with him again. *See? Hussy.*

My fingers reach down and fist his hair, trying to move him to where I want him, but he holds off. Delayed gratification, my ass. I want him now.

He slips his fingers into the corners of my shorts and panties, wriggling them off. They land somewhere behind him, but I couldn't care less at this point. He's all I see. I reach out, tugging impatiently at his tee. I need him out of this shirt as soon as possible. Remington smirks at me before dragging it up over his head and tossing it to the side.

He spreads my knees wide with his thighs and I don't hesitate to let them fall open. His eyes trail up my completed naked body, and chills run up my arms. Not from the cold, but from the need.

His breath is warm against me as he peers up my stomach at me and winks. "You ready?"

"Eat me, Rem. I need your mouth on me."

"Mmm... I love it when my fiancé talks dirty to me." My response is nonsense. I gasp and arch my hips as he works me up in the best way possible.

Remington's tongue lashes out to flick my clit as his fingers enter me.

I have zero shame when I find myself riding his face to climax. I combust like an explosion and Rem clamps down on my hips, keeping me in place to ride it out. I've never felt this desperate need to be with him, to connect before, and I can't say I'm complaining. He willingly gives whatever I silently ask of him.

I'm panting as I lay there, trying to get my breath and watch as he licks his lips, then wipes the remainder on the back of his hand. For some reason I find it super-hot.

As my eyes trail down, I see he's sporting a full-on erection pressing against the zipper of his jeans, begging to let me at it. He hasn't asked me to suck his cock since we officially reunited, but I want to anyhow.

He climbs up my body, his tip tracing over my center. As much as I want him to plunge into me and take away the ache, I want him in my mouth more. Pushing him away, I shake my head. Confusion fills his eyes as examines my face, determined to figure out why I'm denying him. So, I give in and let him know.

My eyes find his cock and I almost salivate with want. I'm so turned on it's not even funny. "I want to taste you first."

He shakes his head. "I don't know how long I'll last babe, I'm pretty on edge already."

I wink. "Well, we'll be here all night."

His eyes light up like a Christmas tree at my suggestion and he hurries to scoot up the truck bed. Kneeling beside my face, his buckle clanks as he undoes it and his pants. His fingers find the corners of his Levi's and boxers and he pulls down, letting them pool around his knees. His cock springs free in my face and all of me tingles at the thrill of bringing him pleasure with my mouth.

He leans over my mouth and his balls are in my face, so I slip my tongue out to lick them. They're saltier than I remembered, but I don't mind. I let one fall into my mouth and run my tongue over it. A groan is forced from his lips, and I do it again, knowing he's liking it. He lifts up, pulling his ball from my mouth, and it slips out with a pop.

Gripping his cock, he bends it down to put it into my mouth. My tongue slips out to lick the tip, and he groans again. His noises only urge me to give him more pleasure. I run my tongue along the underside of his cock, over his overly sensitive vein, and he curses. His fingers find my hair and tighten me to him.

His cock surges into my mouth and my throat works as I swallow around the thick intrusion. He is silky and soft, yet harder than steel. The skin on his shaft tastes like sweat and man and it's the biggest high.

My moan is muffled around Remington's length. I keep sucking him, my mouth clenching around him tighter.

Remington leans down as I'm sucking his cock and pulls my

nipples with his fingers. It lights me up, sending need directly to my pussy.

His groans and moans urge me on. His cock slips past the back of my throat and I breathe in through my nose. I'd forgotten how thick he was, my mouth almost sore from giving him head. His fingers trail down my body and find my pussy, circling the clit and slipping down my seam. He starts working my clit as I keep sucking him. His hand in my hair tightens, and he starts thrusting faster into my mouth, his cock hardening. I know he's close and I aim to complete the task at hand.

I moan around his cock, and the vibrations set him off. Hot streams of cum line the back of my mouth and slide down my throat, warming my belly. He pulls out and I lick the tip, getting all of his taste.

"God, babe. That was..."

"Mmmhmm."

"You'll have to give me a little time to recover. I can't remember the last time I came so hard."

He flops onto his back in the truck bed and reaches out, pulling me into his side. Our breaths are both ragged. The stars twinkle and shine above us, luring me into a daze of happiness.

Remington's hand finds mine at our side and entwines his fingers with me, pulling my hand up to kiss it. His lips are firm, yet soft. "I love you, Rem."

"Always yours, Faith. You remember the last time we had a night like this, just you, me, and an open space?"

"No, but it sure is nice. I didn't realize you had a crick at the back of your property too."

"First, it's our property, babe. Secondly, yep. Same crick as the one we used to sit beside in McCoy's field."

I can hear it behind us, water trickling and splashing over rocks. Crickets play their own little tunes. Animals we can't see scamper through the tall grass around us and the breeze has died down. I'm thankful for it because we're both butt ass naked lying here. I'm not afraid of anyone seeing us like this because we can't even hear any cars from the road this far back. It's literally only us.

I roll onto my side and place my hand on Remington's chest, my leg over his thigh. My fingers run through the rough patch of hair scattered between his nipples and I trace my name tattooed in cursive on his chest. The ba-dump of his heartbeat is slowing down finally. He leans over and kisses my forehead. One of my favorite things he does. It's like a little reminder of how much he loves me.

I can't help but admire the features of his face as I ask the next question. "So, when do you want to get married?"

He smiles, and the moonlight illuminates his white teeth. "I want to call you my wife as soon as possible."

"Big or small wedding?"

He shrugs. "I don't care, as long as you're there with me. I have a feeling we won't be the only ones getting married soon."

"Really?"

"Yep, sounds like Beau is awfully serious about Cassidy Mae. I'd bet there's a proposal in the next couple of months."

My eyebrows raise. "You think she's ready for a proposal?"

He shook his head. "I guess we'll find out."

A couple of hours later, I woke up to Remington covering us up with blankets. The chill had crept in and dew was starting to settle onto the grass. Today was the best day and I couldn't wait to spend more of them with the boy I fell in love with when I was fifteen years old. We may have had a shit show of a way to get to this point, but I'd do it over and over again. I fell back asleep in his arms, ready to take on the world.

FAITH

Warm sun bathes my face as I slowly blink my eyes open. Insects are buzzing and birds are singing from the trees. The water splashes and swirls as it cascades over stones in the crick. Remington is stretched out beside me and we're still naked under the blanket he covered us in last night.

Raising my hands in front of me, I stretch out and yawn before wiping the sleepies from my eyes. Hot breath hits my ear as Remington whispers, "Good morning, fiancé."

"Good morning, you." He leans up and kisses my bare shoulder, his scruff scraping across my skin, but not in a painful manner. Rolling onto my back, I find gray-blue eyes staring back at me. He grins, those cute little dimples surfacing. Remington's lips meet mine a few minutes later, it's a long kiss, a hot kiss promising there's more where the first came from, but we don't have time for more this morning.

The sun is already halfway into the sky and it's no longer early morning, which means we need to make our way to the stables sooner rather than later. I groan, "Can't we stay here today?"

"I have no complaints, personally, but Beau may miss me."

I wink at him. "Well, what if I need you more?"

"Don't tempt me, babe." He smirks, and I feel the press of his erection against my hip. *Naughty man.*

"Do you know where my clothes are?" I sit up and search around.

"Somewhere around here, wasn't at all concerned with where they landed last night while I was devouring the sweet, sweet pussy in front of me."

"Not helping..."

He leans up and peppers kisses to my shoulders and spine. "Then stay a while..."

"Rem..."

"I know, I know. Maybe today will be an easy day at the barn and we can sneak away to the hot springs or something. Maybe I'll drag you into one of the stalls and kiss you crazy just because I can." I love how he's acting like a schoolboy all over again. It's like we're back in the crush phase and can't get enough of each other. I'm not complaining in the slightest.

He held my shirt up to me, but whenever I reached for it, he pulled away and made me kiss him. Eventually he relented, but I couldn't help the wide smile as it took up most of my face. I scrounged around under the blankets and found my shorts and panties, while he found his jeans and tee. He didn't even bother to put on his boxers, claiming easier access for later on, and then winked. *His damn wink.*

Working together, we cleared up the back of the truck bed fairly quickly and loaded it all into the truck and headed back toward our house.

Our house.

I still couldn't wrap my head around it. This whole place was ours now.

We took about thirty minutes to get showered and dressed before we were in the truck again, headed toward Willow Springs. Beau had texted me earlier this morning and let me know the only lesson I had scheduled had cancelled and I wasn't needed unless I wanted to hang out at the stables.

Rem had to stop by the barn to help with mowing the fields and mending some things around the barn. I liked the idea of being able to openly ogle Remington without a shirt on while he was being all manly and sweaty under the heat of the sun.

———

Beau and Rem met at the barn, and he turned to give me a wave and wink before they headed off to do whatever was needed. I stood and stared at the barn, and I swear today seems like I have fresh eyes. I survey the tall double doors, the rough wooden walls with hooks holding halters and bridles. A spare pitchfork sits unattended in the middle of the aisle. A wooden ladder leads up to the hay loft.

Some horses were still inside today. Mostly the new horses or the boarders who kept their horses with us. Not all boarders liked the idea of all day turnout. Maybe their horse had skin allergies or if the horse was light colored, they worried about a sunburn. Crazy how a white horse could get a sunburn, but their skin underneath was a pink color and easily burned.

I start filling up the water buckets in each stall and checking the salt lick blocks for each horse. I picked up some stalls, the scrape of the pitchfork loud against the quiet sounds of horses happily munching on hay only a stall or two away.

The sound of a horse rubbing its backside against the creaky wooden board of its stall door told me I needed to figure out who it was and stop them. It could seriously mess up a tail. The new horse, Napoleon, was the guilty party, and I pushed him away from the door. You couldn't tell him no because he didn't understand, so I'd have to watch him.

Koko was in the barn, still from not being turned out earlier with the others after my lesson cancelled, so I walked over to her stall.

After inquisitively nuzzling my pockets to make sure I didn't have any hidden sugar cubes, she laid her chin on my shoulder. The bristles under her muzzle are prickly, like a small cactus running over my skin. I leaned my head against hers and inhaled the familiar scent of horses and straw. I loved Koko with all my heart, but I truly wished for my own horse.

Remington and I had moved into our own place and had so much space that we could move the horses home to live. It'd be nice to see them grazing outside from my kitchen window as I made cookies or dinner.

I hadn't noticed until this morning, but there was a swing on the back porch as well. It made me think of the perfect spot to sit while the horses munch away, listening to their chewing sounds and the swishing of their tales, as the sun disappeared beneath the horizon. I'd sit beside the love of my life, maybe eventually a kid or two.

Koko nuzzled me again, reminding me I'd spaced off again. I grabbed her halter from the stall door hook and walked her out to the pasture. Her pasture mates came running with whinnies as they saw her standing at the fence. I opened the gate and removed her halter. She waited a minute and then busted out at a gallop, the other horses following in hot pursuit.

Across the way Remington was aboard a bright red tractor mowing the pasture. His shirt hung from the back of his pants and his tattooed chest was on full display, being kissed by the sun. I had to be honest. I was completely jealous of the sun.

My mind slipped back to last night where I kissed my favorite tattoo on his chest, my name. Since he'd been tattooed the first time, he had ink added to it, and I couldn't help but smile. His body was a walking, talking work of art, and I enjoyed licking and tasting every inch of his skin. He wiped his brow with his forearm, and it was the sexiest thing I'd seen since last night.

Hello, horny lady alert.

Shaking my head, I found my way over to the arena. Cassidy Mae and Oakley were running barrel patterns, and I wanted to watch. Dust kicked up as she took the barrels fast. It was crazy to see a horse get so low to the ground as she bent her shoulder in toward the barrel.

I was mesmerized watching them work together as a team.

I didn't realize how much time had slipped away from me, when strong arms encircled me from behind and warm breath skated across my naked skin. "Hey, you."

"Hey, done already?" I spun around to face him, and he backed me into the fence.

"Yep, pasture is mowed, and the damaged stall is mended. How're they doing?" he asks, nodding toward Cassidy Mae and Oakley.

My eyes find Oakley and Cassidy Mae back in the arena. "I can't wrap my head around how athletic it all seems. I wouldn't think a horse could get so low to the ground, but she does it with each barrel."

"They're a great team."

Turning back to Remington, I notice how blue his eyes are today. Like a gray blue dancing in the sunlight. He'd put his shirt back on before sneaking up behind me and I think for our friend's sake it was a fantastic idea. I wasn't sure I could keep from fondling him, if not.

Beau came up behind us and smiled. "We're taking the afternoon off to swim at the lake. Y'all in?"

My eyes lit up, and I bounced on my feet. "Hell, yes, we're in!" I say it way louder than I need to, for sure, but I don't care. I know how much fun lake days are around here.

Remington leans in. "We don't have swimsuits here anymore, babe. I moved your clothes home to our house. So we'll have to stop there first."

I nod. "Right."

Rem walked toward Beau and clapped him on the shoulder. "Hey man, we need to run home and grab swim clothes and we'll meet you there. Sound all right?"

Beau smirks. "Yeah, see you there. Cass and Reagan are changing now and then we'll head out."

We head toward the truck and Rem opens the door and helps me into the passenger side. Ten minutes later, we're pulling up to our house. I still get chills when I think about it. I'm not sure I'll ever get used to it.

As we get out, his blue eyes find mine.

"All right, I'll grab trunks and you grab a suit and we'll be ready."

"Yes, sir," I say, rubbing my hand seductively up his arm. A groan slips from his mouth, and I knew he'd probably been thinking the same thing I was.

"Don't say those types of things, Faith. We don't have time right now."

I winked. "Who said we have to show up right when they do?"

I barely made it in the house before his eyes were half lidded and desire pooled within them.

"Naughty..."

"You're complaining?" I reach to the hem of my shirt and pulled it up slowly over my head, followed by my bra. Slipping my thumbs into the corners of my shorts, I turn and shake my ass provocatively as I slid them down my legs, bending over. Peeking behind me, I notice how much he is enjoying the show and giggle.

He tilts his head, watching. "Oh, damn babe. You're not helping me be appropriate right now."

"Why do you want to be good when you're so amazing at being bad, Rem?"

He chuckles. "You aren't going to win right now. It'll make it all the better later, delayed gratification and all." His hand met my ass as he walked past me and kept strolling away. "Get your suit, babe. We have places to be."

I growl out loud, stalking away in a huff. "Unbelievable."

I traipse off to my dresser and pull out my swim suits, trying to decide which one would expose the most skin. I'd drive him bananas simply because I could.

Slipping off my panties, I then tossed them into the laundry hamper. I picked up my renegade skimpy bikini set and put it on. Turning in the mirror, I gave myself a once over and smiled.

Perfect.

Remington was in the bathroom showering the dirt and dust from himself so he didn't see me slip in behind him until he felt my hand on his hard cock. He moaned as I fisted his cock and started to stroke it. "What did I tell you, Faith? You're on your way to being spanked for bad behavior."

"You want me to stop?" I ask, moving around to the front and then dropping to my knees in front of him. I licked my lips, and his eyes flamed with desire.

"Fuck no." His head fell back as I put my mouth on him.

Water streamed down my face as my tongue swirled around the head of his cock. He reached down and pulled on the string holding the top of my bikini to my tits, exposing me. His hands found my nipples, and he pulled and squeezed. I moaned around his cock, and a groan flowed from his lips.

My hands cascade up his body, following his happy trail up to where I feel his sexy abs beneath my fingers. The water is hot, almost scalding, but I don't care. I need this, I need him. All these months of fighting and bickering has led us to this moment. We need this, this contact, this intimacy, this love.

"Need you now, babe," he said huskily.

"We don't have time," I argue back, using his words against him.

He smirks. "I can be quick." Hands under my armpits, he pulled me up his body to stand. His fingers found the hem of my bikini bottoms, and he pulled them off. "You honestly think I'd let you out of the house wearing it anyhow? This body is for my eyes and my eyes only, baby."

I'm wet for him already, completely primed for his cock. His mouth finds mine, devouring me and making me needy before he puts his hands under my ass, lifting me against the wall. It's cold compared to the flames building within me. I take a deep breath, getting used to the temperature change.

Without another second to waste, he presses himself inside me in one long stroke. His groan is earth shattering, and I feel it too. Shifting his hands on my ass, he slides in a little farther and I'm lost to the sensation of being filled by Remington. I wrap my legs around his waist, my feet pushing into his ass, letting him know I need more. He rewards me with deeper, faster thrusts. "Yes, fuck, oh Rem."

"Mmm... I love it when you say my name, babe. I'm so fucking hard for you right now. Grinding down on this wet little pussy. Delayed gratification is overrated."

"Yes..." I pant out. He's slamming into me now. I clamp down around him as an orgasm hits, like a crashing wave pulling me under. Three more thrusts and his body starts jerking around mine, releasing himself deep into my core. It's warm against me. I should be thinking about how we haven't been using condoms, but I'm on birth control so I'm not worried. He's told me it's only been me and I believe him.

He doesn't pull out immediately, simply stands there, head pressed against mine as we pant, our hearts beating furiously. His lips find me, and his kiss is sweet. "I can't get enough of you, babe. The best part is I have you all to myself for years to come."

"Hells yes. Now, you ready to go to the lake?"

"Yeah, let's do this." The water is starting to get cold, so he cranks up the nozzle. Pulling shampoo from the shelf, he washes my hair for me first, then follows with soaping up my body.

It feels nice having someone else wash you. I wouldn't trade it for anything. I return the favor and five minutes later the shower is being turned off and we're drying off our bodies, ready to fully enjoy this lake day without the sexual tension in the way.

My swimsuit is completely soaked, so I put on a simple red bikini. "Is this one better?" I inquire.

"I mean, I'd prefer you to be wearing a one piece where no one else gets to see your sexy body, but... I'll be there to ward off any men who can't keep their eyes to themselves. So, you do you, babe."

"How very generous of you." I wink, and he swats my ass again.

He grabs swim trunks and bends down to put them on. Remington is definitely a shower, not a grower. His cock hangs heavily between his legs as I watch him pull up the trunks, and it disappears beneath them. I'm going to want it again later, but now for a lake day!

———

We pulled up to the lake about twenty minutes later, sunscreen on, sunglasses on, ready to bask in the sun and chill with our friends.

Beau was standing over to the side with Cassidy Mae and Reagan. Rea was obviously giving him a hard time and Cassidy was doing the same thing, but in a different way. You couldn't hide Beau's hardon a mile away. Not like I was going to say anything about it to Rem.

Rem parked the truck, and we headed toward the water. It was hot out today, so a dip in the lake seemed like the perfect remedy. Rhett was already in the water by himself, but the smile on his face as he admired Reagan was something you couldn't miss.

He'd been hanging out with Reagan a lot lately, and I wondered how Beau would feel about his best friend dating his sister. My guess was he wouldn't be cool with it and from the posturing occurring quite regularly, I am probably right.

We were standing in the water with Rhett when we heard

Reagan say, "Come on, Cassidy. Let's get away from this party pooper. Swim time." They both stood up and walked toward the lake, lemonade coolers in their hands. Wading into the water, they came our way. Rhett said something about the way Reagan filled out her suit and Beau shot him a dirty expression. We couldn't help but laugh. Yep, he definitely has a problem with it.

A few minutes later, Beau joined us in the water, unable to take his eyes off Cassidy Mae. She had other plans, though, as she splashed him in the face with a spray of water. All of a sudden, water was flying all around us. A water fight ensued.

———

We'd been invited over for dinner at the farm tonight. We were told all our friends would be there, and it'd be nice to have them together again. What we didn't expect was all the decorations put up once we arrived. I saw Nova out of the corner of my eye, smiling at us, and my Spidey senses tingled. I bet one hundred percent she had something to do with this.

As we exit the truck, a chorus of congrats shouted around us and I can't help beaming from ear to ear. We hadn't told anyone except Beau and Nova, but I wasn't shy about wearing my ring, so putting two and two together, they had to know.

Nova walked over and wrapped her arms around me. "I'm so damn happy for you. You happy?"

"I'm so overwhelmingly happy." The emotions hit me full force, and I find myself wiping my eyes.

"We wanted to do something small to celebrate you two this evening. Most of it is set up in the bunkhouse since it's emptied out."

"I appreciate you, Nova."

She nodded and walked over to where Jameson was standing, waiting for her. He wrapped his arm around her waist and pulled her in, kissing her on the temple. It was a sweet gesture, and I gave her a thumbs up when Jameson wasn't looking my way.

Rhett, Reagan, Beau, and Cassidy Mae all came over and said congrats as well. It made my heart sing with joy over all of our friends being so excited for us.

They led us into the bunkhouse and it was filled with decorations. A future Mr. and Mrs. banner hung above the fireplace. Four tables were set around the room, three for all of us, and the last one filled with cupcakes and engagement party games. It wasn't a very big deal, but it meant the world to us.

Remington squeezed my hip as my eyes trailed around the room. Grey-blue eyes peered back at me as he mouthed the words, *I love you*. My heart skipped a beat. The expression of love painted across his face was priceless and something I'd commit to memory.

Nova passed out champagne and gave a speech to toast to. A small sound system sat in the back of the room, and country music beat slowly throughout. We sat down to enjoy the snacks provided and enjoyed the evening with our friends. Occasionally, my eyes would find Remington's and he'd smile. I'd smile back, and he'd wink. Even if it took us forever to get here, I'd do it all over again. He was worth it. We were worth it.

We sat back and listened to our friends chatting. It felt like it'd revolved full circle. From teenage sweethearts to getting married we'd seemed to survive the good and the bad. Now, we just had to plan the wedding, and I have the perfect idea.

Epilogue - Faith

S ix months later

"Come in," Cassidy Mae hollers from inside the room. Reagan and I figured she may have some pre-wedding jitters before the ceremony.

"We just came to check on the beautiful bride." She turned as we walked in behind her as she stood in the mirror. "You're something, Cass. You look amazing in this dress."

"You don't think it's too simple?" she asks quietly, turning to face us.

Regan shakes her head with a smile. "No, it's perfect on you and I know once Beau sees you, he's going to freak out at how gorgeous his wife is today."

My mind replays back to the day Remington and I said our vows two months ago. It was a small ceremony composed of only our friends. We gathered down by the hot springs, one of our favorite places that had captured so many memories.

I wore an off-white simple lace tulle wedding dress with a sweetheart neckline and Remington wore Levi's with a button-down shirt, cowboy hat, and boots. It'd been perfect. The sun was out, a small breeze blew through the trees. Our horses grazed nearby.

Remy and Annie now live at the house with us. All the space out back converted into a small barn and field for them. Annie is the perfect little palomino mare, her hair is a golden yellow color with three white socks and a white star on her forehead. Her mane and tail are the purest white. We'd bought her from an auction so she didn't get sold to someone who wouldn't appreciate her as much as I do.

I wanted to save her, like Remington had done with Remy. Rescues were the fastest way to a full heart. It was a strong bond between a rescue horse and an owner. I think they instinctively know deep down you're saving them from the depths of the world. You'd give them a home, a forever home, and love them until they died.

Reagan's words bring me back to the present. "Hey, don't be nervous. That man out there has been in love with you since the first day he saw you. He will love you until you die, and you'll probably be holding each other's hands. You want to wait in here any longer or are you ready to marry your man?"

A smile paved its way across my face, reaching my eyes. I remember Reagan had said something similar to me as her and Nova had helped me get ready the morning of my wedding.

She nods. "I'm ready. Wait, how does he look?"

Reagan made a face before responding. "Well, I won't comment on my brother's looks but..."

I'd seen Beau on the way in, and he seemed nervous. He was rubbing his hands on his thighs and pacing, but I wasn't about to say it. So instead, I said," I ain't never seen him in a tux, but dang that man fills one out nicely." I smile at her, so she knows I am telling her the truth. "He looks good, Cassidy Mae."

We left the room, and I watched as she walked down the stairs and met her father at the bottom. His eyes shined with unshed tears, and I was so happy for her. My father hadn't been at my wedding. Mom hadn't heard from him in months after he ran off with a woman half his age. *Today wasn't about me,* I thought, before shoving my issues into the back of my brain.

The field had been lined with chairs, not many like our wedding, but enough to seat their friends and family. The canopy sat at the front layered in red and purple flowers, a bright pop against the light blue sky. A light breeze trailed over my shoulders, and I breathed in the fresh air.

Reagan and I walked down the aisle in our low-cut bridesmaid dresses, and I couldn't help the smile as it formed or the tears as they went streaming down my face. So many emotions racked me today, and I refused to keep them in. First Remington and I getting our shit together. Now, Cassidy Mae and Beau. Nova had driven up today to celebrate with us and Jameson couldn't seem to keep his hands off her. I wondered if they'd be next.

As I lined up behind where Cassidy Mae would stand under the canopy, my eyes caught Remington. He exuded sexiness in his tux and he was all mine, finally. I still preferred the tee shirt wearing, Levi jean hugging, backward hat wearing, boot toting Remington version, but this one was pretty nice too.

Blue eyes found mine, and he radiated the happiness I felt. My body came alive under his gaze, his eyes following each curve and dip. He winked, and I knew the promise it held for later.

I mouthed *naughty* and he waggled his eyebrows. *This man.* I still couldn't believe we'd found our way back to each other after all this time. He was mine.

Our friends and family stood as Cassidy Mae walked down the aisle. She strolled, looking exquisite in her wedding gown. Music played, and I drifted off into my own memories.

. . .

Our friends stood as I walked down the aisle. Remington stood at the end, smiling back at me, tears in his eyes. There he stood. My forever. All I had to do was get to the end of the aisle and say yes.

My eyes trailed over our guests and I realized there was nowhere else I'd rather be than surrounded by friends and family. Mom sat in the front row, and for once she seemed happy. After Remington and I officially got back together, she finally gave her blessing, and we've been eating dinner at her house every Thursday since then.

My father wasn't there to walk me down the aisle, but Beau stepped in to give me away. Jameson had gotten ordained to do our vows. We walked slowly as we approached the canopy. "Don't let me fall." I'd said to Beau, and he gave me a cheesy grin.

"Never. You've got this, Faith."

I made it those ten steps to Remington, and he leaned in to kiss my forehead before we said our vows, right before we said I do to the rest of our lives. His smile could light up the sun. It made the moon shine a little brighter that night.

We danced the night away under the stars, my head pressed against Remington's chest. His chin against my head. I remember thinking this was the best day of my life. We had so much life ahead of us. I could finally see it now. Our new house, the horses out back, a couple of kids running around. The only thing missing was a goat named Elvis.

People clapping around us brought me back to the moment, and I clap along with them as Beau and Cassidy Mae kissed.

Remington and Jameson had tacked up Apache and Zeus for Cassidy Mae and Beau to ride off into the sunset with. It was a beautiful wedding, and I was so happy for our friends.

The reception was held in a tent at the farm, but Cassidy Mae and Beau snuck out long before the reception ever started. They'd spent time thanking each person for coming and being here to share their special day with them.

Halfway through the wedding reception, I pull Nova to the side. "Hey, I need you to walk with me for moral support."

Her eyes widened. "Moral support for what? Are you okay? Oh God, it's not Rem, right?" she says in a rush as I pull her away from the crowd.

Once we were away from the tent, I headed to the car and grabbed my bag from the backseat. "Faith, you're scaring me. Wanna tell me what's happening right now?" I opened the backpack and showed her the contents.

"Eeekkkkk, really?!" She bounced on her toes.

"Shhhh... keep it down!" I whisper-shouted.

Her eyebrows hit her hairline. "Wait, does Rem not know?"

I shook my head no and bit my lip.

"Oh, sweets. Let's do this." She holds out her hand, and I grab it as we walk toward the bunkhouse. It already held so many memories for us. Why not add another one?

Nova found her way to the couch as I headed back down the hallway to the bathroom. I was terrified, but a part of me was also thrilled about the idea of having a baby with Rem.

I held my fancy dress up as I peed into a cup and set it on the sink. I didn't think I could pee on a stick the size of a big pencil. It wasn't happening.

Three minutes longer. Three minutes stood between a non-pregnant me and a pregnant me. A tear slipped down my face and I couldn't hold it back, so I let it out. A knock on the door a couple of minutes later, and Nova popped her head in. "Hey, you. Wanted to check and see how you were holding up."

"What if I can't do this, Nova? What if I'm not cut out to be a mom?"

"Shut the hell up. You finally have your life together. You waited around and fought for a man who'd forgotten who you were other than the fact that you left him. You sat in his hospital room and waited for him to wake up. You are the kindest, most patient person I know. You'll be a kickass mom. Who knows... maybe Auntie Nova will be moving here soon?"

My eyes widen. "Wait..."

"I know!" She screamed. "Jameson asked me to move in with him."

I double blinked. "You're moving to Moonshine Springs?"

She held my hands as she bounced around. "Yes, I'll be right down the street from you. Now, there's no excuses. We're doing this. Even if your stick says no right now, I'll still be here for future little Remington and Faith babies. I love you, girl. This is what best friends are for, we're here til the end."

I beamed proudly. "I'm so happy right now."

She nodded in agreement. "Me too."

"All right," she shrugs. "Are you ready to find out if you're growing a little Rem bean in there?"

"No?"

"Okay, we're doing this anyhow."

"I can't..."

"I'll do it for you." I nod, bite my lip, and wait for her to tell me two little words. She walked behind me and found my test on the sink. Rubbing my shoulder, she said the words I'd been waiting to hear. "You're pregnant."

Tears streamed down my face, crying a river of joy. We've come full circle, high school sweethearts, to Rem building us a house, to getting married, and now we were having a baby.

The door on the bunkhouse creaked as it opened and my heart stuttered in my chest. *Shit.* "Faith, babe, you in here? Jameson said you and Nova snuck in here. Everything o..."

He walked down the hallway and found us in the bathroom. His eyes found the stick in Nova's hand and stopped dead. I wondered if he was even still breathing. "Babe?" His eyes found mine.

"Rem, I have something to tell you."

"Okay..."

"You may want to sit down..."

His finds found my face as he started inspecting me. "Faith, just tell me. Are you okay? You're kinda freaking me out right now."

A tear slips down my cheek as concern draws across his face. "Rem, do you want kids?"

"Wait, is it yours?" His eyes widened finding the pregnancy test in Nova's hand and I nodded.

My eyes dropped to the ground. I didn't think I could stand it if I peered up, and he was frowning. "Yeah, it's mine, Rem."

"Why did you drop your eyes? Aren't you excited? What's it say?" My eyes find his as a small smile crept across his face as he fiddled with his hands, anxiety taking over.

I raise an eyebrow. "What do you want it to say?"

He reached over and pulled me into him, kissing my head. "I want it to say hell yes, babe! I want to have a baby with you, Faith."

I pulled back and peered up at him. "Really?"

"I didn't want anything else or anyone else. You're with me for long term, babe, and I want to build a family with you. Our whole life has led up to this and I'm so excited to see what happens next."

"Then, I guess we're having a baby." I smiled and Remington reached down and picked me up, spinning me around.

"Fuck yes, Faith. I'm gonna be the best dad ever!"

"I love you, Rem."

"I love you too. We're having a baby." He stoops down, rubbing my still flat stomach. "Hey in there, little girl or guy, I'm your dad." Then he stood back up and placed a hand on my cheek. "I'm so happy, Faith. Over the moon. I came in here because I have a second surprise for you tonight. Can you walk with me for a minute?"

I narrow my eyes at him. "I'm not sure what else I can handle right now, Rem. In case you haven't noticed I'm a little emotional."

"I think you'll like this one. Follow me." He reaches down and entwines his fingers with mine.

I quickly glance over at Nova, and she squeals. "We're having a baby! I'm so excited for you two."

Letting Remington's hand slip for a second, I walk back to Nova and hug her. "Thank you."

"I'm so proud of you, Faith. You can do this, and I'll be just down the street if you ever need Auntie Nova to babysit. Now, go."

Remington held his hand out, and I took it. One more peek over my shoulder, and Nova gave me a smile and shooed me along.

He leads me out of the bunkhouse and toward the barn. Soft country music floats toward us from the reception and some overly happy drunks stand laughing outside the tent. He shouts to no one in particular. "We're having a baby!"

"Hell yeah, congrats!" A chorus of people shout back.

"Rem, shhhh."

"What? I'm ecstatic. I want to shout it from the rooftops, Faith." I stored the picture of him so excited in the moonlight to memory as we walked. His profile, even at night, was handsome.

Rem lets my hand fall only long enough to pull open the doors to the barn and let us slip inside. The barn was dark as we felt around for the light, finally turning it on.

He grabs my hand again, almost afraid he'd lose it, and walked me to the end of the barn, stopping at the last stall. The small sound of bleating came from behind the door, followed by the rustle of hay. I turned and quirked an eye at Rem, and he shrugged his shoulders as if to pretend he had no idea. As I peered over the stall door, I saw a small brown and white baby goat.

"Surprise, babe. Do you like him? His name is Elvis," he whispers in my ear and I turn to face him, tears littering my eyes.

"You bought us a baby goat?"

"Yeah, babe. It was all part of the plan, right? A house, a couple of horses, a few kids, and a goat named Elvis?"

"You remembered?"

"How could I forget? I remember everything about our future. I plan to make sure you get it all, anything you've ever wanted. I made you a promise and I intend to keep it."

"You're too good to me, Remington Cole."

"I won't ever be enough for you, Faith, but I'll make you the happiest wife alive."

He opens the stall door for me, and I follow him in. The little baby bleats again, and I bend down to rub his head. He instantly jumps into my arms, and my heart melted. "Welcome to the family Elvis Cole," I whisper to the little fur baby in my arms.

I stand up and Remington comes up behind me, talking to Elvis in a baby voice and there went my ovaries, done for with this man. He reached around to rub the little guy's head and I leaned back into his arms, breathing in the scent of baby animal hay, and the all too familiar smell of my man - sandalwood and musk with a touch of dust.

"You happy, Faith?"

"I couldn't be happier, Rem. This is perfect."

"You're perfect. This, us, the things in between. We're building a family now and I wouldn't want to do this with anyone else because it's always been you and me against the world. Are you ready to head home and introduce Elvis to Annie and Remy?"

"It's too cold out, Rem. We can't leave him by himself in the barn, he's just a baby. Can we let him stay in the house, please? Goats are trainable." I gave him my best pout face.

He smiled. "See, you're gonna be the best momma. We can do whatever you want, Faith."

"I love you, Rem."

He puts his hand up to my cheek and leans in to give me a kiss. "I love you too. When we were sixteen, I fell in love with a shy, beautiful girl and now I'm head over heels in love with the same girl. Only now, she's my wife. Maybe those love letters kept us together all those years. It was something to hold on to even though you weren't here. But now you're here and instead of those love letters, we're writing our story live instead of with ink and paper."

I frown. Why is he acting like it was the end of them? "I loved those letters. You can't ever stop writing them."

"I'll still write you love letters. It won't change. We'll stick them in the back of our closet and pull them out occasionally, just to remember all the things we had to work through to get to this point."

"Not all of them, right?"

"How about only the sexy ones and the sweet ones?"

"Deal."

"Glad it's settled. Now let's head home and get our celebration on. We may just have to kick the little guy out of the bedroom for a couple of hours because I have some big plans." He winks with his devastatingly handsome face, dimples showing, and I couldn't say no.

"Sorry little guy." I said to the baby in my arms and he just maa'd me. "Well, you talk an awful good game, Rem. Let's see if you can live up to it. What are we waiting for?"

"After you," he says, moving aside for me to get by. I walk by and he pats my ass. *Oh, this man.*

I remember the first time I ever laid eyes on six-foot blue-eyed Remington Cole. I knew I'd never love another boy the same way and boy was I right. You could say there's a time in everyone's life where a first crush changes everything and it's true. We've changed. We aren't the same people we once were. We've grown up, evolved since then, but one thing remains the same. I love him with my whole heart, young, old, forever.

Remington Cole was my first crush, my first kiss, my first love, and now he would forever be always mine.

I hope you loved Remington and Faith's story with all the twists and turns it took. There's a few more books coming in the Moonshine Springs Series, featuring the rest of the Willow Springs characters finding their own happily ever afters. Even though this book can be read as a standalone, some of the characters will interconnect to the other books in this series.

If you haven't read about Cassidy Mae and Beau's road to happily ever after, you can download Written in the Sand today! Jameson and Nova, plus Rhett and Reagan, will be getting stories too. Saddle up, these cowboys are about to show you what love is all about!

OTHER TITLES BY ZOEY DRAKE

Sweet and Sexy Standalones

Second Chance Rescue

Topsy Turvy Kinda Love

Melting Wynter

Moonshine Springs Novels

Written in the Sand

Written in Love Letters

Dark and Taboo Standalones

Dirty Monsters

Holiday

A Whiskey Run Christmas Young Adult:

A Small Town Christmas Romance

Anthology Shorts

The Myth of Love - Part of Beyond the Love: A BRAE Anthology

Caige - Part of Hot Boy Summer: A Charity Anthology (6/7/22)

Azalea Blooms - Part of JOCKS Anthology (7/12/22)

Reckless Legend - Part of Kiss & Tell: An Amaryllis Media Anthology
(9/6/22)

Written in the Sand

http://bit.ly/WrittenintheSand - Amazon

http://bit.ly/WITSZDrakeGR - Goodreads

Catch up today:

I always believed my happily ever after came with the words "I do."

I'd been happy once. In love. Until one night changed everything.

Changed us. The love of my life, or so I thought, had become my own worst nightmare.

So here I am...

Back in Moonshine Springs. A place I wouldn't return to unless absolutely necessary. But that's not the biggest shock. Waiting for me with open arms and a safe place to stay is my high school best friend's brother, Beau. He's told me I'm his, but starting over isn't as easy as creating a new happily ever after. My past isn't done with me and soon enough, bleeds in

My name is Cassidy Mae and this is my chance to begin again...

This book is for adults only and contains scenes featuring specific issues which may make some readers uncomfortable. For further details, I have listed the trigger warnings specifically on my website: www. zoeydrakebooks.com

MELTING WYNTER

Weston Croix

Okay, so I might have a few playboy-like tendencies. That tends to happen when you fall in love and don't end up with the happily ever after of your dreams. I built a wall around my heart and decided to have a little fun instead.

Now, I've found myself falling for the ice queen herself. Did I mention that she's also my editor-in-chief?

She's not interested in me or being an us, but when our best friends start dating, we can no longer escape our insecurities or the fire burning between us.

I guess I'm just going to have to turn up the heat and melt her heart.

Wynter Carlisle

I've got the perfect job, an apartment in NYC's elite The Gardens high rise and life as I know it is great.

If there's one thing I've learned over the years, it's that people are fickle and love isn't always permanent. I'm the only one I can always count on, well except for my best friend Addison.

I had a plan to protect my heart. That was, until Weston – the cocky columnist who works for me...in more ways than one.

Can we really break down our own barriers or will our destiny go up in flames? We're about to find out.

Second Chance Rescue

http://bit.ly/SecondChanceRescue1 - Amazon

http://bit.ly/SCRonGR - Goodreads

Catch up today:

The plan was simple. The results are anything but...

I've lost too much to even think about opening my heart to anyone again. Grief consumed my life, and all I wanted was to be left alone so I could drown my sorrows while trying to find a sliver of relief at the bottom of a bottle.

But my father saw right through me, throwing me a curveball I never saw coming. Go back to working at our family's law firm, or take a wife. If I don't, I can kiss my inheritance goodbye.

Luckily, I have another card up my sleeve—and her name is Macy. She's shy, sweet, with curves in all the right places. She's also the perfect solution to my problem *if* I can convince her that what I'm proposing will end up benefiting us both.

It's easy. She needs money, and I need a wife. It's a win-win situation.

The way I see it, it's just another business transaction. No commitment. No strings. Zero complications. What could possibly go wrong?

Topsy Turvy Kinda Love

http://bit.ly/TopsyTurvyKindaLove - Amazon

http://bit.ly/TTKLonGR - Goodreads

Catch up today:

BROOKS

I ran under the cover of darkness with only a duffel bag to my name.

Once you leave the compound, you're spiritually dead, outlawed, excluded.

I wanted more to life outside of everything I'd ever known.

What I found was Mia.

I can see my ring on her finger.

Her heart in my palm.

Her name on my lips.

My child in her belly.

And I'll do just about anything to get it, even sex lessons if that's all she'll give me.

MIA

I'm your average bartender with a bad little habit.

I won't deny it, I like a little weed while I paint.

Creative juices and all.

My life is just fine until I meet him.

He says he only wants sex lessons, but I know that's a lie.

He wants me,

To wear his ring.

A white picket fence and two point five kids.

But I'm not sure how to love and I'm not sure I want to try.

We'll see if Brooks is up to the challenge of calming this cotton-candy haired badass.

Dirty Monsters

Co-Write with Katie Rae

https://bit.ly/DMGRKRZD - Goodreads

Https://books2read.com/u/baGdY8 - Universal

Catch up today:

Sex, drugs, alcohol....

I used anything it took to make the pain go away.

Was I an addict?

Maybe.

But more than anything, I was lost...

One stupid mistake landed me in rehab.

Some place that's supposed to make you learn how to cope and handle things better.

Instead, I found myself craving a fix, but getting high in rehab wasn't easy.

Until I found a dark, tall, and sexy nurse who could take away all the pain.

I could get high on him alone.

How was I supposed to know the secrets he held?

That he was the last person I should use for my next rush?

Didn't matter.

His darkness called to me like a beacon in the night and I was hooked.

Once I realized how forbidden he was, I only wanted him more.

Even if there was a chance we may destroy each other in the process.

I was willing to risk it.

This book is for adults only and contains scenes featuring specific issues which may make some readers uncomfortable. For further details, I have listed the trigger warnings specifically on my website: www. zoeydrakebooks.com

A WHISKEY RUN CHRISTMAS
YOUNG ADULT: A SMALL TOWN CHRISTMAS ROMANCE

https://amzn.to/3sAYhEe - Amazon

https://bit.ly/3mn1TbT - Goodreads

Catch up today:

Willow

Christmas is everything. New beginnings, a time when anything can happen.

The only thing missing for me?

Someone to share the joy of the season with.

I've tried it all. Speed dating, setups, nothing ever sticks.

Then I met a handsome stranger... well, ran into him, literally.

Oliver

Christmas has taken over Whiskey Run, and I can hardly stand it.

New to town, I didn't realize the holiday would shove itself down my throat.

But a chance encounter with a beautiful woman who spilled her holiday cheer all over me has me rethinking my distaste for the season.

As I let her show me around the festivities, one after another, I realize there's more to us than just some holiday libations.

ACKNOWLEDGMENTS

2020 was a hard year for most of us. The pandemic, staying at home, being unable to socialize for fear of this nasty virus. When the clock struck midnight on January 1st this year, I was excited and ready for the new year and all it would bring with it. The possibility of being able to see friends, restaurants opening back up, and life getting back to some semblance of normal.

I wasn't writing much at the time. Here and there I'd open my laptop and I'd stare at it until words formed, but it was nothing to take my breath away with, if anything. Some days the mouse sat blinking on the screen in front of me for hours. So, I decided that maybe 2021 wasn't my year, maybe I would take a year off from releasing books until I was ready.

Well, 2021 has been the worst year I've had in many, many years. In March of this year, I was walking into work when I slipped on black ice and busted up my leg pretty badly. I dislocated my entire knee, tore all of my ligaments, fractured my tibia and fibula, strained muscles, and caused nerve damage. You name it, I probably did it. Needless to say, I was told I would need reconstructive knee surgery, but only after my fractures could finally heal which would take about 6-8 weeks.

So doped up on pain meds my brain started yelling at me and words started forming. Little by little I was starting to write again. Words were flowing endlessly across my screen and I couldn't contain my excitement. Finally, I was doing something productive.

If you've ever been on bedrest, you may know how that feels.

Finally getting the chance to be productive and complete something. It's hard on you physically and mentally, so when I finally wrote the words "The End" on this story, I literally cried. Tears of joy because I just didn't think it would happen this year. In fact, I was convinced it wouldn't.

I have good days and bad days. This story is a rollercoaster and that's because I was on a rollercoaster of emotions while writing it.

I read through this book while I was editing and I thought I was crazy because I really liked what I was reading. Writing through the fog of pain meds is hard, but I did it. I. Finished. it.

Let me start the thank you's off with my husband. You've been the most supportive person in my life this year. Every time I can't do something, you tell me it's okay. From surviving a broken leg, through surgery, making me meals, handling life without me right beside you, and holding me when I got bad news in July, I'm amazed at your strength and optimism. You are my rock, the other part of my soul and without you I would be utterly lost and helpless. Ride or die, baby!

Lori, momager, moda – our fearless momma bear! You were with me every single damn step of the way on this book. There to bounce ideas, tell me my ideas didn't suck, and send me encouragement and help along the way. You're a true friend and friends are the family we choose. Love ya!

Katie – oh gosh, where do I even start? Thank you just doesn't seem like the right words. You lit a fire under my ass with this book, writing on the other end of the computer screen. Cheering the loudest when we reached our word counts and telling me it was okay when we didn't. From all the tiktok videos to the funny hospital stories I had, and even the okbie's I can't believe I've found a writing buddy as cool as you. LOVE YOU, GIRL!

Sarah, Julie, Autumn, Norma, Liv – these authors keep me smiling! You ladies... all the check ins and messages these last couple of months have meant more than you will ever know. Your brightness is a light in this otherwise dull time and I hope it never disappears! You keep me motivated, inspired, and thankful that I've met you along the way! I wanna be y'all when I grow up. Thank you so, so much!

TALIA! Thank you for not murdering me over the amount of times I asked you to redo the spine of this book haha. Also, thank you for always making my story come to life!

Lindee – these images of Travis and Sabree are phenomenal and I can't thank you enough for the perfect shot on this cover!

Travis and Sabree – thank you for posing for these photos. They were absolutely perfect in bringing these characters to life.

Amy – I can't say thank you enough for working with me this time, after all the delays and issues I've had. Thank you for rescheduling me without complaint! And editing this monster!

My beta team – Jill, Celia, Denise, Katie, Lori, and Norma. You were amazingly helpful with all your comments and suggestions! The angry messages, sad messages, happy messages, and GIFs completely made my day! Here's to hoping the rest of romancelandia likes WILL as much as you did! I couldn't have done this without you!

Last, but not least, Zoey's Lit Ink Lovers and my readers! You guys are my soul! Your love for my books inspires me to write more. Without all of your support, sharing, and taking a chance on me I wouldn't be able to fulfill this dream of writing and sharing the stories I have tucked away in my brain.

The best is yet to come... I can feel it!

Made in the USA
Middletown, DE
24 May 2022

66109375R00194